A TRIAL OF SOULS

THE GODLING CHRONICLES

A TRIAL OF SOULS

BRIAN D. ANDERSON

4 Horsemen
Publications, Inc.

DEDICATION

For George Stratford, whose amazing hard work and dedication made the timely release of this novel possible.

CONTENTS

PROLOGUE

Weila crept silently atop the dune. Keeping as low as possible, she peered down over the vast expanse of the Soufis camp.

The blood from the sentry had sprayed everywhere, and sand was now sticking in ugly, irritating clumps all over her arms and clothes. She wiped the bloody grime from her forearm in disgust, at the same time silently cursing herself for her carelessness. The man had turned around just as she was about to slit his throat; she could count herself very fortunate indeed that she'd been able to silence him before he could raise the alarm.

The sound of obscene songs and gruesome laughter drifted up from the camp, fueling her hatred for the slavers to even greater heights. A grim little smile formed as she took careful note of their positions and numbers. When the dawn came, they would be silenced forever and the sands would be rid of the Soufis plague once and for all. Though repulsed, she continued to watch for another two hours as the merry-making rose to a fever pitch. During that time, six slaves were killed by their drunken masters, and a dozen fights erupted, three of which ended in death.

"Animals," she muttered, sliding back down the side of the dune and retrieving her bow.

She returned to the body of the sentry and buried it in the sand. The two other Sand Masters who had accompanied her on this mission were planning to scout the area west that led to the flat, hard sands of the Crystal Plains, then rendezvous with her five miles north of the Soufis encampment. The route across the Crystal Plains would enable the Soufis army to reach Dantory in less than two weeks. If that happened, the people there would certainly be slaughtered. They would never expect such vast numbers to march on them from the deep desert. In their minds, civilization ended beyond their own doorsteps: the Soufis, nomadic human tribes, and especially the elves of the deep desert, were nothing but rumors and myths to all but a very few of Dantory's citizens. And even if they did know what was coming, there would still be no hope of stopping the onslaught. An army of this size would be able to destroy their towns in hours, killing any who resisted, and enslaving those who did not.

Bands of elves had been gathering for weeks at the Waters of Shajir. Twenty thousand were already there, and another thirty thousand were expected to arrive once word reached the southeastern tribes—more than enough to defeat the Soufis. And once these long-standing enemies had been dealt with, the march from their beloved home would begin. Darshan had come, and a new beginning was on the horizon.

As she made her way through the darkness to meet up with the others, Weila wondered what life a Sand Master could find in the West. The idea of a forest or an ocean didn't disturb her. It was the thought of being without purpose that caused the most concern. In the desert, she had responsibility and direction. Her people looked to her for guidance.

What would she be without that? Cursing herself for useless despair, she pushed these thoughts from her mind.

As Weila approached the rendezvous point, she caught a foul scent. Ducking behind a low dune, she inched around the base until she could see what had alerted her. Only a few yards ahead were the two other Sand Masters, both of them on their knees with hands bound behind their backs and faces beaten and bloody. Leolo was young and strong but had only just become a full-fledged Master. Sherindi was nearly as old as Weila and very capable. Three Soufis warriors stood over the pair, silently pacing back and forth. How they had ever managed to capture two Sand Masters was a mystery, but that was of no consequence right now. The Soufis had sealed their own fate with their actions.

Weila drew her knife and prepared to free her comrades. Her muscles tensed, but just as she was about to charge in, another figure appeared from the darkness. Its long black cloak and fluid movements told Weila that this must be the Vrykol Darshan had spoken of. Her heart sank. The dagger she wielded was far too small to have any chance of beheading the creature, and arrows would be useless.

One of the Soufis kneeled in front of Leolo. "I still think they're lying. There's bound to be more of them about."

The Vrykol took a long sweeping look around. Weila froze.

"Then perhaps a bit of gentle persuasion might help," the creature said. In a single rapid motion, it spanned the distance between itself and the helpless elves. Its hand shot out. There was the glint of steel, and Leolo gasped loudly in shock and pain. A series of desperate gurgling sounds followed. Seconds later, he slumped over, blood still gushing from his throat and down his chest.

The Vrykol looked down at Sherindi. "Your death will be considerably harsher unless you tell me where the rest of your companions are."

Sherindi glared defiantly and spat on the ground at its feet. "Vile creature. Save your threats."

The Vrykol laughed. "I make no threats. I only wish to spare you the torment of being taken back to the Soufis camp. I can only imagine what they would do to such a lovely elf woman. I offer you a quick death, here and now—nothing more. All you need do is speak the truth."

Sherindi lowered her head. "Do what you will."

Taking her bow, Weila notched an arrow. "Forgive me," she whispered after saying a brief, silent prayer. Her hands trembled for a moment as the bowstring drew tight. She could feel tears running down her cheeks. Sucking in a deep breath to steady her aim, she let loose the arrow. It struck home with a solid thud, piercing Sherindi's heart. Weila instantly sprang to her feet and ran off into the night, hatred filling her soul.

As she wound her way between the dunes, she glanced back regularly for signs of pursuit. The Soufis had no chance of catching her, but she was concerned that the Vrykol might be able to. After half an hour, she halted and listened carefully. Her path would have been difficult to follow, even for another Sand Master. Soon she smiled, satisfied that she was alone.

"You are a difficult prey," came a voice from the darkness.

Weila's smile vanished. She drew her dagger. "Come closer and you'll find out exactly how difficult I am." She could see the outline of the Vrykol slowly closing in.

It stopped a few feet away to push back its hood and reveal elf features. "Do not fear. I only wish to speak with you."

"I have nothing to say," she shot back angrily. Darshan had told them that there was a Vrykol in elf form, but that still hadn't prepared her for the reality of actually seeing one.

The Vrykol smiled, its white teeth gleaming in the darkness. "That is just as well. For I wish you to listen."

"You have nothing to say that I would hear." Her voice was hard and steady.

"I could kill you where you stand," it said, sounding amused. "Or you can listen."

Weila paused for a long moment. "Then speak and be gone."

"I want you to tell your people to leave the Soufis alone," the Vrykol instructed her. "In return, the Reborn King promises to leave your desert in peace from this day until the end of time. Furthermore, we pledge to prevent the Soufis from ever returning. Once my master is finished with them, they will be destroyed and trouble you no longer." He took a step forward. "Is that not what you want? To live free in your desert?"

"You offer what we already possess," said Weila. "We do not need your master's leave to be free."

"You think not?" He shook his head and chuckled. "You cannot possibly understand the forces that will be arrayed against you should you hinder the plans of my lord. You may very well be able to defeat the Soufis, but your forces will be diminished. And once the war in the West has been won, the Reborn King shall cast his gaze east. He will sweep down upon you like a plague and hunt down every last elf that breathes desert air. There will be no one left alive to know that you ever existed. Do you not see wisdom in my words? Would you see your people annihilated, fighting a battle that is not your own?"

"You think to persuade us to be idle while you seek to dominate the world?" she scoffed. "You expect us to allow evil to reign? Know you nothing of the people whose body you have polluted with your foul spirit? You cannot be so stupid."

"We will not dominate the world," he replied, his voice turning into a deathly whisper. "We will burn it to cinders. Nothing shall remain. Your precious desert will seem a paradise by comparison, and there is nothing you can do to stop us."

He turned his back to her. "Should you attack the Soufis army and attempt to leave your lands, none of you will be spared. Darshan will still fall, and the elves will be wiped from memory. To this, I swear. Deliver my message to your leaders." With this final demand, he stalked away, disappearing into the night.

Weila stood there for several minutes, doubt slowly sneaking its unwanted way into her heart. She could not help but wonder how much truth there was in the Vrykol's words. Was this Reborn King really so powerful as to make good on his threats? She shook her head and steeled her wits. She would not allow darkness and despair to rule her. Regardless of what the creature had just said, Darshan was their salvation, and he would fulfill the prophecy.

She reached down to pick up a handful of sand, squeezing it tightly. As the grains seeped out between her calloused fingers, the gritty texture calmed her, soothing her heart. The sands were eternal, and no matter where she would travel, she belonged to them. Should the end come and the fire of the elves be snuffed out, they would meet that destiny without fear. And tomorrow, she would have her vengeance. The faces of Sherindi and Leolo, and the cruel way that the Vrykol had brought about their end, burned fiercely in her mind. It was enough to erase all doubt and bolster her courage.

Opening her hand, she released the sand and raced off into the night to join her people.

CHAPTER 1

Gewey woke to the sound of heavy pounding on his door. His eyes cracked open and he could see that Kaylia had already gone.

"Come in," he called, rubbing the sleep from his eyes.

It was Ertik. He was dressed uncharacteristically in black wool pants, together with some old and badly worn leather armor. "It is time, my Lord."

Gewey held back a laugh. The armor was far too big for Ertik's slight frame, and the pants had been made for a much shorter man. "Don't call me my lord. And please put on normal clothes."

Ertik flushed. "If I am to go to war, then surely I should have some protection. I do not intend to wear this all the way to Skalhalis. I'm merely attempting to get used to the fit." He smiled down at himself and shrugged. "Or lack of perhaps? But this was the only spare armor available that even came close to fitting me. The rest had already been distributed to the soldiers who needed it."

"Who says you're going to war?" asked Gewey, still amused. Ertik was by far one of the most capable and serious-minded of all the people in Valshara. It was almost impossible to keep a straight face to see him thus attired.

"I am to represent Amon Dähl," he explained, head held high. "I may be no soldier, but I have been an agent of my order for longer than you have been alive, and have faced death many times, though not in battle. I also have other skills that could prove to be useful."

Gewey held up his hand and lowered his head. "I do not doubt you for a moment. But..." He peeked up and was unable to contain a grin.

Ertik looked down once again at his ill-fitting attire before meeting Gewey's eyes. There was a brief pause—the pair of them then simultaneously burst into laughter.

"I think perhaps I'll forgo the armor after all," said Ertik, shaking his head. A moment later, he was serious again. "Kaylia sent me to tell you that the army is assembled and ready."

Gewey's humor instantly evaporated. He sprang up from the bed, cursing. "Why didn't she wake me earlier? I need to check my gear and..."

"It's all been taken care of," said Ertik. "Your horse and sword are already prepared and awaiting you outside, and your clothes are in your wardrobe." He gave a disapproving look that was accompanied by a sigh. "I must tell you, I do not like that you intend to go into battle without armor."

"I think Kaylia would agree," remarked Gewey as he walked to the wardrobe. "But I have no intention of coming close enough to enemy swords to need it."

"Still, you should use caution," Ertik retorted.

"Perhaps I could borrow yours," said Gewey, smirking roguishly. He could see Ertik was not amused. "Don't worry.

If at any time I feel in need of protection, I'll put some on. I'm certain Kaylia will have made sure that I have it available should I change my mind."

"I'm sure you're right," said Ertik. "She is a remarkable person. You are lucky to have someone like her watching over you." He drew a deep breath. "Anyway, your breakfast and bathwater are being brought as we speak."

Gewey nodded. "Thank you. I'll join you as soon as I'm ready."

Gewey examined the clothes Kaylia had left for him: an open-necked crimson shirt and black pants; both made from Elven cloth and tailored to his form. Sewn onto the shirt's breast was the image of a silver sword set against a full moon. He had been told that this was the sigil of Amon Dahl given to the knight chosen to protect the Sword of Truth. He tried on the soft leather boots. They were polished to a mirror shine and hugged his feet like a pair of suede moccasins. His belt had been cleaned and rubbed with oil that gave off a sweet scent much like maple syrup. This immediately reminded him of mornings in Sharpstone with his father. He smiled inwardly, seeing the man's kindly face in his mind.

A few minutes later, his food and bath water were brought in, and soon he was dressed and making his way through Valshara. The halls were quiet and solemn. Those he passed bowed low, though none were able to meet his eyes. With the exception of Kaylia and High Lady Selena, his name was now Darshan to everyone within the temple walls. These were the only two who were seemingly still unaffected by the dramatic way in which he had used the flow of the spirit to establish his control over the doubting council members.

It hadn't taken very long for him to become aware that the consequences of his use had not been contained to the receiving hall. The entire temple suddenly knew of the name given to him by Gerath, and they began to all but worship at his feet. He realized that Aaliyah had hit upon the truth.

The flow of the spirit was by far the greatest of all the powers. That the Reborn King had gained such a vast following in such a short time could be easily explained if he had gained this ability as well.

As Gewey exited the temple, he found his horse awaiting him, along with six guards—three elves, and three humans. All were wearing gleaming steel plate from head to toe and held long spears adorned with a small banner matching the sigil on his shirt. Each man had been carefully handpicked by Kaylia and Aaliyah to be his personal guard.

Gewey was surprised by how close the two elf women had become in so short a time, considering that they had been rivals for his affections only a matter of weeks before. The bond he'd created with Aaliyah in the desert had given them a common goal—his safety. Though indeed odd, he was pleased that the situation had not caused jealousy or resentment.

He mounted his horse and urged it toward the gates, his guard keeping pace on either side. The few people about in the yard lowered their heads and closed their eyes as he rode by. To Gewey, it looked disturbingly like they were praying. Not that he minded prayer, but he had the uneasy feeling that the prayers were to him, and not for him.

When they reached the end of the passage leading from Valshara, Gewey halted. Facing him were fifteen thousand soldiers in tight formations of one hundred men. Just beyond these were ten thousand elf fighters, and in the distance he could see the heavy cavalry who were flying the Valsharan banner of the sword and moon. Along the cliff wall were dozens of wagons carrying provisions.

The moment he was spotted, the army let out a thunderous cheer so loud that Gewey wanted to cover his ears. He had heard stories about armies and warfare, but nothing could have prepared him for this. His heart raced as he raised his fist high in the air, prompting the soldiers to cheer even louder.

While casting his eyes over the scene, the sheer scope of what was to come began to set in. Urgency had meant they were unable to wait for their full strength to muster, so the enemy would most likely have superior numbers. Nevertheless, what they did have assembled was still impressive. And even though Angrääl may have more soldiers, they wouldn't have ten thousand fierce elf warriors fighting on their side. Gewey allowed a small amount of the flow to pass through him. What's more, this army would have a god leading it.

The soldiers made way for him as Gewey spurred his horse to a quick trot. At the vanguard, he saw Kaylia, Aaliyah, Nehrutu, and King Lousis. He had hoped to have Lord Chiron and Lady Bellisia riding with him as well, but they had both decided to march alongside their kinfolk.

The elf army would be in front and the humans used to reinforce them should the lines break. As he rode along, Gewey noticed the differences between the two allied forces. The humans wore heavy steel plate and carried thick broadswords and large square bronze shields. In contrast, the elves wore light leather and long, thin swords, and only those on the front line carried small, round wooden shields.

The cavalry was made up entirely of humans, mostly men from Althetas, though a few were from the other kingdoms. Their armor was even heavier than the infantry's, and they carried long, steel-tipped spears.

That Gewey insisted on such a quick departure had sent the generals into a frenzy. Though none said it directly, he knew they thought him a fool. But it was clear they had already waited too long. Scouts had been sent ahead, though the army would most likely be nearly there before any of them returned with information. The only thing he could hope to learn was whether King Halmara marched on Althetas or Valshara.

King Lousis had supported Gewey's decision when he'd arrived the day before, mostly because he was afraid for his people. Thanks to his strong leadership and Lord Chiron's experience in the Great War, they accomplished in days what should have taken weeks. Fortunately, the wagons carrying construction materials had arrived a week earlier and were able to be loaded with provisions from the temple.

His guard fell back as he approached Kaylia and the king.

King Lousis was clad in finely woven chain mail, on top of which he'd donned gleaming steel plate with the crest of his city displayed proudly across the chest.

Kaylia wore deep green Elven leather armor with a long knife attached to her belt on each hip. Her hair was braided and wrapped tightly. Gewey thought she looked every inch a warrior, and a beautiful one at that.

Gewey bowed his head to the king. "We march on your command, Your Highness."

Lousis bowed in return, grinning boyishly. Drawing his sword, he held it aloft. The air became still and quiet; for a moment or two, the only thing that could be heard was the soft rustling of banners and the snorting and stamping of horses.

His voice then thundered over the field. "Now let Angrääl tremble in fear at our wrath! To war!" The army erupted once again, with the name of Darshan ringing out everywhere. The king turned his horse and slowly the army began to move forward.

"How far is it to Skalhalis?" asked Gewey.

"Three days to the city," replied Lousis. "But if they are heading to Althetas, we may be pressed to catch them."

Gewey nodded. "I thank you for your help. If you hadn't arrived when you did..."

"If I hadn't arrived when I did," interrupted Lousis, "there is a chance my city would be besieged and undefended. It is I who should thank you. You are the one who urged immediate action. If it were left up to the generals and nobles, we would still be sitting on our backsides."

Gewey laughed. When meeting the king two days earlier, he'd liked him at once, and it appeared the feeling was mutual. Lousis had not been present at the receiving hall when he'd unleashed the flow of the spirit, and as a result, Gewey found that he was more comfortable with the king than with most of the others at the temple. He knew Lousis's kindness and good nature were genuine, rather than a result of the flow's influence.

"You can thank Lord Chiron more than me," said Gewey. "That he fought in the Great War carried a lot of weight with the commanders. His insistence that I was correct went far to sway them. Not to mention that he knew how to organize the army quickly."

"I know," said Lousis. "He told me that he once marched with fifty thousand elves, with only a single day to muster." He shook his head with a slight smile. "How humans ever defeated them, I cannot imagine."

"The human armies of old were vast and powerful," interjected Kaylia. "I read many accounts of the battles when I was a child. Their generals became quite adept at anticipating elf tactics." She flashed a wicked grin. "Angrääl will not have that advantage."

By midday, the sky was overcast, and a bitter chill was in the air. Ertik joined them for a short time before returning to a mixed unit of Amon Dahl knights and Althetan soldiers. Gewey smiled at the fact that he had removed the ridiculous armor and now wore just a set of simple leathers, with a short sword at his side.

Shortly after Ertik withdrew, Gewey spotted a man on a horse riding hard straight for them. As the rider neared, he recognized him as one of the scouts the king had sent.

"Your Highness," said the scout, his voice urgent. "The armies of Skalhalis are heading this way."

"Are you certain?" asked Lousis.

"I am," he replied. "Fifty-thousand infantry and a thousand heavy cavalry. They'll be upon you in less than a day."

Lousis immediately ordered a halt and called for the generals and elf commanders. After a map was laid on the rocky ground, they all gathered around while the scout showed them from where Halmara approached.

As the scout pointed to their location, Chiron smiled broadly.

"What is it?" asked Lousis.

"They have numbers," Chiron replied. "But clearly whoever commands has no notion of elf tactics." He pointed north and south of the enemy's position. "On either side, there is flat, even terrain." He moved his finger to the middle and drew invisible lines. "They march in straight line formations, with heavy horse in front and bowmen at the rear in order to overwhelm our inferior numbers. Which means they intend to shoot volleys of arrows into our ranks until we are forced to advance our outnumbered cavalry. Once the cavalry is defeated, their horsemen will then withdraw and attempt to flank us while their infantry presses us back."

The generals nodded in agreement.

"And what does this have to do with elf tactics?" asked Lousis.

Chiron smiled and glanced back at his kin. "This is the same mistake the human armies made when the Great War began." He stood tall. "An elf army is not a brute force. It is a swift death. The moment they are in sight, we can divide our ranks and flank them before they know what has happened. The heavy horse only need occupy the enemy long enough for us to engage. By the time they figure out what we have done, their left and right flanks will be decimated. The flat terrain will increase our speed and make it impossible for them to adjust in time."

Lousis laughed heartily. "A bloody fine strategy." He reached out and squeezed Chiron's shoulder fondly. "If this works, we will lose few men."

Gewey stepped forward. "I do not want the cavalry to engage."

"But..." began the king.

"Forgive me, Your Highness," said Gewey, cutting him off. "But I promised that the enemy would see my wrath, and I intend it to be so. Once the elves split off, I will show them the true meaning of power." He looked at Chiron. "When I'm done, you will only need to keep them from escaping." His voice rumbled and his eyes were fire.

"And if the Vrykol attack?" asked Kaylia.

"Then, and only then, does the cavalry move," he replied. "Keep them at bay until I have done what needs to be done."

"And what is that?" asked Chiron.

A wreath of flame erupted just above his head. "I will burn them all." He felt Kaylia's hand touching his arm and allowed the flame to disappear. The rage had begun to fill him again. The hatred. He looked into Kaylia's eyes and calmed his spirit.

King Lousis stared in disbelief. "I was told of this power. It was witnessed by the council at my home. But to see it for myself..."

Kaylia took Gewey's hand. "I need to speak with you privately."

Gewey followed her for a few yards until they were just out of earshot. He could feel her concern through their bond. "There is nothing to worry about," he told her.

Kaylia placed her hands on his cheeks, cradling his face. "Your anger keeps building, and each time with less prompting. I fear you may lose control."

Gewey nodded. "I fear it as well. But there is not much that I can do. I told you ... I'm changing."

"Changing into what?" she asked. "I would not see you completely become Darshan."

He took her hands and kissed them gently. "The part of me that is Darshan loves you just as much as the part of me that is Gewey. But I promise to be careful."

Kaylia smiled. "I will hold you to that."

The commanders passed on the battle plan to their troops, and soon after, they were underway. Gewey could feel his anxiety increasing as they came ever closer to the enemy. He thought back on the stories of ancient battles his father would tell him as a child, and of the great heroes who fought. He wondered if someday stories would be told of this battle. How would he be remembered? As a warrior and savior, or as a bringer of death and destruction?

By late afternoon, Gewey could sense the approaching army and focused on finding the Vrykol. Finally, he felt their foul presence spread throughout the ranks.

"The men we face are afraid," he said. The words were out before he even realized he had spoken.

King Lousis laughed. "Such a battle has not been fought in many generations. I doubt anyone is without fear on this day."

As the enemy came near, Lousis raised his arm. In response, a trumpet sounded, calling for a halt. The banners of Angrääl flew high and the glint of steel and polished leather glimmered even in the dim light of the overcast sky. Their lines were twice as long, and much deeper, too. Led by the cavalry, they moved like a great, lumbering behemoth.

"I hope you can do what you say," whispered the king to Gewey. "Or I'm afraid that even our elf allies will be of little help."

Gewey flashed a confident smile and dismounted. Aaliyah, Nehrutu, and Kaylia followed close behind as he strode out several yards beyond their lines. The elves had already begun to move into position, splitting their numbers into two smaller groups.

From the enemy lines, four men began making their way to the center of the field. They were carrying a red banner with a broad white stripe diagonally across it.

"It means they wish a parley," said Kaylia.

Gewey nodded. "Then let us meet our foe." He waited for King Lousis to join them and then started out.

Two soldiers in heavy plate armor with the broken scales sigil across their breastplates stood as guards, each holding a tall banner. In the middle left was a man in superbly crafted gold plate armor; a great eagle gripping a fish in its talons emblazoned across his chest. A long rapier with a gold hilt crowned by a large sapphire hung at his side, and a thin gold band sat atop his wrinkled brow. Despite his splendid attire, his aging features gave him a ragged appearance, and his eyes were vacant and lifeless.

The man next to him was, in stark contrast, youthful and strong. His black curling hair was oiled and pushed back. Instead of armor, he was dressed in a fine light-tan linen shirt and black pants. A long, thin blade hung from a polished black belt, and his black leather boots looked as if they had never felt the touch of the road. He stepped forward, at the same time flashing a friendly smile. "Greetings." His voice was smooth and cultured.

Lousis ignored him. "King Halmara. I see that not only have you given over your kingdom to Angrääl without a fight ... you also now allow others to speak for you."

Halmara refused to meet Lousis's eyes. "I have given nothing. Yanti speaks on behalf of the Reborn King."

"So you are Yanti," said Gewey, steel in his voice. "I was hoping to meet you before I destroy your army and send you to the afterlife."

"Ah," said Yanti. "Gewey Stedding, I presume. Or do you prefer Darshan?"

"It doesn't matter what name you use," said Gewey. "I just wanted you to see the instrument of your doom. Savor your final moments, because, by the time the sun sets, I will kill you and hang your mangled body from the walls of Valshara." He stepped forward, his face only inches away from Yanti's. "But before I do, you will watch your people die, and your master's hope for conquest disappear."

Yanti was unmoved. "I see you are every bit the young godling: fierce and powerful. It is a shame you have chosen to ally yourself with this sad lot. If only your wisdom matched your heart."

The ground began to shake as Gewey drew in the flow. His anger swelled, threatening to burst forth. "We shall see who is wise when I am bathing in your blood."

"Perhaps," said Yanti. "But before you do, I think there is something you should see." He waved his hand in the air. From the Angrääl lines, two soldiers came forward at a quick jog.

Even in armor and helm, Gewey recognized them at once. "Killian? Chancy? What the hell are you doing here?" There stood Killian Hedgpath and Chancy Jerrison—from Sharpstone. He had grown up with both boys. Up until the death of his father, after which his full attention was needed to run the farm, he had spent many hours in their company.

"Gewey?" they said in unison.

Yanti held out his hand, silencing them. "I just thought you should know exactly who it is you will be slaughtering."

"How many of you are there?" Gewey asked, looking at Killian. They had been close as children.

Killian looked nervously at Yanti, who nodded his consent. "There are twenty of us from back home."

"How in blazes did you end up here?" asked Gewey. He glared at Yanti, who simply smiled in return.

Killian swallowed hard. "They came to Sharpstone not long after you and Lee left. They told us we could see the world—and that the pay was good. Three times what we make back home. I didn't know…"

"That's enough," said Yanti. "Return to your posts."

The two boys hesitated for a moment, but a quick glance from Yanti sent them running.

"And what do you think is going to happen now?" asked Gewey. "Do you imagine we'll just turn around and go home because you parade my childhood friends in front of me?"

"Not at all," Yanti replied. "I merely wanted you to understand the cost of war and the reach of my master. By now, your little village belongs to him, along with all of its inhabitants. Their fate is now tied to that of Angrääl. And no matter how powerful you are, before this war ends, you will lose everything you hold dear." He stepped back and shook his head. "Is it really worth it? Through the power of the Reborn King, you have the ability to save all those you love. Why will you not understand this?"

"At least you admit it's a war," remarked Lousis with disgust.

"Of course, it's a war," said Yanti. "But not with you. And not with your people. It is you who are making it so. This is a war against the lies told by the gods. The Reborn King merely seeks to free people from their yoke so that they may live as equals, unburdened by fear and petty hatreds."

Gewey stared silently at Yanti for nearly a full minute, then burst out laughing. "The silver tongue you possess has turned to brass. I think you did not expect me to be here.

You thought I was still in the desert. And if you imagine it's wise to tell a god that you wish to destroy the gods, then your stupidity is laughable." He stepped forward, putting his face right into Yanti's. For the first time, Yanti looked uneasy. "I am not the boy who left Sharpstone. And if need be, I will not hesitate to kill those from my village who have joined you." He moved forward again, forcing Yanti to step back a pace. "I have finished wasting my time with you. Run. Run now, or die where you stand."

Yanti glared furiously. Then, regaining his composure, he bowed. "Come, Your Highness. It appears this parley is concluded."

Gewey watched as they walked quickly back to their lines.

"Are you all right?" asked Kaylia.

Gewey looked at her and smiled. His eyes glowed with power and his body filled with the flow. "I am perfect," he said. He turned to the king. "You should go, Your Highness. I would ask you to protect Kaylia, but as I know she will refuse to leave my side…"

Kaylia grabbed his hand, squeezing it tight. "I knew you were becoming a wiser man."

"Aaliyah and I will remain as well," said Nehrutu. "Should the Vrykol attack, we may be needed."

Gewey nodded and drew his sword. The familiar heat felt comforting in his hand; the flow of earth and air increased tenfold. Thousands of elf voices screaming their battle cries erupted behind him.

At that moment, thousands of arrows from Angrääl bows came streaking across the sky in a high arc, like a cloud of death. Gewey grinned viciously and raised his sword above his head. A ferocious blast of wind spun into a massive vortex that rose up to meet the attack. Stopped in mid-flight, the arrows scattered like straw, tumbling down and littering the field between the two armies. The Angrääl soldiers shifted uneasily, sending out a spike of their fear into Gewey's mind. He smiled with satisfaction.

With astonishing speed, the elves were already halfway across the ground, separating them from both Angrääl flanks. Gewey took a moment to marvel that so many could move in unison at such speed. Another volley of arrows from the enemy shot skyward, but Gewey blasted it again, this time with even greater force.

Now the Angrääl horseman began to advance. In response, Gewey closed his eyes, and the earth began to tremble. With an almighty roar, a massive ball of flame, at least thirty feet in diameter, burst into life. The charging horses immediately slowed, but Gewey moved the fireball rapidly toward them. It exploded outward with an ear-shattering boom. At least half of the soldiers and horses were instantly engulfed and burned alive. The rest scattered in a desperate attempt to flee back to their own lines. Gewey roasted as many as he could before they disappeared within the infantry.

Rage like he never thought possible filled Gewey's spirit. He could see that the elves had already reached both sides of the enemy force, who, suddenly realizing the threat, were hastily turning to engage them. Gewey stepped forward and sent another ball of flame crashing into the enemy lines. Screams of horror carried over the field. Gewey was pleased.

From the heart of the fire, a dozen black cloaks emerged.

"Vrykol," said Nehrutu.

But instead of attacking, the Vrykol formed a tight circle and began to sway back and forth rhythmically. Gewey felt a chill wash over him, but it was not a chill in the air. It was within the flow itself. He reached out and tried to upheave the earth beneath them, but nothing happened. He looked to Nehrutu and Aaliyah. They nodded with understanding and reached out together, but still to no effect.

A horn blast rang out, bringing a third volley of arrows from the Angrääl archers. This time Gewey was helpless to stop them and could only watch in despair as the deadly shafts slammed into the Althetans. Wails of pain reached his ears. Consumed with blind fury, he gritted his teeth and prepared to run straight at the Vrykol. But, just before he was out of reach, Kaylia caught hold of his arm.

"No!" she cried. "You cannot!"

Gewey roared, nearly jerking her off the ground.

"Come," said Aaliyah. "We must pull back."

Gewey at first refused to move. His hatred was beyond measure. It took the combined efforts of all three companions before they were eventually able to convince him to withdraw.

"We must hurry," said Nehrutu.

Yet another volley of arrows came over, covering the sky like a veil.

Gewey spun around, all the while trying desperately to stop the oncoming death. "This isn't over," he cried out, his voice an unearthly deep growl. He watched helplessly as the arrows struck home and more men fell.

The cavalry began its charge just as he and the others reached their lines. Gewey's guard immediately surrounded them. Nehrutu and Aaliyah both drew their weapons— Nehrutu also picked up the shield from a fallen soldier and pulled Aaliyah close.

At that moment, King Lousis strode up, a grave expression on his face. His guard followed, struggling to keep pace. Gewey saw blood trickling from a wound on the king's neck.

"Are you hurt?" Gewey asked.

"A mere scratch," replied Lousis. "What happened?"

"The Vrykol have somehow completely blocked my powers," Gewey told him, scowling.

A horn blew, signaling the Althetan bowmen to let loose their own arrows ahead of the charging horses.

"We must move aside, Your Highness," interrupted one of Lousis's guards. "The infantry will attack soon."

Lousis grunted. "Come. He's right, we must move."

Across the field, Gewey could see the Angrääl footmen and their remaining horsemen clashing with the Althetan cavalry. At the same time, the elves attacking the enemy flanks were relentlessly squeezing them back inch by inch. Arrows streaked through the air from both sides, one burying itself with a deep thunk into Nehrutu's shield.

Gewey looked at Kaylia. There was no fear in her eyes and none reaching him through their bond, only rage. It was then that he realized his anger was reflected in her.

"We must hurry," urged the guard.

Gewey allowed himself to be led through the ranks until just beyond the range of enemy bows. The dead and dying he passed fueled his determination. By the time they neared the wagons, his anger was like a white-hot ball in the center of his chest.

"Don't worry," said Lousis, placing his hand on Gewey's shoulder. "Thanks to your initial attack and the speed of the elves, we will still win the day."

"Perhaps," said Gewey. "But my failure has cost lives."

"If not for you," countered Nehrutu. "Many more would have perished this day. You all but destroyed their horses before the Vrykol were able to stop you."

This did little to ease Gewey's mind. "We must send word that every effort should be made to engage the Vrykol. If their circle is broken, I can end this battle quickly."

Lousis ordered one of his guards to spread the word to the commanders. "There is nothing for you to do now but wait."

Gewey looked out on the battle and snarled. "We'll see about that." He stormed off to the wagon that was carrying his gear and quickly found the leather armor placed aside for him. Kaylia walked up just as he was putting it on.

"You are allowing your wrath to dull your wits," she said sternly. "We will win this battle without you putting your-self in danger."

"It is not me that will be in danger," Gewey shot back. "I have no intention of dying today. But I cannot simply stand by while people are being killed."

"Then I will..." she began, but a fierce glance from Gewey stopped her short.

"You will remain here," he told her. As if with a mind of its own, the flow of the spirit swelled up within him and then spilled out. It entered Kaylia, and she closed her eyes.

"Do not try to influence me as you do others," Kaylia said angrily. But when she opened her eyes, Gewey was gone. She reached out to him, but their connection was dull and weak. Cursing, she hurried back to their group. "Have you seen Gewey?" she asked.

"He was with you, was he not?" replied King Lousis.

Kaylia explained what had happened.

Aaliyah nodded slowly. "His powers continue to grow. And that he is able to hide his mind from his bonded mate says that he is determined."

"I must find him," said Kaylia, fear seeping into her voice.

"No," said Aaliyah sharply. "He may still be able to feel your bond clearly. And if he feels your fear, that could weaken him." She took hold of Kaylia's hand. "Come. Together, we will lend him our strength."

She led Kaylia to a space behind the wagons where there was a soft patch of grass. Lousis had sent two soldiers to protect them, but Aaliyah instructed them to stand several feet away and remain quiet. She sat down, crossed her legs, and gestured for Kaylia to do the same.

"As you know, when Gewey saved my life in the desert, it created a bond between us," she said.

"Yes," said Kaylia. "He told me what happened."

"Then you know that this was partly the reason why I gave up my efforts to become his mate," Aaliyah continued. "I could feel what he felt for you, and it made me realize that regardless of how strong I am, you will always be stronger. Your heart and your spirit give him greater power than ever I could." She took Kaylia's hands. "We will use this to help him. Though my connection to Gewey is different and far weaker, together we can enhance it." She closed her eyes.

Kaylia became aware of Aaliyah's spirit surrounding her and pulled her close until both bonds became visible. Slowly, she allowed Aaliyah to make them as one. As they melded together, she could feel Aaliyah guiding her strength, urging it to reach Gewey. Love ... power ... devotion. The words took form and sprang forth. In that moment, Kaylia understood completely what she must do.

Pushing aside all fear and anxiety, she steeled her mind so that she could ensure Gewey's survival.

CHAPTER 2

Gewey made his way through the formations of soldiers who were awaiting the order to advance. Arrow after arrow continued to thud into their upheld shields, and the cries of the wounded, together with the clash of steel from across the battlefield, sounded ever more loudly. He could feel the men's desperation. Every second they remained where they were increased the chance that an arrow would find a piece of exposed flesh. The Althetan archers were returning the assault in kind but in fewer numbers.

His thoughts turned to Kaylia. The moment he'd released the flow of spirit through their bond, it was as if she'd been turned to stone. At first, this had frightened him, but when he reached out to her, a realization dawned. She was unharmed. It was his will—his desire for her to stay out of harm's way—that had caused this thing to happen. Some elusive part of him had instinctively known what needed to be done. Yes, the dark veil he had placed between them had created feelings of uncontrollable sadness, but he could not allow her to come after him. He must do this alone, and her love for him would undoubtedly drive her to follow if she could locate where he was.

The roar of battle grew louder as he finally neared the vanguard of the reserves. The instant he stepped beyond the front line of men, it was as if he had been struck in the chest by a blacksmith's hammer. He staggered dizzily for a moment as a huge rush of passion and love suddenly swept away all his feelings of sadness. He knew at once that it was Kaylia. After quickly regaining his footing, strength flooded through his limbs. He looked out at the melee and smiled. He had yet to draw in the flow, but he was already feeling as strong as if he had.

"I love you," he whispered, unsheathing his sword. Power, as he had never imagined, swept over him, saturating every part of his being.

By now, the Althetan cavalry and infantry were pushing back the Angrääl lines. The Vrykol had retreated out of sight, but Gewey could still feel their presence. He turned to face the reserve forces and raised his sword.

"Forward!" His voice boomed and echoed, as though within a great cavern. "Let this be our enemy's doom."

The response was instant. Every single soldier facing him began banging his sword against his shield and repeatedly crying out the name of Darshan. Gewey turned back to the fray. An instant later, his legs burst into violent life.

With Kaylia's strength now combining with the flow of earth and air, he was able to cover half of the distance to the enemy lines while the Althetans following were still managing their first few steps. The men fighting and dying ahead—no matter whether they were friend or foe—appeared to Gewey as insects. The rage had returned, and the power he held increased its intensity.

The first Angrääl soldier he reached was cut down as if made of parchment. Gewey's sword barely paused as it sliced through armor, bone, and flesh. Again and again, his enemies fell to his blade. Most scarcely knew he was upon them before his cold steel carved them to pieces.

He continued cutting a swath through the enemy lines, relentlessly pushing on toward where he knew the Vrykol were gathered. The carnage he left in his wake was causing terror among the Angrääl soldiers. Many began to flee the battle, only to be met by the advancing Althetan reserves.

Swords pressed in on him from either side, but he easily avoided them and made each attacker pay with his life. By the time the Vrykol finally came into view, his fury was so great that not a single Angrääl soldier dared to approach him. Many began throwing down their weapons the moment Gewey's eyes fell upon them. Those who could not run, frozen in his path by their sheer terror, were shown no mercy. Soon, the number of men whose life he had ended that day was beyond counting.

He glared at the circle of still swaying Vrykol standing only a few yards away. Letting out a mighty roar of fury, he bared his teeth like a feral beast.

At that moment, Yanti stepped into his path. His face no longer bore any trace of arrogance or smugness. His lips were twisted into a vicious snarl, and his eyes were dark and dangerous. In his right hand, he held his long sword, and in his left, a small triangular dagger.

"It would seem I underestimated how strong you have become," Yanti said. His voice was even and tempered, but his anger bled through.

"And yet you still stand in my way," Gewey responded, inching forward. "You will die a fool."

Yanti let out a snake-like hiss and then charged. He was far faster than any opponent Gewey had ever faced before, and the tip of his blade cut deep into Gewey's arm before he could twist and spin away.

"We will see who dies," said Yanti. "My master may have to live without his prize."

Gewey spat before moving in, swinging his sword in a low, tight arc. Yanti deftly avoided the blow and quickly countered with a short thrust. Gewey deflected the blade and brought up his hilt at Yanti's jaw. Yanti turned his head and ducked. Pain shot through Gewey's leg as the dagger cut across his thigh. Blood poured freely from both of his wounds.

Yanti stepped back and laughed tauntingly. "I have always desired to see the blood of a god. Disappointing, really." He smiled darkly. "Perhaps it tastes better than it looks."

Again Yanti's blade sought flesh, first feinting right and then coming down hard at Gewey's neck. Gewey was only just able to block the blow. Sparks flew, and the sound of steel on steel was ear-piercing. Spinning, he brought the back of his fist crashing into Yanti's temple, sending him stumbling back. Without hesitation, Gewey followed this up with his boot, kicking his opponent hard just under the heart. With a deep grunt, Yanti landed flat on his back. In an attempt to finish things, Gewey stabbed at his chest, but his sword found only earth as Yanti rolled away and sprang up. His face was contorted and flushed.

Gewey felt the flow swell as he pressed home his attack. Again and again, he struck at Yanti, each time his blade came closer to its target. His lips turned upward into a confident smirk, relishing the furious look on Yanti's face as he desperately dodged and parried all of his attacks.

Finally, Gewey saw an opening. Stepping sideways, he brought his blade across the hand holding the dagger. Yanti winced as it fell from his grasp. Without pause, Gewey moved in. Each time their swords collided, the sparks flew higher and brighter, bursting into tiny balls of white flame.

Yanti's face began to betray his fatigue, which only made Gewey's attacks more ferocious and determined. Yanti began to lunge desperately, trying to force Gewey back on his heels, but to no avail. Gewey cut twice in rapid succession, one to Yanti's shoulder, and the other to his chest.

The sight of blood gushing from the deep wounds he had inflicted caused the rage in Gewey's heart to explode. He raised his sword and brought it down with a powerful, sweeping stroke. Time slowed as the blade closed in. It was only then that Gewey saw the smile flashing across Yanti's lips.

Yanti stepped in and to the left. Gewey had over-extended, leaving himself wide open. Now he understood his opponent's plan. He wanted him to think he had won. He wanted him to strike hard and carelessly. His head jerked back as the hilt of Yanti's sword smashed into his jaw. Gewey stumbled, trying to bring his blade in front of him, but pain filled his gullet. He looked down. Yanti's sword had run him through.

Yanti pushed the blade in deeper. "And so ends Darshan," he said, his voice calm and confident. Gewey tried to raise his sword, but it fell from his grasp as Yanti gave a vicious twist to the blade inside him. He then ripped the sword free and stepped back, his arm lifted high in readiness to take Gewey's head.

Gewey sagged to his knees, glaring defiantly, chin raised. But just as the final strike was on the verge of delivery, an arrow shot through Yanti's wrist. He cried out, dropping his sword.

Spinning around, Yanti was able to see hundreds of elves closing in. They had broken the Angrääl lines; some of them had already begun engaging the Vrykol. Another arrow buried itself in Yanti's chest, sending him staggering back. Gewey clutched at his stomach—blood was gushing out, creating a crimson pool at his knees. He struggled to his feet and reached down to pick up his sword, but his head was swimming, and his vision was blurring. He fell to one knee. Even as he dropped, he saw three more arrows strike Yanti. His enemy's expression was now a strange mixture of pain, anger, and sheer bewilderment over how this had been allowed to happen to him.

Yanti collapsed in a heap.

Gewey looked up. The Vrykol had been overrun and were falling one by one, their heads rolling from their shoulders. Three elf warriors clad in blood-stained leather armor ran up to him.

"You are hurt, Darshan," said the first elf, his youthful features made grim and macabre by a mixture of blood and dirt. "We will help you back to the healers." He waved over six more of his kin and ordered them to guard their passage through the battlefield.

Gewey was too weak to argue. The flow was slowly draining from him. "I must retrieve my sword," he said, pain shooting through him with each word. The elves held him tight as he picked up the blade and wiped it clean on the leg of Yanti's pants.

Leaning heavily on the shoulders of his elf escort, Gewey looked out over the field. The forces of Angrääl, unable to stop the elf advance, were now falling back and attempting to regroup a few hundred yards to the south. Thousands of bodies lay amongst the dark puddles of blood blackening the battlefield.

They were only halfway across the field when Kaylia and Aaliyah appeared, racing toward him in a dead run. Gewey's guard was trailing far behind.

Gewey managed a weak smile as they approached.

"Fool!" cried Kaylia. "Damn fool!" Pushing the elves aside, she lowered Gewey to the ground.

Aaliyah kneeled beside him and placed her hands over the wound to his stomach.

"Only stop the bleeding," ordered Gewey. "Save your strength for those in dire need. I have survived worse than this."

Aaliyah frowned. "As you wish."

Gewey gasped as he felt the bitter cold of her healing touch. The flow reached inside him and he could feel his wound beginning to mend. He pushed her away after only a minute. "That's enough for now."

The elf fighters helped Gewey to his feet and then slowly walked him back to where Nehrutu and King Lousis waited. There, Kaylia dressed the wounds on his arm and leg. Already, hundreds of the injured and dying had been brought back from the battlefield and were being laid out in rows directly in front of the wagons. More were pouring in every minute.

Lousis was surrounded by ten guards, while Nehrutu was a few feet away, speaking with the healers and preparing to tend to the maimed and dying. When they caught sight of Gewey, both shot him a disapproving glance.

"You're a bloody fool," said the king. "You know that, don't you?"

Nehrutu only nodded at Aaliyah, cheerlessly.

"I must help Nehrutu," said Aaliyah. Without waiting for a reply, she followed him and the healers as they set to work.

Gewey was led to a wagon just behind the king and sat down. Kaylia settled beside him. The elves all bowed before speeding off to return to the fray.

"Bloody fool," Lousis repeated. He shook his head and stared angrily for a full minute. Gradually, though, his mouth turned up into a smile. He then let out a soft chuckle. "But fool or no, songs of your deeds will be sung for generations to come."

"What do you mean?" asked Gewey. "I failed; far too many have died."

"Failed? Are you not thinking clearly?" Lousis took a seat next to Gewey and leaned back on the wagon. "Never have I seen such power. Your mad charge opened the way for our men to break through. And let's not forget what you did to their heavy horse." He grabbed Gewey's shoulder firmly and gave him a fond squeeze. "This battle would have happened regardless of your presence. But had you not been here, we may well have been defeated—even with the elves at our side. You saved thousands of lives this day."

This did little to console Gewey. He smiled at the king and closed his eyes. "I'm sorry for what I did to you, Kaylia."

Kaylia took his hand and placed it in her lap. "We can discuss that later. For now, you must rest."

Gewey allowed himself to drift to the edge of sleep. The sounds of the battle still carried over the field, and for several hours he lay still and quiet. From time to time, reports would come back to Lousis. The enemy was not surrendering but was still being pushed back ever further. They had managed to regroup, but most of their archers had been slain and they had only a few horses remaining.

An hour before sunset, a messenger arrived with news that King Halmara had been killed and that the remaining generals were asking for terms of surrender. Lousis bowed his head and said a quiet prayer.

"Tell them to lay down their arms," Lousis commanded. "Those who comply will be imprisoned until this war ends. Those who do not will die. Any who attempt to flee will be put to the rack before they are hanged."

The messenger hurried away.

Gewey smiled up at Lousis. "You are far kinder than I might have been."

Lousis shook his head sadly. "I don't know how kind I am. War causes hardship and famine. Those men who surrender will likely starve before our victory comes." He sighed and walked away.

In that moment, Gewey felt pity for Lousis. Even though he had known him for only a short time, he realized that the king cared deeply for his people, and the thought of their suffering weighed heavily on his heart. The harsh days ahead would take its toll on everyone.

Gewey felt Kaylia's comforting presence within him and allowed himself to drift off deeper and deeper until sleep overcame him.

He was already accustomed to the odd sensation of waking up inside the dream world. His mind had changed from the moment he'd first felt the touch of the flow. Sometimes, though, it was difficult to recognize the difference between the spirit world and the realm of his own mind. He'd even managed to pass from one to the other while returning from the desert when Kaylia had reached out and pulled him to her. This time, however, he was alone within his dream. He could still feel the connection, but it was distant and faint.

He was standing beside a shallow ravine surrounded by rolling hills that were covered by tall pines and great oaks. He reached down to touch the rich black soil and gazed up at a cloudless sky. The sun hovered just above a far hill, but the light cast no shadows and was as bright as that of high noon. The scent of honeysuckle and pine needles carrying on a warm, gentle breeze brought a smile to his lips. Looking out over the landscape, he spotted a thin wisp of smoke rising from the trees atop a distant hill.

Well, I suppose that's where the dream wants me to go, he thought with amusement.

When he was a child, the Sharpstone village mothers would tell him that dreams were windows where the soul could be revealed and the future told. Vera Tarver, wife of Walt Tarver, a master mason, was said to be able to interpret their true meaning. On more than one occasion, his father had taken him to Vera after a particularly bad nightmare. He remembered how comforting her words had been. Of course, when he was older, he soon realized she had only said what he needed to hear in order to calm his fears.

Now, having been within the spirit world and having seen so many wonders, he no longer paid heed to dreams. To Gewey, they were merely his fears and desires coming to the surface of his mind. Even so, when they were not bringing horrifying images of war and death, he found them to be quite enjoyable. And being able to experience them as if they were real made the pleasant ones a welcome respite.

On entering the cluster of trees at the top of the ravine, he found himself walking along a narrow trail that wound its way up and down the steep hillsides. As he moved on, he increasingly felt that he had trodden this way before. The trees seemed somehow familiar. He passed by a thick willow, its curved drooping branches hovering low over the trail. Leaning against the trunk was a gnarled and twisted branch that made Gewey think of Felsafell's walking stick. He then understood why this place seemed familiar. He was dreaming of the Spirit Hills. He half expected to see the old hermit appear.

I wonder where he is? he thought while ducking under the willow.

"I am here," said a voice from behind him.

Gewey spun around. There stood Felsafell, clad in his worn buckskins and smiling his crooked, friendly smile. He walked with long strides to the branch and picked it up. After looking it over for a moment, he returned to the trail.

"And what does a child of heaven want with poor old Felsafell?" he asked. "I heard your call and swiftly to your aid, I come ... yes, oh yes. Could it be that power found satisfies not? Does the awakened god have questions? I think he does, or I think he dies."

"I didn't call you," said Gewey. "But I do have questions."

"Then let us walk and talk," he replied. "We will wander the dream. But all answers, I have not. More questions you will have ... once our time is done."

Ahead, the trail broadened enough to allow them to walk side by side, and they continued along at a leisurely pace. Gewey was quiet for a time. He had contacted people through their dreams before, but it was always a bit unsettling. His troubles had begun in Sharpstone when his dreams were invaded by the Dark Knight. Kaylia was always welcome, but anyone else felt like an intruder, regardless of intent.

"Where did you go when you left The Chamber of the Maker?" asked Gewey.

"I journeyed through snows and mountains," he replied. "So I could see the cold, dark with my own eyes. The king in his castle. The enemy of my kin."

Gewey stopped short. "You went to Angrääl?"

Felsafell's usual cheerful countenance turned sour. "His face I viewed, though I remember it not. His name I heard, but the memory vanished."

"Why did you go there?" he asked, unable to hide his suspicious tone.

Felsafell laughed. "Please, have no fear. I am not his. Though his power is great, a mortal man, I am not. He cannot trap my soul. I asked him to free my kin and let them fade." He lowered his eyes. "The Reborn King refused my plea. His servants they will remain until his destruction."

Gewey shook his head and sighed. "You didn't really think he would do that, did you? He would never give up the Vrykol." He noticed Felsafell's surprised expression. "I know what has happened to your people." He told him about his time in the desert and the Black Oasis.

"Far have you come in a short span of earthly life," said Felsafell. "But farther still have you to go. The king in the north has stolen the souls of the innocent. Trapped them and bound them ... enslaved them, he has. He thought to do the same to poor Felsafell. But only a dying mind can fall under his spell, and mine can last as long as the stars."

"I'm amazed he let you live," remarked Gewey.

"Kill me, he cannot," said Felsafell. "But I think he was unaware his power had failed. I think he believes me trapped like the others." He met Gewey's eyes. "Beware those who have looked upon his aspect. For they are his, and his alone. They cannot betray him, nor fail to answer his call."

"How does he do this?" asked Gewey.

"I think you know ... Darshan." Felsafell laughed wistfully. "But perhaps the knowledge bringer knows not. How merry a laugh the thought brings. But you shall know all too soon."

"He must use the flow of the spirit," Gewey mused.

"Indeed, he must," agreed Felsafell. "A power you have neglected. Your strength ignored. Air, earth, and water are but toys. The spirit is where true power lives. The dark one knows this. Oh yes, he knows this all too well."

"But how can I use it to fight him?" asked Gewey. "War is fought with swords and spears. I can't defeat armies with the spirit."

Felsafell raised an eyebrow. "So strong in body and young in mind. War can only be won with spirit. What is a sword without the will to use it? Just shiny metal. Neither man nor elf will make war without the heart to fight, or a leader to follow. Soon you must raise the hopes of the world, and all must flock to your banner, or they will surely flock to his."

Gewey frowned. "But how? I don't know how to use it. At least, not in the way you're saying."

"Then learn you must before time has faded." He continued to stroll down the trail.

"Can you teach me?" asked Gewey.

"The powers are unknown to me and mine," he replied. "You must be your own master."

"What about the Book of Souls?" asked Gewey. "Are the answers there?"

"Answers, yes. But the question may not be the same."

"Then where should I look?" he asked.

"I do not know," said Felsafell. "My kin are gone and cannot whisper in old ears. But have faith that things will unfold as they should. The fates have brought you love and fortune. I do not believe they will abandon you now." He looked up at the forest and sighed woefully. "It is good to see my home again … even through your eyes."

"Where are you now?" asked Gewey.

"Far away," he replied. "Far from home and comfort. But you shall see me soon enough. But now you must wake. Your destiny calls and you must pay heed."

Gewey opened his eyes. Kaylia was still beside him, sipping a cup of wine. King Lousis approached, followed by Chiron, Ertik, and Bellisia.

"The enemy has surrendered," said Chiron. "The armies of elf and human are victorious. The King of Angräal is cast out." His face shone with pride.

Bellisia did not look as pleased. "Yes. But at a great cost. Thousands lay dead upon the field. Thousands more are badly wounded."

Gewey felt guilt strike at his heart. "I am sorry. I did not suspect the Vrykol could have such power. Nor did I expect Yanti to be so strong."

Bellisia gave Gewey a compassionate smile. "I would be a fool to blame you. Every elf knows that you ensured our victory and that without you, many more would have perished. I am just saddened by the death of so many brave souls."

"We all mourn," said Lousis. "But it is also a time to rejoice. More shall join our cause when they hear of Angräal's defeat."

Gewey struggled to his feet, wincing from the wound in his stomach. Kaylia was instantly at his side. "Your people have good reason to celebrate," he said. "But I cannot join them."

"I don't understand," said Lousis. "This is your victory."

Gewey shook his head. "No. My victory comes later." He told them about his dream. "I believe what Felsafell says, even if I don't fully understand. I must learn to use the flow of the spirit."

"What will you do?" asked Chiron.

Gewey shrugged. "I'm not sure. I think first I shall read the Book of Souls and hope it will give me some guidance." As he spoke, his legs faltered, and he was forced to lean on Kaylia.

"But for now you will rest and heal," said Kaylia sternly.

All nodded in agreement.

Gewey smiled. "I wouldn't dare to argue. Once Aaliyah and Nehrutu are finished treating the wounded, tell them I would speak with them."

Kaylia led Gewey away to a soft bedroll and helped him lie down. It wasn't long before Althetan soldiers and elf warriors began seeking him out. Some asked for his blessing, which he reluctantly gave, while others came simply to thank him for their victory. After a time, Kaylia ordered the guards to turn them away.

"They don't see my failure," muttered Gewey.

Kaylia looked displeased. "I think you are the only one who sees it as failure. No one expected you to destroy an army alone. Only you would be so foolish as to imagine you could." She cupped his face in her hands and forced him to meet her eyes. "You must know that there will be more battles ... and more death. If you wish to stop it, you cannot do so alone. Gerath knew this. That's why he gave you his gifts, and why they were meant to be passed on to those who love you."

Gewey leaned in and kissed her. "You're right. I know you are." He lowered his eyes. "And I'm sorry for what I did. I didn't intend to use my powers on you. And when it happened, I shouldn't have taken advantage of it."

Kaylia frowned. "That is true. And if you had not already gone through battle, I would most certainly be making you feel as though you had." Her features then softened. "But for now, I will just be happy that you live."

Gewey rolled onto his back and closed his eyes. This time his dreams were of home—with Kaylia at his side.

CHAPTER 3

Theopolou and Mohanisi strolled casually together down a broad forest path. Theopolou guessed that it had been made by a human woodsman for transporting lumber to nearby villages, where it would then be turned into building materials. Fortunately, the path appeared to be abandoned at the moment.

For two weeks, they had been forced to wind their way through the forest unseen, Theopolou fearing that a premature encounter with elves from the Steppes might end their mission before it had even really gotten started. A chance meeting with humans did not concern him so much. From what he had learned, most of the northern cities were similar to Althetas with regard to their attitudes toward elves.

He and Mohanisi had spoken at length about the fears of the southern cities. Elf lands stretched out east from their borders, and humans were not suffered to pass. This forced most to conduct all their trade by sea, virtually cutting them off from the central kingdoms. Even by ship, the human traders were forced to sail near the western isles of Lymbos, off the coast of the Tarvansia Peninsula. More than one vessel had ventured too close and found themselves under elf knives.

"It is a wonder there is any peace at all," Mohanisi had remarked.

Theopolou couldn't help but agree. For centuries, he had resisted the idea that the world must be shared with their former enemies. He had not seen the inevitability of what was now coming to pass. Even without a foe such as the Reborn King, it was always going to be only a matter of time before the old hatreds spawned another war—a war that would have broken the elves completely. Whatever honor remained within their race would have been lost forever. And though their doom may still be at hand, at least they will not have rotted away from the inside.

It would be two weeks yet before they reached the Steppes, so Theopolou was taking full advantage of his time with Mohanisi. He yearned to hear about the original land of his people, and Mohanisi was perfectly willing to tell him whatever he wanted to know. The more Theopolou learned, the more he found it difficult to imagine ever leaving such a wonderful place. He began longing to see it for himself.

At midday, they decided to rest for a few hours. Theopolou had determined early that he would not waste his strength by pressing the pace. A shadow had been growing over his heart, and he could not shake the feeling that he may be marching off to his death. If that was the case, he would not hurry to meet it. Though he did not fear death, the idea of not living long enough to see his people restored brought him great sadness.

They found a small clearing peppered with fragrant yellow wildflowers. Mohanisi built a small fire and heated some leftover stew he had saved in a tin.

"Do you think our brethren will pay us heed?" he asked.

"I think we shall be fortunate to return alive," Theopolou replied, giving a weak smile. "The closer we come to the

Steppes, the darker my soul becomes. With each step, my hope fades."

"I feel it as well," said Mohanisi. "But I do not believe it is your hope fading. We approach something evil, and possessing an unyielding power. It corrupts the flow and causes the spirit to wither."

"What could do such a thing?"

Mohanisi shook his head slowly, staring into the flickering flames. "I do not know. Never have I heard of anything that could do this. Not even in legend." He stirred the stew with his dagger. "But if this is what has caused our brothers' hearts to blacken, then I think our quest will fail unless we find it ... and destroy it."

After the meal, they continued on until shortly after sunset.

As they were setting up camp, Mohanisi suddenly stiffened. He listened carefully. "Two elves approach from the north."

"Do they know we are here?" asked Theopolou. He strained to hear them but was unable to detect anything.

"No," Mohanisi replied. "Not unless they possess the same power as I. Not even your seekers can match me in the wild." He continued to listen. "If we remain here, they will find us."

Theopolou thought for a moment. "Then let them find us. I do not think two lone elves would seek battle. If anything, they are scouts, and I think your use of the flow will be enough to discourage any aggression."

Mohanisi frowned. "I am loathe to use such power against an elf—even a misguided one. But I believe you are correct. And if they are scouts, we should know who sent them and why."

A few minutes passed, after which it became clear that the approaching elves had now sensed their presence. They immediately halted and remained absolutely still for nearly half an hour. Finally, they crept closer to the camp.

Just before they were in view, Theopolou stepped forward and called out. "Come and join us as friends. Warm yourselves by our fire. We mean you no harm."

"Your accent is that of the south," came back a deep male voice. "Yet you venture to the Steppes. I would know why."

"Join us and we will be pleased to speak of our journey," said Theopolou.

There was the sound of steel sliding free—also the creak of a bowstring being drawn. A single figure stepped into the light of the fire. He was short and stocky for an elf, with close-cropped auburn hair and a ruddy complexion. He was clad in thick buckskin pants and a vest, together with a pair of tan moccasins. A tiny silver horsehead hung from a chain against his chest. Theopolou recognized it as a charm worn by the elves of the northernmost tribes. His narrow brown eyes and thin lips gave him a sinister quality that most humans would find disturbing. He was wielding a short sword with a polished bone hilt.

"Why draw your weapons?" asked Theopolou. "We have not drawn ours. Are we not kin?" He took a tentative step forward. "I am Theopolou, and this is Mohanisi."

The elf stared for a long moment. "I am Strydis, and my companion aiming an arrow at your heart is..."

Out of the shadows appeared an elf woman with a bow drawn. As Strydis had said, her arrow was pointing directly at Theopolou's heart. "I am Jylia," she said.

She was dressed in the same buckskin pants and moccasins as Strydis but wore a well-fitted tan cotton shirt. Her shoulder-length honey-blond hair was wrapped in a dozen small braids tipped with black beads. Her face was youthful and fierce, with eyes dark and intense. Theopolou guessed that she was no older than Kaylia.

"Unless you intend to kill us, I would ask you to put away your weapons." Theopolou's voice was stern and commanding.

"I beg your forgiveness," said Strydis, without lowering his blade. "But we have been pursued for many days. And I must be certain you are what you seem."

"We should kill them," said Jylia. "We cannot risk..."

"How dare you!" roared Theopolou. "You threaten your kin with death?" Jylia stepped back, but Strydis was unmoved.

"My sister should not have suggested such a thing," he said. "But do not pretend you are unaware of what has happened between our tribes. My people have struck at yours. Even were that not so, we would still have reason to be wary."

"I was at the Chamber of the Maker when elf made war on elf," Theopolou affirmed, calming his tone. "But do not speak of it as if our people are separate. I was alive during the first split. I understand far better than you what has happened, and what this means for our people. That is why we have come."

Slowly, Strydis relaxed. His eyes bore immense sadness. "Then you have wasted your efforts." He sheathed his sword and turned to Jylia. "I tire of fear and hate. Away with your bow. If they are false, then so be it. I no longer care."

After a few moments, Jylia sighed and lowered her weapon. "I hope you have not doomed us."

Strydis walked toward the fire. "We were doomed long before now."

Theopolou and Mohanisi offered them to sit. For a time, they all did so in silence.

It was Mohanisi who spoke first. "From whom do you flee?"

Strydis's lip curled in disgust. "From the black heart that now dwells in my people. We flee from the poison of the Reborn King. He has brought hatred and death to every corner of my beloved land. He has enslaved our elders to his will, and made the very air we breathe a fume of evil."

"How has he done this?" asked Theopolou.

"I do not know," he replied. The anger in his voice was combined with deep sorrow. "We were once a proud and free people. Masters of the Steppes, riding our great stallions, we were under the yoke of no one. Humans feared to tread near our borders, and the Creator had blessed our people with plenty. Then he came—or at least his ambassadors did. They spoke warnings of human plots to drive us from our lands."

"And you believed these lies?" asked Theopolou, incredulously.

"No," he replied. "Not at first. But they convinced our elders to journey to Angrääl to seek the truth. They promised that they could show evidence of the plans that were being formed against us. Each elder that returned was somehow changed. Not long after that, strange rumors began to fly. Rumors of an elf/human alliance in the south bent on our destruction."

"Surely, even with the word of your elders, you found this hard to accept?" said Theopolou.

"Most of us refused to believe that our kin, no matter how removed from our lives, would do such a thing." Strydis rose to his feet and turned his back to the fire. "But then a dark shadow fell upon our souls. One by one, my people began to fall into despair and madness. They became obsessed with the idea that humans had corrupted our kin and intended to march armies north."

"But something must have caused all this," said Theopolou. "No elder has this much power over their clan."

"Were that so, Jylia and I would still be warm in our beds," said Strydis. "Something has stolen their will. And those who refused to follow the elders' insanity were cast out. Or at least, we thought they were being cast out. The discontents were told to leave and made to promise that they would not join our brethren in the south." He looked down at his sister. "When we heard of the plan to attack the Chamber of the Maker, a group of us decided we could no longer bear to remain. We swore our oath, then left our homes behind. Twenty of us set out." He bowed his head. "We are all that remains."

"What happened?" asked Mohanisi.

"A day into our journey we were set upon," said Strydis, his anger returning. "By foul creatures cloaked in black hoods. They reeked of death and fought like demons."

"Vrykol," whispered Theopolou.

"We have heard this name from our legends," said Strydis. "And perhaps that is what we encountered. I cannot be sure. Whatever they were, they slaughtered us like sheep. We barely escaped with our lives, and the beasts have been tracking us ever since."

"How do you know they were sent by your elders?" asked Theopolou.

"One of them spoke the name of Ryslotis," he explained. "He is a chief among our people. They vowed to bring him our heads as proof we were slain. It was then we realized just how dire our plight had become." He faced Theopolou and Mohanisi. "If you seek to reconcile, then you will find yourself surrounded by foes. You should turn back and return to your people, lest you find a deadly reception."

"We cannot turn back," said Theopolou. "We are honor bound to liberate our kin from this evil."

"Then you will perish," said Strydis, darkly. "For no honor remains on the Steppes. They are no longer your kin." He sat back down.

Jylia took her brother's hand and placed her head on his shoulder.

"There is hope," said Mohanisi, his face awash with compassion. He told them where he was from and why he had come.

Strydis and Jylia stared in utter amazement.

"Can it be?" said Jylia. She leaned forward, carefully scrutinizing Mohanisi. "Have the fathers and mothers returned? Do you have means to support this claim?"

Mohanisi nodded. "Beyond my word, there is this." He held out his palm and a tiny ball of flame appeared. "My people possess powers that yours have forgotten. Does this prove me to be true?"

Jylia flushed. "Please. I meant no offense. But if you wish to convince those snared in the jaws of Angrääl, you will need more than words."

Mohanisi allowed the flame to vanish and smiled. "I take no offense. You are kind to advise us."

"Where shall you go?" asked Theopolou.

Strydis shrugged. "I do not know. We had thought to settle in the wilderness south of the Spirit Hills, near the ruins of Santismal. I have heard rumors that there are still elves that dwell there. Perhaps we can find peace and forgetfulness among the broken tombs of the ancient kingdoms."

"You could journey south to Althetas," suggested Theopolou. "There you would be welcomed by your kin. Although, as war has come, I cannot promise safety."

Strydis nodded. "It would be good to be among brethren whose hearts are still true." He looked into Theopolou's eyes. "It is clear that you are an elder among your people. Why they would send you on such a hopeless mission, I cannot fathom." He removed his necklace and handed it to Theopolou. "This will gain you audience. It will not save you, but it will allow you to approach the elders unharmed."

"Thank you," said Theopolou gratefully.

Theopolou felt pity for his kin, so for a few hours they spoke of happier times. Mohanisi regaled them with tales of his home and the wonders of his people. The next morning, they bid Strydis and Jylia a fond farewell and continued north.

"There has to be something causing this," mused Theopolou as they walked on. "Some power being used to alter their minds." His voice grew firmer. "As you say, Mohanisi, if we are to have any hope of succeeding, we must discover the source of this curse and destroy it as quickly as possible."

He paused before adding: "Let us pray that we can find the power to do so."

CHAPTER 4

illet gazed out on the market square of Sharpstone. Three
armed thugs stood at the far end, near the entrance to
the docks.

Dina and Randson had returned with a dozen sell-swords
and two knights of Amon Dähl. He had hoped for more, but
word had reached them that Valshara had fallen. Most of the
knights had traveled west to aid the High Lady. In fact, it
was all Millet could do to keep Dina from doing the same.
But her duty was here, and at least they had the benefit of
not being entirely supported by paid swords.

Most of the people indebted to the faithful jumped at
the chance of having their debts paid off, and in less than a
week, support for Millet had swelled. The faithful reacted by
sending a delegation to the king, but Millet had anticipated
this and made certain that they never arrived.

Once it was clear that the stakes had risen and Millet was
not to be taken lightly, the faithful took great care to ensure
that all of their movements were witnessed publicly. Millet
had been successful in creating fear among them, and with
the town no longer under their control, they were becoming

increasingly nervous, even in crowded places like the market. There were those who had more reason than most to despise the servants of the Reborn King. More than twenty of the best young men in the village had left home to join the armies of Angrääl, and there were many parents who feared their children would never return.

Millet knew that soon the faithful would send for soldiers of their own, but a fauna bird had delivered a message to the temple of Gerath in Helenia stating that Lord Broin and Lord Ganflin were sending help. Moreover, Linis was to come as well. This news made Dina in particular brighten with joy, making it clear to Millet that she had feelings for the elf. It showed in her eyes during their late-night conversations, and her reaction to his impending arrival told him that it was far beyond a passing fancy.

"You should not be out here alone," called a gruff voice from behind.

Millet glanced back to see Bevaris, one of the Amon Dähl knights. His face was weathered and scarred from years of rough living and fighting, and his skin burned permanently brown from the sun. Though not exceptionally tall, his shoulders were nearly as broad as those of two men, and his dark brown hair was cropped short and even. A massive two-handed sword, far too heavy for the average man to wield, was strapped across his back. The many notches on its blade told of the countless battles it had been involved in.

"Everyone is out at the Stedding farm today," Millet explained. "And you were tending the horses."

Bevaris scowled disapprovingly. "Then you should have waited." He looked at the thugs. "Yours?"

"No," replied Millet. "Perhaps the faithful are desperate for protection."

Bevaris laughed. "They would have to be to hire brigands and thieves. From the look of those three, they'd be as likely to rob their paymasters as to protect them."

Millet nodded in agreement. "Still, we should find out if that is, in fact, why they're here."

Bevaris grunted and strode toward the trio. Millet watched as he proceeded to quietly interrogate them. Each glanced up nervously at his massive blade as they spoke in hushed tones. After only a few minutes, Bevaris returned, looking satisfied.

"They claimed at first that they were heading to Helenia to join a caravan west," he said. "Of course, when I assured them that their journey would end right here unless they spoke truth, they then told me quick enough that they are on their way to Baltria. Apparently, Angrääl is preparing for war, and the city is ripe with fools who are too careless with their gold."

Millet bowed his head thoughtfully. "We should watch the river more closely. If Angrääl sends troops down the Goodbranch, they may bypass Sharpstone. We need to be able to send word to Gewey and the others about the enemy's movements."

"We should also prepare the house for an assault," said Bevaris. "If they land in Sharpstone in strength, it is certain they will come for us. And we should send word to Helenia."

"I'll send Randson in the morning," said Millet.

Randson, son of Barty Inglewood, the gardener, had shown himself to be far more capable than Millet could have guessed. In spite of his reserved nature, he was shrewd and well-read. To his credit, Barty had seen to it that Randson had received a good education. In fact, it was Randson, and not Dina, who had managed to gain an audience with the king.

As they returned to the manor, people shouted out greetings and grateful blessings. Millet smiled inwardly to see Sharpstone's folk so happy, even though he knew it wouldn't last. Two black-cloaked faithful scurried to the side of the avenue at their passing, only to be tripped by Martha Tredall.

"Oh, dear! How clumsy of me," said the cooper's wife.

Millet couldn't prevent himself from laughing, which brought angry stares and curses from the two men.

"You really do love to antagonize them," remarked Bevaris with amusement. "You should just let me kill them. I could be in and out of their house before they knew what had happened."

Millet's smile vanished. "I may do that soon enough. But I need to know if they have information that could help us, and dead men cannot speak."

"I'll take a dead enemy over a live one," said Bevaris. "And I suggest you do not wait too long to strike. If soldiers come..."

"If they come, they come," snapped Millet. His moods had become more volatile lately. He took a deep breath. "If they come, then we will need to move quickly. I'll have the docks watched for signs of trouble. The moment an Angrääl soldier steps foot in Sharpstone, the first thing we do is wipe out the faithful. But you're right in that we should not delay too long, regardless."

On approaching the manor, Millet immediately noticed that the front door was ajar. Bevaris drew his sword and grabbed hold of Millet's arm.

"Better to be safe," said the knight. Creeping to the door and peering in, he sheathed his sword and drew out a long triangular dagger.

Millet followed as close as he dared. Just inside, two dusty packs had been pushed against the wall. Bevaris listened for signs of anyone moving within the house.

Then a familiar voice came from behind. "I suppose I should have sent word ahead."

They spun around to see Lee Starfinder smiling broadly. Millet let out a short laugh and embraced his old friend warmly.

"By the gods," he cried. "It's good to see you."

"And you, my lord," Lee replied.

"Is Jacob with you?" he asked.

Jacob entered. "I'm here."

Millet introduced Bevaris, who was looking none too pleased.

"I am honored to meet a knight of Amon Dähl," said Lee. "Please forgive me if I surprised you."

Bevaris bowed. "No need. My anger is directed at myself. I must be getting old to have not heard you."

Lee laughed heartily. "Take comfort in the fact that Jacob and I have spent several weeks moving silently, so we've had quite a lot of practice." He looked around. "Where is Dina?"

"She'll be along before sundown," Millet replied. He looked Lee and Jacob up and down. "In the meantime, I think you'll be wanting to clean up. We can talk after."

Millet was relieved when Lee led Jacob directly to the guest rooms rather than the master's chambers, thus avoiding the awkwardness of making the reversal of roles obvious. He was just about to start heating water for bathing when Barty and Randson returned, along with three other hands and six hired swords.

Millet waited in the main hall until the bathing water was ready, then went to his chambers to wash and change. By the time he returned, Dina was back and sat on the sofa alongside Lee talking merrily. Jacob was sitting in a chair by the hearth, staring glumly into the fire. Lydia could be heard barking orders at poor Trevor, who, in spite of the fact that Millet had hired someone to assist the old man in the kitchen, still appeared to do most of the work himself.

Millet smiled at the sight of Lee back inside the manor. But he looked different—sadder and more careworn—as if age and the many miles of road traveled had finally caught up with him. His simple dark blue pants, shirt, and low-cut suede boots, though typical for Lee to wear while lounging, appeared ill-fitting to his current disposition. Millet could see behind the smile to where the pain lived. He had known the man far too long not to notice.

Millet took a seat across from them. He saw that Dina had already cleaned up and changed into a linen dress with bright yellow floral patterns and blue buttons down the front. "Did the mayor's wife insist on you using her shower again?" he asked.

Dina laughed. "Yes. And she practically forced me to take this outfit. She said that if I'm to be a lady of Sharpstone, I should look like one."

Lee glanced at Millet inquisitively.

"Dina mentioned about showers to the mayor's wife not long after we arrived," Millet explained. "She liked the idea so much that she had one built in her house. Now, she likes to show off by allowing visitors to use it—especially visitors from elsewhere. For some reason, she suspects Dina of being a foreign noble in disguise, so she steals her away at every opportunity."

Lee chuckled softly. "I did so miss this place." He called Jacob over, who forced a smile and joined them. "Forgive my son's melancholy. But we've been through quite a lot."

Jacob's smile slowly vanished, returning to a sullen stare as his eyes shifted past the gathering and to the wall behind them. "Yes. Once I've settled my mind and rested, then I'll be more like myself." These words seemed to shake him to life, and he looked at Millet with a hint of cheer returning. "Though perhaps a touch less spoiled and angry than you may remember."

Millet did not return the levity. "My lad, you and your father escaped Angrääl, and I believe that alone earns you a bit of rest. And though this is not Hazrah, it is your home nonetheless, so long as it stands."

Jacob bowed. "I thank you." His voice was emotionless.

Millet could not help but wonder why Lady Penelope was not with them. "If you are able, I would hear of your journey," he said to Lee. "Unless you would rather wait until after..."

"No. It need not wait." Lee's face darkened and his jaw tightened. He told them of the events after they had parted ways. "We made our way south through the wilderness until we were well away from Angrääl," he concluded, "then gained passage on a boat heading to Baltria on the Goodbranch."

Tears streamed down Millet's cheeks upon hearing of Lady Penelope's fate. "My heart breaks at this news. Do you think this Captain Lanmore spoke truth? Could she still live?"

Lee shrugged. "Perhaps. I cannot be certain. If she does, it's as a slave to the King of Angrääl. Whatever the case, my course is clear; I must fight until one of us is destroyed. If my wife still draws breath, then that is the only way to free her. If she does not, it is the only way to avenge her."

"What can I do to help?" asked Millet, fury boiling up in his voice.

"Allow Jacob and I to enlist into your service," Lee replied earnestly. "To give you aid in the fight that will surely come."

"The fight has already come," interjected Dina.

Millet nodded and told them of the faithful, and of the news coming in from the west. "Valshara is retaken and your mother is in command of Amon Dähl. Beyond that, we know nothing."

Lee thought on this for several minutes. "It is good that Lord Ganflin and Broin have sent help, but the fact is that the army Angrääl will send here will crush any resistance we can offer."

"There is one other thing," said Millet. "Two days ago I received a message that an elf army is marching from the desert beyond Dantory."

Lee raised an eyebrow. "Then the rumors we heard all those years ago were true."

Millet nodded. "So it would seem. When Linis arrives, I have considered sending him east to plead for their aid. But that won't be for some time. Several weeks at least."

Lee grinned. "Linis travels swiftly. And though slowed by human soldiers, I suspect he will find ways to motivate them."

Millet's concern showed on his face. "Yet even with his assistance, should Angrääl land here in force, we will be heavily outnumbered and may have to surrender Sharpstone." His frown grew deeper. "The king has been resistant to raising an army, and the lands surrounding Baltria are already subdued. The cities and towns west of Kaltinor are in turmoil. It will take time to reclaim them from the Dark Knight's influence. I have begun to send gold to our allies, but I fear we may be too late."

"If we are overrun," said Lee. "You must decide which direction to take."

"I have given it much thought," said Millet. "The lands east from here to the desert have been largely ignored by the Dark Knight. It seems he intends to cut the land in half, and with his forces engaged in the west, I believe he will focus his attention there first."

"So you will go east?" asked Jacob.

"I hope to stay here," replied Millet determinedly. "But yes. Should it come to that, I think east would be the wiser course. We can gather support along the way. Your father and I have spent many years in the hills and valleys east of the Goodbranch and have many friends there."

"So what do you need to prepare?" asked Lee.

"It will help that you are here," said Millet. "I have driven the faithful to the brink, and your presence will further unravel them. Aside from that, you can coordinate a defense with the two knights of Amon Dähl. I think you will find them quite capable." He smiled warmly. "Of course, there is the question of your lands and title to be resolved."

Lee shook his head and held up his hand. "There is nothing to resolve. You are lord of the House Nal'Thain, not I."

Millet laughed. "This is true. And I have no intention of returning them to you." His eyes fell on Jacob. "Once our duty is fulfilled, my intention is to pass over lordship to your son."

"That is not..." began Jacob.

"I am an old man," said Millet, cutting him off. "I was honored to wear the mantle of Lord Nal'Thain when your father found himself unable to do so, and at the time, there was no one else. But it is clear that you are not the confused boy you once were. The look in your eyes and the expression on Lee's face tell me that. I will retain the manor in Sharpstone as reward for my service. But once this war is over, I hope to have earned a peaceful retirement." He reached out and patted Jacob's knee. "But don't worry. For now, you are free of the burden."

Lee nodded with satisfaction. "This is agreeable. And I think by then we will both have earned some peace." He looked at Jacob. "I know you will do honor to our family."

Jacob sighed heavily, then chuckled. "We'll all probably be dead soon, anyway."

Lee let out a full-on belly laugh. "Good point."

"I think we've had enough unhappy talk for now," said Dina. "I've missed your stories, Lee. For all his talents, Millet would make a wretched bard. Regale us with an exploit of your youth. The more fantastic, the better."

Lee leaned back and smiled. "How can I refuse?"

His tales told during the hours leading up to dinner were indeed astounding, though the occasional quiet cough from Millet exposed a few small exaggerations. Lee quickly corrected these by adding in Millet's bravery as well.

The meal was just as pleasant. All the hired hands, plus as many of the sell-swords as they could accommodate, gathered around the large dining table. Songs were sung and stories were told. For the first time since Millet and Lee had left Sharpstone, the manor felt warm and alive again. Even Lydia joined in and sang a sweet lullaby she had learned as a child.

By the time the meal was over, Millet felt as if years of hardship and worry had been washed away. And though he knew this was only a passing moment, he savored it nonetheless. Lee had taken over the burden of seeing to the patrols around the manor, and Bevaris knew what needed to be done along the river and docks. With these responsibilities in safe hands, Millet felt secure enough to allow himself just one carefree evening.

It was truly good to have his former master home. And even though danger loomed, he was glad to be facing it surrounded by friends.

CHAPTER 5

Millet, Lee, Dina, and Bevaris sat quietly around the fireplace. The second knight, Tristan, a younger though not inexperienced man, was with Jacob, Barty, and Randson scouting the area around the house occupied by the faithful. The hired swords were patrolling the manor and keeping an eye on the docks and river. During the last two weeks, they had spotted hundreds of river vessels flying the banner of Angrääl heading south. Every one of these had been packed with troops and machines of war.

Millet was becoming anxious for the arrival of Linis. With each day that passed, the gnawing feeling of impending conflict increased. He looked up at Lee, who was sitting with his cup between his knees, eyes fixed on the flickering flames.

"You are doing the right thing," said Lee, feeling Millet's stare. "It's the only thing you could do."

"Don't worry, my lord," added Bevaris. "I have every confidence in Tristan. It will be clean and quick."

Millet glanced up at Dina, who nodded her agreement.

A knock at the door made them all jump, prompting Lee and Bevaris to reach for their daggers. Dina calmly stood up and answered the door. It was Mayor Freidly. Dina invited him in and offered him a seat by the fire.

"So tonight's the night," whispered the mayor.

Millet nodded somberly. "Indeed it is, your honor."

Freidly looked around at the assembled group. "No offense, but I never imagined such a night in Sharpstone. Too much blood and hardship for my poor town. If we had known what they were about when they arrived, we would never..."

"Never what?" interrupted Lee. His tone was harsh. "Never allowed them to buy you like a cheap blanket? Never allowed them to make slaves of the people you swore to protect?"

"That's enough, Lee," snapped Millet. "The mayor is here on my invitation, and you will show him courtesy."

Lee clenched his jaw for a moment but then relaxed. "Of course. Please forgive me."

Freidly's face was flushed, but he seemed to be more in awe of the fact that Millet commanded Lee than offended by Lee's words. In fact, most of the town was still gossiping about this reversal of roles. "No need to apologize," he said. "You're right. I allowed this to happen."

"There was nothing you could have done," said Millet. "If you'd resisted, you would have found yourself in an early grave." His eyes fell on Lee. "And the people of Sharpstone have no experience with such evil men."

Lee sighed. "I know. But as you have told me all of my life, I allow my passions to govern me." He stood and walked to the window. "It can sharpen my tongue if I'm not careful."

"You fear for your son?" remarked Bevaris.

"I can't help it," affirmed Lee.

"Tristan will keep him from harm," Bevaris said confidently.

Lee forced a smile and turned to the mayor. "See to it that all is ready. More and more soldiers pass this town each day. If they land here and we are defeated, you must ensure that the people comply with Angräal."

Freidly nodded.

It had been decided several days ago that, should Millet and the others be driven away, the people of Sharpstone would not continue to fight. Millet and Lee knew that they would be slaughtered. There was no time to build an adequate defense, and farmers and merchants would be of little use against hardened soldiers. Much better for them to be occupied and await liberation. Naturally, encouraged by what Millet had already achieved against the faithful, this was a bitter pill. But he had eventually convinced them of his wisdom.

"Tell us, your honor," said Dina, smiling girlishly. "What juicy gossip is there to be heard? Surely these things reach the mayor's ears."

"You can't be serious," said Freidly, taken aback. "You want to hear such things on an evening like this?"

"I think it is the perfect time to hear gossip," Dina replied.

"I agree," said Bevaris. "I miss the gossip and chatter of my own home. I would be reminded of such carefree days."

"And where is your home?" asked Freidly.

"Xenthia," he replied. "East, below the foothills of the Weeping Mountains."

"I've been there," said Lee. "King Vistylis reigned at the time. He kept an estate as lavish as any in the West."

"His son, Luccia, still does," said Bevaris. "He spends most of his time there and has practically made it the new capital. He prefers the quieter atmosphere. The estate is now twice as opulent as his official palace in Nashis."

"A grand city also," said Lee. "Though I have only ever seen the palace from outside the gates."

"Should we ever find ourselves there," said Bevaris, "I can see to it that the king allows us entry." He leaned back and took a sip from his cup. "Now, my good mayor, if you would be so kind as to lighten heavy hearts with the intrigues of your fair town."

Mayor Freidly bowed and began reporting the local gossip. The mood in the room lifted at once, and a few laughs were even heard. He had just gotten to telling them of how Naomi Sweetwater had caught her husband trying to seduce the wife of Jack Venturia, a pig farmer, when Tristan burst in.

In contrast to Brevaris's bull-like build, Tristan was tall and lean, and also quite handsome. His curly, blond hair fell nearly to his shoulders, and his chiseled features and ice-blue eyes had already turned the head of more than one farmer's wife. He was clad in a black shirt and pants, together with soft leather boots. On his belt hung a short sword and dagger; both hilts were spotted with blood.

"What happened?" asked Bevaris.

"It is done," Tristan replied. "The faithful are dead."

"Was anyone hurt?" asked Lee.

"No," said Tristan. "But I have ill news. One of the towns-folk spotted us on our way back and told us they had seen a large number of men camped ten miles north of here."

This news brought the room to its feet.

"Did he say how many?" asked Millet.

"He thought it to be a hundred, maybe more," replied Tristan. "He said he couldn't tell in the dark and was afraid to get closer. I sent Randson and Jacob to find out more."

Millet could see a flash of anger on Lee's face. He touched him on the shoulder. "Jacob will be fine. Randson knows the woods and trails better than anyone. And you've taught your son well." He turned to Tristan. "Gather the men and send the workers to the Stedding farm."

"I should alert the town council," said Freidly.

Millet nodded. "But tell them not to do anything until we know more."

The mayor took a deep, nervous breath and left.

"Even if the count is accurate," said Bevaris. "One hundred is too many unless you enlist the townsfolk."

"No," shot back Millet. "I will not involve the people."

"But it may buy us time to gather more men," Bevaris countered. "In a month we could..."

"We have no guarantee it would buy that much time," said Millet firmly. "Otherwise I would agree."

"There are no guarantees in war, my lord. Only risks."

"And it is a risk I am not willing to take."

"I think you are allowing your love of this town to cloud your judgment," Bevaris told him.

"Perhaps," agreed Millet. "But if Sharpstone is lost, it is much better that we have living spies in an occupied town rather than see it destroyed. Better for the enemy to think they fought a rogue lord who stood against the will of the townsfolk than perceive the entire town as a threat."

"But..." started Bevaris.

"We have no time for this," Lee snapped at the knight. "The lord of this house has spoken. We must prepare."

Bevaris sighed and shook his head. "Very well. Come, Tristan. It is time we put our armor to use."

Bevaris and Tristan hurried to their room. A few minutes later, they reappeared in polished black leather armor. Bevaris had his huge sword strapped across his back, and a dagger hung on each hip. Tristan wore a long sword with a silver hilt crowned by a single black opal. Across his chest was a strap holding six small throwing knives.

Tristan gathered the men in front of the manor while Bevaris readied the horses. About an hour before sunrise, Jacob and Randson returned.

Before Millet could open his mouth, Jacob spoke. "Two hundred men are on our heels. They'll be here in minutes."

"The sell-swords will flee," said Bevaris.

"Then don't tell them," said Lee. "From where do they approach?"

"Half from the north," Jacob replied. "The others have already circled around to the west." The look of fear was in his eyes. "Father ... there are Vrykol among them."

"How many?" asked Lee.

"At least three," he replied.

Lee turned to Millet. "I think we should leave now."

There was a commotion outside. Millet went to the window. "That time is past," he said. "They are here."

Silhouetted through the gate by the lamps at the entrance of the main yard stood a black-cloaked figure. Millet turned and picked up a short sword he had leaned against his chair.

"Please," said Lee. "Stay with me and Jacob. You may be a far better lord than I ever was, but a warrior you are not."

Millet smiled and grabbed Lee's shoulder fondly. "If I am to face my end, it will not be cowering. And I don't think that even you can protect me from two hundred soldiers."

"Then let us meet our end together," said Lee. He walked over to Jacob and embraced him. "I'm sorry I have failed you. But I am honored to have known you, and I am proud you are my son."

Jacob squeezed his father tightly. "You have not failed me. I'm happy we will meet death side by side."

"We're not dead yet," said Dina. Her voice was steel. She wore a leather tunic over her tan cotton blouse and carried a long dagger in her right hand. "They face the son of Saraf and the knights of Amon Dähl. Even vastly outnumbered, such opponents are to be feared."

"Come then," said Millet. "Let us make them pay dearly for their foolishness."

Millet had considered asking Dina to remain hidden, but one look at her face told him it would be useless to do so. Their fates were tied together, for good or ill.

The group filed out into the yard. The sell-swords were clearly terrified, and Tristan was doing everything he could to keep them from fleeing. Only Barty and Randson remained steadfast.

"Listen to me," shouted Lee. Everyone went silent. "If you run, you will most surely die. Our only hope is to fight them off until they withdraw. When they regroup, we'll take the horses and break out. The path will only allow about ten men through at a time, so their advantage will be much lessened. We can do this if we stay together."

The men shifted, muttering curses. But they could see the sense in his words, and none chose to run. Lee positioned himself between Dina and Jacob. Bevaris insisted on being near Millet, while Tristan was at the opposite end, keeping the men in formation.

Millet had ordered the fence surrounding the estate raised and doubled two weeks earlier, making it difficult, though not impossible, to climb or break down. The main gate would only allow room enough for ten men to pass at once, but it was not designed to hold off any type of determined assault. The enemy would be able to break it down as if it were made from clay.

Dozens of torches could be seen approaching from out of the darkness. Moments later, the sound of countless heavy boots striking earth thudded in their ears. Then, one by one, the torches went out. The air suddenly went still, with only the shallow frightened breaths of the sell-swords breaking the silence.

The piercing blast of a horn rang out, followed by the roar of battle cries.

"Here they come," muttered Bevaris, a wicked grin on his weathered face. His sword, gripped in both hands, was nearly as long as he was tall.

The gate flew open as the first wave of soldiers battered it down with a felled tree. Ten men clad in heavy plate, the sigil of Angrääl across their breast, dropped the ram and, scrambled through. Behind them, row upon row of others awaited their turn to enter the fray.

Lee led the charge to meet the attack head-on. As the two forces met, the air filled with the sound of steel blades violently clashing. The enemy was driven back almost at once.

Lee cut down three men in quick succession. Bevaris placed his massive shoulder in front of Millet, pushing him back out of harm's way. His mighty sword swept down, nearly cleaving a soldier in twain and forcing Bevaris to kick the body away from his blade. Jacob tried to maneuver himself in front of Dina, but she deftly slipped by him and gutted an attacker.

On the other end, Tristan, Barty, Randson, and the sell-swords were faring just as well. They had already killed four men, with only a few minor cuts between them suffered in return. Millet's hopes lifted at the sight, but these hopes were short-lived.

As quickly as they fell, the fallen soldiers were being replaced, each new attack becoming more ferocious than the last. It wasn't long before Lee and the others found themselves being driven back toward the house. Very soon now, the attackers would be able to spread out and flank them. Two sell-swords had fallen and Tristan was bleeding from a deep gash on his left forearm. Dina was surprisingly capable with a blade, her light attire allowing her to easily avoid the clumsy thrusts of the Angrääl soldiers.

When another sell-sword fell, the left side gave way and Tristan was forced to withdraw. Soldiers began to pour through the gate, attempting to surround them.

"Fall back to the manor!" shouted Lee.

Just then, another blast from the enemy horn sounded. In response to this, amazingly, the soldiers began to retreat. Within moments, they had all passed back through the gate and disappeared completely into the darkness. Millet and the others stood where they were for a full minute, utterly confused and unable to speak.

"Why did they stop?" asked Jacob, breaking the stupor.

"I don't intend to find out," said Millet. "Let's fetch the horses and get out of here." He turned to the sell-swords.

"You men should ride with us. Once we're far enough from here, you can either come along or go your own way."

They dragged the bodies of their fallen comrades away from the main path and retrieved the horses. No sooner had they mounted than Lee's back stiffened. He drew his sword.

"Someone approaches," he said. "Whoever it is, they're alone."

"Perhaps they want to negotiate a surrender," offered one of the men.

"Then they're bigger fools than I thought," said Lee. "The moment he enters, kill him and follow me."

A minute later, a lone hooded figure walked cautiously through the broken gates. Lee was just about to sound the charge when the figure threw back his hood.

It was Linis.

Lee, Dina, and Millet immediately leaped from their horses. Linis smiled warmly. "I see I have arrived a little late."

They all took turns in embracing the elf, Dina lingering longer than the rest.

"You're just in time, my friend," said Lee, not hiding his relief. "How many men did you bring?"

"I had fifty," Linis replied. "But I lost nearly half of them driving away your foes. Mostly they fell to the Vrykol." He glanced over his shoulder. "The men are about a quarter mile back. We surprised the enemy and were able to cause enough confusion to break their ranks, but I think it is certain they will regroup and return."

"We're ready to ride now ... if you are," said Millet.

"Good," said Linis. He gave Dina a quick smile. "Then let us be gone."

Linis led them down one of the many paths leading away from the manor. Millet could hear whispers from the sell-swords about Linis. Clearly, they had never seen an elf before.

"Are your men mounted?" asked Lee.

"Yes," replied Linis. "I do not enjoy travel by horse, but it was the only way to move so many men quickly. I have little in the way of supplies, but Lord Ganflin and Lord Broin sent gold."

Millet nodded. "That is good. We will need it." He had packed as much gold as could be carried himself.

As Linis had said, the men awaited them a quarter mile away. Most wore either light leather armor or thin chain mail with the sigil of a sword and moon.

"They have fled west to the river, my lord," said one of the men. "Along with the one remaining Vrykol." The word Vrykol came out like a curse.

Linis turned to Millet. "You know these parts better than I."

"We should go southeast, through the forest," interjected Randson. "It's slower, but it avoids town and will put us well beyond the Stedding farm."

"Lead on," commanded Millet.

Randson spurred his horse forward, guiding them into the outlying forest and down a narrow hunting trail. Lee fell back to the rear to listen for signs of pursuit, while Linis stayed at the front. By dawn, they were well away, and clearly, the Angrääl soldiers had no desire to catch them. They stopped in a clearing to rest their horses. Millet removed a pack from his mount and pulled Randson and Barty aside.

"I need you to go to Baltria," he told them.

"If you think to keep us from harm," objected Barty.

"I intend to put you in harm's way," interrupted Millet. "I need eyes and ears there. Someone I can trust and who no one knows. You cannot return to Sharpstone. If you do, it will be quickly discovered that you fought with us." He handed Barty the pack. "Here is enough gold to bribe whomever you must, and to keep you fed and housed once you arrive. Find Jansi. He serves Lord Lanson Brimm. There is a letter in the pack that will prove to him you are a friend. He may be able to aid you."

"How shall we contact you?" asked Barty.

"Do not try," said Millet. "When the time comes, I will contact you. Until then, learn what you can. If you are found out, make your way to Althetas and go to King Lousis. He will take care of you."

After saying a brief farewell to the others, Barty and Randson rode off south through the dense forest.

"You are becoming ruthless, my old friend," said Lee. "Far more so than I. I don't think I could send them into such peril."

"Perhaps," said Millet. "But I need them there." He took a deep breath. "I do not like who I have become, Lee. But I think that fate has chosen this path for me for a reason, though it may be at the cost of my soul."

"Where are we going?" asked Linis, smiling as he approached.

"To Dantory," replied Millet. His tone was firm and commanding. "We have received word that the elves from the deep desert mass for war. We will join them, gathering what support we can along the way."

Linis raised an eyebrow. "Then let us meet these desert elves. We can tell our tales as we travel."

CHAPTER 6

The journey back to Valshara had been difficult for Gewey to endure. Fighters, both elf and human, came to him in a ceaseless stream to thank him for their resounding victory. King Lousis did his best to keep his men away, but his mind was on other matters. Most of the prisoners were from Skalhalis. The generals from Angrääl had refused to allow their men to lay down their arms, and only after King Halmara was slain did his commanders kill the Angrääl leaders and order the surrender. Lousis had decided to force the prisoners to construct their own prison. When that was completed, he would release those from Skalhalis and allow them to return to their families.

One thing deeply troubling Gewey was the disappearance of Yanti's body. He had personally searched the battlefield for more than an hour and found no trace of him. The thought that the man could still live caused his anger to resurface. He had later considered looking for the men from Sharpstone but dismissed the idea. If any survived, they would be safer in prison.

Word of their victory had already reached Valshara, ensuring that the entire temple was outside greeting them when they arrived. Gewey, Lousis, Kaylia, and Ertik rode abreast into the yard as cries of "Long live Darshan" echoed from the walls. Both men and women openly wept at the sight of him as he passed. Gewey did his best to be gracious and smile.

High Lady Selena stood at the door in her ceremonial robes. Her face was a mixture of relief and sadness. "We thank the gods for your victory. Tonight, there shall be a celebration banquet to honor you all."

They dismounted and bowed in unison.

"It was hard fought," said Lousis. "But the true honor goes to Gewey."

"So I have heard," said Selena. "Songs are already being sung throughout the temple about his deeds."

"I'm sure they are exaggerated," said Gewey.

"Perhaps," Selena countered. "But you give people inspiration and hope. You may very well have to accept the myth that is surrounding your name."

Her words struck a chord with Gewey. Suddenly, he was filled with a sense of urgency.

"What is it?" asked Kaylia, sensing his feelings.

"I need to have the Book of Souls brought to my chambers as soon as possible, High Lady," said Gewey.

Ertik stepped forward. "I will see to it."

Selena turned and opened the door. "Water and food are already being brought to your rooms." She glanced over her shoulder. "Kaylia, I would speak to you as soon as you are able."

Gewey moved to take a step forward. As he did so, pain shot through his stomach where Yanti's blade had struck. Aaliyah and Nehrutu, who had been riding only a few yards behind him, were at his side at once.

"You have delayed healing long enough," said Aaliyah sternly. Still weak from healing the wounded on the battlefield, her face was pale and her eyes tired.

"I am in no danger," said Gewey.

"Perhaps not," she said. "But I can feel your agony through our bond. For Kaylia, it must be far worse. Would you allow your stubbornness to cause her pain?"

Gewey closed his eyes and nodded his consent. "Very well. Allow me an hour to wash and change, then come to my chambers."

Kaylia walked him through the halls to their room. Stares of awe were evident on the faces of all they encountered. A tub of steaming hot water and a meal of bread and veal awaited them. Gewey and Kaylia washed, changed into soft cotton robes, and took their meal. They were sipping on a cup of wine when Aaliyah arrived with Nehrutu. Gewey allowed them to lay him on the bed and complete the healing. His spirits lifted immediately.

"Thank you," he said. "I'm sorry for being so bullheaded. I was just concerned for you both."

"No need to apologize," said Aaliyah. "But you must learn to accept the help of those who love you. You cannot protect everyone. There are times when it is you who need protection."

Gewey smiled warmly. "You're right, of course. But right now, it looks like it's you two who need to care for yourselves."

Nehrutu laughed. "I believe you are right." He touched Aaliyah's shoulder. "Let us go."

Soon after they'd left, Ertik arrived with the Book of Souls. Gewey sat on the edge of the bed and ran his fingers over the box.

"Do you think you will find the answers you seek there?" asked Kaylia.

"According to Felsafell—no," he replied. "Though I believe it may show me where to begin."

Kaylia took the box and placed it inside the wardrobe. "Then you will begin tomorrow. We should rest before the banquet."

Getting into bed, she pulled Gewey down beside her. As she kissed him, mutual passion exploded through their bond.

"But perhaps rest can wait for a while," she murmured.

Ertik returned at sunset to inform them that the banquet would be beginning soon. Selena had ordered the court-yard cleared and made ready; even the receiving hall could not accommodate all the many people eager to celebrate their victory.

Gewey wanted to wear simple elf attire, but Kaylia wouldn't hear of it, instead dressing him in a snow-white silk shirt with a raised collar and silver buttons. His matching pants fit almost too snuggly, accentuating his muscular form. Completing the ensemble was a formal black jacket with silver embroidery along its broad collar, together with boots and a belt polished to a mirror shine. He decided to leave his sword behind and wear a plain dagger that contrasted with the elegance of his attire, giving him an approachable and less arrogant quality.

Kaylia wore an emerald green satin dress that hugged her curves and flowed with her graceful movements. Two maidens came and adorned her hair with delicate white flowers. Gewey was amazed at how easily she could transform from a beautiful warrior into a breathtaking goddess. Human women would take hours painting their faces and dressing themselves in extravagant gowns, and still only become a shadow of the loveliness he saw before him.

Just before they left the room, he took hold of Kaylia's hands and looked at her with heartfelt approval. "I feel like a peasant next to you."

Kaylia leaned in and kissed him lightly on the cheek, smiling impishly. "That is good. Let us hope that feeling lasts forever."

When drawing near the temple entrance, they saw two guards in gleaming plate mail, each holding a banner bearing Gewey's crest. They snapped to attention and pushed open the door the moment they saw the couple approaching.

The sound of music and laughter poured in. As they stepped over the threshold into the open air, they could see hundreds of finely dressed humans and elves talking and drinking. The sheer myriad of colors from all the widely differing outfits was stunning. Enhancing this, warm torchlight filled the yard with a pleasant glow.

Selena had arranged for dozens of long tables to be set in neat rows on either side of the courtyard near the curtain walls; a raised platform had also been erected close to the main gateway. Flowers festooned the statue of the sword, which was surrounded by six brass braziers. Four musicians—in actual fact, three temple priests and a soldier—were playing merrily while people danced and sang along to their music.

The blare of a trumpet heralded the new arrivals. Within moments, the banquet drew quiet as all eyes fell on Gewey. Then a single voice cried out, "Darshan." This was immediately followed by another. Then another—and another—until the entire yard was roaring out his name.

Gewey could feel the wave of emotion washing over him from the crowd. The faint sound of a child's laughter and hundreds of tiny bells drifted down, filling his mind. As when the anger and rage had flowed through him, he felt immensely powerful. Yet this time it was not the unbridled torrent of before, but a steady, controllable surge. The flow of the spirit illuminated the entire yard. It was as if he could see through every soul there. The temptation to reach out and touch them was almost irresistible. Gewey raised his fist high. The crowd erupted afresh.

Kaylia leaned over to whisper into his ear. "You have given them hope."

Her words brought him back, allowing the flow to subside. He took Kaylia's hand, and they walked into the crowd. People beamed, making way for them as they passed. A few moments later, Nehrutu and Aaliyah approached.

Aaliyah was wearing a flowing red silk dress with deep crimson beads sewn in undulating patterns along each side that wrapped themselves around her delicate waist. Her black hair was tied back in a thick braid, interwoven with a red satin cloth.

Nehrutu wore a white, loose-fitting, open-collared shirt, trousers, and black suede boots. A gold belt studded with emeralds held his short sword and was wrapped atop a black sash.

They bowed low and smiled warmly. Gewey and Kaylia returned the gesture.

"It is good to see joy after such hardships, is it not?" said Aaliyah.

Gewey nodded. "I wish it could last."

"A fleeting joy is a joy, nonetheless," said Nehrutu.

"Come," said Aaliyah. "High Lady Selena wishes you to join her."

They made their way through the crowd to the platform where Selena, Lord Chiron, and Lady Bellisia stood talking quietly.

"The hero of Valshara has arrived," said Chiron. "Along with his lovely unorem."

Gewey gave an embarrassed laugh.

Selena leaned in and kissed Kaylia on her cheek, then looked at her approvingly. "You are a jewel on the crown, my dear."

Selena was dressed in her ceremonial robes, with her hair falling loosely down her back.

Kaylia smiled graciously. "I thank you."

Both Chiron and Bellisia were wearing the white robes of the elf elders; the same ones Gewey had seen when he first met them at the home of Theopolou.

"I hope you have prepared something to say," said Selena. "You will be expected to give a speech."

Gewey's sudden wide-eyed stare of terror brought a laugh to them all.

"Then I suppose he will need to rely on the same wit and cunning that brought elf and human together," said Bellisia teasingly. "If he can bring me to change my stubborn ways, this crowd should cause him no difficulty at all."

"I think Theopolou deserves the credit for that," said Gewey.

The mention of the old elf's name brought a moment of respectful silence as they were reminded of the danger Theopolou was currently putting himself in.

"I thought King Lousis was with you," remarked Kaylia.

"He will return soon," said Selena. "The main army is celebrating near the entrance of the pass. He couldn't resist joining his soldiers for a round of ale."

The conversation turned to the battle itself: they spoke of the bravery of those who'd perished, and of how their comrades had died. Gewey was uncomfortable with the subject at first, but Kaylia quietly told him that it was common for elves to do this. They felt it honored the memory of those lost.

After about an hour, Selena excused herself and stepped up onto the platform. Another trumpet blast quieted the crowd. She stood silently for a moment, her face solemn.

"I thank you all for joining us in this celebration," she began. Her strong voice carried easily throughout the courtyard. "It is good and proper that we rejoice in this marvelous victory. And though there are many difficult days to come, we now know that the evil that threatens to destroy us is not invincible. More importantly, our enemy knows it as well.

"Many of you here tonight will have lost friends and family. Our kin and comrades have fallen to the foul beasts of Angrääl. And though we repaid them tenfold, this still does not fill the emptiness left in our hearts by their absence."

She lowered her head and took a breath. "I wish I could tell you that your losses are at an end. I wish I could say that you will suffer no more. But that would be a lie. Many more will perish before this so-called Reborn King falls. But I swear to you that we will see victory. And we will rebuild this world.

"Bonds once unimagined have been formed between elf and human, and a new kinship will rise from the ashes of destruction. The first Great War ushered in an age of mistrust and hatred that lasted for five hundred years. That time is now at an end. This second Great War will see the annihilation of the evil that plagues us all and bring about the birth of a new age; an age of understanding and cooperation. Together, we have already found a common cause and a reason to set aside our misgivings. Blood has been shed and friendships, both old and new, have grown stronger. I believe that these friendships will guide us through the crucible and become the weapon that ultimately drives away the darkness."

Many heads nodded in agreement as Selena began her conclusion. "The enemy we face is strong and his armies are vast. But they will not prevail. They lack the one thing they need for victory. The spirit and will to see this world reborn in the image we determine. They cannot conquer us with hatred and malice. And they cannot stop the storm that they have unleashed. Our destiny is now, and forever will be, in our own hands."

Selena looked out over her audience, then bowed reverently. Cheers erupted and swelled with thunderous applause. She motioned for Gewey to join her. The moment he stepped up, the already deafening volume of the crowd doubled in intensity. The flow of the spirit illuminated the yard and Gewey once again could hear the bells and laughter. It filled him completely, caressing his body and mind with a firm yet pleasing touch. Its seductive power grew with each passing second until he felt every bit the god people saw him to be.

"I know many of you believe that I was the reason we were victorious." His voice boomed and echoed off the stone walls like a thunderclap, startling and silencing the crowd. "I have heard the songs you now sing. But know this—it is I who sings your praises. It was you who conquered the foes that sought to destroy you. It was the power of your hearts that crushed their will.

"Many of you have come to believe that I am here to save you. You know what I am, and think that I alone can mend a world that has been broken by war, hatred, and suspicion. But I tell you now that it is the spirit I see before me that has the real power. It is you who will give me the strength to do what must be done. I am in awe of your courage and humbled by your determination."

Each word he uttered swelled the flow within him. The lights danced furiously in every corner and began to pass into those listening. Instantly, he could feel their will bending to his.

"I rejoice in the knowledge that I have such passion and heart at my side. The time will soon come when I must do battle with the Reborn King. We will face one another and our fates will be decided. This is my sole purpose. It is why I am here. It is why the gods created me. But should I succeed, it will be because of the power I gain from you. You give me the strength to meet my destiny. And in payment for your kindness, I will give you all that I am. I am at your service and in your debt from this day until the end of days."

At that moment, the flow of the spirit burst forth. Dozens of humans and elves dropped to their knees in worship.

Others wept openly as hundreds of voices cried out in unison, repeating again and again the name of Darshan. Without a thought, Gewey unleashed the flow of the air around him, allowing his body to be lifted several feet above the platform. A pillar of fire sprang to life above his head, shooting skyward and piercing the night. He was a god in both body and spirit as he gazed down upon the people, bathing in their adoration.

A voice entered his mind like a distant echo. *Enough.* He tried to ignore it, but it was relentless. *Enough! Enough!* He realized it was Kaylia calling to him through their bond. Reluctantly, he allowed the power to drain away and drifted slowly back down to the platform. By then, all but Kaylia and his friends nearby were on their knees, chanting his name. Even Chiron and Bellisia had tears streaming down their cheeks, while Nehrutu was clinging desperately to Aaliyah. Kaylia and Selena were standing close to each other, a severe look of dread on both of their faces.

"We should return to our room," whispered Kaylia.

Gewey could still feel the ecstasy of the moment lingering in his mind. He turned to Selena. "You wanted me to be an inspiration, did you not?"

"The gods stay in heaven for a reason," she replied, motioning toward the crowd. The entire banquet was still kneeling and chanting. "Do you desire worshipers? Do you think that is why you were sent here?"

Gewey looked unblinkingly into Selena's eyes. "I have enough questions. What I need are answers. Can you provide them?"

"No," she admitted. "But I believe you must find them soon before you lose that part of you that is human."

Gewey held her gaze for a moment before turning away and striding toward the temple, Kaylia at his side. Those he passed lowered their eyes. Some reached out to touch his leg. Despite this overpowering display of mass devotion, by the time they reached their chamber, he was already starting to revert back to his normal self.

"I should apologize to High Lady Selena," he said, sitting down on the bed and staring at the floor.

Kaylia sat beside him and took his hand. "Tomorrow."

"I don't know what's happening to me," Gewey said. "It's like I can't control what I have become. When it was just anger and rage, I could at least make sense of it. But this is different."

Kaylia stroked his cheek. "I am here. Do not forget, my love, I feel what you feel. The power of the spirit is seductive beyond anything I could have dreamed. But I know you are strong enough to resist."

"But should I resist?" His voice wavered. "Is this not what Felsafell said I must learn to use? If I am to believe what he told me, it is only through the flow of the spirit that I can defeat the armies of Angrääl, and with them, the Reborn King."

Kaylia looked at him with pity and compassion for several seconds. Finally, she got up and retrieved the Book of Souls from the wardrobe. "Perhaps this should not wait," she said.

Gewey nodded and took the book over to the table. As he opened the box, dim light poured out like a thin fog. The lettering on the cover was the same as before, but this time it was immediately understandable to him as if written in his native tongue. He removed the book and opened it. Kaylia lay in bed watching him while he read page after page, until eventually, he heard her even breaths as sleep took hold.

Gewey continued reading until dawn, only stopping then to eat breakfast and change into his more comfortable elf clothing. At midday, after Kaylia had departed for a lesson with Nehrutu, he decided to seek out Selena to offer his apologies. Stepping outside of his room, he paused for a moment, astonished by the dozens of flowers and baskets of fruits that had been placed just outside his door. Sighing, he moved on to seek out Selena's quarters. But directions were not so easy to come by. Most of the people he encountered were simply too overawed to even look at him, let alone speak—one soldier even fell face down on the floor as he approached. It was only after some time that he finally managed to get the instructions he needed.

He knocked softly and heard a calm voice telling him to enter. Selina was sitting quietly in a plush chair, reading a book. She was wearing a soft cotton robe and slippers. Putting down the book, she smiled warmly.

"If you've come to apologize, there's no need," she said. "I know you must be very confused by your power."

Gewey took the chair across from her. "I admit it is confusing at times. I don't fully understand how it all works, or how I should use it." He leaned forward. "The powers of earth, air, and water are complicated, but at least I know what to do with them. The spirit is very different."

"I'm certain you will figure it out," she said. "Your makers would not have sent you otherwise."

Gewey took a moment to scrutinize her. "I couldn't help but notice that you were unaffected. I understand why Kaylia and Aaliyah can resist because of the bond between us. But you..."

Selena let out a merry laugh. "I did not become the High Lady of Amon Dähl without learning to govern my own mind. I am indeed affected by your power. In fact, last night it took all of my strength not to fall to the ground just like everyone else."

Gewey felt embarrassed. "I'm glad you didn't. You were right. I don't want worshipers."

"That is good to hear," said Selena. She paused to raise an eyebrow. "Kaylia told me you were reading the Book of Souls. What have you learned?"

Gewey shrugged. "So far, I don't understand most of it. It speaks of names and places I have never heard of before.

But of course, I've only just begun. I'm hoping it will make more sense as I read on."

Selena nodded. "I'm sure it will, and I think it's vital that you finish it."

Gewey stood up. "That is what I intend to do now."

"You will be sure to tell me what you learn, I hope," she said, picking up her book once again.

Gewey bowed and returned to his room.

For the next four days, he did nothing but read. During this period, Kaylia spent most of her time with Nehrutu and Aaliyah. Keen to help, Aaliyah was now assisting Nehrutu with Kaylia's lessons. At the end of each day, the offerings at Gewey's door had to be cleared away, and soon a guard was placed outside to discourage those wanting a blessing from the great Darshan.

On the morning of the fifth day, Gewey sent word that he urgently needed to speak to Selena, Aaliyah, Nehrutu, Chiron, and Bellisia. He also wanted Lousis there but learned that the king had returned to Althetas with Eftichis and Ertik to meet with the Southern rulers. He was worried that the elf elders would be offended by his words but had decided that he must risk their displeasure. What he had to say would change what both races believed forever.

Kaylia could sense his uneasiness, but to Gewey's relief, she did not press him to explain the reason for this. Instead, she began to pack for a journey. It eased Gewey's mind greatly to know how well she understood him and even more that she would not allow him to be alone.

CHAPTER 7

Theopolou and Mohanisi stood at the edge of the last tree line and looked out at the grassy expanse of the Steppes. The treeless flat plain gave Theopolou an uncomfortably exposed sensation. He had visited the elves that lived here many times in the past but had never once enjoyed the occasion. He was always anxious to return to the familiar sights and smells of the forest.

The humans that shared this land were an odd and unpredictable people. They had no cities or towns, instead choosing to wander in small groups, hunting bison and gathering roots. Though they generally tended to stay clear of the elves, their nomadic nature meant that occasional confrontations were unavoidable. Some of these ended in violence, but as they had no social structure beyond their small groups, nothing had ever seriously escalated.

The elf lands hugged the coast, though there were no ports to speak of. Unlike the southern, forest-dwelling elves, they cared little for boats and felt uneasy on the water. They did, however, possess a great love of horses, and boasted some of the best breeding stock in the entire world. Though

Theopolou's tribes, along with most others, did, in fact, use horses, they much preferred to travel on foot.

The elf villages were a three-day walk across the open plain. The humans kept mostly to the northeastern areas but were known to occasionally venture south in pursuit of the herds. Even with Mohanisi's abilities at their disposal, Theopolou had no desire for a battle. Should the humans run across two isolated elves, there was a very good chance they might try to take advantage of their apparent vulnerability.

The first two days were uneventful. The only life they ran across was a small herd of wild horses and an eagle screeching high above in a cloudless sky. Usually, the elves would send small parties to scout the outlying regions, mostly to keep the humans in check, but so far, there had been none. The town of Lan Silsia was the first they would encounter. It was sparsely populated, and in the past, had been quiet and peaceful. Mostly, the inhabitants concerned themselves with their small farms and herds of sheep, caring little for the politics concerning the rest of the tribes. It made Theopolou think of Gewey and the small village of Sharpstone he had told him about. A part of Theopolou wished he could show Gewey just how similar elf and man really were. He laughed inwardly that such obvious things had escaped him for most of his life.

On the evening of the second night, he mentioned this thought to Mohanisi.

Mohanisi cocked his head. "Why would this surprise you? It was the elves who taught the humans culture and civilization in the beginning. And both races were tempered by the same land. It is natural for you to see yourself reflected."

"I see it now," said Theopolou. "But for so long, the hatred has blinded us; the devastation of the Great War was kept fresh in our minds by elves like me."

"I do not pretend to understand how it must feel to live through such horrors," admitted Mohanisi. "But it is good to see that even old hearts can be mended."

Theopolou smiled. "I must say that it feels right to forgive ... both the humans and myself." He glanced sideways at Mohanisi. "And what of your kin? You have said many times that we seem as different to you as the humans do to us. What will the rest of your people think of us?"

"When I arrived, I was doubtful that our people could ever be reunited," he replied. "And I still believe it will take time for us to understand you completely. But more and more, I discover the grace and nobility I was hoping for. And the fact remains that you are our kin as much as any elf who dwells in my own lands. It was no fault of your own that you were separated from the place of your ancestors, and it would be wrong to judge you harshly."

They spoke quietly for a short time longer, then slept until dawn.

The following morning they had been walking for only an hour when they heard the sound of distant hoofs approaching from the north.

"It is a human," said Mohanisi. "He is alone and, as of yet, unaware of us." He closed his eyes and furrowed his brow. "He is afraid."

"Can you sense Vrykol?" asked Theopolou.

Mohanisi shook his head. "No. But I think we should find out what has terrified him. From what you have told me of the humans here, it would have to be something truly dire."

"We risk a fight," said Theopolou. "But I think you are correct. We must know what has happened."

With the grass just tall enough for them to lay down unseen, they positioned themselves directly in the path of the oncoming horse, springing up when it was only a few yards away from their hiding place. The horse reared, nearly throwing the man from his saddle. Theopolou quickly grabbed the reins.

The rider was clad in leather pants, a shirt made from bison hide, and a grubby wool jacket. His russet complexion and weathered appearance spoke of how hard life was on the Steppes. His deep-set, dark eyes opened wide in alarm as he reached for a rusty curved sword attached to his saddle. In an instant, Mohanisi seized the man's arm and jerked him roughly to the ground.

"We mean you no harm," said Theopolou.

The man glared at them, trying to mask his fear.

"If we wanted to kill you, we would already have done so," Mohanisi stated calmly. He stepped back and allowed him to regain his feet.

"What do you want of me?" asked the man.

"First, I want to know your name," Theopolou replied.

"I am called Rinzo," he said, holding his head high.

Theopolou bowed. "I am Theopolou, and this is Mohanisi. From what or whom do you flee?"

"I flee nothing," Rinzo replied. "And I fear nothing."

"I will not waste time with lies," said Theopolou. He nodded to Mohanisi.

Mohanisi held out his palm and a ball of flame burst to life above it.

Rinzo hurriedly stepped back, gasping in astonishment. "What are you?"

"I am nothing more than what you see before you," Mohanisi replied. The flame grew and moved toward the now terrified human.

"Please," Rinzo begged. "Enough. I'll tell you what you want to know."

Mohanisi smiled, and the flame disappeared.

"What caused you such fear as to make you ride blindly across the Steppes?" asked Theopolou.

Rinzo steadied himself and straightened his shoulders. "I flee a monster that massacred my clan. It tore them limb from limb. Some were even stripped of their skin. I had just returned from the well when I found them. If I had been there when the monster arrived, I too would have suffered the same fate."

"What would do such a thing?" asked Theopolou.

"I only caught a glimpse of it," said Rinzo. "It was wrapped in a black cloak and carried a long, jagged blade. If not for the speed of my horse, it would have caught me. It moved so fast that it would have run down a lesser steed."

"Vrykol," muttered Theopolou. "Are there any other elves nearby?"

"Not that I've seen," replied Rinzo. "Lately, your kind has kept to their villages."

Theopolou thought for a moment before backing away. "You are free to leave. But be sure you tell your people that the elves had nothing to do with the death of your kin."

Rinzo looked at them for several seconds with a perplexed expression. Then, without a word, leaped back on his horse and sped away.

"We should be cautious," said Mohanisi while watching Rinzo disappear into the distance. "If the Vrykol are slaughtering humans, they may well be doing the same to elves."

"It would take many foes to truly threaten the tribes here," said Theopolou. "I fear our enemy is trying to make it seem as if the elves are to blame, and so trick the humans into fighting."

"Do you believe the Reborn King would enlist these humans to his cause?" asked Mohanisi.

Theopolou shook his head. "It is doubtful. The humans of the Steppes would be of little use to him. They are a wild people and would be a liability in an organized army. The most he could hope for is to have them conduct hit-and-run attacks. Even then, their numbers are few. Any attack on an elf village would be suicide."

"A possessed mind can be driven to many things," Mohanisi pointed out. "We must take all into account until we know more."

Their mood darkened as they continued; the feeling of corruption they had been sensing was becoming ever stronger. At midday, they heard the approach of an elf patrol. Seekers of the Steppes were capable and dangerous—a point proven by the fact that Mohanisi sensed their presence only a few minutes before the patrol sensed them and turned to intercept.

Very soon, six elves came into view. They were dressed in tan leather shirts and pants that blended well into the grass of the plain. Each wore a long knife at his side and a short bone bow across his back. Theopolou waved a greeting, but the seekers did not return the gesture.

When they were about thirty yards away, all but one stopped. The elf that continued to approach had short-cropped silver hair and an ivory complexion. His bright green eyes were narrowed by the midday sun and stared unblinkingly at Theopolou.

"I am Shen, seeker and protector of Lan Silsia," he said. His voice was cool and emotionless. "What business do you have here?"

"What has happened to the hospitality of Lan Silsia that kin are treated as strangers?" said Theopolou firmly.

"Do not feign ignorance," countered Shen. "That there are just two of you is the only reason you still live." He stepped forward menacingly. "I will ask you one last time. What is your business here, Lord Theopolou?"

"So you know me," said Theopolou. "That is good. We are here to discover the reason for the attack on our tribes by our brothers and sisters of the Steppes."

Shen scrutinized Mohanisi for a moment, apparently ignoring Theopolou's words. "You have a strange look about you. From what tribe do you hail?"

"I am not from anywhere you would know," he replied.

Shen sneered. "So you say." His eyes drifted back to Theopolou. "As for your so-called reason, I think you will find that we are not easily deceived. You come to sue for peace more likely. Or to gauge our true strength. The silver tongue of Lord Theopolou is well known to us. But it will not avail you here."

"I wish to speak to Jillianis," said Theopolou, pulling out the necklace Strydis had given to him. "You cannot deny me."

"That trinket will get you nothing, and Jillianis is no more," said Shen. "Her life ended nearly six months ago. Her sister, Oliana, has replaced her as village elder."

"This trinket may be worthless," countered Theopolou. "But I am an elder, and that should be enough for you, seeker."

Shen scowled and turned to walk toward his companions. "Follow," he ordered.

The other seekers filed in behind them as they headed northwest. After a few miles, the tall grass gave way to a mixture of yellow sand and multi-colored pebbles. The crashing of the sea against the rocks carried on the wind, and fresh salty air left a pleasing taste on Theopolou's lips.

As the village came into view, Theopolou was reminded of the first time he had visited the place. It was just after the end of the Great War. The split had begun. He and his father had come to convince the elves of the Steppes to join them in their fight against those who would continue to attack the human cities. They failed to sway them; their northern cousins instead chose to remain neutral. Soon after this, the estrangement of their tribes began.

The village of Lan Silsia was simple and rustic by Southern standards. The round houses were made mostly from finely woven grass attached to wooden frames and sealed by oil from the red hanso bush. Though simple in design, the craftsmanship was amazing. The weaving was so fine and intricate that it was easy to mistake it for linen—smooth to the touch; it kept the dwellings warm at night and cool in the day. The outside walls of each house were decorated with breathtakingly beautiful murals, mostly depicting the day-to-day life of the village. They were so lifelike that the first time Theopolou saw them as a young elf, he imagined them to be at an actual moment frozen in time.

"Lovely," remarked Mohanisi. "Your artisans are to be congratulated."

Shen nodded curtly but said nothing.

The street was tiled with a cream-colored slate, each stone etched with ancient Elven script. The few elves who were about stared at the newcomers with intense interest, gathering into small groups and whispering, their eyes full of suspicion.

Eventually, the group arrived at an empty market square. In its center was an ebony statue of an elf sat astride a powerful steed and holding aloft a long blade.

"Why is the market empty?" asked Theopolou.

"Save your questions," snapped Shen.

"This place feels strange," said Mohanisi, his voice loud enough to carry to all. "Something bad has happened here."

"I feel it as well," said Theopolou.

Their words caused the seekers to tense.

Beyond the market, the buildings became noticeably larger. Some were still of the woven grass variety, while others were Southern-style wooden buildings. Though most were similar in size to a typical human dwelling, their outside walls were decorated in the same fashion as the others in the village.

At the end of the street, however, stood a large, single-story structure quite different from anything else around it. Built with black stone, its red tile roof sloped sharply before flattening out and extending by around ten feet. Here it was supported by a series of round wooden beams. The front door was stained to a deep crimson and bore a carved relief of four stallions.

Theopolou glanced over his shoulder. Elves were coming out of their houses and following at a distance.

When they were at the door of the black stone house, Shen motioned for them to wait there and went inside. The other seekers stood silently in a group close by. A few minutes later, Shen returned and ushered them in.

Glowing orbs on thin brass pedestals provided only dim lighting. A thick, brown rug covered the floor, and several large round pillows were arranged in a circle at the center. To the left, a fire burned in a hearth. Several tiny statuettes of elf maidens placed in a neat row graced the mantle above. In the far right corner of the room, a beaded curtain was draped over a narrow doorway. The walls were decorated with stained wooden carvings of various animals of the Steppes, together with vibrant charcoal drawings of landscapes and villages.

They placed their packs and weapons near the entrance and followed Shen to the pillows. He grunted harshly before striding across the room and disappearing behind the curtain.

"They lead a simple life," remarked Mohanisi. "It is very different from your people."

"They live a life we claim to desire," said Theopolou. "But I wonder how many really do wish it. I often find myself missing the comforts of my home."

Mohanisi smiled. "I understand. I, too, long for home."

A sensation of darkness and evil washed over them both.

"Something taints the flow in this place," whispered Theopolou. "And it is drawing near."

"I feel it as well," said Mohanisi. "Do not allow it to enter your heart."

Theopolou nodded sharply.

The clatter of beads echoed throughout the room and a tall, slender elf woman appeared from behind the curtain. Her long, straight, red hair flowed carelessly over her shoulders and down her back. She wore a tan linen shirt and pants, both well fitted to her form, together with a brown leather belt that held a small, black-hilted dagger. Her ice-blue eyes reflected the dim light, and her ivory complexion gave her the illusion of possessing a faint aura.

Shen followed close behind, carrying a round wooden tray with a bottle of wine and four clay cups. Theopolou and Mohanisi rose to their feet and bowed low.

"It is good to see you again after so many years, Oliana," said Theopolou. "Though I mourn the loss of your sister."

Oliana frowned and motioned for them to sit, her finger rubbing the hilt of her dagger. Shen gave each a cup and poured the wine.

"I do not think you have come to offer your sympathies," said Oliana. Her voice was thin and raspy.

Theopolou frowned. "No. But you have them nonetheless."

"Do not waste time, Theopolou," she told him. "State your business."

He sighed. "Very well. I have come to discuss the unprovoked attack on my kin by the elves of the Steppes. I hope that together we can resolve this very serious matter before more lives are lost and more damage is done."

Oliana continued to finger the dagger. "You dare to say we were not provoked?" Her tone was surprisingly calm, though her mood was betrayed by the fury in her eyes. "You claim kinship, yet plot against us at every turn."

"We do nothing of the sort," said Theopolou. He glanced down at the way Oliana was continuously fidgeting with her dagger. It was not of elf make. Nor was it in the fashion used by the humans of the Steppes. A wave of dread washed over him. It was the same feeling of corruption and malice that he and Mohanisi had experienced before, only this time, it was almost palpable. "We were gathered within the Chamber of the Maker when attacked by your tribes. We had done nothing to warrant such a vile act."

She turned to Shen. "You see how he lies? His own kin confesses and yet still he thinks to deceive us." She met Theopolou's gaze. "I have spoken to the one called Malstisos. He has told me of your treachery and blasphemy."

"You have seen Malstisos?" said Theopolou. "Where is he?"

"That is not your concern," she snapped. Her eyes fell on Mohanisi. "And where is it that you are from?"

Mohanisi looked to Theopolou. The old elf closed his eyes and nodded.

"I am from across what you call the Western Abyss," he said flatly. "Though from what I have seen thus far, I doubt you will take my word on this."

Oliana hissed a laugh. "And why should I not take your word? I can feel your power. You are like no other elf I have encountered. Certainly, you are gifted even beyond the wise and mighty Theopolou." Her tone was mocking and vicious. "But your presence is not unexpected. We have been told of a new enemy arriving on our shores."

"The only enemy I have seen is the one that has blackened your heart," said Mohanisi. "I can see through you. It is clear to me that you only offer us hospitality as a matter of formality. Your true intention is far more severe." He put down his cup and turned to Theopolou. "Do not drink. She has poisoned our wine."

Oliana grinned maliciously. "It is only a sedative to keep you docile. I feared you may do something foolish."

"Then we are to be killed?" asked Theopolou. He poured the wine onto the floor and tossed the cup to Shen. "Will you not hear us?"

"You will be heard," she replied. "Then you will face judgment." She rose to her feet. "The elders shall convene and decide your fate." She looked down at Mohanisi. "As for you...

I think I will enjoy our time together." She stalked away and passed through the beaded curtain.

Shen stood. "You will come with me. Do not attempt to flee. You will only succeed in getting yourself killed."

Theopolou frowned as he and Mohanisi rose. "It would seem that fate was intended for us from the moment we arrived."

Shen led them from the building. Just outside, dozens of armed elves had gathered, their eyes full of suspicion and anger. They were escorted to a small brick building just a short distance away and told to go inside.

The interior was plain and undecorated, furnished only with a small table and three chairs. Their packs and weapons were tossed inside after them, and the door slammed shut. Only a single flickering glow orb strapped to the ceiling lit the room.

"They seem unconcerned that we are still armed," noticed Mohanisi. "Perhaps they wish us to try to fight our way free."

"I think they simply have no fear of us," said Theopolou. "And that in itself is troubling." He took a seat at the table. "I believe I have discovered the source of the Reborn King's control."

"Yes, the dagger Oliana wore," said Mohanisi. "I felt it as well. But I have never heard of such a thing."

"I have," said Theopolou. "At least, in legend. It was said that in the early days of creation, the gods fashioned objects of great power and placed them in their temples throughout the world. It was believed that to be near one could trap your mind and spirit, breaking your will and enslaving your soul. The gods, displeased with what they had done, hid them away, thus freeing the people of the world."

"It sounds like a child's tale," remarked Mohanisi.

Theopolou smiled. "It is. But since Gewey has come into my life, I have been forced to re-examine the truth behind legends and myths. I don't think that the gods created the dagger Oliana wields, but perhaps the Dark Knight has found a way to make such an object into an extension of his own power. We both could feel its foul influence and see how she obsessed over it."

"Then we must find a way to destroy it," said Mohanisi, his voice fiercely determined. "The power of the Creator must be cleansed."

"To destroy it, we must first possess it," said Theopolou. "And I can think of only one way to do so."

Several hours passed without anyone coming to see them. Finally, Shen appeared with a large plate of lamb and a bottle of wine. Without a word, he placed them on the table.

Theopolou stopped him just as he reached the door to leave. "Tell Oliana I challenge her right to lead this clan, as well as her authority to hold me. By my right, as an elder and leader of my tribe, I demand her answer."

Shen stared at Theopolou emotionlessly and nodded. As he departed, Theopolou bowed his head. His body suddenly felt very bent and old.

Mohanisi walked over and gently placed his hand on Theopolou's shoulder. "What happens now?"

"If she accepts," he explained, "and tradition dictates that she must, we will face one another in single combat. We are only allowed to carry one weapon each, and I don't think she will leave the dagger behind. If I am victorious, I will claim what is hers and destroy it." He sat down at the table and began to eat a small piece of roast lamb. Of course, she has the right to choose a champion. In that case, he must use a weapon of hers in combat, and unless I am wrong, she will not willingly relinquish the dagger to another."

"But what happens if you are wrong?" asked Mohanisi, taking the seat across from him.

He gave a sad smile. "Then an old elf will die quickly at the hands of a young seeker."

A few minutes later, the door flew open, and Oliana stepped inside. Shen and three other seekers were just behind her. Her face was flushed red with anger and her hand rested dangerously on the dagger.

"You think to use trickery?" she shrieked. "You have no right to challenge my rule. You are not of my tribe. You cannot…"

"I am still an elder." His voice thundered, silencing her. "And I have not been found guilty of any crime. You cannot deny me. Or do you intend to ignore our traditions and laws?"

"Such a thing has not been done since the first split," she countered, trying to regain her composure.

"A conflict your father wisely chose to stay out of," said Theopolou. "But the fact remains, it is my right to challenge your leadership."

"To challenge me, you must show just cause," she shot back. "You have none."

"You have imprisoned your kin without provocation," he told her. "That is enough."

Oliana laughed maliciously. "I have cause to imprison you. The elders of the Steppes have deemed your tribes our enemy." She turned to leave. "You have nothing."

"Mohanisi is not of my tribe," said Theopolou. "Or of any other tribe your elders have wrongly accused. By your own words, you have admitted this to be true."

She froze and stood for a long moment. When she finally spoke, her voice was a thin whisper. "Prepare yourself. Tonight, you will join your ancestors." Pushing by the seekers, she left.

"What just happened?" asked Mohanisi.

"You are not guilty of any crime," said Theopolou. "Nor do you stand accused under our laws. That she has detained you unjustly is enough for the challenge."

"What happens now?"

"Now we wait and see," he replied solemnly.

CHAPTER 8

Theopolou spent the next few hours resting in the far corner of the small room, his pack beneath his head for a pillow. The glow orb became dimmer and dimmer until it was but a faint light on the ceiling. Mohanisi sat at the table, awash in the flow, searching the emotions of those who passed near the building. He could feel only sadness and dread.

The door opened and Shen entered. Theopolou rose to his feet and allowed the flow to rush through him. His muscles flexed and stretched with renewed strength. He checked his dagger and said a silent prayer.

"I shall act as your second," said Shen.

Theopolou looked at him skeptically. "I assumed I would choose my own."

Shen shook his head. "As you pointed out, Mohanisi is not a member of any tribe. This makes him the offended party and unable to act as second. Oliana does not want you to think she will not hold to our laws, so she chose me to second you as a sign of good faith."

"Am I to be allowed to witness?" asked Mohanisi.

"You will," he replied. "But you must not speak or act on Theopolou's behalf."

"And if I fall?" asked Theopolou. "Will Mohanisi be afforded safe passage?"

Shen bowed his head. "You have my word on that. I will see him to the borders myself. But understand that even if you succeed, you will still likely face the judgment of our elders once they arrive. The leadership of this village cuts your ties to your own tribe and forfeits your protection as elder of your house." He looked into Theopolou's eyes. "But of course, you knew this."

Mohanisi stepped closer to Shen and shut his eyes. "I sense a great conflict within you. The darkness has not consumed you completely. You still fight it."

"You see much," admitted Shen. "But do not think to turn me against my own kin. I have seen the ships off our coast and heard the elders speak of the plots against us. And though I did not agree with the decision to attack your people, it was inevitable. Humans have ever sought our destruction, and it was the gods who brought us to this pass. For five hundred years we have lived as exiles in our own land because of the very people Theopolou's kin now call friend. An alliance between the elves of the south and the humans can only mean one thing."

"It was not my tribe, nor any other, that brought the evil now infesting your land," said Theopolou. "You are a seeker. Surely you can feel the corruption of the flow. You think we are capable of such a thing? It is the Reborn King who has done this. The ships are his, and he is the source of the corruption. Have you not seen the vile Vrykol that serve him?"

Shen's lips tightened. "I have seen them. But they do not trouble us. They are forbidden to enter our village."

Theopolou pulled out the horse pendant. "The elf who gave me this was fleeing the Vrykol. He and his sister were the sole survivors of an attack planned by Ryslotis, the elder of his tribe. They were exiled. But once away from their village, they were attacked anyway."

"That is a serious claim," said Shen. "One, I doubt you can support."

Theopolou sighed. "Beyond the word of an elf, I have no evidence."

Shen stiffened his back. "Then we have spoken enough. Oliana awaits."

He led them from the building onto the street. The air was cool with a breeze that brought the sea to their nostrils. Hundreds of torch-carrying elves lined the avenue on either side. They walked at a steady pace east for a distance, then turned south. As they progressed, the elves lining the street filed in behind them.

"She is making quite a spectacle of this," remarked Theopolou.

"This is the first time in living memory that a leadership has been challenged," Shen replied. "Oliana did not need to coax anyone to witness it."

They wound their way through the streets until they reached the outskirts of the town. Ahead, hundreds of elves already awaited them around a great circle of torches. Oliana stood at its center beside a figure in a white hooded cloak. As they entered the circle, the elves that followed spread out and joined the other spectators.

"Wait at the edge," Shen instructed Mohanisi.

They approached Oliana and her second until they were only a few yards away. She was wearing a loose-fitting red tunic, brown leather pants, and a pair of suede moccasins. Her hair was tied in a tight braid, with a silver band resting on her brow. She thumbed her dagger anxiously as she met Theopolou's eyes.

"Is this your champion or your second?" asked Theopolou.

"I shall be the one to face you, Theopolou," she hissed with contempt. She touched the cloaked elf beside her and he pulled back his hood, revealing blond hair and a cold expression. "Have you met Malstisos?"

"I have not," Theopolou replied. "But I know his family and I have spoken to Sister Maybell about him. She was quite concerned."

The mention of Maybell caused Malstisos to shift uncomfortably. "Human feelings and fears are irrelevant," he said in a low voice. "I kept my word and delivered her to safety."

"That you did," said Theopolou. He reached out to him with the flow but was thrown back at once.

Malstisos's hand slid to the dagger at his side. He glared furiously. "Do not try that again."

Theopolou bowed slowly. "My apologies. I did not know you were attuned to the flow. That is unusual, considering you are not a seeker or an elder. Someone has been teaching you."

"Enough!" said Oliana harshly. "We are here to settle a challenge, not to speak of matters that do not concern you." She stepped forward. "I give you this one chance to withdraw and await the judgment of the elders. I have no desire for this futile pursuit to end your long life." She met his eyes and flashed a malicious grin. "But I can see that your mind is set."

"Then draw your weapon and let this be done," replied Theopolou. "I think you will find that my age has not slowed my body."

Oliana sneered and turned to face Malstisos. "See that his remains are afforded all proper rites."

Malstisos and Shen bowed to each other, then walked to opposite ends of the circle.

Theopolou drew his dagger and stepped back. With legs parted and slightly bent, he eyed Oliana cautiously. He knew better than to underestimate her. Though not a seeker, all the elves of the Steppes were well trained in personal combat, and he did not know what extra power the dagger might be giving her. His already keen senses sharpened as he allowed the flow to enter his body.

Oliana pulled her dagger free, her expression turning to a stone calm. An instant later a shadow appeared, surrounding her body and hiding her features from clear view. As she moved slowly to her left, a swirling wind flowed around the circle.

"Now do you see, Lord Theopolou?" Her thin voice suddenly carried an echo. "The power of the north has given the elders of the Steppes the strength to prevail. And he will return to us our kingdoms."

Theopolou could feel the corruption of the flow penetrating him—sapping his strength. Only with a great effort was he able to push it out and follow her movements. "Does your heart hold nothing of what you once were? Look at yourself. Can you not see the evil that binds you?"

She did not reply. The shadow around her became darker, and the wind rose. With effortless grace, she sprang forward, slashing at Theopolou's neck. He leaned back and spun right, but still, the blade cut a long gash just beneath his left ear. Theopolou countered, thrusting low and swift, but Oliana easily twisted away and brought her dagger across his shoulder.

"You have become old and slow, Theopolou," she jeered, dancing away. "Though you never were a warrior—isn't that right? Words are your weapons. How are they serving you now?"

Blood soaked Theopolou's shirt from his wounds, but he ignored the pain and fought to keep his focus. Easing back slowly, he waited for Oliana's next attack. She moved forward to match him, then struck low, barely missing his right thigh. In response, Theopolou brought down the hilt of his dagger, grazing her cheek. She countered upward, slicing open his shirt, but Theopolou was already leaning back and the blade missed his flesh. Again she pressed, but this time Theopolou grabbed her sleeve and pulled hard, bringing her stumbling forward.

She spun to face him, the shadow around her fading slightly to reveal the hatred in her eyes. Without hesitation, she charged once more. Theopolou again used her aggression against her, backing away and landing a blow with his empty hand on her exposed jaw. This only served to intensify her anger. Letting out a hideous scream, she attacked again, this time even faster and more furiously. Her blade cut into Theopolou's arms and chest several times, but he moved ever back, preventing the steel from biting too deep. Even so, he was losing too much blood and knew he would soon weaken. Oliana struck at his neck, and he was forced to duck and roll away. Her growing frustration was making her thrusts wild, but he needed something more.

"It would seem words are not my only weapons," he taunted. "Perhaps you should yield before this ends ill for you."

The shadow darkened, and the wind went wild. Oliana's face was contorted with fury. "I shall cut out your heart and send it to your kin."

A dark blur shot at Theopolou. But this time he stepped forward, twisting his torso to the left. Oliana's dagger plunged into his chest, just to the right of his heart. Theopolou gasped and pulled her to him, at the same time sinking his own blade into her throat. Blood sprayed from her mouth, covering his face as they both fell to the ground.

Theopolou rolled over, jerking her dagger free from his chest. He could feel his life slipping away. The weapon pulsed in his hand, and he could sense the darkness growing around him. He looked over at Oliana. The coughs and gurgles of her death throes were made even more gruesome as she tore feebly at the blade protruding from her mangled flesh. After a few seconds, the shadow vanished, the wind died, and she became still—her eyes vacant. Theopolou dropped her dagger and clutched at the wound in his chest.

In seconds, Shen and Mohanisi were at his side. Mohanisi placed his hands on Theopolou and allowed the flow to pass into him. But after only a brief time, he stopped.

"There is something sinister at work," he whispered. "The wound will not close. There is nothing I can do."

Theopolou nodded with understanding. "Destroy the dagger." His voice was shallow and weak. "Do it now."

Mohanisi nodded and stood up. Kicking the dagger several feet away, he closed his eyes and held out his arms. A flame burst to life around the blade, growing hotter and hotter until its heat started to blister his skin. For a full minute, the fire raged until a faint crack and pop could be heard. This was immediately followed by a loud explosion that sent black smoke shooting out in every direction. The sheer force of the shockwave pushed both Mohanisi and Shen clean off their feet. The cloud of smoke billowed and expanded until it filled the entire circle. There it paused for a moment, as if suspended in time. Then, with an almighty roar, it collapsed inward and disappeared completely.

Blind panic instantly set in. Screams of pain and despair erupted from all those assembled. Elves began tearing at their skin and running aimlessly around, many colliding with each other and falling stunned to the ground. Some curled themselves up into a ball and wept uncontrollably, others pounded their fists into the earth while shouting endless streams of curses. Shen was on his knees with tears flowing freely down his face.

Mohanisi stared in horror at the chaotic scene.

"They are free," muttered Theopolou. "But they are wounded."

Theopolou's words snapped Mohanisi to attention. He crawled over to the old elf's side and once again tried to heal the wounds. This time, the flow entered, but the destruction of the dagger had greatly weakened him. He managed to stop the bleeding, but Theopolou's life was still slowly fading away. Desperately, he ran to Shen and roughly pulled him to Theopolou's side.

"You must help me," Mohanisi commanded. But Shen did not respond. His tear-filled eyes stared out into nothingness. Mohanisi let out a roar and slapped the seeker hard across the face. This time, Shen blinked and gasped. "Help me!" Mohanisi repeated, this time with as much force as he could muster.

Shen looked down at Theopolou. "I ... I don't..." His voice was weak and distant.

Mohanisi grabbed Shen's hands and placed them on Theopolou's chest. "Your brother is dying. Now you must lend me your strength."

Slowly, Shen regained his wits and allowed the flow to pass from himself into Theopolou. But he was weak and was soon drained. "Will he live?" he managed to ask.

"I do not know," Mohanisi replied.

Theopolou's eyes were closed; his breathing was shallow and labored. Mohanisi looked out on the field. Some of the elves had ceased their screaming and were now just sitting motionless. Others rocked back and forth, muttering incoherently. A few were bleeding from self-inflicted wounds.

Summoning up all of his remaining strength, Mohanisi lifted Theopolou in his arms and stumbled toward the village. Shen followed, though his confused expression and short, uneven steps suggested he would be of little help. Once they had reached the street, Mohanisi approached the first house he came to and kicked open the door.

Inside, the dwelling was lit by a fire in a round hearth set at the center of the room. A small stove was to his left, and a mahogany table and chairs to his right. The walls were decorated with charcoal drawings of bison and deer. A pedestal stood on either side of the room—one holding the bust of an elf man, the other an elf woman. An archway to the rear was covered by the same beads as those in Oliana's house.

Mohanisi pushed through the beads and into a narrow hall. There was a door on both sides and another at the end. Steadying Theopolou's body, he bent down and opened the door on his left. Inside was a small bed with a soft mattress and large white pillows. He gently laid Theopolou down and grabbed a blue wool blanket that was folded neatly in the corner. After covering him, he turned to Shen.

"I need roots and herbs from your healers," he said urgently. "Go now."

Shen stood there for a second with a glazed look in his eyes, then nodded and left. But fifteen minutes later, there was still no sign of him returning. Mohanisi was growing more and more desperate. He had managed to keep Theopolou's life from completely fading, but his own weakened condition was making it impossible to do more.

When Shen finally arrived back, he appeared to be more like himself. He handed Mohanisi a small flask. "Drink this. It will restore your strength so that you can heal him further."

Without a thought, Mohanisi opened the flask and quickly drank every last drop. Almost immediately, heat rushed through his veins. He felt his strength returning, though not completely. But it was enough for now, and he renewed his efforts to heal to Theopolou. More and more he passed the flow until he was once again on the verge of collapse. It was then that Theopolou's eyes fluttered open.

"That is enough, my friend," whispered the old elf. "Please, no more. You will only injure yourself. My wounds are far deeper than you know, and you cannot heal them."

Mohanisi smiled. "That is nonsense. Your body is nearly mended."

"It is not my body that is dying." Theopolou breathed heavily and closed his eyes. "Oliana's dagger has caused my spirit to wither. Its dark power has killed me."

Mohanisi refused to believe what he was hearing. "There must be something that can be done," he said, tears welling in his eyes. "It cannot end this way. You are still needed."

Theopolou opened his eyes once again and took hold of Mohanisi's hand. "It has not ended. My journey through this life has been long and my tasks are complete. I die knowing that my final act has freed my kin from eternal night." He winced and shifted in his bed. "My people still have the spark of grace within. Do not abandon them. They need your light to show them the way."

Mohanisi nodded slowly as a tear fell. "I swear to you, I will never abandon our kin. I will see them restored."

"I would have liked to have seen your home." Theopolou's voice grew weaker. "I would have liked that very much."

"Your name will be sung atop the spires of every city," Mohanisi replied. "All will know of your sacrifice, and of your love for our people."

"Tell Kaylia that I love her most of all." Theopolou's grip lessened as his eyes closed for a final time. "And that she has made me very proud."

Mohanisi kneeled beside the bed for the next hour, weeping softly until the very last bit of life had left Theopolou's body.

"He saved my people," said Shen.

The seeker's voice startled Mohanisi erect. "And your people need you. See to them. I will join you as soon as I am able." He struggled to his feet. "There is still much to do if we are to honor Theopolou's courage."

"There must be other objects such as the one Oliana carried," said Shen. "They must all be destroyed."

Mohanisi nodded. "When your elders arrive, it will be done. And though I may be forced to do something I never thought possible for me to do, I will not fail." He pushed by Shen and opened the door on the other side of the hall.

"Wake me in four hours. I should have regained some of my strength by then."

Shen bowed and left.

Mohanisi lay down on the bed and shut his eyes. The image of Theopolou's dying body burned into his mind.

I will not fail.

The same thought echoed again and again until sleep finally took him.

CHAPTER 9

Gewey sat quietly on the edge of the bed, awaiting the arrival of the others. Extra chairs had been brought into his room and arranged in a semicircle. Kaylia sat beside him, eyes closed, holding his hand.

"I have not asked what it is you have discovered," she said. "But I sense it is troubling you. Are you certain the others need to hear it?"

Gewey nodded resolutely. "The truth can no longer be hidden from view. I gather only those close to me so they can decide for themselves how to tell their people." He paused for a moment, prompting Kaylia to open her eyes and squeeze his hand. "I'm getting tired of meeting people who hear my words as if they are divine. Right now, I want only my friends with me. Yes, I am Darshan, but when I am with them, I am still Gewey as well."

"You will always be Gewey to me," said Kaylia. "I will never see you as anyone else. And though I know you must use the god inside of you to defeat our enemies, I will always keep your human self in my heart. And there you will never be lost."

He leaned over and kissed her cheek. "As long as you are with me, I can stay strong." He chuckled. "It's funny. So much has happened in such a short time. I forget that not so long ago I was running with Lee like a scared rabbit, leaving everything behind. It makes me wonder if I'll ever see my home again. I used to long to see the world. Now all I think about is my house and my fields."

"When our duty to this world is done," said Kaylia, "you will return. And Sharpstone will become my home as well."

This brought amused laughter from Gewey. "I can't wait to see the look on the village mothers' faces when I return with my elf bride. We shall certainly be the talk of the town."

Kaylia laughed as well. "I had not thought of that. I suppose I must learn the ways of your village so not to cause too much of a scandal."

There was a knock at the door, and Selena entered, together with Chiron and Bellisia. Gewey offered them seats. A moment later, Aaliyah and Nehrutu arrived. Gewey served them each a cup of wine before sitting down himself.

"I take it you have brought us here to discuss what you have read in the Book of Souls," said Selena.

Gewey nodded. "Yes. And I want you to convey to the other elders and nobles that I mean no offense by not inviting them." He grinned at Bellisia and Chiron. "I know they do not enjoy being left out."

Chiron laughed. Bellisia did not.

"You do as you feel proper," said Bellisia. "The other elders will understand."

"And who would dare to question the will of Darshan?" added Chiron.

Gewey frowned. "I asked you here because it is not Darshan that you know. My blunder at the feast has isolated me from almost everyone. Only you, my friends here in this room, still keep my human self in your minds above that of the god. And it is that human side that needs your friendship more than ever."

Aaliyah stood. "I believe I speak for everyone when I say that our friendship shall never be something you will want for." She sat back down and took Nehrutu's hand.

Gewey smiled warmly. He could feel the bond between them combine with that of Kaylia's. "Then I shall tell you what I discovered within the Book of Souls. I'm not sure what you may think or how people will react. But I do believe that if a new world is to rise, it must be built on a foundation of truth."

Gewey took a sip of wine, then sat the cup on the floor beside his chair. "Understand that much of what I read was confusing. It mentioned names and places I've never heard of. It told stories of heroes and kingdoms that are far beyond my knowledge of lore. And the book isn't written in order. It jumps back and forth in time. It was all I could do to piece everything together.

"It begins with the firstborn of the world. Those of you who know Felsafell can count yourself among the few people to have met one of this race. He is the last of his kind, and the oldest being that walks the earth."

"But Felsafell looks human," said Chiron.

"He does now," said Gewey. "But the Book mentions the changes his people went through, both culturally and physically. And though it doesn't say exactly how they once appeared, I'm certain he looked quite different long ago. And when I say long ago..."

He rose to his feet and stood behind Kaylia's chair. "The Book of Souls speaks of history in terms of tens of thousands of years. It says that the Creator gave life to the firstborn more than one hundred thousand years ago. Immortal, they wandered the world and watched the lands change and the mountains rise. Rivers turned to dust and fertile plains became barren deserts. But as time passed, they forgot about the Creator. Their prayers went silent, and they soon fell into despair.

"Where once they had no notion of time, the eons began to weigh on their hearts. Each day of life was like torture. They wandered aimlessly, seeking relief, but were trapped by their own immortality. In their anger, they began to burn the world around them. They warred on each other for no other reason than distraction. They no longer bore children and cared for nothing, and soon all the lands became an endless battleground.

"It was when their hearts were at their most corrupt, and all they knew was hatred and sorrow, that the Creator took pity and sent the gods to help them."

"Does it say when the gods were created?" asked Chiron.

"No," Gewey replied. "Only that they resided in heaven and were given the power to shepherd the world out of darkness. Whether they were created for that purpose, or they already existed before that, it doesn't say. Or maybe I wasn't able to understand it properly. I'm not exactly a scholar."

He reached down and picked up his cup. "What came next was hard to decipher. It says that the gods came down from heaven and gave the firstborn the Word of the Creator, and that the power of her name stopped the wars and chaos."

Selena raised an eyebrow and grinned. "It refers to the Creator as her?"

Gewey nodded. "I hadn't thought about it before, but it always refers to the Creator as her—never him. It does say that the power of her name carries with it the power of heaven and earth. It was with this power that the gods brought peace to the firstborn.

"For thousands of yeears, the gods lived among them. They took physical form and built temples to honor the Creator. But the more time they spent among the firstborn, the more like them they gradually became. Their returns to heaven grew less frequent. In time, they began to take wives and lovers for themselves. The children of these unions were of a different race. Immortal, they were bound to earth like the firstborn, but like the gods, they could feel the power of the Creator within them.

"As these children grew, they learned to use that power to create wondrous objects and change the face of the world. But they became distant from the firstborn and separated themselves from their earthly parents. This drove the firstborn mad with sorrow; they begged the gods to grant them the same power as their children. But try as they might, the gods could not change the nature of what the Creator had made. A thing forged by her hands will remain forever unchanged.

"Their despair grew until they no longer took joy in anything. Many began to wither and decay. But, as immortals, they could not die. Overcome with pity, the gods offered them release from their pain ... through death."

"You mean the gods killed all of Felsafell's race?" asked Selena, appalled.

"They didn't slaughter them," said Gewey. "They simply offered them a way out. Though the gods could not change what they were, they did have the power to kill their physical bodies and free their spirits. But once done, the gods discovered that they could not bring them into heaven. So instead, they created a realm where they hoped the firstborn could be happy. This became the spirit realm.

"One by one, the firstborn were released, and eventually all but Felsafell vanished from memory. The gods were pleased with what they had done and dwelled with them in the spirit realm. For thousands of years, they didn't return to the earth, leaving it in the care of their children.

"When they did eventually return, they were horrified to discover the fate of the firstborn re-emerging in their offspring. Wars had begun. But by wielding the power of the Creator, the devastation was far worse than before. Lands were laid to waste, forests burned, and mountains leveled. The gods prayed to the Creator for guidance, but none came. Some wanted to kill them and send them to the spirit realm with the firstborn, but others refused to slay their own children. It was Gerath who came up with the solution. They combined their powers and banished their children to a distant land. But they knew that would not be enough to stop the madness. So they took the one thing from them that they still could—their immortality. And as they were not forged by the hand of the Creator, it could be done.

"Angry and betrayed, the children made war on their parents. But now they were mortal and no match for the gods. For the very first time, the gods witnessed true death. They wailed at the agony of losing their children and desperately tried to undo what they had done. But they couldn't. Their children were destined to remain in a cycle of life and death for all time." Gewey drained his cup and poured himself another.

"What became of them?" asked Aaliyah.

Gewey stared into his wine and paused, then with a sigh, continued, "The gods mourned for many years, forsaking both heaven and the spirit world. Finally, they felt a call to return to heaven, and that was when they made a wondrous discovery. The spirits of their children had not died but had found their way into heaven. The gods rejoiced. They thanked the Creator for her kindness and begged forgiveness for their lack of wisdom. The Creator told them to return and watch over her new creation.

"When they saw the world once again, a new race had arisen from the ashes of their children's destruction. Humans!"

There was a short silence as those present thought on what Gewey had told them. Aaliyah was the first to see the full picture.

"I think I understand," she said. "And you are right to be wary of telling this tale." She looked at Chiron and Bellisia.

"We are the children he spoke of. We are the creation of the gods and the firstborn."

"Is there more?" asked Bellisia. Her voice trembled.

"Nothing that your history doesn't already tell," Gewey replied. "The humans populated this world until the elves returned and enslaved them. The gods intervened and created the Great Barrier. But as I said, these things you already know."

"I don't see how this changes anything," remarked Selena. "Why would this news upset the elves?"

Aaliyah met Selena's eyes. "The faith of elves, both here and in my homeland, is based on the belief that our people were given life by the Creator. We are taught from childhood that she breathed life into our bodies and gave us our souls. Also, that we are favored above all her works. This is why she allows us to feel the flow. In gratitude, we see ourselves as guardians of her world and protectors of her faith."

A look of realization slowly crept across Selena's face. "And now it appears that you were not given life by the Creator at all, but by the gods and the firstborn. In truth, it was we humans who were given life by her, not the elves." She shook her head and held up her hand. "I'm sorry, I did not mean to suggest..."

Aaliyah smiled. "I know you meant no offense. But you are correct. Where once we were noble, now we are mongrels."

"You are not mongrels," snapped Gewey.

"I know this," said Aaliyah. "But many will be shattered when faced with such a truth."

"Perhaps it is time we did exactly that," said Chiron, his countenance uncharacteristically grave. "I must admit, this shakes me to my foundation for the very reasons Aaliyah has just stated. I was taught my faith and believed my history. I saw my race as the light of creation and all that is best in the world. To know that I am not a child of the Creator I have worshipped all my life sends darkness into my very soul."

He looked at Gewey. "But knowing that my true forbearer has returned to me and my kin to fight at our side gives me hope. And though it will take time to banish this darkness, I will build on that hope."

"What say you to this, Bellisia?" asked Gewey.

Bellisia sat in silent thought for a moment, staring intensely at the stone floor. Finally, she looked up. Her eyes fixed on Gewey and there was a fire in her gaze. "I do not see how this changes anything I believe. I trust that the words you spoke are true, and can accept that the elves are the product of a union of two races. But I cannot, and will not, believe that the gods created my soul. You said yourself that the gods thought their children dead until they found them in heaven."

She rose to her feet and kneeled in front of Chiron. "Do not let the darkness in. These fragile bodies are but shells in which our greater self resides. That is at the core of what I have always believed. It is our soul that is eternal, and it is our soul that was given true life by the Creator." She took his hands and kissed them tenderly. "Let that be our task; to show our kin their true immortal selves."

Chiron gave her a fragile smile. "Your words comfort me and I thank you."

Bellisia returned to her chair, looking determined and strong.

Gewey touched Kaylia's shoulder. "And you?"

Kaylia shrugged. "I care nothing about how my people came to walk this earth. I believe as Lady Bellisia. And even if it is not so, what does it matter? My life is here and now with you. Whatever the origin of my spirit may be, it is bonded to yours, and I am satisfied."

"What will you do now?" Gewey asked Bellisia.

"I will tell my people the truth," she replied firmly.

"As will I," said Chiron.

"And what about you, Gewey?" asked Selena. "Did you find the answers you need in the Book of Souls?"

Shaking his head, Gewey removed a piece of parchment from his pocket. "Only more questions. I copied out the one passage I found that might mean something, but I'm not even sure it's really about me. It says: 'And with her Word, she will bring life to the creation of heaven. From the dust he shall rise, and with him the world. To cast down the foes of heaven shall be his payment for her generous gift. For she has sacrificed so that he may live.'"

He frowned. "Like I said, I'm not even sure it's about me. But one thing I do know for certain. I will not find the answers I seek here."

"What will you do?" asked Nehrutu.

"I think I must find Felsafell," he replied.

"Do you know where he is?" asked Selena.

Gewey shook his head. "No. But I do know where he once lived, so I will begin there."

"I loathe to think of your absence," said Chiron. "You serve to galvanize the resolve of the people. Without you..."

Gewey held up his hand. "Without me, there is still a war to be fought and an enemy to prepare for. Our first battle was waged with only a portion of our strength. You and the other elders, together with High Lady Selena and King Lousis, must gather all of it. Felsafell told me that we will only achieve victory if I discover how to use the flow of the spirit, so I must leave you to seek out this knowledge."

"Then Aaliyah and I will come with you," said Nehrutu.

"No," said Gewey. "You are needed here. Both of you."

Kaylia stood. "Do not fret. He will not be alone. I will protect him ... even if it is from himself."

"When do you intend to depart?" asked Aaliyah, her concern bleeding through her bond with Gewey.

"Tomorrow," he replied. "But before I go, there is something I wish to give Lady Bellisia." He went to the wardrobe and retrieved the staff presented to him by Gerath. "I had intended to give this to Lord Theopolou. But now I think it was always meant for you."

The moment it touched her hand, her eyes grew wide. She gasped, and for several minutes simply stared at the staff in wonder. "I thank you for such a treasure," she finally said.

"I hope it serves you well," said Gewey. "I have seen your gift at healing. With this, you can do even greater good."

"If Lady Bellisia will allow me," said Aaliyah. "I would be honored to instruct her."

Bellisia smiled and nodded. "The honor would be mine."

For the next hour, Gewey read out some of the tales from the Book of Souls. Though much of what he related appeared to be new to his audience, certain names he mentioned did indeed draw flashes of recognition from Aaliyah and the others. By the time everyone was ready to retire for the evening, it was decided that, once the war was over, Gewey would write down all the stories so that the elders and other scholars could study them. He enjoyed thinking forward to a time when there would be no more struggle and killing.

Once everyone had left, Gewey drank another cup of wine and then climbed into bed.

"Are you sure the Spirit Hills is where we should start?" asked Kaylia as she lay next to him.

"No," he admitted. "But I can't reach Felsafell to ask him. I've tried, but he only seems to appear when he decides."

"It is difficult to fathom," she mused. "That he could be over one hundred thousand years old is beyond my comprehension. I will certainly be asking him about this when we find him."

Gewey turned on his side to gaze lovingly at her. "I'm so glad that you'll be with me."

Kaylia smiled. Her eyes twinkled in the dim candlelight. "You have taken your very last journey without me by your side," she told him.

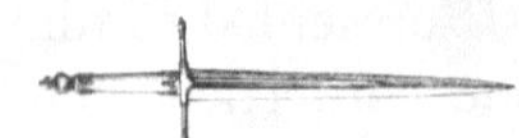

They rose an hour before dawn the next morning and pre-pared for the journey. Hoping it would help them to leave unnoticed, Gewey had found a hooded cloak for each of them to wear. After a brief meal, they said their farewells to Selina and the others and left the temple. A horse-drawn wagon awaited them just outside. Gewey knew that they could travel much faster on foot or horseback, but should any curious passerby question them, it would be far easier to claim they were a couple simply leaving the war-torn west. The wagon would add credibility to this lie.

As they wound their way through the narrow passage, Gewey was reminded of when their journey had begun and Kaylia had drugged him with jawas tea.

She laughed, seeing his thoughts in her mind. "You deserved it at the time."

Gewey shrugged and grinned. "I don't know about that. You could have just told me what I wanted to know."

"Then what mystery would have remained?" Her voice was light and musical.

The bright morning sun and crisp, cool air lifted their spirits. Gewey urged the horse on and leaned back. "I just realized. This will be our first time alone on an adventure."

"Then I think I will make the most of our time," she replied, taking his hand.

Gewey thought back to the intensely fierce elf woman she appeared to be when they first met. Little had he realized at the time how intricate her spirit really was, or how deep her emotions truly ran. And though their bond allowed them to share the innermost aspects of themselves, he was still con-tinually amazed by how much more there was to discover. It was as if he could feel her growing and changing, strength-ening their connection with each passing day.

He tried to imagine what their life would be like if they returned to Sharpstone. After all that had happened, and all that was still to come, would it be a life they could realistically hope to lead?

Suddenly, an image of his home flashed into his mind. He knew that it had come from Kaylia. He was wearing his comfortable elf clothes, sitting in his father's chair, and sipping a cup of wine. Kaylia was close by in his mother's rocker. She was dressed in a white satin robe and holding a small bundle in her arms. At first, he couldn't tell what the bundle was, but as she rocked forward, he could see the tiny face of a sleeping baby. His heart was filled with love and tranquility.

"You would have such a simple life?" asked Gewey.

Kaylia looked confused. "What do you mean?"

"The vision you just showed me. It was beautiful."

"I did nothing," she replied.

He described it to her. "I thought it came from you. I felt it through our bond."

She smiled. "Then let us hope it is a vision of the future."

CHAPTER 10

Gewey knew that the journey to the Spirit Hills would take them at least four weeks by wagon, and he intended to use that time by learning as much as he could about the flow of the spirit. However, his thoughts were becoming increasingly troubled the farther away from Valshara they traveled, making it nearly impossible for him to concentrate. The enemy could certainly strike back very soon, and without him there, the battles would be far more costly. He was also concerned that King Lousis intended to sail a fleet to Baltria once Skalhalis was secured. Most of the Angrääl ships had escaped, so word of their defeat would reach the Reborn King quickly. More than once Kaylia scolded him for worrying about things he had no control over, but it was hard to not think about them, anyway.

They planned to make their way to the Old Santismal Road. When they reached Vine Run, they would sell the wagon and head into the wild on foot. He thought about the night he had spent at the inn there with Dina.

"I'll have to explain to Minnie why I have a different wife," he teased.

Kaylia did not find it amusing and poked him hard in his ribs.

They had camped for the first few days but decided it best to take rooms in towns and villages once they were far enough away from Althetas for Gewey to pass unrecognized. Kaylia had a red silk head wrap Selena had given to her to hide her elf features. Gewey did not like that she needed to conceal who she was, but Kaylia assured him she wasn't bothered by it. Besides, it was necessary if they wanted to pass unnoticed.

Gewey spent most of their time alone asking Kaylia about her childhood, and very soon came to realize just how little he knew about her life. Each new tale caused him to feel closer to her. Now he truly understood just how much she loved her people and cared about their future.

On the eighth day, they came upon a small caravan of ten wagons camped along the roadside. Each one was piled high with furnishings and other personal possessions. The people looked haggard and weary, barely noticing as they approached.

"This is what comes of war," whispered Kaylia. "We should stop and find out to where they flee." She glanced up at the darkening sky. "It will be night soon, anyway."

Gewey pulled up just beyond the last wagon. Most of the people had gathered around a fire close to the side of the road, over which a large iron pot was suspended. A short, round-faced man approached. His curly salt and pepper hair was unkempt and matted. He wore a lightweight cotton shirt and a pair of torn, brown trousers—clearly clothing not made for cold climates. His dark complexion masked his aging features well, but his uneven, awkward steps and bent posture spoke of many years of toil.

He smiled politely. "I welcome you, friend. But I must tell you that if you seek food, we have little enough for ourselves. And no coin to purchase more."

Gewey reached into the wagon and pulled out a large sack of potatoes. "In that case, we will share what we have with you. We only want to warm ourselves by your fire."

The man's eyes lit up. "Then you are most welcome indeed." He bowed. "I am Andren. Please, warm yourselves." He looked at his own thin rags. "I can tell you, it does get cold at night."

Kaylia retrieved a sack of salted pork and they followed Andren to the fire. Most of the people gathered around it were women, children, or elderly. They looked up suspiciously, whispering softly to each other.

Gewey glanced into the pot at the thin soup inside. He threw down the potatoes. "I think these might be better." He took the pork from Kaylia. "This as well."

His offerings instantly changed their mood. In moments, the sacks were opened and laughter could be heard from everyone. Each took their turn to thank Gewey and Kaylia for their kindness.

"There is far too little generosity of late," said Andren as they settled down by the fire. "And we are truly grateful. Though I hope this will not cause you hardship."

Gewey shook his head and smiled. "Not at all. We are happy to help. But I must ask why you are here and in such dire straits?"

Andren's face was strained. "We flee the wrath of Darshan."

His words caused Gewey and Kaylia to tense.

"Darshan?" Gewey repeated, feigning ignorance.

Andren cocked his head. "You mean you haven't heard? King Halmara provoked the wrath of a god. They call him Darshan, but who knows which one it really is? Most think it's Gerath or Saraf being called by a different name." He shrugged. "Not that it matters. Though I am surprised you haven't heard. I assumed you were fleeing the war as well."

"We are," said Gewey. "But I heard nothing about a god."

"The story I heard was that he marched his followers against King Halmara and Angrääl," said Andren. "Then he told his people to halt and bear witness as he destroyed an entire army with a wave of his hand. It is said that he burned ten thousand soldiers in an instant."

"That's hogwash," cut in a thin old woman wearing a shabby blue dress. "My son was there. He was one of the few who escaped back to Skalhalis after the battle. He told me that whatever it was that attacked them, it only destroyed the horses with fire. After that, King Lousis and the elves did the rest." She spat, scowling. "Anyway, it was those bastards from Angrääl who brought this down on us. If they had never come, there would be no war. And I would still be in my own house in front of a fire instead of being out here in the cold, turned into a beggar."

"So, are all of you from Skalhalis?" asked Kaylia.

"Yes," said Andren. "We were the first to leave. But I can promise you that this road will soon be flooded with refugees. The Reborn King will return. You can count on that. And when he does..." His voice trailed off for a moment and he shook his head sadly. "When Darshan and Angrääl meet again, I wager they'll lay waste to the entire coast. I, for one, have no intention of being there when it happens. I'm too old to fight, and I refuse to watch my city burn."

The pain in the man's eyes sent a pang of guilt shooting through Gewey. Already his name was becoming a symbol of destruction and fear. Kaylia touched the back of his hand with keen understanding.

The earlier bright mood was now completely gone as the people thought of their lost homes and the loved ones left behind. Mothers without children, sons without fathers, wives without husbands. And this was only the beginning. They finished eating in silence, then prepared for sleep.

From the west, Gewey heard the sound of furious hoof-beats and the rattle of steel approaching. He guessed it was at least three riders. He glanced over at their wagon; his sword was just behind the driver's seat. Kaylia shook her head ever so slightly.

Moments later, three Angrääl soldiers in full armor came into view. Everyone stood huddled together, clearly afraid.

"I'm sorry," said Andren.

"For what?" asked Gewey.

Before Andren could respond, the riders halted and leaped from their saddles. All bore the sigil of Angrääl on their breastplates. The tallest had a gold chevron on each shoulder. Pushing aside the refugees, he peered inside the iron pot.

"You are welcome to share our meal," said Andren. "And to warm yourselves by our fire."

The leader removed his helmet, revealing dirty blond hair, a square jaw, and deep-set brown eyes. The scars on his face told of many battles, while the worn and chipped hilt of his broadsword suggested that it had spilled much blood in the past. Without any word or provocation, he walked straight up to Andren and backhanded him across his jaw, sending him crumbling to the ground.

"I am Captain Lott Grusta," he shouted, surveying the camp. "And you have no right to offer what already belongs to the Reborn King."

Gewey reached down and helped Andren to his feet. Blood trickled from his nose and mouth.

"There is no need to hurt anyone," said Andren. "We have no weapons. Take what you want and leave us in peace."

Grusta's eyes fell on Gewey and Kaylia. "These two look as if they may not be as helpless as the rest of you rabble. Which is your wagon?"

Gewey leveled his gaze. He felt his muscles tense. "You will not be leaving here with anything. Nor will you harm these people. Get on your horses and ride away ... while you still can."

The captain stepped in close so that their noses were virtually touching. He was broad in the shoulder, though not quite as broad as Gewey. The other two soldiers slowly moved their hands to their swords.

"Perhaps an example must be made," he growled.

Gewey flashed a wicked smile. The flow filled his body. Just then he felt Kaylia through their bond, pleading for him to restrain himself. Instead of releasing the flow of earth or air, he allowed the spirit to enter him. The night sparkled with countless flashes of tiny light. He could see the fear and desperation inside everyone there—including the soldiers. He reached out and touched their spirits, willing their fear to grow stronger.

"You should leave now," he whispered.

The captain began to tremble. Slowly, he backed away and mounted his horse. He looked at Gewey one last time before spurring his horse to a gallop. The other two soldiers followed in close pursuit.

For several minutes, the people remained still and said nothing, as if expecting the soldiers to return.

Finally, Andren spoke. "I have never seen anything like that. They could have killed you where you stood."

Gewey shrugged. "They were just cowards preying on the weak."

"Well, it was cowards like them who robbed us of our provisions," said Andren. "They're the reason we are half-starved." He slapped Gewey on the shoulder. "But now that you are with us, perhaps they'll leave us be."

"I think we were lucky," remarked Kaylia. She turned and walked to their wagon, Gewey following close behind. "That was foolish," she whispered, once she was certain no one could hear. "You could have revealed yourself."

Gewey placed his hands on her shoulders. "But I didn't. Even better, I used the flow of the spirit to put fear into their hearts."

"I know," she replied. "I felt it. It was different from that at Valshara. It was as if you reached into their very souls and twisted them to your will."

"If I could do that to all the armies of Angrääl, the war would end quickly." His voice contained childlike excitement. "Imagine the lives that would be spared."

Kaylia nodded but with a skeptical look in her eyes. "Indeed, it could. But first, you need to master this skill, or there is no telling the damage you may do."

He took her hands and smiled. "I'll be careful. I swear."

They returned to the campfire. Andren and the others were talking and laughing, and before everyone went to sleep, they even mustered enough enthusiasm to sing a few songs. Gewey's heart was glad to see their spirits lifted. The hardships that the war had already brought to people weighed heavily on his mind. But his encounter with the soldiers gave him hope.

The next morning, they packed their gear and filed in behind the other wagons. Though traveling with a caravan of displaced women, children, and elderly was sure to slow their progress, it would certainly mask their presence to any who sought them.

By midday, a cold breeze was coming down from the north. Gewey passed out the few blankets he had brought with him to the neediest of the refugees, at the same time distributing the dried meat and fruits among the entire group. He knew that the farther from the coast they went, the colder it would get.

He began to think of Sharpstone. Likely the first snows would be falling there soon, if they hadn't already. Even without Angrääl soldiers traveling down the Goodbranch, business from the north would have all but ceased by now, and the grain suppliers from the Eastland kingdoms would have already finished their year's trading. He hoped his farm was in good order. That such mundane thoughts still entered his mind made him chuckle softly to himself.

After a short midday meal, they continued on their way. Andren had told him that most of his group intended to seek refuge in the Eastland, where it was said that the Reborn King had yet to invade. They asked hopefully if Gewey intended to accompany them the entire way. Not wanting to cause them despair, he evaded the question. It was obvious that his and Kaylia's presence made them feel safe. He even considered using the power of the flow to lift their spirits, but Kaylia sensed his thoughts and gave him a scathing glance.

"Do not be a fool," she hissed. "You cannot control it. You will end up with a caravan of worshipers, and I, for one, do not want this lot following us into the Spirit Hills chanting your name."

Gewey was surprised by how much of a child she could still make him feel. "You're right, of course."

It was nearly an hour before sunset when they came across a riderless horse grazing at the side of the road. Gewey recognized the saddle and gear to be from Angrääl. After searching the area, he very soon came upon the soldiers who had visited their camp the day before. Their bodies were heaped upon the ground, with blood staining the sur-rounding earth from the savage wounds on their faces and throats. He ran back to the wagon and grabbed his sword.

He told the others what he had found. "I'll make sure that whoever did this is no longer nearby."

Kaylia grabbed her long knife and followed him to the bodies. She examined the gruesome scene for several min-utes, then nodded with understanding.

"There are no signs of bandits or rogues about," she said bitterly. "What was done to these men ... they did to themselves."

Gewey stared at the bodies, stunned and mouth agape. Guilt and regret stabbed at his heart as he realized what he had done.

"This is why I tell you to be cautious," said Kaylia coldly. "And this is why Felsafell said that the spirit is your true weapon."

Gewey wanted her comfort, but she offered none. It pained him to feel her anger and disappointment. "I didn't mean for this to happen," he told her.

"I do not think you did," said Kaylia. "But even after what happened in Valshara, you still insist on using a power that you have yet to understand." She pointed to the dead soldiers. "What if this was someone other than the enemy? Could you have borne the guilt?"

Gewey looked again at the bodies, the terrified expressions of their last moments frozen on their faces. Suddenly he felt ill. He turned to Kaylia, but the instant their eyes met, he felt a sudden rage rush through their bond. It was unlike anything he'd felt from her before. She clenched her fists and stormed away into the nearby brush. Gewey stood there, dumbfounded. After a few minutes, she returned, a look of remorse on her face.

"I'm sorry. I swear I will not use the flow of the spirit on anyone again until I understand it better," Gewey promised.

She shook her head. "It is I who should apologize. I do not understand why I became so angry. For some reason, I lost control of my passions."

Gewey smiled sympathetically. "You're just tired. And with everything that has happened, I think you're allowed to get angry from time to time." He took her hand. "Besides, if you can't vent your frustrations on me, then who can you?"

She did not smile back. "Perhaps you are right. Still, it was an unusual feeling."

He looked once again at the bodies. "We should not tell the others that they killed themselves. The truth would only frighten them."

She nodded, then pulled away from him and began rifling through the soldiers' clothing.

"What are you doing?" asked Gewey uneasily.

"We are at war," she replied flatly. "They may have information." She pulled a small coin purse from the captain's belt. "And this can replace the stolen provisions."

Gewey turned away from the ghoulish scene and made his way back to the caravan. He told the others that the soldiers had been killed by bandits, and also that the bandits had left a trail headed north. This brought forth sinister smiles and nods of satisfaction. When Kaylia returned, she gave Andren what coin she had found, then got back into the wagon.

"They had no information about their masters," she told Gewey once they were underway. "Only a few personal letters and mementos. But even these can tell us something. Those men were from Gath."

Gewey looked at her, eyes wide. "That could mean the armies of Angrääl have already begun to march west."

"At minimum, the Reborn King must have some sort of hold there," she offered. "We may have even less time than we thought."

From that moment on, the slow pace of the caravan was painful to bear. At night, Gewey tried desperately to reach Felsafell, but to no avail. By the end of the second week, they were well down the Old Santismal Road and he was in a constant state of anxiety. Kaylia was faring no better. She was having repeated outbursts of rage that grew ever more frequent. Though mostly directed at Gewey, on a few occasions she had loosed her anger at the refugees. Soon, none cared to speak to her at all and avoided her whenever possible.

Gewey began to notice the ruined pillars and broken statues of the ancient kingdoms along the roadside. He recalled the stories Dina had told him when they had first left the Spirit Hills. The Book of Souls had mentioned the cities of the firstborn, and he now wondered if these were, in fact, ruins from that time. If so, he marveled at the construction. For something to stand for so long, even as a ruin, spoke of skill beyond his imaginings.

Midway through the third week, the weather became increasingly cold, with snow falling briefly a few times. The towns they passed, though unwilling to allow the caravan to stay within their borders overnight, at least provided them with a place to purchase blankets and warm clothes. Gewey had given his fellow travelers a few extra coins to add to those Kaylia had taken from the soldiers. That evening, after finding a clear spot to camp, the refugees huddled together around their fire, sipping on cups of hot soup.

Kaylia was unpacking their blankets when Gewey felt a flash of keen awareness through their bond.

"Elves are near," she said before he could ask.

Gewey allowed the flow to fill him and reached out. In moments, he heard them. Six elves were camped in the woods a half mile from the road. They were aware of the caravan but showed no signs of aggression.

"Whoever they are, it seems they wish to stay unnoticed," said Kaylia in Gewey's ear.

"Still, we should find out who they are," he said. "If they're from the Steppes, we need to know."

Kaylia nodded in agreement. "If they are, we should try to avoid conflict. At present, they are not interested in the caravan, and I would not want that to change." She reached into the wagon and grabbed her weapon. "I should speak to them alone."

"I don't like it," said Gewey. "Your last encounter with the elves of the Steppes didn't exactly go well."

"I don't think they will attack me," she said. "If I can sense them, they can certainly sense me, and they have still shown no sign of interest. I have the feeling they are not those who attacked the Chamber of the Maker."

"Even so," said Gewey, his tone hard and unyielding, "I will be nearby."

Kaylia nodded in agreement and handed Gewey his sword. The eyes of the camp followed them as they made their way into the forest, but none dared to question them. As they drew near, Gewey could sense that the elves, nervous of their approach, had begun to prepare themselves for an attack. One look at Kaylia told him she had sensed the same thing. In spite of his promise to her, he felt a strong temptation to ease their minds with the flow but fought against it. Should they show aggression, he would use air and earth. When they were one hundred yards away, Gewey halted and allowed Kaylia to continue on alone.

Through their bond, he could feel her apprehension. Flashes of her capture and time in captivity shot into his mind. He reached out and touched her, sending comforting thoughts, but this was met coldly. Something was troubling her. Her harsh reactions and ill temper had no source that he could understand. Whenever he asked about it, she insisted that nothing was wrong.

He allowed the flow to surge through him, all the time concentrating hard. At first, he could hear the birds flitting through the trees and brush, their sounds mixing easily with the rustle of windswept leaves in a perfect chorus of life and harmony. But slowly he filtered all of these things out until the only sounds to reach him were the breathing of the elves and the nimble footfalls of Kaylia.

"What do you want with us?" asked a rich, powerful female voice.

"You are from the Steppes," said Kaylia. "I would know why you are so far from your lands?"

"Do not feign ignorance," said the woman calmly. "You know as well as I that there is a second split. We simply do not wish to be a part of it."

"So you venture east?" remarked Kaylia.

"As do you," she countered. "Though we do not disguise ourselves as human. Nor would we travel among them."

"Then you share the same feelings as the rest of your kin?" Her voice showed sudden signs of irritation.

"We do not choose to live as you or your people," she replied. "Nor will we bend to the will of the Reborn King, believing, as many do, his false promises of a return to our past glory."

"So you have fled?" asked Kaylia.

"We seek peace and a return to our old ways." Her voice was now sad but determined. "Though I do not hold much hope for this. Many who have tried to leave the Steppes have been pursued by foul beasts and slain. I fear that, no matter where we go, they will find us. Some have taken refuge among the ancient ruins south of here. As I understand, the humans believe them to be possessed by spirits and rarely go there. But I doubt such rumors will keep the Vrykol at bay."

The word stuck in Gewey's mind. He had hoped not to encounter the Vrykol this far from the sea. It would surely mean that the armies would soon follow, and that time had run out.

"Do they pursue you now?" asked Kaylia.

"No," she replied. "Though I know they have spent much of their time preventing the elves from leaving the Steppes. We were fortunate. Our elders would have us believe it was the humans who ambushed our people. But we know the truth. Large numbers of those exiled, and those like us who simply chose to leave, have been set upon by the Vrykol and had their bodies desecrated. Many of them decided to join your kin in the south. I think the fact that we went east instead may have saved us."

Gewey could feel Kaylia's fury.

"Your elders know this is happening?" Her voice was steel.

"Their minds are trapped by the Reborn King," she replied in obvious anguish. "As are the minds of many of our people. A dark curtain has fallen over the Steppes. Those who are not overcome by it are forced to leave."

There was a long pause before the elf continued. "Your human companion moves well to hide himself from us. But I hear him now. It was wise not to bring him into our camp with you."

"He worries for my safety," said Kaylia. "And considering what has happened, for good reason."

"He needn't worry," she said, amused. "Our intent is to avoid bloodshed, if possible. But still, it was unwise to come at all considering you are..."

There was another pause, during which Gewey could feel Kaylia's confusion.

"Come," the elf woman continued. "Walk with me. We should speak alone."

He heard their gentle steps fade, and to his relief, the other elves made no move to follow. Soon, they were beyond his ability to hear their words. He was tempted to move closer but did not want to provoke them. Though he didn't know what was being said, he could feel Kaylia's confusion turning to panic and fear. He clenched his fist, trembling with the desire to find her and keep her safe. Finally, after several agonizingly long minutes, they returned.

Without another word, Kaylia came back to him, and they made their way back to the caravan.

"What did she say to you?" he asked.

"Nothing I care to speak about," she snapped. "And do not try to pry the information from me through our bond."

"I would never do that," he protested.

She looked at him sideways. "The important thing is that these elves do not mean us, or anyone else, any harm. We will leave them be."

That night, when Gewey tried to reach out with his spirit as they slept, she held him at bay. Though not forcefully, she made it quite clear to him that she intended to keep whatever secret the elf from the Steppes had given to her.

As they neared Vine Run, Gewey told the others that he and Kaylia would be staying there for some time, and would therefore no longer be traveling with them. This caused great sadness and anxiety. He gave them what provisions he had remaining, and most of his gold, but this did little to soften the blow. Several of the mothers begged them to stay, even going so far as to send their children over in an attempt to sway them. By the time the dilapidated vineyards came into view, Gewey and Kaylia were cringing every time someone spoke to them.

When the caravan reached the outskirts of Vine Run, they said their goodbyes and turned their wagon into the heart of the town. They could feel the tear-filled eyes watching them as they left, and the sound of called-out farewells followed them far down the street.

Vine Run looked much the same as it had the last time Gewey was there. None of the burned buildings had been repaired, and the streets were in even worse condition than before. Only a few villagers were about—their tattered clothes telling him all too clearly that times had become even harder. A few flakes of snow were beginning to fall, and a bleak gray sky promised a great deal more to come.

"How do these people survive?" muttered Kaylia.

"Not easily," said Gewey.

The inn was the only building in town that looked sturdy enough to keep out the cold. He could see Minnie, the sweet old innkeeper, standing just outside. She and her husband were hanging pumpkin vines on the front door. Her chubby, round face lit up as she spotted Gewey.

"Well, I'll be," she called out merrily. "It's so wonderful to see you again." She tilted her head to look behind him. "I see your friends aren't with you this time. Such a pity." She shot her husband a stern glance, and he immediately guided the wagon to within a few feet of the inn's door. Minnie's eyes then fell on Kaylia. "And who is this lovely creature? It's none of my business, but I'm surprised your wife isn't with you."

Gewey could feel Kaylia's irritation.

"This is my wife," he replied. "The woman you met before was a friend. We posed as a couple so as to pass through unnoticed. I apologize for the deception."

She burst into laughter. "No apologies necessary, young man. With all the strange happenings, I understand you not wanting to draw attention." She held out her plump hand to Kaylia as she stepped down off the wagon. "And you are the vision of loveliness, my dear. You will light up the inn tonight."

The pumpkin vines made Gewey think of the festival of Gerath. "Is there a celebration?"

"Indeed, there is," she replied. "Our reserve stores of wine have been purchased for ten times what they are worth. That'll be enough gold to see the town through the winter."

"That is good news," said Gewey. "Who bought them?"

"The Reborn King, of course," she said, smiling.

Gewey and Kaylia stiffened.

"Are his soldiers here now?" asked Gewey.

"Certainly not," replied Minnie. "Why would they want to stay here? They just came to purchase our wine. In fact, you missed them by only a day. They left here with ten full wagons. Almost everyone in the village was bought completely out." A stiff breeze carried a flurry of snowflakes. "And not a moment too soon, I'd say. I was afraid we'd starve this year." She stepped over to the door and opened it. "Now come along. My old goat of a husband will see to your wagon and horses."

After retrieving their personal packs and weapons, Gewey and Kaylia stepped inside. The common room was warmed by a fire burning brightly in the hearth, and a dozen or so women were decorating the rafters and tables with pumpkin vines, various berries, and flowers. Some of them quickly recognized Gewey from his last stay and called out warm greetings.

Minnie showed them to their room. Once inside, she took a long appraising look at Kaylia. "If you would permit me, I have a dress that would suit you very well." She glanced down at her own round figure and laughed. "Long ago, it fit me. But I think I would enjoy seeing it on you. That is, assuming you'll be joining us tonight." She reached out and grabbed hold of Kaylia's hands. "Please tell me you will."

Kaylia forced a smile. "Of course."

Minnie flashed a satisfied grin and left them.

Gewey and Kaylia tossed their packs in the corner and leaned their weapons against the wall next to the bed. A few minutes later, Minnie returned holding a square cloth bundle. She was accompanied by two young women carrying a brass basin of hot water and two towels.

"I'm sorry I don't have shoes for you," said Minnie. "But you'll look gorgeous, anyway."

After they left, Gewey and Kaylia washed up. Minnie's husband brought them a plate of roast beef with boiled potatoes, along with a bottle of sweet wine. When he had gone, Kaylia looked at the food and curled her lip.

"I think I will pass on this fare," she said. "And I am in no mood for wine."

Gewey looked at her with concern. Her feelings were erratic and confused. "I'll fetch you some tea and bread," he said.

Before she could protest, he opened the door and hurried to the dining hall where Minnie was still hard at work preparing for the feast. Musicians had arrived and were gathered around the fireplace, tuning their instruments. Minnie happily made tea and gave him a small loaf of flatbread.

When he returned to the room, Kaylia was frowning at the dress Minnie had given to her. It was made from deep blue satin and decorated with a white orchid print that spiraled up its length.

"Not to my taste," she remarked.

"I think you'll look beautiful," said Gewey. He put the bread and tea on the table. "Of course, you always look beautiful to me."

Kaylia laid the dress on the bed and gave him a warm smile. "Then I suppose I will be satisfied with Minnie's gift."

After a short rest, they changed clothes and ventured into the main hall. Gewey had donned a simple green cotton shirt and brown trousers. He'd also made a passable attempt at polishing his belt and boots. Minnie's dress fitted Kaylia surprisingly well, the smooth fabric shifting around her curves as she moved. She continued to wear the red headscarf to cover her elf ears, though there was little to be done about concealing her striking eyes and obvious superior grace. In light of the recent visit by the Angrääl soldiers, Gewey felt uneasy about leaving his sword behind but knew the sight of an armed stranger may well cause more problems than he cared to deal with.

The hall was already filled with cheerful townsfolk. The musicians were playing a jaunty melody and the center of the hall was alive with people dancing and singing. Minnie spotted them right away. Throwing up her hands and beaming with delight, she pushed her way through the crowd to give Kaylia a warm embrace.

"I just knew you would look wonderful in that dress," she said. She winked at Gewey with a playful smile. "Though your husband could use a bit of refinement." She took Kaylia's hand and led her to a group of women talking on the far side of the room. Gewey did his best to follow them without knocking people over.

"This is Malorie, Bellia, and Cheriel," said Minnie. "Good friends of mine, and probably the only people here who you will be able to have a decent conversation with." The women smiled politely. "As for you," Minnie continued while turning to Gewey, her plump cheeks rosy and her eyes filling with mirth, "you can stand quietly and listen."

Kaylia looked at the women awkwardly before introducing both herself and Gewey.

"What a lovely dress," said Malorie, a woman of about forty with wavy, black hair gathered in a loose ponytail that was tied in place by a silver ribbon. She was wearing a long blue cotton dress with tiny white beads sewn in a criss-crossing pattern from the shoulder to her waist. "One of Minnie's perhaps?"

Kaylia nodded. "She was kind enough to allow me to wear it for the celebration."

"Kind?" Malorie laughed. "The woman has more clothes than a princess. Most of which she hasn't been able to wear in years. Every time a cloth merchant comes to town, she gets the tailor to make her another one. And it's not like she has them made to fit." She leaned in and whispered. "The poor dear still thinks she's going to regain her youthful figure."

Gewey could tell that Kaylia did not like this woman.

The other two women were dressed in a similar fashion, though their dresses lacked the intricate beading. They looked to be younger than Malorie by a few years and were far less talkative. The conversation centered mainly on petty gossip and rumors about the townsfolk. Kaylia kept silent and nodded politely. She was just about to excuse herself when Malorie grabbed her arm and motioned for the others to come closer.

"Have you heard?" she asked in a half-whisper. "Elves have been spotted in the woods south of the Spirit Hills."

"I heard that too," said Bellia. "I even heard they're planning to settle there."

"Well, you know that they live right next to humans out west," said Malorie. "Someone told me that they're even taking wives."

The other two women gasped.

"Have you been out west?" Cheriel asked Kaylia.

"Yes," she replied. Her voice was cold and steady.

Gewey didn't like where this was going. He could feel Kaylia's temper rising.

"Is it true?" asked Malorie. "Are elves and humans living together?"

"It is," Kaylia affirmed.

"Well, I would be terrified if an elf lived next to me," said Bellia.

"And why is that?" Kaylia asked, tilting her head slightly.

"You know how much they hate us," she replied. "I'd worry that they would kill me as I slept. And the gods help me if my daughter were to take one as a husband."

The others nodded in agreement.

"First of all," said Kaylia, "if an elf were to kill you, it would not be while you slept. And second, if your daughter caught an elf's eye, it would speak well of her."

"I'm sorry, dear," argued Malorie. "But I happen to know that an elf can't be trusted. If they were to settle here, it would only be a matter of time before the killing began." She patted Kaylia on her shoulder. "You're too young to understand, but they have hated us for hundreds of years. My mother told me the stories about the Great War. They'll never forgive us for defeating them." She looked at the other two women. "It's a shame the old stories aren't told to children these days."

Gewey knew what Kaylia was about to do only a split second before she did it.

"I think you have nothing to worry about," Kaylia told Malorie, pulling off her scarf and revealing her elf ears. "If I have not harmed you after such an insult, I think you have little to fear from my kin. The old hatreds are a thing of the past, as you can plainly see."

The three women gasped in unison, staring in sudden terror.

Gewey quickly stepped forward and pulled Kaylia away.

"We should return to our room," he told her.

"Nonsense," said Kaylia. "I have watched my kin die to protect these people's meaningless lives, so I have earned my place at this feast. Especially being that it was bought with the gold of our enemy."

She jerked free from his grasp, pushed her way through the crowd, and took a seat at a table near where the musicians were playing. Gewey sat down beside her, nervously scanning the crowd for a reaction.

It was not long in coming. In well under a minute, everyone else who had been sitting at their table was on their feet and backing right away, as if suddenly confronted by some terrible demon. As more and more people began staring in Kaylia's direction, the dancing and singing gradually faded. Finally, the music stopped altogether. Only anxious murmurs of fear could now be heard in the otherwise deathly silent room.

"Oh my, oh my!" Minnie's voice came from behind them, cutting right through the tense atmosphere. She rounded the table and sat directly across from Kaylia. "I wish you had mentioned you are an elf, my dear."

"What should it matter?" Kaylia shot back coldly.

"Well, for one thing, I could have prepared the folks for it," she replied. She reached over the table and lightly touched Kaylia's hand. "But as things are—so be it. Pay no mind to these gossips and dullards. You are my guest and that's that." She stood and addressed the crowd. "Do you hear me? Kaylia is my guest. Any of you who don't like it can leave now." Her eyes fell on Malorie. "And that includes you."

Malorie stiffened her back and huffed.

Minnie's husband walked up. Holding out his hand, he bowed. "I've always wanted to meet an elf, Miss Kaylia. I would be honored if you would dance with me." He grinned at Minnie. "And just so you know, my name is Vernin, not old goat."

Kaylia sat motionless for a long moment, then took the old man's hand.

"Music!" shouted Minnie. "You're not being paid to gawk like idiots." She kissed her husband's cheek. "And don't you go hurting yourself."

After a few seconds, the music resumed, allowing Vernin to escort Kaylia onto the dance floor. The crowd watched in silence as the two danced and spun with the rhythm. Vernin moved surprisingly well for a man of his advanced years, leading Kaylia expertly around the room. Gewey could feel Kaylia's anger and apprehension dwindling.

"He really is a sweet old goat," said Minnie. "And you two don't need to worry about this bunch. They'll warm up soon enough once the brandy sets in."

The song ended with Kaylia hugging Vernin and kissing him fondly on the cheek. He bowed in return before making his way through the still-silent crowd to the bar. Kaylia rejoined Gewey and sighed with satisfaction.

"You know that was foolish," he said.

"Yes," she admitted, smirking. "But tomorrow we can lose ourselves in the Spirit Hills, so I imagine there is little harm done. And I did enjoy silencing that hag, Malorie."

Seeing her spirits lifted was enough to make Gewey smile. Slowly, the people returned to their merrymaking. Before long, they began coming over to introduce themselves to

Kaylia. Mostly it was a simple hello and welcome, but bolder villagers were keen to know about her and her people. In less than an hour, she was completely surrounded by eager townsfolk asking a myriad of questions.

Gewey recalled when he'd first met Kaylia, and of how unwilling she had been to say anything about herself or her people. Now, she seemed perfectly happy to do so. A few of the village men, apparently not wanting to be outdone by an old man, even dared to follow Vernin's example by asking her to dance. Kaylia was pleased to oblige. A handful of people, such as Malorie and her two friends, still chose to keep their distance, but before the night was over, Gewey could easily have imagined that elves were commonly seen in Vine Run.

It was well after midnight before the celebrations died down. No one wanted to leave while Kaylia was still there. Reluctantly, she and Gewey said goodnight and retired to their room. As they approached, Gewey noticed that their door was ajar. His muscles tensed and he instinctively pushed Kaylia behind him. The flow filled his limbs as he burst inside.

There, sitting cross-legged on the bed, smiling his customary crooked smile, was Felsafell. He wore his usual buckskin clothing, and his gnarled walking stick lay across his lap.

"A lovely sight," said Felsafell. "Bonded elf beauty and her handsome mate."

Kaylia entered and shut the door.

Gewey breathed a sigh of relief. "You have no idea how happy I am to see you."

"I think you are," said Felsafell. "And indeed you should be. Wasting time looking for an old man's house you could never find would only serve to frustrate an eager mind. Nothing there but keepsakes and memories. None worth a copper to anyone but me." He hopped up nimbly and looked Gewey in the eyes. "The power you used is not as you had hoped. Dangerous and vile, yet with it you must do what seems impossible."

"I don't understand," said Gewey. "When I use the flow of the spirit, it doesn't feel evil or vile, but the results are terrible and unpredictable."

"Temptation is seductive, oh yes, it is," said Felsafell. "Pleasing and soft. And though evil it is not, vile, it remains. Long ago did the gods abandon it. A world of the mindless and soulless was all they could create. Yet you must do what they could not."

Gewey recalled the people in Valshara leaving offerings at his door and shuddered at the thought of the hordes of worshipers he could create. He told Felsafell of this, and of the encounter with the soldiers.

"Then you have seen what must not be," said Felsafell. "And now you understand your foe's greatest weapon." He turned his back and lowered his head. "Strong it is." His voice was oddly somber. "And a weapon he has mastered. He steals your time and hope, and he will certainly overcome this world unless you can thwart your own nature."

Gewey cocked his head. "My nature? Are you saying that my being a god is a weakness?"

Felsafell shrugged gawkily. "You could say that. Yes, you could. Your foe is human, though a god he wishes to be. It tempers his power, it does. Makes it easy to control. No worshiper does he create, nor do his victims drive themselves mad. Ensnares their hearts, he does. Oh yes. Through loyalty, his strength grows, but it is a loyalty taken, not given."

"So must I learn to be more like him?" asked Gewey incredulously. "Must I be able to ensnare the will of others without turning them into sycophants?"

Felsafell laughed. "Were it only so simple. A shame it is not. You must break his power without imposing your own. You must turn a hammer into a needle. A blacksmith must be a jeweler." He smiled at Kaylia. "And your bonded mate must be at your side. Or the earth will be lost to your spirit."

"That part will be easy," said Kaylia. "I will never leave his side."

Felsafell raised his eyebrows and smirked. "Easy you think? Will time and circumstance spare you a jagged path and a hard choice? Long I have lived in the world. I see much though learn less. But hard-learned lessons are never forgotten. Sometimes love is an enemy when shared too deeply."

"I share my love with many," countered Gewey. His voice was unwavering. "But none do I love more than Kaylia."

"I can see that told him you have not," said Felsafell, his eyes shooting between them. "But tell him you will, or our journey together ends here. The Child of Heaven cannot march to his destiny in ignorance." He took a step back, his face grave and resolute.

Gewey turned to Kaylia. "What is he talking about?" He could feel her sudden anxiety threatening to overwhelm her.

A tear fell down her cheek as she glared angrily at Felsafell. "I would have told him in my own time." She looked back at Gewey and took his hands. "I ... I am with child."

Gewey remained silent for a moment, dumbfounded. He blinked hard and shook his head. "Are you sure?"

"The elf woman from the Steppes was a healer," she replied, her voice wavering. "She knew of my condition at once and made it known to me. That is why I have been unable to govern my anger."

Gewey felt a rush of elation, but it was mixed with fear. "Why did you hide this from me?"

"We are on a dangerous road," she explained. "I worried that your mind would be distracted from what must be done. I was afraid you would abandon your duty in order to protect me and our child. Please forgive me."

The trace of fear inside Gewey vanished as he listened to her explanation. Now, an uncontrollable wave of pure joy rushed through him. "You never have to apologize to me. Whatever I may face, I will face it with you by my side. I will not let our child be a source of fear and doubt." He reached out and pulled her to him in a tight embrace. "Our child will be a source of strength. I swear it."

"I was afraid you would try to send me away," she said. Her tears of happiness flowed freely.

He gently eased her back. With a tender smile, he touched her cheek. "I could never send you away. If our child is to be safe, you must be where I can protect you."

"That is well and good," said Felsafell. "For she is needed, and I am satisfied." He moved to the door. "And even an old man knows when to leave young love to their rapture. The morning will find us among the hills I call home. With the dawn, I will return." He shot them one last crooked grin and left.

Gewey and Kaylia slept very little that night. Instead, they lay staring into each other's eyes, whispering softly and bathing in the love that flowed between them.

CHAPTER 11

The road east from Sharpstone led directly into the Jerrica Hills that bordered the Eastland kingdoms. After Lee and Linis had satisfied themselves that they were not being pursued, they decided it was safe for the group to take the main road. If a large force were to approach, they would easily hear it and have time to get everyone out of sight.

All of their remaining sell-swords had collected their pay, along with a bit extra, and had turned south to the coast. Lee didn't mind losing men whose loyalty could be bought, though he did have concerns that a loose tongue might bring an enemy searching for them.

He had always disliked traveling eastward. The road snaked through endless hills and shallow valleys, and the terrain was deceptively rugged. Tall grass hid the rocks and pitfalls from view, making a cross-country journey perilous and even more time consuming than usual.

Most of Lee's time was spent with Millet in quiet conversation. Millet again recounted the events after they had parted just north of Baltria, while Lee spoke of his journey in more detail, although not of the fate befalling Penelope.

Linis, when he was not laughing and talking with Dina, kept himself busy by training Jacob in the ways of the seeker. As for the soldiers, they were a hardy and loyal group, with most of them having served Lord Ganflin for many years. Bevaris and Tristan took it upon themselves to see to their needs, and soon Linis insisted that the knights should take over command, saying that they understood human tactics and methods far better than he. Bevaris seemed most pleased by this.

On the fourth day, they ran across a small caravan of merchants heading west to Helenia. Lee managed to discover that although Angrääl had not yet sent any significant forces to the Eastland, word had spread about the gathering of their armies in the north. The people were afraid, and the various kings and queens had sent tributes in the hope that they would be spared.

The snow had begun to fall in earnest by the end of the first week, forcing them to take refuge in Lathila, a small farming village, in order to purchase warmer clothing and blankets. Most of the soldiers were accustomed to the warm climate of Althetas and were ill-prepared for such a harsh cold. The small inn didn't have enough rooms to house the entire party, so Lee paid a local farmer to open his barn. Dina was allowed to stay in the farmhouse and sleep with the farmer's two young daughters. That evening, Linis and Jacob convinced Millet and Lee to accompany them to the local tavern.

The tavern was typical of a small village. Hearths burned brightly on opposite sides of the room, and a long bar spanned its width from corner to corner. Cheerful townsfolk occupied most of the simple wood tables and benches, leaving only a few still available. An old man was playing a lute beside the bar; his lack of skill told Lee that he was most likely just a local making a bit of extra coin rather than a true traveling minstrel. Still, it was a welcome change from the biting cold of the long road.

Concerned about drawing additional attention to their group, Linis had wrapped his head in a wool scarf to disguise his elf features.

"I do not like that you must hide," grumbled Millet. "Not after everything you've done and sacrificed."

"The time is coming when I will no longer have to hide," Linis told him. "But for now I must. Though I admit living openly among humans in the West has made it difficult for me to go back to the way things were. Only now do I realize the effect it has had on me."

Lee ordered a round of ale and a hot meal. It wasn't long before songs were heard throughout the hall and Lee was telling tales of his youthful exploits. Jacob listened with interest, especially when Millet stopped his former master to see to it that he was telling the story accurately.

It was almost time for them to depart when Lee and Linis stiffened. Their hands slid to their weapons as the door opened and a tall, cloaked figure entered.

"Vrykol," hissed Lee.

At once, Jacob leaped to his feet, but Linis grabbed his arm.

"Do nothing," the elf said. "Wait until your father or I make a move."

The Vrykol scanned the hall before slowly approaching their table. It stopped only a few feet away and pushed back its hood. Linis let out an audible gasp as the face of an elf was revealed. Its black hair was tied in a ponytail and its dark complexion was a stark contrast to its ice-blue eyes.

"Such a shame that these fine people know not of the greatness in their presence," said the Vrykol, bowing. "It is indeed fortunate to run into you here."

"Shortly, you will not consider yourself so fortunate," said Linis.

The Vrykol tilted its head and frowned. "Now, now. It would not do if we fought here and innocent villagers were to be hurt." Its face turned to a slight smile. "Besides, I only came to greet you. Can enemies not be civil to each other?"

"You are an abomination," seethed Linis. "I will offer you no kindness—only the edge of my blade."

Lee looked around the room. A few people were already taking notice of the Vrykol, believing it to be an elf. "Say what you have to say, then I would flee if I were you."

"Bold and rash," said the Vrykol. "Just as I have been told. But you need not worry. My business, as well as my master's, is done in this part of the world ... for now. If you seek aid or allies, you will be sorely disappointed. And the elves of the desert are all but destroyed by now."

"So you seek to turn us back?" asked Millet.

The murmurs grew as more people began noticing the newcomer.

"No indeed," it replied, amused. "As I said, I only wanted to meet you and your brave companions. The fierce Lee Starfinder, son of Saraf, and his loyal servant Millet Gristall." Its eyes shifted slightly. "And this must be Jacob. I have heard good things about you as well. It is no small matter to betray your own father."

Jacob's face turned red with rage.

"Leave now, beast," growled Linis. "Or the crowd will be no protection for you."

The Vrykol ignored the threat. "And the name of Linis is certainly known to me—a legend among the elf seekers, to be sure. Only Berathis could surpass your skill. But alas, he is slain. By Lord Starfinder I heard."

Lee shot up from his seat, his sword drawn in a flash. The Vrykol stepped back, holding out his palm.

"Kill me if you will," it said. "But know that I am not alone. If I do not return to my comrades, the woman Celandine will die. At this very moment, I have men outside the farmhouse where she awaits your return."

The veins on Lee's forehead bulged. "And if she is harmed, I will..."

The Vrykol gave a sneering laugh. "Save your threats. I have not harmed her. She is of no interest to me other than as a means to ensure my safe passage from this tavern." He strode gracefully over to the exit. "I am truly honored to have met you. And I suspect we shall meet again."

The moment the door closed behind him, the tavern erupted. Shouts and curses from frightened villagers combined with speculative whispers about Lee and his companions. Not that their opinions were of any concern to him at that very moment. Brushing the locals aside on his way out, Lee ran as fast as he possibly could back to the farmhouse, the others as close on his heels as they could manage. To their great relief, they found Dina sitting quietly on the front porch, wrapped in a thick wool blanket and sipping a cup of warm cider.

Linis immediately headed to the barn and roused the men, while Dina went inside the house to retrieve her long knife. Within a few minutes, the house was completely surrounded by Ganflin's soldiers. After satisfying himself that the men were in position, Linis went to look for signs of the Vrykol. He returned a half hour later.

"They were watching from about two hundred yards away," he said. "They must have arrived just after we left, otherwise I would have certainly heard them."

"How many?" asked Lee.

"Only ten as far as I can tell," Linis replied. "All were human except for the creature. They headed west only a short time ago."

By now, the snow was coming down hard. Lee knew that if they intended pursuit, a decision needed to be made quickly. He addressed the party. "I say we forget the Vrykol and press on. We have much distance to cover, and I will not allow the words of that fiend make me think our efforts will be fruitless."

"And if elves have come out of the desert, I intend to meet them," added Linis.

"Will we stay here tonight?" asked Bevaris.

"Yes," replied Lee. "But I fear this may be the last time we feel warmth until we reach the desert region. I will no longer risk endangering the innocent with our presence."

Millet made his apologies to the farmer for the commotion and gathered everyone inside the barn. Bevaris and Tristan kept watch on the house while Linis patrolled the perimeter. By morning the sky was clear, but nearly a foot of snow had fallen.

Travel was slow once they set out, with only Linis's keen senses keeping them from wandering off the road. Lee hoped that the snowfall did not extend too far east, otherwise the horses could be in real danger. Without taking shelter in the towns they passed, it would be difficult to keep their mounts fed and rested.

After the fifth day, Lee had to risk sending Millet and a few of the men into the village of Henna, another small farming community, for grain and extra supplies. When they returned, Millet reported that the rumors of a coming invasion from the north had already gripped the village with fear.

"This is the Reborn King's intention," said Millet. "To make the east too afraid to fight so that he can focus his assault on the west."

"Then we will have to alleviate them of this fear," said Linis. "Once we join with the elves, then we can show them that they do not fight alone."

"Sadly, I think they may fear an elf army as much as the one from Angrääl," said Lee.

"Then we shall have to show them differently," Linis retorted.

Lee noticed how closely Linis was standing to Dina. He smiled. "I think your example may help to show them the way."

"We should begin with King Luccia in Xenthia," suggested Bevaris. "My sway there may help us. And he is by far the wealthiest ruler in the Eastland. If we gain his support, the others could well follow."

"Then that is where we will begin after joining with the elves," said Lee.

After a few more days, the snow on the ground had dwindled to little more than an inch, allowing tufts of grass to peek out. The cold wind, however, was biting and relentless. When they were a day outside the city of Theodim, it was decided to take the risk of traveling cross-country; the terrain was now beginning to flatten, and the ground held far fewer hazards.

Bevaris, being a native of these lands, took the lead and guided them toward the Xenex Valley. From there, they would head southeast along the border of the kingdom of Comodaro until they reached the outskirts of the desert. Beyond the valley, the knight explained, warm air from the Sea of Gertharis overcame the frigid north wind. The land there, though thick with tall pine forests, was flat and much easier to traverse.

The Xenex Valley was reputed to be a sanctuary for wandering brigands and outlaws. Its difficult approach from the north, coupled with multiple exits to the south, made it a perfect refuge for anyone who wanted to evade capture.

It took them almost two weeks to reach the narrow path leading down into the heart of the valley, by which time they had nearly exhausted their supplies. The charred remnants of old signal fires from bandit lookouts confirmed that its reputation was well earned. Once lit, such a fire could be seen for miles.

As they rounded a rocky bend, the whole valley came into view. The flat grassy ground was dotted with thin patches of snow. Here and there, a few withered trees sprung up, their bare limbs stretching out like dead fingers reaching for the dull gray sky. Thousands of jagged boulders were scattered all along the base of the east and west rims, providing excellent cover for anyone wishing to conceal themselves. To the south, in the far distance, they could see the hazy visage of the gentle upward slope leading away from the valley. Lee guessed that it was at least a two-day trek away.

"If there is anyone here," said Bevaris. "They will have seen us by now." His voice was filled with worry.

"Is something wrong?" asked Lee.

"Bandits would have lit a signal fire and fled," he explained. "If anyone is about, they do not fear us. We must be wary."

"Could someone have come up from the south?" asked Linis.

Bevaris shrugged. "Possibly. But not likely. At least, not in winter."

They followed the path until it leveled out and broadened; the land before them looked desolate and uninviting. Linis and Lee rode ahead with Bevaris, looking and listening for signs of foes, but the rise and fall of a howling wind overwhelmed all other sounds.

"The earth here is dead," muttered Lee, with a hint of revulsion.

Linis nodded in agreement. "Yes. The flow is weak. Something dire once befell this place."

"It is said that the gods fought over the dominion of man on this very spot," said Bevaris. "Poisoning the valley for all time."

"Whatever the case," said Linis. "It will make detecting danger difficult."

"We should cut straight through the center," suggested Lee. "At least that way we'll be able to see anyone coming from a way off."

In spite of its level appearance from the top of the valley, the ground was uneven and rocky, and it took more than an hour to find a decent clearing in which to make camp for the night. Linis and Lee were not the only ones who felt uneasy. None of the men slept well, and all of them were eager to depart more than an hour before the sun broke over the valley's rim.

A few low clouds drifted down from the north, bringing with them an occasional flurry of snow. By midday, the entire company was chilled to the bone. Linis stayed close to Dina, who was being uncharacteristically quiet and reserved.

"This place is foul," she whispered, just loud enough for Linis to hear. "Something evil lurks."

"Do not fear," Linis assured her. "If the Vrykol are here, we will cut them down."

"It's not the Vrykol," she replied. Her eyes darted back and forth. "I felt something like this once before when I was in the Spirit Hills with Gewey. But this is far more intense."

Just then, a horrifying scream sounded from somewhere in the east. Everyone in the group turned to see a lone figure running toward them. It stumbled and fell every few yards, then scrambled to its feet and kept advancing.

Lee leaped from his saddle and quickly drew his sword. In an instant, Linis and Tristan were at his side. Bevaris ordered the rest of the men to form up and keep an eye on their flanks and rear.

As the figure drew closer, Lee was surprised to see a man in a black turban and facial scarf. He was clad in a flowing black robe, and in his right hand, he held a broken scimitar. His dark eyes were wide with terror.

"I don't think he even sees us," remarked Linis.

"I agree," said Lee. "His fear has blinded him to all but his flight. But something is odd. I am sure he is from the desert. I recognize the dress."

When the man was only twenty yards away, he finally caught sight of the party and came sliding to a halt. He spun around to look fearfully behind him, then faced Lee and the others again. His breathing was labored and his eyes showed signs of madness. An instant later, he set off at a run again, this time attempting to circle around them. Bevaris spurred his horse, at the same time drawing his massive sword. In only a few seconds, he caught up and smashed the flat of his blade over the man's head, sending him sprawling and unconscious. Bevaris sheathed his blade and slid down from the saddle. Grabbing the man by the scruff of his neck, he dragged him to Lee and tossed him roughly to the ground.

Linis kneeled down and allowed the flow to bring the man back to consciousness. The moment his eyes opened, he let out another terrified scream and tried to rise to his feet. Lee planted his boot on his chest, holding him still.

"Calm yourself," Lee said. "What has frightened you so?"

"It's coming!" he cried desperately. "It's coming! It will kill you all! Please, let me go!"

Lee nodded to Bevaris and Tristan. "Hold him." He lifted his foot as soon as the man was in their grasp. "You can leave once you tell us what we need to know."

The man's eyes were wild. "No time! It's coming!"

Dina stepped forward and gently placed her hands on their terrified captive's cheeks. "Calm." Her voice was musical and soothing. "No harm will come to you."

The man's breathing gradually steadied. His eyes locked on to Dina's, though he still trembled with fear. "The beast tricked us. Led us to slaughter." His eyes shot to Linis as if seeing him for the first time. "He led us to our doom so that the elves could kill us all. Now he has a monster finish what is left of us."

"Who are you?" asked Dina.

The man's gaze did not leave Linis. "I am Alluzal, of the Soufis. But the elf already knows this."

Linis raised his brow, taken aback. "I have never heard of the Soufis."

Alluzal snarled. "Liar! Our people have fought with yours for generations."

"He is not from the desert," said Dina calmly. "We are from the west."

His eyes shot from Linis to Dina and then back again. "It matters not. They are all the same."

"I have heard rumors of the Soufis," said Lee. "But your people never leave the deep desert. Most others don't even know you exist."

Alluzal spat. "We don't bother with borderland scum. They are weak and useless. They are not even fit to be slaves."

"So your people are slavers?" asked Linis. Alluzal only glared at him. "Then I understand why you would fear my desert kin."

"I fear no elf," he shouted in protest. "I have killed dozens of your kind." He struggled against Tristan and Brevaris's hold. "Let me go and I'll kill another."

Linis smiled fiendishly. "You know not what you ask. Your head would leave your shoulders before you took a single step." In a blur of motion, his blade was at Alluzal's throat. "Now tell me this instant what pursues you."

Dina touched Linis's shoulder. "He will tell us. There is no need for threats."

"And why would I do that, woman?" Alluzal mocked.

"Because we will allow you to go free," she replied, unaffected by his tone. "And unharmed."

Linis lowered his blade and backed away.

Alluzal's jaw tightened. "You will all die soon, anyway. The creature that took my brothers will come for you, too." He looked back in the direction he had come. "My people were deceived by the one called the Reborn King." Alluzal looked at his captors and grinned. "I see you've heard of him. Well, he promised my people that he would rid us of the elves once and for all if we helped him take the lands west of our desert."

This brought a growl from Linis.

"He promised us sixty-thousand of his own soldiers," he continued. "But none came, and the elves attacked us without warning. Slaughtered us, they did. I was among the few who escaped. The one we called the dark elf was supposed to lead us west, but when the attack came, he and his guards had disappeared."

"He must be speaking of the Vrykol we encountered," remarked Lee.

"I don't know what you call it," said Alluzal. "It looks like an elf, but it's not. Me and thirty of my brothers caught up with him and he convinced us to follow him west. He led us here, then told us to wait for his forces to arrive." His eyes were ablaze with hatred. "But instead of an army, we were left to be killed by a demon."

"What attacked you?" asked Dina.

Alluzal began to tremble again. "I don't know what it is. But it killed us one by one. Tearing us limb from limb and ... and..."

His words trailed off.

"And what?" pressed Lee.

"It feasts on the flesh of men." His voice wavered and tears welled in his eyes. "It ate my brothers. We tried to go back, but it wouldn't let us. It toyed with us like we were nothing." He heaved an unsteady breath. "You will see it soon enough."

With these ominous final words, Alluzal straightened his back. "I have held up my end of our agreement. I know nothing more. Release me."

Lee looked deep into his eyes, then waved his hand. Bevaris and Tristan let him go. Without a moment of hesitation, Alluzal dashed away north as fast as his legs could carry him.

Lee watched him until he was out of sight. "I know you would rather see him dead, Linis."

"No," he replied. "We hold to our bargains. And now we know that the Vrykol lied about the destruction of the desert elves."

"Yes," said Lee. "But I am still concerned about..."

Dina gasped. "Something approaches. Something foul."

Lee listened hard, but neither he nor Linis could sense anything.

Linis placed his hand on her shoulders. "Can you tell what it is?"

"No," she replied. "But I can feel its presence. It is wild and full of wrath, like a rabid wolf with only one intent."

"What intent?" asked Lee. He peered out, but could see only the grass bending with the bitter wind against the rocky backdrop of the valley's edge.

"Death," she whispered. "That is the only thing it desires. To cause death."

Lee pulled Jacob to his side and turned to the soldiers. "Keep your ranks close," he commanded. "Whatever is out there may try to separate you from your comrades."

"Look!" yelled Jacob, pointing to where they had first seen Alluzal.

A pale figure had suddenly appeared. Hunched and deformed, with a face that was twisted and mangled, it stood there, swaying slowly. Stringy black hair fell over its hulking shoulders, and its thick muscles seemed to be on the verge of bursting from its ghostly skin as they rippled and tensed. It held no weapon and wore nothing but a tattered pair of black trousers.

Jacob gasped. "What is it?"

Before anyone could answer, a shadow engulfed the creature. In a blur of darkness, it vanished.

"I think it may be a half-man," answered Lee, snarling. "I encountered something like it many years ago in the Dashivis Pass." He turned to the men. "This creature is faster and stronger than anything you'll have ever fought against. It will cast a shadow that will blind you and raise a wind that will deafen you. But do not flee or you will die." With a face like stone, he narrowed his eyes and scanned the area.

Lee could see the fear in Millet's eyes. Both of them had very nearly been killed in the caves of Dashivis Pass by a half-man driven mad by the Jewel of Dantenos. In later years, he'd discovered that the jewel was likely a creation of the gods that had been endowed with their powers and placed in the temples during ancient times. If this creature possessed such an object, it would be strong, fast, and exceedingly difficult to kill.

Twenty yards away, a shadow flashed from east to west before vanishing again. A moment later, the wind picked up and swirled around the entire company. The horses reared and bucked, throwing some of the riders from their saddles. Those who weren't thrown were forced to dismount.

"Here it comes," roared Lee, clenching his blade tightly. Glancing left to Jacob, then right to Millet, he felt a chill knotting in the pit of his stomach.

The wind howled and the shifting darkness suddenly engulfed the entire group, leaving no one able to see even a single inch ahead. At first, there were cries of confusion and fear from some of the men. Screams of agony quickly followed, even rising above the ever-increasing roar of the raging tempest. For a couple of minutes, everything was utter chaos. Then, as suddenly as it had started, all became quiet again. The wind died, the darkness lifted, and their vision was restored.

The scene revealed was gruesome. Three soldiers lay dead, their throats ripped out with unimaginable savagery. In addition, Tristan lay bleeding from a gash beneath his right ear. Bevaris immediately rushed to his side.

"I'm fine," the younger knight said, waving his friend off and regaining his feet. "Bloody thing only scratched me."

The other soldiers shifted nervously, their eyes shooting down to their fallen comrades.

"There will be time to mourn them later," shouted Lee. He breathed deeply and closed his eyes. When he'd faced the mad half-man all those years ago, he had been little more than a boy off on his first adventure. Now he was ready. He filtered out the sound of the wind and the panicked breathing of the men, searching only for the creature. He could tell that Linis was doing exactly the same thing.

Then he heard it—the slightest of footfalls off to his left. Almost immediately, the darkness surrounded them once again. This time Lee knew where it was, but the creature was too far away for him to reach it in time. The strangled gurgling of throats being torn apart echoed grotesquely in his ears as two more men fell. Linis had located the creature's position as well and moved quickly forward. A ghastly cry pierced the air as the elf's long knife found flesh.

Then, for a second time, the darkness was gone.

"I wounded it," said Linis, a pleased expression on his face.

A deep, rumbling, primal roar came from their left.

"I think you did," agreed Lee. "But this thing is not easily slain and will heal in an instant."

Lee had barely finished his sentence when the beast attacked again. This time it came at them in full view, out-pacing the shadow that trailed behind him. Lee barely had time to react as a pale hand reached for his neck. He ducked and stepped away, but before he could strike back at the crea-ture, it shifted direction toward the soldiers. In almost no time at all, another one had fallen dead and two more were severely wounded.

Linis threw a small dagger, but the creature twisted away from it and charged at the seeker. Another blade flew over Lee's shoulder from behind. This one found its mark, burying itself deep into the beast's chest. It staggered for just a split second before resuming its attack. Linis leveled his blade and stepped right. His knife sliced into the creature's exposed ribs. Lee knew that this was his chance—possibly the only one he would get.

He leaped forward, striking with his sword just as a clawed hand was about to seize Linis by the throat. Shockwaves ran up Lee's arm as if his blade had hit solid rock instead of flesh and bone. No matter. The creature wailed and turned on Lee, its deformed face contorted into a vicious snarl. Its arm, severed at the elbow, was hanging by a single piece of white flesh. Black smoke rose from its wounds, and the air was filled with the putrid scent of death.

Bevaris stepped up from behind, swinging his great blade. It stuck halfway through the beast's neck, sending it to its knees. More acrid smoke spilled out as the knight kicked it in the back, freeing his sword. The scrape of steel on bone sent shivers up Lee's spine.

The smoke continued to rise, driving the men back, coughing and wheezing. Lee rolled the creature onto its back. Through the haze, he could just make out the glint of something metallic buried in its chest, just above the heart. It was round and smooth, about the size of a silver piece. He reached down to grab it, but the second his fingers made contact, he fell to his knees as if struck by lightning. Linis and Millet rushed to his side.

"That is what has changed him," Lee told them, steadying himself. "Pry it out with your knife. But don't touch it."

Linis pulled the dagger from its chest and dug the object out. Tearing off a piece of cloth from his shirt, he carefully picked it up. A second later, the creature's body began to convulse. Millet pulled Lee to his feet and led him away. They had only gone a few yards when the body burst into flames. Everyone stared with a combination of horror and wonder as the white-hot fire shot up, forcing them even farther back. Slowly, the flames died away, leaving nothing of the creature but a small pile of gray ashes.

Bevaris immediately began treating the wounded while the others gathered the bodies of their fallen comrades.

Linis held up the cloth containing the metal object with the tips of his fingers. "What is this?" he asked.

"I'm not sure," replied Lee. "It's different to what I encountered years ago. At least, it feels different. The object I saw then was…" He hesitated. "Well, I guess you could say it had a mind of its own. It possessed a half-man and drove him completely mad. But with this thing, I feel nothing but malice and fury."

"What should we do with it?" asked Dina.

"It's too dangerous to take with us," said Lee. "I don't know what it could do to me."

"Can we destroy it?" asked Millet.

"We have no tools," replied Linis. "I think we should bury it."

Lee nodded in agreement. "Yes. But be sure to mark where it lies. I will return and destroy it later."

Linis walked a few yards north and dug a hole with his dagger, leaving a small piece of cloth wrapping sticking out of the ground.

After retrieving their mounts, they covered the fallen men with stones and said a few reverent words of prayer before continuing south. Morale was low and nerves were shaken. Lee decided that they would risk going into a town once they'd left the valley. He looked at Jacob and smiled inwardly at the bravery of his son in the face of such a dreadful encounter. It was Jacob's dagger that had slowed the beast and saved Linis's life. As much as he feared for the boy's safety, he was also truly happy to have his son by his side.

His mind drifted to Penelope and the sight of her lifeless body in his arms. At that moment, he was grateful that the Dark Knight was not there to tempt him with an offer of a quiet life with his family.

He might well accept it.

CHAPTER 12

The moment they crested the southern slope of the valley, Lee felt a blast of warm air wash over him. The entire company sighed with relief and began packing away their blankets.

Bevaris spurred his horse forward to pull alongside Lee. "If you still intend to take a short respite, the city of Molsans is less than a day south of here."

Lee thought for a moment. "Yes. I've been there. It's large enough for us to pass unnoticed." He glanced back at the men. Their shine and polish were gone, replaced by the tatters and ravages of a long road and a hard battle. "Molsans is almost due west of Dantory," he continued. "We can re-supply and perhaps gather information. Several desert towns trade there, though not usually at this time of year. Still, we may get lucky."

They followed the trail south from the valley. By midday, they came to a well-traveled road leading southeast. They passed a few merchants and tradesmen along the way, but their wary eyes told Lee that conversation was unwise.

"It would seem things have changed here as well," remarked Millet. "I remember the people of the Eastland being far friendlier."

"Yes," agreed Lee. "We can only hope that we do not run into trouble before we leave."

They arrived in Molsans just as the sun was sinking below the horizon. The warmth had lifted their spirits, and the promise of a soft bed, a hot meal, and good wine helped considerably. The city itself was small by Western standards—not even a quarter the size of Baltria or Althetas. The gates were open wide, though guarded. After a brief discussion with the sentry, together with the bribe of a few coins, they were allowed to pass.

Most of the buildings were single-story and constructed of dense red brick. The cobblestone streets were clean, well-maintained, and lit by a series of oil lamps held high by wrought iron poles. The merchants and vendors had already closed for the day, so the streets were populated mostly by those returning home or heading out to seek entertainment. The casual dress of thin cotton shirts and trousers worn by the local men was typical for warm climates, though the multitude of bright colors reminded Lee of the elaborate silks woven in Dantory. The women wore mostly short dresses or loose-fitting pants and blouses and kept their hair tucked beneath round cloth caps.

They made their way through the city to an inn with a large oval sign that read: "The Wandering Pilgrim." As Lee dismounted, a young waif of a boy approached.

"Stable your horses, sir?" he asked.

Lee took out a silver coin and handed it to him. "See that they're well-tended."

The boy whistled loudly. Within seconds, three of his friends promptly rounded the corner of the building. Lee sighed and gave a coin to each one of them.

"You never could say no to a child," said Millet, smiling.

"Let's just hope this inn has enough rooms for us all," remarked Bevaris humorlessly.

The inn was indeed large. In fact, the main room was as spacious as anything most lords could claim to have in their house. Sturdy tables and chairs were lined up in neat rows, and a hearth burned brightly on either side of the room. Dozens of brass lanterns hung from thin chains on the ceiling, illuminating the hall with a cheery glow. The few locals scattered about immediately took notice of the newcomers.

A comely young woman holding a round wooden serving tray quickly came up to them. Her mouse brown hair was tied in a loose ponytail, and her bright blue dress was stained with ale and wine. She smiled happily, setting her tray down on a nearby table.

"Welcome strangers," she said in a voice so high that it twittered like the chirping of a finch. Her eyes opened wide as the rest of the band filed in. "So many." She shrugged. "No matter. We have room enough for all."

Once everyone had been allocated a room, they all sat down for a tasty hot meal of roast pork and carrots. The wine was good too, and soon the men were thoroughly relaxed. Lee was pleased to see smiles and laughter becoming the order of the evening.

Linis, Dina, and Millet were sat with Lee, while Tristan and Bevaris had placed themselves among the soldiers.

"I just hope we can get to Dantory without more trouble," said Millet.

"I wouldn't count on it," said Lee. "If the elves have chased these Soufis out of the desert, we could run into more of them."

Linis scowled at the mention of the Soufis. "Slavers! I can only hope they slaughtered the lot of them."

"Actually," said Millet, "we can use this to our advantage. That Angrääl would recruit such allies may sway the Eastland to our side."

Lee nodded. "They may well fear enslavement more than the Reborn King."

"It's hard to imagine that these people could go unnoticed for so long," remarked Dina.

"The desert is vast," replied Lee. "There have always been rumors of the people who dwell there. Some claim to have seen them firsthand, but no one dares to venture very far into the emptiness of the sands. The people of Dantory and the other towns that border the desert trade with the west, so they have no reason to look east to lands so inhospitable."

"In fact," added Millet, "they have always taken comfort that the desert was at their backs. No army would dare try to cross it, so it served as a natural defense."

"Though apparently, not as good a defense as they thought," said Linis.

Millet was about to reply when the front door flew open and two tall figures wearing white turbans and thin, tan cotton robes stepped inside. The white scarves covering their faces revealed only deep blue eyes. At each of their sides hung a long, curved blade and a waterskin. They scanned the room for a moment, then removed their scarves. Even with the turban still covering their ears, Linis knew at once that they were elves.

"How did they enter without me sensing them?" he muttered. Jumping to his feet, he quickly made his way to the door.

The elves smiled when they saw him approach.

"Greetings, brother," said the elf on the left. "I am Milu and this is Lolin. It is good to see an elf of the west at last."

The young barmaid approached, smiling brightly. "Are these more of your friends?"

Linis turned, suddenly aware that the scarf hiding his own ears was slipping back. "Indeed, they are."

"Wonderful," she replied. "I'll see to their rooms right away. And, as it seems they carry no packs, I will have food brought."

Linis motioned for the two elves to follow him back to the table, where he introduced them to Lee and the others.

"I would advise you be cautious," whispered Linis. "Humans here are not yet accustomed to the company of elves."

Milu laughed. "I have already noticed that. Though we are told such is not the case farther west."

"So you are from the desert?" asked Lee.

"We are," affirmed Milu. "We were sent to scout ahead of our march west."

Linis took a moment to look at the newcomers closely. With a satisfied nod, he then told them about their encounter with the Soufis, as well as what the Vrykol had said.

Milu and Lolin both sneered. "The Soufis fought fiercely, and many elves lost their lives. But they were no match for us, and our army is not significantly diminished."

"Where are they now?" asked Dina.

Milu eyed her curiously and reached his hand across the table. Dina at once withdrew.

"Why do you pull away?" he asked. "Do you fear I will discover that you are half-elf?" He let out another loud laugh. "Then ease your mind. Darshan spoke of you to our people. The name Dina is well known to us. Weila is the Sand Master I follow; she told us of you, and others such as the half-man, Lee Starfinder."

"I am Lee Starfinder," said Lee.

Milu and Lolin exchanged glances.

"Then fortune is indeed on our side," said Lolin. "Darshan spoke of your courage and wisdom."

"I assume you mean Gewey," remarked Lee.

"Yes," Lolin replied. "He is also known by that name. And to answer your question, my people have gathered north of the human city, Dantory. We await word from Darshan to begin our march from the sands."

"Then your wait is over," said Lee. "Our enemy is on the move. If your intent is to aid us, now is the time."

"It is our intent," said Lolin. "We will fight alongside our kin and restore ties long forgotten. Our destiny is at hand and we meet it gladly."

"Your aid will be most welcome," said Linis. "In the morning we will ride east to meet your people." He leaned forward. "But I must ask how you managed to approach the inn without my sensing your presence."

"I think you will find we are different in some ways," explained Milu. He told them of his people's rejection of the flow and their long life.

Linis and the others marveled when Milu told them that he was nearly seven hundred years old.

"Until we spoke with Darshan and Aaliyah," he continued, "we did not know that this was unusual. And whatever the reason is for it, we did not perish once we left our desert home."

Having only recently heard about the desert elves and their powers from Linis, Lee was both curious and keen to meet them. "How many are you?" he asked.

"By the time we return, our number will have reached at least forty thousand," replied Lolin.

"It's hard to imagine so many elves hidden away for so long," said Dina.

Lolin smiled. "We were not hidden. Just unsought."

"Our stories tell of the lost tribe of exiles," said Linis. "But I thought it was just a legend. Of course, much of our lore has been forgotten. Only the scholars know the tales in full, and even their knowledge is incomplete."

"Then perhaps once our two peoples are reunited," said Milu, "we can put the pieces of our past back together."

Lee knew that there were urgent matters to be discussed, but he allowed the conversation to drift on to more pleasant subjects. Dina moved her chair closer to Linis, and they all listened as Lolin and Milu told them about life in the desert, and of how Gewey's appearance had inspired them to seek out their brethren in the West. As they spoke about the battle with the Soufis, Lee could see a definite look of satisfaction on their faces.

"Sand Master Weila told us about her meeting with the Vrykol," said Lolin. "And of its ludicrous offer. It must have known we would refuse. But it became clear when we attacked that it had not warned the Soufis of our intent. They were taken completely off guard. Even so, we were greatly outnumbered, and many lives were lost during the battle. Some had wanted to wait until we were at our full strength to attack, but it was feared the Soufis would march west before that could happen. The human cities would have been defenseless."

"That human lives mean so much to you, speaks well of your people," said Dina.

"The Soufis are not the only humans in the deep desert," said Lolin. "Long have we shared the sands and traded in peace. The Creator does not give us the right to decide whose life is important and whose can be wasted. All should live free upon this world."

"I wish my kin had held the same understanding," said Linis, regret and sadness in his voice. "It has taken the threat of annihilation to open our minds and cleanse our hearts."

"Then let them be cleansed and rejoice," said Lolin. "The end times are upon us, and a new world will be born. Old hatreds will vanish, and the world of elves will become one with the Creator's design. Together, we will see that our people never again forget the ties that bind us." He smiled warmly at Dina. "And we will become parents of a new race. Perhaps one that will have our strengths and leave aside our weaknesses."

"I hope you are right," said Linis. "But before that can happen, we must defeat those who seek to destroy us."

"Indeed," agreed Lolin. "We can be with my kin within a week if we press our pace."

"Then that is what we shall do," said Lee. "Do you have mounts?"

Milu smiled and shook his head. "I assume you mean the beasts I see humans ride. We have no experience with such animals. But do not fret. We can keep pace on foot over this terrain. In fact, I would wager it will be you who struggles to keep up with us. Running over this hard ground is nothing compared to traveling through the deep sands."

"Good," said Lee with satisfaction. "Then we leave with the dawn."

They talked well into the night before finally retiring. Linis and Dina left the inn for a time to stroll through the city together. The men were more at ease now, and the trials of the long road were like a distant memory—a tale to be told to their children.

Lee couldn't help but wonder what kind of reception an army of forty thousand elf warriors marching across the land would get from the Eastland kingdoms. Should such a thing have happened in Hazrah, panic would surely have gripped the city. But that would be dealt with in due time.

The next morning, Milu and Lolin were already outside waiting when Lee and the others left the inn and took their mounts. With Millet and Bevaris having already procured fresh supplies from the innkeeper and distributed them among the men, they were ready to go.

As they made their way from the city, Linis removed his headscarf, allowing his elf features to be plainly visible. Though it drew several stares from passersby, no one dared to make a comment. Once outside the city, the desert elves immediately broke into a quick jog, leading them away from the main road and into the thin brush beyond. A few sparse patches of trees and bushes were the only things that broke the flat grassland.

The heat of the morning sun wrapped around them like a blanket, while a stiff west wind cooled their faces. The cold of the hills had been hard to bear, but Lee knew the scorching heat of the desert could be far worse. In less than a week, most of the foliage they saw now would be gone, and the dry cracked earth and blazing sun would start to become oppressive.

"It has been a long time," remarked Millet, dabbing his forehead with a piece of cloth.

"Yes it has, my friend," agreed Lee. "And we were both a great deal younger last time we faced the desert sun."

"I can create a cool breeze," offered Linis. "The elves from across the Western Abyss showed me how."

Lee shook his head. "We'll need to get used to it. Besides, I don't intend to stay there for long."

Linis told Lee how Aaliyah, Mohanisi, and Nehrutu had taken it upon themselves to instruct him and the others in the ways of the flow.

True to their word, Milu and Lolin easily pressed the pace. Often the horses had to break into a run to keep up and were forced to rest long before the elves had tired.

Morale was high on the first night of camp. Linis and Dina spent much of the evening talking with Milu and Lolin, while Lee, Jacob, and Millet discussed strategy for their return march with Bevaris and Tristan. There was no way to avoid alarming the Eastland with their crossing, so Angräal would certainly learn of it quite quickly.

"The best we can hope for is that Angräal decides not to stop us," said Lee. "And that the Eastland sees us as friends."

Millet drew his dagger and scratched a rough map in the dirt, showing the land from the desert to the Goodbranch. "If we are met by resistance before we reach King Luccia in Xenthia, we should head south, and then west."

Tristan rubbed his chin in thought. "That puts us dangerously close to Baltria."

"Yes," said Millet. "But the crossing there is narrow. And with forty-thousand elves who have likely never seen a river before..."

"I see what you mean," said Tristan, nodding.

"And if we manage to see King Luccia?" asked Bevaris.

"Then it will depend on what he says," replied Millet. "If he joins our fight, we will decide what to do then."

"I should ride ahead," suggested Bevaris. "I can quell their fears of an elf attack."

They all nodded in agreement.

"I will come with you," called Lolin, striding up. "I would like to meet the human king and convey our good intent."

Bevaris looked unsure. "An elf riding openly into an Eastland city may not be wise."

Lolin sat beside him and slapped him on the shoulder. "They will need to know us sooner or later, and I say the time is now."

"I agree," said Millet. "There is no more use in hiding. When the elves march, their banners should fly high."

Lolin laughed. "We carry no banners. But perhaps we shall make some."

By the time they reached the outskirts of the desert, the heat was close to intolerable. All of their water supply had been exhausted in three days, and if not for Lolin and Milu's experience in finding water in the most unlikely of places, Lee guessed that at least half of the men would have died of thirst.

Being that the elf camp was well north of Dantory, it was considered best if they avoided the city altogether. Milu told

Lee and Millet that supplies were plentiful, and there was no need to trouble an already frightened people.

The thought of there being life-sustaining food and water in any significant quantity within such a barren wasteland boggled Lee's mind. He had once traveled two days into the desert and it had nearly killed him. Of course, he was young and inexperienced at the time, but he could still feel the burn on his skin and the swelling of his tongue whenever he thought about it.

Nights were equally uncomfortable as the temperature dropped to near freezing. Lolin assured them that once they arrived, there would be comfort and cheer enough for all.

The day they were due to arrive, Lolin and Milu called for a halt after only a few miles.

"We will go ahead and announce our arrival," said Lolin.

After several hours, they returned with twenty more of their kin, all dressed in similar fashion, and all carrying long scimitars on their waists. Lee dismounted at once, signaling for the others to do the same.

"We have brought refreshment for weary souls," announced Lolin.

Without a word, the elves began handing out tiny leather flasks, which the men accepted greedily. Only after draining them dry did they stop to thank their benefactors. When Lee opened his flask, the scent of sweet honey filled his nostrils. As the cool liquid soothed his parched mouth, he felt renewed strength shooting through his limbs. He was unable to stop drinking until every last drop had been consumed.

"We will provide you with suitable attire once we reach the camp," said Milu.

The elves walked among the men as they made their way north; conversation was warm and friendly, and with the help of the elf flasks—of which there seemed to be plenty— the blaze of the sun was all but forgotten. The land had now become virtually devoid of plant life, with only a few hardy shrubs and tall cacti able to survive the conditions. At first, the ground was cracked and brown, but as they continued, it gave way more and more to ever-deepening yellow sand. In the far distance, tall dunes could be seen, rising and falling like waves on a vast ocean, given life by the heat reflecting on the horizon.

"We're here," called Lolin.

Linis and Lee stared out at the empty sands.

"What do you...?" began Lee, but then the faint outline of tents came into focus.

"Amazing," whispered Linis to himself. "To keep so many hidden."

Before them were hundreds upon hundreds of unevenly spaced tents. Their rounded tops and yellow coloring, combined with the way in which they'd been arranged, gave them the illusion of being an actual part of the landscape. Thanks to their nimble, almost fluid movements, the multitude of elves within the camp also blended in equally well. In fact, Lee had to focus with all of his might merely to keep any one of them in sight for more than just a few seconds.

"I think this is a skill we'll need to relearn once we leave the desert," said Milu. "I doubt the green lands of the west will provide us with the same advantage."

Lee rubbed his chin. "Actually, it could work very well on the plains and in the forests. It's brilliant—and simple. With the right materials, you could do it, I'm sure."

"I doubt it is as simple as you think," corrected Linis. "But it is certainly worth a look."

Soon thousands of elves began walking toward them at a slow, deliberate pace. The sound of greetings and salutations carried loudly over the flat sand. When they were about one hundred yards away, the elves halted, allowing the company to approach them the rest of the way.

"The Amal Molidova will wish to see you at once," Lolin said to Lee. "Your men shall be well cared for, your beasts too." He patted Lee's horse gently on its sweat-soaked neck. "I know nothing of horses, but I imagine they are in dire need of care."

"They are far heartier than men," replied Lee. "These steeds are of strong stock. But you are right. They do need care."

"Who is the Amal Molidova?" asked Millet.

"She is our leader," answered Milu. "At least, she leads us in times of great need." He cracked a smile. "Unlike the people of the west, we have little use for chiefs and kings. But when one voice is needed to guide us, the Amal Molidova is who we look to. But worry not. She is kind and wise. It was she who first recognized Darshan for who he is. She spilled a drop of his blood into the Waters of Shajir and revealed to us our destiny."

As they entered the camp, the sounds of singing and laughter filled the air. Scattered between the tents were small fires surrounded by elves drinking and smiling in the familiar way that only kin share. Lee marveled at how people could find so much happiness in such a desolate place. Eyes fell upon them as they passed by—not eyes filled with suspicion and distrust, but with a welcoming joy that lifted Lee's spirits.

They dismounted and Lolin told some of his nearby kin to tend to the horses. They stared at the animals in fascinated amusement before leading them away.

"Tristan and I will see to the men," said Bevaris. "No need for the whole lot of us to see this Amal Molidova, I think."

Lee nodded curtly.

"And who shall speak for you?" asked Lolin.

Lee gestured to Millet. "Lord Millet Nal'Thain is the wisest among us—except for perhaps Lady Celandine." He grabbed Linis's shoulder fondly. "I am a servant of Lord Nal'Thain's house, and my dear friend serves the Lady."

Linis shot Lee an annoyed glance. But a moment later, he burst into laughter. "Quite right," he agreed.

"I would like to come too," said Jacob. "If that is all right?"

Lee grinned at Jacob. "My son is always welcome by my side."

Lolin and Milu led them through the immense camp to its very center. There, a circle of wooden blocks surrounded a large cloth pavilion, held aloft by black wooden poles. Beneath this lay a group of round pillows, atop one of which sat an elf woman clad in sky-blue robes. Her angular features were framed marvelously by her golden hair, and her sparkling green eyes were made even more striking by her flawless alabaster skin.

She rose to her feet as they entered and smiled brightly. "Ah, the friends of Darshan have arrived." Her voice was musical and free of troubles. "I am Lyrial. Please, sit with me and take your ease. We have much to discuss."

"Thank you, my lady," said Millet. "I am Millet Nal'Thain. This is Celandine, Linis, Lee and Jacob. The rest of our party is enjoying your hospitality."

"And they are most welcome," she replied.

They all sat. Shortly, an elf boy brought them each a cup of wine and then hurried away. Lolin and Milu bowed low and also excused themselves.

"I am told you are the half-man, Lee Starfinder," said Lyrial, looking deep into Lee's eyes. "You are the mentor and companion of Darshan."

"I am," he affirmed. "Though I'm sure he no longer needs my guidance."

Lyrial let out a childlike laugh. "We all need guidance. Even a god must look to those wiser than himself."

"Then I hope he has found someone wiser than me," he replied.

She smiled. "And you bring your son. He has your strength. I can see it."

Jacob gave a respectful bow of the head. "My father is a great man—a fact I have only recently come to realize. So I thank you for your compliment, my lady."

She bowed her head in return before looking to Millet. "And Millet, Darshan mentioned you in his tales as well. You have the look of one with great conscience and care. But it would seem that you are now lord rather than servant."

"I am Lord of the House Nal'Thain," he said proudly. "Though Lee once held that honor."

"And Linis, chief among seekers," she continued. "Darshan holds you in high regard. He spoke of your great skill, and of the friendship you offered when first he journeyed from his home. We will certainly be in need of your instruction once we are beyond our beloved desert."

"I would be honored," said Linis. "That you and your kin are now known to me is a gift from the Creator."

Lyrial nodded, then looked closely at Dina. "I have very much desired to meet you, Celandine. Darshan spoke of your courage when you rescued him from the servants of our enemy." She reached out and touched her hand. "When this business is done, we must speak in private."

Linis stiffened.

"You need not fear," assured Lyrial. "We have no ill intent. This I swear." She took a sip of wine. "I think we should now speak of what we can do to aid Darshan."

"Indeed," said Millet. "Unfortunately, time is becoming our enemy."

"Then we shall move swiftly," said Lyrial. Her tone was strong and commanding. "Our battle with the Soufis is over. Their remnants are scattered and without hope. At this moment, we are ready to march west until we find the sea."

Millet explained their intention to win over the Eastland kingdoms.

"Then we shall follow you to that end," said Lyrial thoughtfully.

"What about the desert cities?" interjected Jacob. His tone was that of a young boy in the presence of his elders, but he kept his head high and his back straight.

"They are too few and disorganized," said Millet.

"He does have a point," countered Lee, trying not to sound like he was coming to his son's defense. "Perhaps we should leave a small company of people behind to try and gather their support."

Millet shook his head. "We cannot afford the time, or the swords. If we can sway the Eastland kingdoms to join us, then we can send men back. But I don't think we should do anything before that." He looked at Lyrial. "How soon can your people break camp?"

"Tonight, if you wish it," she replied boldly.

"That fast?" The surprise on Millet's face was clear. He chuckled. "I think perhaps we will rest at least one night ... unless you have objections."

Lyrial shrugged. "I have none."

"Then Lee will explain our route," said Millet.

For the next hour, Lee explained how they would travel. Bevaris had rightly suggested some days earlier that they should go north and skirt around the Xenex Valley. It would add a few extra days to their journey, but if Angrääl had sent forces, they wouldn't want to be caught in the valley with an army guarding the narrow and steep path that was the only way out. Even if the enemy numbered in the mere hundreds, they would be sure to lose many elves before fighting their way through.

Lyrial told them of their supplies and weapons. They traveled light, much like the elves of the West, and each warrior was able to carry enough food and drink to last at least two weeks and still stay strong. They wore no armor, so speed would certainly be on their side.

Lee was concerned that should they run into heavily armored troops, they could be overmatched. But as nothing could be done, he dismissed the thought.

The night had come, and the temperature was dropping quickly by the time they were finished. An elf girl brought them thick red blankets and a bundle of elf robes.

Lyrial stood. "The blankets will serve you well during the cold nights, and the robes will keep you cool until we are no longer in the desert." They thanked her in turn. "Then, if there is nothing further," she continued, "I will have you taken to your comrades." She took Dina's hand and held her fast. "Stay."

Dina smiled at Linis, clearly amused by his over-protective look.

Lee slapped his shoulder. "Come, my friend. Let us find some wine and meet more of your kin."

Millet and the others bowed, and two elves led them away.

Once they had left, Lyrial released Dina's hand. "I know of your story." Her voice was low, and her face grave.

Dina tilted her head and frowned. "That I am half-elf is no secret. And you've already made it clear that you know of this."

"It is no secret, as you say," she replied. "And I do not imply shame. But this is not what I speak of." Lyrial leaned in closer. "I know of how you came to be—and of how you came to live among humans. I also know of the role Linis played."

Dina looked mildly surprised, though not angry or uncomfortable. "I'm surprised Gewey remembered to tell that tale. I suppose he left out no detail of our adventures."

She shook her head. "Gewey ... as you call him, did not tell me of it."

A cold chill seized Dina's spine. "Then who did?" she whispered.

"It was me," came a soft voice.

Dina stood up and spun around. Before her stood a tall elf woman wearing soft, white linen robes. Straight, black hair fell most of the way down her back. Her features were sharp and beautiful, with lightly tanned skin that glistened in the moonlight. But most noticeable of all at this very moment were the tears welling in her hazel eyes.

Dina knew instinctively who she was. A loud gasp slipped out. "Mother!" she cried. Her body trembled and her mind reeled. Her breaths were shallow and quick.

"Yes, my love," she replied. "It is me."

"How...?" She stepped forward but became faint and lost her balance. Hands gently supported her.

"You should sit, child," said Lyrial. She eased Dina carefully down.

Dina's mother sat across from her, tears falling one after the other. "I have missed you so much."

Dina was unable to speak. The sight of her mother's tears and the sound of her voice were overwhelming. A million emotions knotted in her throat as she swallowed down her sobs. A full minute passed before she was able to say anything at all.

"How is it you are here?" she eventually asked.

"I do not know how much you have learned of what happened, and why I had to leave you," she said.

"Linis told me everything," she whispered.

Lyrial stood. "I will go now." She looked down at Dina's mother and nodded. "Nahali. You know where I am if you need me."

Dina blinked and shook her head. "Nahali?"

Her mother smiled lovingly. "That is my name here. You may use it if it is easier for you."

"No," said Dina. Her own tears now began to flow. "You are my mother." Moving across, she embraced Nahali, clinging desperately to her as if afraid she would suddenly disappear.

Nahali held her close as they both wept for joy. "You cannot know the happiness I feel."

Dina had no idea of how much time had passed before they finally let go of each other and sat back. Dina took a cloth from her pocket and dried her eyes. Nahali did the same.

"Linis is with you, I hear," said Nahali.

Dina nodded. "Yes. And I am certain he will be pleased to see you."

Nahali smiled. "I would very much love to see him as well. But first I would tell you of what happened to me. I have been in agony all these years, knowing that you thought me dead."

"Linis told me that he spared you," said Dina. "But he didn't know where you had gone. I wanted to look for you but..."

Her tears returned. "I should have..."

Nahali held up her hand, her eyes full of a mother's love. "You did what you had to do. Had you sought me out, you would never have found me. That you followed your path has brought you to me, and for that, I thank the Creator." She took a deep breath. "But now I must tell you how I came to be here."

"Please—tell me everything," Dina said.

Her mother began. "After Linis spared me, I fled north along the Goodbranch River, hiding among the humans in their towns and villages. I found it easy to deceive them. Your father had told me of the people in the east and their manner of dress, so I wore a scarf to hide my features and told people I was from the desert. Most believed it, and those who doubted me took it as a sign I was hiding from someone. But none suspected the truth. I moved from place to place for a time, but it became more and more difficult to keep going. I had no gold and was forced to hunt and trap in the wild. I knew my kin would eventually discover me if I didn't keep close to the towns, so I continued farther north, beyond where our people roam. When I neared the mountains, I tried to lose myself in the surrounding forests. The game was plentiful and humans seldom ventured too far from their homes, so it was easy to remain hidden. I stayed there for several years. But then, something happened." Her eyes grew distant.

"What was it, mother?" asked Dina. "What happened?"

"I was called away." Her voice seemed disconnected, as if she had somehow stepped outside of herself. "I felt an irresistible pull to the east. It was as if I was being called home. I tried to resist, but the more I tried, the stronger it became. Finally, I relented and left the mountains. Each step I took seemed familiar, and each day my heart was less burdened. The guilt and loss I felt remained, but I could feel strength renewing my spirit. Eventually, I arrived in the desert."

She smiled and glanced over her shoulder. "As desolate as it may appear, I could feel life springing forth from the sand. It was like I could almost reach out and touch the Creator." She laughed softly. "Of course, I had no idea what to do next, so like a fool, I wandered off into the deep desert. With one flask of water and three days of food, I was near death in less than a week. If the elves of the desert had not found me, I surely would have died. At first, I thought I was dead. I had given up and laid myself down for a final time on the scorched earth. Then I heard the sound of cheerful elf voices coming to me like a distant echo. They carried me to an oasis where they had camped and nursed me back to health.

"At first I was afraid. I kept asking myself: 'What if they know of my crimes?' Foolish perhaps. But I had lived for such a long time in constant fear, and it was difficult to let those feelings go. However, I soon realized that they knew nothing of me or my kin. These were elves, unburdened by the hatred of my people. I have lived among them ever since."

"So, did you tell them why you were there?" asked Dina.

Nahali's smile was sweet, but her eyes were sad. "No. I told them nothing. I still feared that my kin could discover me. But it did not matter. They asked me nothing and simply accepted me as one of their own. In fact, it was not until Darshan spoke of you and his story spread that I went to Lyrial and told her my tale in full." She reached over to touch Dina's cheek. "And now you are here. My beautiful girl is here." She smiled and sighed. "I have missed so much of your life. And now that you know what became of me, I would hear all about you."

Dina related all the details of her life, beginning with her induction into the order of Amon Dähl. While recalling her first encounter with Linis, she had to pause and take a deep breath in order to hold back the sobs. When she was finished, she embraced her mother once more. "Did you ever discover what it was that called you here?"

"In a way," she replied. "There are spectacular wonders in the deep desert. Things that I can scarcely believe exist. I have never been able to completely understand much of what I have seen, but it is clear to me that the hand of the Creator is directly involved. I am certain that is what called me here, and what makes it difficult for me to leave."

"If you ask it of me," said Dina. "I will stay here with you."

Nahali shook her head. "No! It is I who will come with you. My exile is at an end, and I will walk hand in hand with my daughter in the land I once called home. And I will do so proudly."

"I would like that," said Dina.

A wry smile crept over Nahali's face. "Tell me—how long have you loved Linis?"

Dina blushed, suddenly feeling very much a child. "Almost from the moment I met him. And he seems to love me in return."

Nahali held her head high. "Naturally. He would be a fool not to." Her serious countenance softened until she began to laugh. "And he is quite handsome as well ... if I remember correctly."

Dina rocked back and forth with laughter. "I would say I haven't noticed, but..."

"He will make a fine mate," said Nahali. "He is noble and strong."

"I can bring you to him if you'd like," offered Dina.

"Tomorrow," she replied. "Tonight is for us, and I will have you to myself."

The rest of the evening, they talked and laughed as if they had never been parted. Dina fell asleep under the pavilion cradled in her mother's arms ... contented.

CHAPTER 13

Gewey and Kaylia rose just before sunrise and gathered their things. Minnie was already about cleaning the common room, but when Gewey told her that they would be leaving their wagon behind, she scolded him harshly for making his wife walk in the snow. However, after it became evident that he would not be deterred, she insisted they have breakfast and sent them on their way with a small bundle of dried fruit, a wedge of cheese, and one of her few remaining bottles of good wine.

A blanket of new snow covered the ground, which, together with the light from the approaching dawn, gave the earth a ghostly glow. The wind had stilled, allowing the vapor from their breaths to billow out. Gewey instinctively wrapped his arms around Kaylia.

Kaylia pushed him off, pretending to be irritated. "I am not fragile. And the cold does not bother me."

Gewey shrugged and stepped away. "Then you are hardier than I." He looked out at the quiet town. The streets were empty, and thin black smoke issued from the chimneys. "Where is..."

"Felsafell is here," came the voice of the old hermit from the corner of the inn. He was wrapped in a thick fur blanket. "And even the very old feel the bitter bite of winter's jaws." He bounded away, waving for them to follow. "Come now. Many miles and many trials ahead."

The road was empty as they left town; the only life they saw was a few squirrels and a white hare searching the ground in the bare vineyards. Felsafell barely left a footprint as he went along, and after only a mile burst into song.

A measured sand in Creator's hands,
A river flows where the spirit knows,
A destined cry of fallen sky,
A heaven sent tomorrow
The herald sings of flightless wings,
The time will come when battles won,
Will lay to rest on creation's chest,
A song that lifts our sorrow.

"That sounds familiar," said Gewey.

"An old song it is," replied Felsafell, his voice still carrying the tune. "Young I was when first I heard it."

"How old are you?" asked Gewey. "The Book of Souls says your people lived over a hundred-thousand years ago."

"Immortal yes," he answered and twirled on his heels. "And old I am. Death cannot find me, but I can look for death. Though I forget too often. An old mind and a weary heart ... oh yes. I forget to seek it."

"So you wish to die?" asked Kaylia.

"When my journey ends and my work is done," said Felsafell. "I will be paid what is owed. Rest and reunion will be my reward."

A sudden realization struck Gewey. "That is what you meant when I saw you in the spirit world after I fought Harlando. You want me to kill you."

Felsafell burst into merry laughter. "No, oh no. I would not burden your heart with such a thing. When evil is vanquished and your father released, I will seek him out. And he will send me to my brothers and sisters. But first, there is much to be done."

By midday, the snow began to fall once more. Gewey responded by using the flow of the air to warm them, and the flow of water to keep them dry.

"A useful skill," remarked Felsafell. "It is indeed."

"Why is it your people can't use the flow?" asked Gewey.

"Why can a deer not fly?" he replied offhandedly. "Why can a snake not walk? The Creator made us, and change, we cannot."

"But the Book describes you very differently than you appear," countered Gewey.

Felsafell shrugged. "One can put a dress on a bear, but a bear it remains. It does not transform into a comely maid."

"I see," said Gewey, his face twisting into a half-frown. "At least, I think I do."

Felsafell halted and sniffed the air. "Into the hills we go." In an instant, he left the road and was moving nimbly into the forest.

The snow-covered ground was riddled with hidden roots and shallow holes, making Gewey grateful for his training. Even so, Kaylia still had to catch him several times.

Just before nightfall, Felsafell led them to a small clearing, where Gewey used the flow to melt the snow and dry the ground. Soon they had a warm fire and were eating the fruit and cheese Minnie had provided for them.

"Night has come," said Felsafell, his eyes cast skyward. "Tonight the stars are hidden, but still I know the way. Sleep while you can. Soon I must show you what you must see."

Gewey and Kaylia covered themselves with a wool blanket and huddled together beside the fire. Within moments, they were both fast asleep. Gewey's dreams held images of Kaylia holding their child in her arms. But instead of delight and joy, his heart was filled with fear and anxiety. Should their enemies gain knowledge of the child, they would certainly try to use it against him. *I must defeat the Dark Knight before Kaylia gives birth*, he told himself. *Whatever the cost!* Fear was replaced by unrelenting determination. At that moment, he was shaken awake.

Felsafell was kneeling beside him. "Wake now, Child of Heaven. The night will reveal the door. And in you must go."

Kaylia was already packing away their blankets. She used the flow to create a short blast of air to douse the fire. Smiling at Gewey, she told him, "You are not the only one with useful powers."

Gewey smiled in return. It still amazed him how much she had learned from Nehrutu and the look of pride and happiness in her eyes warmed his heart.

Felsafell led them to a narrow trail. Oddly, the snow had not settled on it, leaving the rough, root-covered earth exposed. Tiny silver pebbles were scattered about, gleaming and twinkling in spite of the fact that the clouded sky hid the moon from view. As they continued, the air grew warmer to the point of discomfort. The trees, covered with tiny flowers and ripe berries, were as lush and healthy as they would be in spring. The trail dipped and turned several times until ending in front of a tall hill, thick with soft grass.

Felsafell stopped and turned to Gewey. "You must go forward alone."

Kaylia opened her mouth to protest.

"We cannot enter," said Felsafell, before she could utter a word. "Only one vision will this place reveal at a time ... and no more. Alone one must enter, and alone must they see." He took Kaylia's hands. "When his is done, you must go alone as well."

"I don't understand," said Gewey. He looked at the hill closely. "There's nothing here. It's just a hill."

Felsafell looked at him critically, his kindly face turned to a scolding stare. "After what you have seen? The wonders you witnessed ... have you learned nothing? I can smell the scent of the sands still on you, where the Creator spilled her blood. And still, you think your eyes tell all?" He shook his head.

Gewey nodded and looked at Kaylia. "I'll be fine," he said.

He took a few steps forward, and the hill immediately faded away. In its place stood a small house built of red cedar. It was about the same size as Felsafell's home. The scent of lavender and honey filled his nostrils, and the darkness of the night had now turned to bright day. He looked up. There was no sun in the sky, just a never-ending blue with wisps of white clouds. The door was ajar, and a warm light from a hearth reflected off the wood. Cautiously, Gewey peered inside.

A gray stone hearth was directly ahead against the far wall. The rest of the room was bare except for a thick brown rug in the center. Sitting cross-legged atop the rug was a young woman in a tan tunic and trousers; her black hair and smooth, ageless skin soaked in the light to create a faint aura around her body. Gewey felt a strange sensation as he looked at her. Something was not quite right. Her dark eyes twinkled as she met his gaze and smiled.

"Come in," she said. Her voice was that of a young girl not quite out of her teens. "I have been waiting a very long time for you."

Gewey took a tentative step forward. "Who are you?"

"You ask who I am," she replied. "But you really want to know what I am. You are not the first to ask this question, but you are the only one who can puzzle it out." She giggled girlishly at Gewey's hesitation. "Don't worry, it will come to you."

Gewey took another step forward. As he did so, his feeling of uncertainty increased. "Are you really here?" he asked.

She cocked her head. "A strange question indeed. But the answer is yes. I am no spirit or phantom. I am flesh and blood and here with you now."

"If you had seen what I have seen then you wouldn't think my question so strange," said Gewey. He took another step, followed by another, and another until he was at the very edge of the rug.

"Then you have already been to the desert," she replied playfully. "You have been to the temple and ridden the blood of the sands."

"You have seen these things yourself?" asked Gewey incredulously.

"I have seen many things," she replied. "Not as much as the old hermit outside, but much nonetheless."

Gewey took another pace, but the moment his foot touched the rug a flash of realization swept over him. "Vrykol!" His voice boomed out and his hand shot to the hilt of his sword.

The girl was unflinching. "In a way, yes. I'm known as the Oracle of Manisalia, but I have had many other names. Vrykol is not among those I enjoy." She leaned back on her elbows. "Do you intend to kill me young godling?"

Gewey was unsure what to do. "How can you be the Oracle?" His voice stammered.

She shrugged. "I am who I am. Though what I am seems to concern you more. And were I a creation of the betrayer, your worries would be justified. But I am not." She nodded to the space in front of her. "Sit and take your ease. I promise I will help you to understand."

Gewey remained still for more than a minute. Finally, he moved closer and sat on the rug. "Know that if you attack me, your head will leave your shoulders before you can move an inch."

Her laughter sounded loud. "A fair deal if ever I heard one. But as I have already said, I have no intention of harming you. I am, as you say, a Vrykol—at least, that's a crude name for what I am. One used out of fear and misgivings by those we tried to help. I was created long ago by Pósix, goddess of the dawn and light, to do her will on this earth. There were once many others like me, but they have long since been slain."

"I have heard that the gods once created assassins," said Gewey. "They were said to be like the creatures the Reborn King has made."

The Oracle frowned. "We were nothing like that. And we were never assassins." Her voice was ice. "We were servants—nothing more. I was given the gift of prophecy by Pósix herself to guide humans through hardship. I have never held a sword, let alone taken a life. History has done my kind a great injustice." Her voice softened. "But that is another tale and matters little."

"Why are you here?" asked Gewey. His heart wanted to believe her, but he knew better than to be too trusting.

"I was forced to flee," she replied sadly. "Had I not, I would have been brought to Angrääl and corrupted. This place is known only to myself and the hermit. All others who could find it died many ages ago. Now, it is all but forgotten."

"Are you to give me a prophecy?" asked Gewey.

She smiled and shook her head. "No. I cannot foretell the future of a god. Your path is hidden from my sight. My duty was to guide the mortal world, though it seems that task is at an end for now. But I can tell you that what you are about to face will not be easy. You have come to test your spirit. And for one such as you, that can be extremely dangerous."

Gewey looked into her unblinking eyes. "Dangerous how?"

"In a few moments, your soul will be revealed to you," she replied gravely. "And for the gods to look so deep is ... well ... a very serious thing." Her smile returned. "But then you are as much human in your heart as those you are charged with protecting. That would be clear to me even had I no eyes to see." She sprang to her feet. "But this is no time for chatter. Your friends await your return, and the old hermit would not appreciate it if I kept you overlong."

As Gewey rose, he noticed a narrow wooden door had appeared beside the hearth. "Will you come in with me?"

She shook her head. "I cannot. Only one at a time can enter. The exposed soul of any person is a private affair. Even more so when that person is a god." She held out her hands. "If it is not too much to ask, I would touch you once. I have spent many years anticipating your arrival, and I would desire that as reward for my patience."

Gewey thought for a moment, then reached out and took her hands. Instantly, he knew she had told him the truth. He could feel the touch of the gods flowing within her. But unlike the vile taint of the Vrykol, her spirit was not trapped unwillingly.

"I am sorry I doubted you," whispered Gewey. "This thing you are is ... beautiful."

"Your doubt is understandable, and I thank you for your kind words," she replied wistfully. Releasing his hands, she danced gracefully to the door. "You should have seen Lee Starfinder when he met me. Poor boy didn't know what to do. I think it might have been the puppy I had that perplexed him." She sighed. "I must ask the hermit for another to keep me company."

This brought a chuckle from Gewey. Suddenly, he missed his friend. "Thank you," he said, bowing low and turning the knob. "And I will ask Felsafell to bring you a new puppy."

The moment the door swung open, the house disappeared. Before him now was a long stone hallway that vanished into the darkness. His footfalls echoed loudly as he walked, and the dusty, stale air dried his throat. He coughed and spat, wishing he had brought a flask. The hall continued on and on until he began to wonder if it had any end at all. He was on the point of turning back when a dim ball of light appeared a few yards ahead. As he drew closer, the ball began to pulse slowly and evenly. Then, when he was close enough to reach out and touch it, there was a blinding flash. After a few seconds, his sight began to readjust.

He looked around. The hallway had vanished. He was standing atop the first in a series of natural rock pillars, each one large enough to hold a couple of dozen men. He walked to the edge and looked down, but was only able to see for about one hundred feet before a dense fog clouded his vision. The sound of a horse snorting nervously came from behind. Glancing around, he saw a great black steed standing near the lip of a massive cliff face. It stamped and shifted, its powerful neck thrusting its head up and down.

"Is anyone here?" His voice echoed repeatedly, but there was no reply. He looked back once again at the horse and sighed.

The next pillar was close enough to jump onto quite easily. What's more, it seemed to be the only obvious way forward. Taking a deep breath, he allowed his legs to spring into life. All was still and calm as he pushed off the edge and flew through the air. However, just as he was about to land, the pillar he was aiming for vanished and transformed into a smooth black granite courtyard surrounded by a one-hundred-foot-high sheer wall. In the center of this stood a ten-foot-tall white obelisk. At the far end, cut into the living rock, was a stairway leading upward. A flickering light shone down these steps, throwing shadows to and fro. Gewey looked behind him. The pillars were all gone. In their place was a dense mist, swirling and twisting over a great chasm.

"Hello!" he yelled. Again, all he could hear was the echo of his own voice.

He approached the obelisk and ran his hand over its smooth surface. There was something familiar about this place, but it was like trying to remember a childhood dream—just beyond his grasp. Shaking his head in frustration, he climbed the stairs. At the top, he saw before him an immense alcove with polished white marble walls inlaid with gold and precious jewels. Scattered across the smooth floor were pieces of a shattered statue depicting a warrior. Gewey could tell that the figure was once roughly ten feet tall and had stood with outstretched arms.

"This was the resting place of the Sword of Truth," came a voice to his left. It was like a gentle breeze over crystal wind chimes. He turned, at the same time reaching for his sword.

Standing before him was a woman dressed in pure white silk robes. Her hair was the color of honey, the tiny ringlets falling over her shoulders and down her back. Her slim figure swayed with unearthly grace, and her ivory skin and azure eyes were perfect in a way that Gewey had never seen before—almost too perfect. Her beauty was so enthralling that he found himself blushing at the sight of her. He had not felt this way since the first time he'd kissed Kaylia.

Finally, he managed to speak. "Who ... who are you?" His voice cracked, and his tongue felt dry and swollen.

She smiled warmly. "I am your guide, Darshan. I am here to show you the path."

"You know me?" he asked.

She laughed a sweet, gentle laugh. Gewey laughed in return, even before he realized what he was doing. "Of course, I know you," she said. "I was there at your birth. I stood beside your father when the divine light helped you draw your first breath."

Gewey's mind reeled. "Are you my ... mother?"

She drew closer. "No, my darling child. I did not have that honor. You know me as Ayliazarah, goddess of fertility and love. But I have had many names." She scrutinized him for a long moment. "This will not do," she said softly, closing her eyes briefly.

As if a spell had been broken, Gewey felt his senses returning. Though still lovely beyond compare, she no longer seemed to exceed the realm of mortal beauty.

"What did you do?" asked Gewey.

"Nothing really," Ayliazarah replied. "I hid my true nature so that you would not be ensnared."

"I don't understand." His tone became suspicious. "How can you be here? I thought the gods were trapped in heaven."

"We are." She stepped forward and took his hand. Her skin was hot to the touch, though softer than the finest silk. "I am as you saw your father—an essence left behind. And like Gerath, I was intended for a specific purpose. I exist as a guide for those who seek to test themselves."

"Test themselves how?" he asked.

"To peer into one's own soul is the ultimate test," she replied, her voice now serious, though still musical and kind. "And it is a test you must now take. For the world depends on you becoming what you must be. As do those trapped in heaven." She waved her arm in a slow arc and her form began to fade. "Fear you not. Though you will not see me, I am still here."

As she disappeared completely from sight, a low rumbling noise began. The ground directly beneath Gewey began to shake violently. He watched as the pieces of the ruined statue crumbled and turned to dust; seconds later, a great pillar of fire erupted from its still intact base in the center of the alcove. The heat was enough to drive him back to the edge of the steps.

A deep, thunderous voice came from within the fire. "And now that the gentle liar has gone, you can know why you are really here."

"What is this?" cried Gewey. Drawing in the flow, he unsheathed his sword. "Who are you?"

"For one so powerful, you know very little," the voice replied. "Do you not know me? We have spoken before."

"You!" he hissed furiously. "What do you want?"

Harsh laughter raked at Gewey's ears. "What does it matter? I have what I want. The war is mine, and so is this world. By the time you return to help your friends, it will all be over. You have lost."

"You lie!" shouted Gewey. "Be gone or face me now."

"I am no liar," he replied scornfully. "It is you and your kind that have lied to the world. Hatred and strife are the result of the sins of the gods. But now it has come to an end. Soon they will all perish. All but you. I offer to spare you and you alone."

Gewey laughed contemptuously. "You have made this offer before. And as before, I tell you this ... I will destroy you."

"You cannot," he said flatly. "I am beyond you now. You can no longer threaten my reign."

Gewey sniffed. "If that is so, why spare me?"

"You are special," he replied. "You are an earthbound god with the spirit of a man. You are far too valuable to waste. In time, you will serve me, though it may take a thousand years for you to relent. But what is time to an immortal? I will watch as you rail against the world—and against me. And when you have exhausted your rage, I will take you unto my bosom. By then, of course, all that you know and love will have become dust, their spirits drifting eternally in the doldrums of oblivion."

Gewey sneered. "That is, unless I join you now, I suppose. You will save all the people I love from certain death. You are a fool if you think me so easily deceived."

"It is not I who will save them," he said. "You will save them on your own. You have the power within you, but you don't know how to control it. I can teach you the flow of the spirit. With it, you can make the people you love immortal."

"Don't listen to his lies!" shouted a familiar voice from just behind Gewey. Before he had time to turn, Lee pushed past him, his blade already drawn.

Gewey almost lost his balance. "Lee!"

"Get back, Gewey," roared Lee, his eyes fixed on the fire. "He's trying to get you to surrender your will."

Mocking laughter burst forth. "Lee Starfinder. The rash fool I have allowed too long to remain among the living."

From the heart of the fire, a spear shot out, piercing Lee's chest. He dropped his sword and fell to his knees. Gewey raced to his side.

"Are you real?" Gewey asked desperately. "Or is this a part of the test?"

Lee pulled the spear free and tossed it aside. He looked at Gewey apologetically. "I'm sorry. The Reborn King has corrupted this place. I would never have allowed you to come here, but I couldn't find you in time." He slumped down, blood soaking his shirt and spilling onto the marble floor.

Gewey eased his friend onto his back and tried to heal him, but the flow was repelled. Letting out a loud grunt of frustration, he tried again. Again, he was pushed back. "I can't stop the bleeding," he cried out.

Lee gripped his wrist. "He won't let you. He wants me dead."

"You can save him." This time, the Dark Knight's voice was tender and compassionate. "If you allow me to show you how."

Gewey reached out and touched Lee's mind. It felt real. His body was warm, and he looked just as he had in Valshara, only more travel-worn.

"I always believed in you," said Lee. His voice was becoming weak and his eyes distant. "You will do what's right."

Gewey drew all the flow he could stand, but it was useless.

"Time is running out." The voice of the enemy was only in his mind this time. "Let me in, and we can save him."

Gewey shook his head furiously. "No!" He drew in the flow of the spirit. The familiar laughter and bells filled the air. He looked down at Lee and could see his spirit rising. He had done this before in the desert—he had saved Aaliyah. But then it was instinctual, and he had no idea how he'd actually achieved it. Even so, he had to try. Summoning up all the resolve he could muster, he tightened his hold on the flow and managed to keep Lee's spirit within its body. But unlike Aaliyah's spirit, Lee's was resisting him. It was trying to force its way out. Gewey held it fast, watching in horror as his friend's body convulsed and jerked in a gruesome dance.

"What is happening?" he cried.

"Did you think all souls are the same?" the Dark Knight scoffed. "How different is a half-man from an elf? Do you even know where to begin? Look at him. Look at what you have done."

Gewey stared in horror as Lee's skin shriveled and blistered. Huge veins bulged from his face and forehead. Suddenly, his eyes popped open. They were black and empty. He let out a blood-curdling screech and scrambled to his feet. Gewey tried to hold him, but he was too strong. Lee ran to the far end of the alcove and began tearing at the marble wall with his nails, shaking his head violently.

"Should I end his suffering?" The Dark Knight sounded like a father teaching a son. "Shall I undo the evil that you have done through your ignorance?"

Gewey couldn't speak. The sight of his friend and mentor in such hellish torment racked him with guilt. Picking up his sword, he slowly approached Lee. He could feel the fear coming from him. Blood ran down the wall where he had ripped off his fingernails in his madness.

"I'm sorry, my friend," whispered Gewey. With a single quick stroke, he took Lee's head. The body continued to claw at the wall for a few more seconds before dropping to the floor. Black ooze poured out, pooling at Gewey's feet. "I reject you," he shouted. "If this is real, then I have more reason to destroy you. If not…"

A howling wind suddenly rose. The light faded until he was in complete darkness. Though he stood tall, he could not feel the ground beneath him. After a few seconds, the wind died and he was alone.

"So it wasn't real?" asked Gewey.

"It could be," echoed the voice of Ayliazarah. "Many things you will face could come to pass. Before you is a road with numerous forks. Your soul is what drives you to your destiny, and that is what you will face. The death of your friend, the corruption of the flow, the temptation to give life— some of these things are real, others could be should you choose to allow it. But beware. This was the doorway. Beyond this place, you will lose yourself. You will forget where you are. You will truly believe that all you see is real." There was a long pause. "Now you must decide if you are to continue and face the truth of your heart."

Gewey took a breath, remembering his first visit to the spirit world. Back then, he had forgotten where he was for a time. As a result, he had very nearly ended up being trapped there forever. And if anything went wrong this time, Kaylia would not be coming to rescue him again.

"And if I fail?" he asked.

His words were met by silence.

It was decided. "Very well. I will go on."

CHAPTER 14

The scent of the mint lamb combined wonderfully with the sweet wine in his glass, making Gewey's mouth water. He picked up the bottle. The label read "Vine Run", prompting him to think of Minnie and her old goat of a husband, Vernin. Taking a sip, he leaned back in his chair, a contented smile on his lips as the warm glow of the fire soothed him. He admired the tapestries and paintings that hung on the walls of the dining room, as well as the plush, blood-red Dantory rug. However, it was the crystal-encased silver lanterns hanging above the mahogany table that he loved most of all. They were a gift from...? He rubbed his chin and chuckled. He couldn't remember how he'd acquired them.

The door opened, and a young maid entered, carrying his plate. The smell of mint filled the room even more strongly, giving everything a wholesome feel. The maid placed his food in front of him and turned to leave. Her red curly hair was tucked neatly under a cloth cap, and the tiny freckles on her nose gave her a girlish quality—not exactly pretty, but cute and sweet.

"Umm!" Her name escaped him. "Thank you..."

The maid stopped and curtsied, her eyes down. "Frannie, my Lord."

Gewey smiled. "Yes, of course." How could he have forgotten? "Frannie, do you remember where I bought those lanterns, or perhaps who gave them to me?"

She looked confused. "You did not buy them, my Lord. They were here when you arrived. But if I'm not mistaken, the king had this house built for you. Perhaps he would know."

"Yes," murmured Gewey. "The king." He waved his hand dismissively. Frannie curtsied again and scurried out.

Gewey ate his meal and finished the bottle of wine. He looked up again at the lanterns. Why couldn't he remember about the bloody things? It was maddening. A few minutes later, Frannie returned with two other servants to clear the table and pour him a snifter of plum brandy. He sighed with pleasure as it touched his lips. To think he had once hated this stuff.

The door opened again, and a man entered. He was dressed in a fine green silk shirt with a ruffled collar, black trousers, and a black satin cape. A thin gold crown rested on his wrinkled brow. Although his frame was bent and he seemed much older than Gewey remembered, he was still able to recognize his visitor as King Lousis. The deep lines on the king's face and the silver in his hair spoke of a man at the end of his days, rather than the proud and strong leader who had fought the armies of Angrääl. But of course! That had been years ago. Gewey laughed at his own absentmindedness.

He stood and bowed. "Your Highness. Welcome." He offered the old king a chair.

Lousis grunted as he sat. "Thank you, Darshan. These old legs are not as strong as they once were. What I wouldn't give to be as I was when the Second Great War began." He chuckled and coughed. "Well ... maybe even a bit younger than that."

Gewey took his seat and poured Lousis a glass of brandy. "To what do I owe the pleasure of your company?"

Lousis raised an eyebrow. "You called me here, Darshan. You asked me to bear witness to the execution." He looked closely at Gewey. "Surely you have not had a change of heart? That blasted elf tried to kill you."

The image of an elf standing over his bed with a knife in his hand flashed through Gewey's mind. He had barely been able to roll away in time and pin his attacker to the ground with the flow. But the elf's face was clouded, making identification impossible. "No! Of course not," Gewey said. "Such things cannot be tolerated."

Lousis looked at him with understanding. "I know he was your friend, and I know you fought together. But he has not been able to accept the peace you have created. He thinks you are a traitor."

It was then that his memory cleared a little. Linis! It was Linis who had tried to kill him. "He blames me for something to do with Celandine. What happened to her?"

Lousis was taken aback. "Don't you remember? She was killed during the second assault on Valshara, just as the war was ending." He shrugged. "It was a confusing time, I suppose, and there was so much turmoil."

The war! It was over? But how ... how did it end? How did Linis ever become his enemy?

Gewey lowered his head. Linis's face appeared in his mind. Hatred and fury blazed in the elf's eyes as he tried to strike him down. "I'm sorry," said Gewey. "I'm not myself today. Tell me about the end of the war."

Lousis straightened. "I beg your pardon? The end of the war? Why?"

Gewey took a deep breath, letting the air out slowly. "As I said, I'm not myself today. I would like to hear the tale ... if you would humor me." He could see the king was unable to refuse. But of course not. Lousis was but a vassal. Darshan was the true authority; that much he knew for sure.

"Well, I guess I should start after you returned from the east," said Lousis. "We had just learned that the elves from the desert had been destroyed by an Angrääl army as they tried to cross the Goodbranch River. We had already been defeated at Baltria, so the Reborn King had us surrounded."

Each word Lousis uttered brought a new memory rushing back. But everything was still distant and surreal. "Yes. I recall now. Kaylia..."

How could he ever have forgotten Kaylia?

"You miss her still, Darshan. I know you do." Lousis looked as if he were afraid to say her name.

Gewey's mind was in turmoil. Where was she? A tear fell down his cheek as an inexplicable sadness washed over him.

"I should go," said Lousis.

"No," ordered Gewey sharply. "Continue."

Lousis stiffened and nodded. "As you wish." He took a large drink of brandy and cleared his throat. "When news of Lord Starfinder's death came, you went into a rage. Kaylia and Aaliyah tried to stop you, but you rode south to where the Angrääl ships had landed at the Tarvansia Peninsula." Lousis smiled. "People still sing songs of that day. The High Lady Selena sent men to follow you, but it was over by the time they caught up. You drove thirty thousand soldiers back into the sea and then burned their ships as they fled. It was said that you flew through the sky casting fire and smoke from above."

It all started coming back to Gewey—the screams of the men, and the stench of burning flesh. But most of all, he remembered his rage. The soldiers had ravaged Lee's body so terribly that Linis thought it best to cremate him and only bring back the ashes. Gewey looked up at the mantle where the urn still rested.

"We thought we had bought time," Lousis continued. "We hoped that such a slaughter would be enough to delay them long enough for us to recover from the defeat at Baltria. But we were wrong. They sailed into our harbor in such vast numbers that even the elf navigators couldn't stop them." This time, a tear fell from Lousis's eye. "They massacred us, burned our city, and drove us north."

Gewey could still hear the sobs of the Althetan children holding onto their slain parents while Angrääl soldiers marched through the streets. Even with all his power, he had been unable to stop them. They were too spread out. The longer he stayed in Althetas, the more people they killed. He remembered weeping as he rode beside Aaliyah and Kaylia when they finally fled the city. He remembered the sorrow he felt from Aaliyah as well. Nehrutu had fallen hours before while trying to save his kin as their ships were sinking into the harbor.

Lousis had stopped talking. Gewey smiled weakly at the old king and filled his glass. "I know this seems odd. But I need to hear it."

"If it helps you, it is my pleasure," he replied, taking another sip before continuing. "Our soldiers and the remaining elves fled to the Steppes. What we found was horror. The Reborn King had sent a vast army and killed nearly every living being there. Entire elf villages were gone; burned to the ground. Fearing that Angrääl was waiting for us farther north, we tried to turn east, but there was nowhere left to run.

"When the enemy finally caught us, we were but forty thousand strong and outnumbered ten to one. Still, with your power on our side, we held on to hope. For three days, we fought, and for three days, we drove them back. They scrambled to place Vrykol where they could stop you from annihilating them, but each time you broke their hold and shattered the lines. By the fourth day, we thought we had won. The army of the Reborn King was weary and disheartened and their losses were mounting. Then ... he came."

Memories raced through Gewey's mind like a river flooded by melting snow. The thought of the battle made him shiver. So many dead. So much blood.

"The Reborn King himself rode onto the battlefield." Lousis's hands began to tremble. "It was as if a great storm had rolled in and splintered the world."

Gewey tried to remember the moment, but it was shrouded in mist. Only the feeling of despair was clear.

"I watched as the bravest and strongest of us fell to their knees and wept." Lousis drained his glass. "Even I was paralyzed with fear. The great king of Althetas—unable to move. With a wave of his hand, five thousand men died instantly, their bodies bursting into white-hot flames. It was then that you stepped forward to meet him. Darshan faced the Reborn King at last."

Gewey bowed his head. The fear still gripped him. Only with a great effort was he able to keep his hands steady.

This time it was Lousis who filled Gewey's glass. "I can still see it as clearly as I see you now. You and the Reborn King, mere feet apart. Two gods at war. I have always wondered what you and he said to each other, though I understand why you never speak of it." Lousis leaned back and paused.

"And?" asked Gewey, desperate to know more.

Lousis shrugged. "And nothing. The war was over. You ordered our surrender and made peace with Angräal. We were allowed to return to our homes and begin rebuilding our lives."

He stared into Gewey's eyes. "You're not all right, are you? It's this business with Linis. But it's not your fault. He could have gone east to the desert with the rest of the elves instead of choosing rebellion. Remember, it was he who tried to kill you, not the other way around."

The rest of the story flashed into Gewey's memory. He had stopped the Reborn King by serving him. The elves, fearing extinction, chose exile to the desert. He had convinced the king to leave them in peace, but some would not accept these terms and felt Gewey had betrayed them. A week after their surrender, agents of Angrääl found a group of those resistant to the peace agreement hiding in Valshara. The Reborn King ordered them all killed. Dina was among them.

He could still see the look in Kaylia's eyes when she found out that he had done nothing to prevent it. The day she left was utter agony. Aaliyah, he remembered... She was the one who had broken their bond. It was as if his heart had been ripped from his chest. Just thinking about it brought a cold feeling to the pit of his stomach.

"Kaylia," he whispered. "I'm sorry."

"Darshan," said Lousis. "Why are you doing this to yourself? Kaylia has been gone for years. She and that witch Aaliyah."

Gewey shot Lousis an angry glance. "Aaliyah was no witch."

Lousis lowered his eyes. "I beg your forgiveness if I offended you. But it was you who swore that you would flay her alive should you ever see her again."

Gewey rubbed his temple. "No. I am the one who should apologize. I think you're right. This business with Linis has affected my mind."

There was a knock at the door. An Althetan guard entered and saluted. "My lords, I have been instructed to tell you that the prisoner awaits sentence in the courtyard."

Gewey sat motionless, deep in thought.

"I know this is hard," said Lousis. "But you must..."

Gewey held up his hand. "Have him brought here. And see to it that his bonds are secure."

The guard looked unsure. "But, my lord. Ambassador Sialo said..." Gewey's eyes silenced him at once. "Yes, my lord," the man said, hurrying from the room.

Lousis sighed. "You know this must be public, don't you?"

Gewey's expression was stone. "I will speak with the elf that was once my friend before I end his life."

King Lousis rose from his seat. He wobbled and gripped the chair with an embarrassed grin. "Too much brandy."

Gewey got up to take hold of the old king's arm. It felt thin and frail. "You've earned your brandy, Your Highness."

Lousis smiled warmly. "Indeed, I have." He opened the door and paused. "I hope you know what you're doing."

Gewey nodded, his face taut. "So do I."

He sat back down at the table and waited, staring at his half-empty glass. He wasn't sure why he was doing this, just that something told him he must. A few minutes later, four guards entered with the prisoner. He may have been in tattered rags, and his face bruised and swollen, but there was no mistaking Linis. The moment he saw Gewey, he tried to jerk free, but even his elf strength was not enough to overcome his tight bonds and four strong men.

Gewey stood up. "Hold him still." He approached the elf and placed his hands on his battered face, using the flow to heal him.

This only served to increase the fury burning in Linis's eyes. "You should just kill me, traitor." His voice oozed hatred.

Gewey ignored his words. "Leave us." The guards looked at each other nervously. "He cannot harm me."

After one more moment of hesitation, they bowed and left.

The second the door closed, Linis charged. But before he had taken more than a couple of steps, Gewey shot a burst of air that threw him back against the wall.

"That is not going to help you," he said calmly.

Linis glared but didn't move.

Gewey sat back down. "Please sit."

Linis remained defiant. "Why am I here?" he hissed. "What do you think to accomplish?"

"I am trying to understand why you hate me so," he replied.

Linis spat. "You know very well why. She is dead because of you. My unorem." Tears welled in his eyes. "My sweet wife. Her body burned and ravaged, all because of you!" His voice raged. "And if that betrayal was not enough, you send my people into exile and ally yourself with the very creature who slaughtered them." He took a menacing step forward. "There are less than ten thousand of us left. Did you know that? Ten thousand! All because of your cowardice."

"It is not my fault we lost the war," Gewey retorted angrily, before regaining his calm. "We would all be dead if I had not accepted the Reborn King's offer of peace. If the war had continued, there wouldn't even be ten thousand remaining. And I've done everything I can to protect the elves. It was I who stopped the king from wiping you from the face of the earth. How is that a betrayal?" He got to his feet. "And there was nothing I could have done to save Dina." He was unable to look at Linis. He knew that was a lie.

Linis laughed contemptuously. "You can't even lie about it properly. The sin is too great—even for the mighty Darshan. And now you will turn a blind eye as your master makes war on the elves across the Abyss."

He met Linis's gaze. "There is no such plan. If there were, I would know of it."

Linis shook his head and gave a wicked smile. "You claim to rule in the name of your master, yet you know nothing? You cannot possibly expect me to believe that."

"I tell you that I know of no such plan," said Gewey. "What proof do you have?"

Linis grunted. "None that you would believe."

"Tell me anyway," he pressed.

"I captured an Angrääl captain," said Linis. His face was proud, yet sinister. "I tortured him for a week and imagined he was you every time he begged for death. The man held out for quite a while actually, but in the end, he revealed everything to me. I saw the ships myself there in Baltria's harbor. They were filled with thousands of Vrykol."

Gewey tensed. Thousands! If that were true, then the Reborn King had broken his word. No more Vrykol were to ever be made ... by either of them. So many of the creatures could easily lay waste to the distant Elven land. "There is one way for me to know the truth," he said, cautiously approaching Linis. "Show me." He closed his eyes and allowed his mind to drift toward his former friend. At first, the elf resisted. "Do not make me force you," said Gewey firmly. Linis eventually relented.

It took only moments for Gewey to see what he needed to. "It is true!" he exclaimed. Fury began to boil inside him. He turned and strode to the other side of the room. "They will have no warning. It will be a slaughter."

Linis huffed. "You speak as if you care. Even with this knowledge, you will still do nothing."

The fury rose. The old sensation he'd once feared, he now willingly embraced. The killing was to end. That was the bargain they'd made. He had sold away his spirit to protect life, and now killing on a scale that made his mind reel was about to happen.

He spun around and faced Linis. His eyes were ablaze. "How long ago was this?"

"Just before I came here to kill you," replied Linis.

Gewey stared at the elf for several minutes, motionless and silent. He then reached in his belt and pulled out a small dagger. Before Linis could react, he crossed the room, spun him around, and cut his bonds. He placed the dagger in Linis's hands.

Ripping open his shirt, Gewey spread his arms wide. "Then kill me now, or once again fight by my side."

Linis did not hesitate. He pushed Gewey with all of his strength, sending him sprawling across the table. Even before the falling wine glasses shattered to pieces on the floor, the blade was at Gewey's throat. Linis pressed the sharp edge into his flesh, sending blood trickling down his neck. For a dangerously long few seconds, the elf's wild eyes reflected his inner turmoil as he battled with conflicting emotions. Then, letting out a primal scream, he slammed the knife into the tabletop and stepped away.

Gewey wiped the blood from his neck while getting to his feet. "I take it you realize you'll need my help?"

"This changes nothing," said Linis through his teeth. "I still hold you accountable for Dina's death. But if you are really willing to help me, my kin must be warned." He clenched his fists. "I will set aside my vengeance ... for now."

"Good," said Gewey. "We will warn them, I swear it. We set sail before dusk." He went to the door and cracked it open. The guards were still outside. "Wait here," he told Linis. "I need to get you clothes and a weapon."

The soldiers snapped to attention as Gewey stepped from the dining room.

"Escort Ambassador Sialo to his chambers," he ordered. But the guards didn't move. He reached out to grab the one nearest to him, but his hand passed through as if the soldier were only mist. He drew back in shock.

The guards faded away into nothing and the world became dark. Suddenly, he remembered everything.

"It wasn't real," Gewey said, the words catching in his throat. But it was real ... he knew it.

"It was what could come to pass," came the voice of Ayliazarah. "You saw yourself as you could be. A betrayer of your friends and servant of your greatest foe."

Gewey fell to his knees. "I would never..." But he knew his words were a lie. "Take me back. I want to go back," he pleaded. He wanted to hold Kaylia and tell her that he would never allow these things to happen.

"This is who you are," she said tenderly. "There is no turning back."

Gewey was struck with dread at the thought of the next trial. Finally, he took a breath and gathered his courage.

"Then so be it," he said. "I am ready."

CHAPTER 15

Gewey stared out at the ruined city of Althetas before lowering his head in despair. The fires had long since died, but the scent of burned timbers still caught the breeze as a reminder of its destruction.

"Why Althetas?" asked Linis.

Gewey looked up. "Why not?" He dismounted. "I can think of nowhere else. Can you?"

Linis shrugged. "I don't understand why you keep trying. They are all gone. There is nothing left to find here."

Gewey closed his eyes. "There is at least one more. It was my failure that caused this, and it is my duty to set her free."

Linis slid from his saddle. "It was no fault of yours. You did what you could."

"I was weak," said Gewey. "Weak and afraid. I fled and left the world to its fate."

"You tried," countered Linis. "No one else could have done more."

Gewey reached out with the flow. Nothing. Still, he had to go on. "Don't you understand? I could have saved them all, but I was too much of a coward. That day when I faced him ... I could have destroyed him. And if I had, they would still be alive. She would have never..."

Linis grabbed Gewey's shoulders and turned him so they faced each other. "What are you talking about? The Reborn King defeated you. I was there. I saw you fight him. He was just too strong."

"No," whispered Gewey. "I was too weak. There was a moment when I could have defeated him. But it would have killed us both." A tear fell down his cheek. "To my shame, I ran away."

Linis looked at him intensely. "That is not true."

"I'm afraid it is," admitted Gewey. "When the moment came, I realized the sacrifice I needed to make, and I ran. What you saw was my shame."

"I refuse..."

"Damn it!" shouted Gewey, jerking free. "Can't you see? I am to blame for everything. All of it."

"Why have you never spoken of this before?" asked Linis. His voice was cool and understanding.

He turned his back. "Because even after all these years, I am still a coward. I feared to lose your friendship. I knew that my shame cost you everything. I was afraid."

"Tell me what happened," said Linis. "I will hear it and make my own judgment."

Gewey's shoulders sagged. "Very well. It was just after Lee and Jacob were killed during the battle for Althetas. You were still fighting in the Steppes with Dina and Aaliyah."

The mention of Dina brought a visible reaction from Linis. Gewey rarely spoke her name, and now wished he hadn't.

"King Lousis had been severely injured, so High Lady Selena took control of the city. We were reeling from the battle and had found out that another Angrääl fleet was on its way. Our defenses were in ruins and our army decimated, so Selena made the decision to abandon the city and retreat to Valshara."

Linis nodded. "This much I know. We received word after the first assault. We were being forced from the Steppes, so I ordered the elves to withdraw and join you."

"Yes," said Gewey. "We hoped you would arrive in time. But as it turned out, it didn't matter. We defended the passage to Valshara for six days. The bodies were piled so high that our attackers were forced to climb over their own fallen comrades just to enter the fray. For a time, it looked as if we had a chance. Then, on the morning of the seventh day, Angrääl pulled back. We prayed that they had given up. But they hadn't."

Gewey wiped away the sweat beading on his forehead. His hands trembled.

"Then he rode onto the field. I knew at once who he was. I could feel his mind pressing in on me. I tried to keep him out, but he was relentless. I knew I had to face him. Kaylia tried to stop me, but the Dark Knight's challenge would not go unanswered."

Linis nodded. "That was when we arrived. I wanted to charge in, but some unseen force held us at bay."

"It was him," said Gewey. "He intended to face me alone and end the war. He knew that if he defeated me, there would be nothing left to stop him."

Gewey pictured the last moments with Kaylia just before he rode out, her face awash with fear. He could still feel her final embrace and the touch of her lips as she kissed him goodbye.

"I failed her." His voice was distant and mournful. "I failed everyone. My horse reared and threw me the moment we exited the passage. I remember the Dark Knight's amusement as his laughter bounced back and forth off the rocks. But even now I can't see his face, only his armor. It was so black it was like it killed the light, leaving a hole in the world. And his sword ... the sword, was gripped tightly in his hand."

"But I saw the rest," said Linis. "I saw you fight him. I saw him disarm you. You only ran because there was no other choice. He would have killed you."

"No," shot Gewey. "You only saw what your eyes told you. When we fought, there was another war being waged within our spirits. He tried to break me, but I fought back with all my strength. I could feel his power surrounding me and pressing in. For a moment, I thought his will would overcome mine, but then I saw his weakness. His desire to destroy me was rooted in his own failures, and it was there that he was exposed. But he was not without defense. If I destroyed his spirit, I knew mine would be destroyed as well. He knew it too and dared me to vanquish him. Welcoming me to join him in oblivion."

Gewey dropped to his knees. "I hesitated, paralyzed by fear. It struck at my heart like an arrow as I saw the nothingness of where my soul would be sent. So I ran. I abandoned everything and everyone and ran. That is my greatest shame and my unforgivable sin." He looked up at Linis, who was staring at him expressionlessly. "Now you know the depths of my cowardice."

Linis said nothing for several minutes. Then he stepped forward and offered Gewey his hand. "Come, my friend. Come and receive my forgiveness."

Gewey looked away. "How can you forgive me? I cannot forgive myself."

"You were little more than a boy," Linis replied. "No one should have expected you to save the world on your own. The entire weight of our sins was set upon your shoulders. Had the elves and the humans not been so shortsighted and selfish—had their hatred for one another not run so deep—the war would never have fallen for you to win alone. It was never right for us to expect so much."

"I wish I could believe that," said Gewey. He took Linis's hand and allowed the elf to help him up. "All I can do now is right as many wrongs as possible."

Gewey had not been back on his feet for more than a second when a flash of recognition struck his mind. He stiffened his back. Unsheathing his sword, he took a step toward the broken gates of Althetas. "She is here," he said, turning to Linis. "I must do this alone."

Linis sighed and nodded. "I wish you luck, my friend. I will be waiting."

Gewey forced a smile before setting off toward the gates.

As he entered the city, he was saddened by the memory of how grand and rich Althetas had once been. Now it was nothing but a burned-out pile of rubble littered with the skeletal remains of the dead. Those who had stayed behind after the siege had hoped the armies of Angrääl would spare them, being that they were not soldiers. What they did not know was that the Reborn King had no intention of occupying the city—or any other city.

Hours later, Gewey was still winding his way through the streets, listening for signs of his quarry. Several times he thought he heard her and reached out with his mind, but could find nothing. He passed by where the manor of King Lousis used to stand. A blackened pit that held the bones of Althetan prisoners was all that remained. He allowed the flow to rage through him and filled it with ruined earth and crumbled rock.

"Why are you here?" The familiar voice came from behind him.

He spun around and gasped. There she was. Her face was twisted and deformed, her clothes ripped and stained, and her once beautiful hair was a tangled mat. Still, he knew her at once. "Kaylia," he said.

"I am no longer Kaylia, you fool," she replied. Her voice gurgled and hissed, and her eyes were black as soot. "She died the day you turned coward."

"I refuse to believe there is nothing of her left," said Gewey. His voice was strong, but the sight of his love stabbed at his heart.

Kaylia let out a hideous laugh. "Why would you care? You abandoned her; you left her to be twisted and corrupted by your enemy." She stepped forward. "What remains of Kaylia knows nothing but hatred for you. Be grateful she cannot speak. You would not want to hear her words."

He could hardly bear to see what she had become. His tears fell freely. "I am sorry, my love. I have come to release you from your torment. Please let me help you."

This brought on more harsh laughter. "You have not the power. No one has. Not even my master can undo what has been done." She reached in her belt and drew a rusted dagger. "But you already know this, don't you?"

Gewey touched her mind but could feel nothing of Kaylia inside. Only pain and death. "Yes." His voice was almost inaudible.

"So you have come to take my head," she mocked. "You think I will be just another Vrykol, easily falling to your blade?"

"No," said Gewey. "I will not take your head, my love."

Her face twisted into a dreadful snarl. "Then you have come to die." She leaped at Gewey, her blade aimed at his throat.

Gewey released a blast of air, throwing her back and flattening her to the ground. Kaylia struggled violently, but he held her down. Then he drew upon the flow of the spirit. Kaylia's black eyes grew wide with terror. She let out a horrifying scream. Only seconds later, her body began to shrivel and curl. Finally, in a burst of power, her spirit was released.

Gewey let out a tortured wail as he saw her. The light of her soul was tainted and broken. He reached inside, desperately trying to touch the part of her that still remained. It was like sifting through an ocean of filth, but nothing was going to stop him. Eventually, he found it—a single point of light. With all his strength, he drew it out and separated it from the clinging, corrupted waste. Carefully, he guided the light toward him, striving to envelop it with his own spirit.

"I must save you," he cried, even though her light was rapidly fading. Desperately, he tried to give her his power. It was useless; she was nearly gone. Her light flickered, but just before it disappeared completely, Gewey finally took her into himself. "Forgive me," he whispered, weeping uncontrollably.

As the light of her soul faded for the final time, a single word echoed in his mind.

"Forgiven..."

Gewey glared up at the corrupted spirit swirling in a mass of evil and malice. With uncontrollable rage, he struck out at it, clawing and tearing until it was ripped apart and out of sight. His rage was now exhausted, his legs wobbled, and he dropped to the ground, still weeping.

The light of the day was dwindling quickly. Choking back his tears, he made his way to where Linis was still waiting patiently by the horses. As he approached, everything began to fade into a thin mist. Gewey ran toward his friend, but before he could reach him, the world suddenly became black.

Once again, his memories flooded back. This time, his heart felt broken beyond repair.

"Why did you show this to me?" he shouted. "Is this what I am? A coward?"

"Yes," called the tender voice of Ayliazarah. "We are all cowards in our own way. The part of you that fears death and loss. The part of you that wants to run and hide. All that walk the earth carry this within them. Only you are different. You hold the fate of us all in your hands. The consequences for you are far more severe should you fail to overcome your demons. For you to know yourself is the only real weapon you have."

"Then these things don't have to happen?" asked Gewey, wiping his eyes.

"I do not know," she replied. "Perhaps—perhaps not. The choices of the spirit are fraught with peril. In the end, only you can know which is the right path."

Gewey closed his eyes and took a breath. "Then let us continue."

CHAPTER 16

He was at home in Sharpstone; the fire in the hearth gave out a pleasing warmth and its dancing light cheered the room. Kaylia was sitting in the rocking chair that Gewey's father had made for his mother. Cradled in her arms, he could see an infant wrapped snuggly in a white cotton blanket. The vision warmed his heart, and this time, his memory remained. A small boy, no older than three or four, was sitting cross-legged in front of the fire, playing with a small wooden horse. His eyes were deep blue and his raven locks shimmered in the light.

"Kaylia," Gewey called out, but she did not look up.

"She cannot hear you," said the voice of Ayliazarah. "Unless you choose."

"Unless I choose?" Gewey repeated. "Unless I choose what?"

"Unless you choose to stay," she replied. "This can be your future. In this place, your enemies cannot find you. You can live here in peace and happiness. You can raise your children and be with your wife forever."

"But it wouldn't be real," said Gewey. "That's not really Kaylia, and those aren't really my children."

"Of course they are," she said with a sweet laugh. "Well, in a way. What you see before you is a reflection of your heart's desire. But should you choose to remain here, Kaylia will be with you, now and for all time."

"You're saying I can make it real?" asked Gewey. The sight before him brought more tears, but this time, they were tears of joy. "I can have this life?"

"Yes," she replied. "But there is a cost. If you remain, you can never leave. The door will lock, and as the gods are trapped in heaven, so shall you be trapped here. The world will be left to its fate, and your enemies will be victorious. But you shall live on forever, with your love by your side."

"But if I leave here and the other visions I've seen come true," countered Gewey, "there will be no hope for the world, anyway. I can see my wife and children before me. They are alive and happy. The alternative futures I was shown tell me that the world is no better off with me in it. Why should I not stay?"

"Perhaps you should. But what you have seen has changed what you will do." Her voice sounded like a swift wind. "You saw your heart, nothing more. The future is always uncertain. You must decide if you will risk all you desire in order to change the future and save the world."

Kaylia began humming softly to the baby in her arms.

"Where's daddy?" asked the boy.

Kaylia looked at him and smiled a mother's smile. "He is on his way, my love. He will be with us soon." Her eyes drifted to the door. Gewey could see a hint of sadness on her face.

His heart felt as if it would burst. He wanted so much to stay. More than anything. Here, he could keep them safe. Here, death and sorrow could not touch them.

"So, the decision is made?" asked Ayliazarah.

Gewey walked slowly to where his son was sitting and kneeled beside him. He reached out his hand but stopped just before it touched the boy's face. "It is made," he said. Rising to his feet, he looked one last time at Kaylia. Her eyes were still fixed on the door. "I cannot stay here."

Ayliazarah's form appeared beside him. She touched his hand and smiled. "Then it is time for you to know the rest."

"What do you mean?" asked Gewey.

The house faded, to be replaced by the dunes of the deep desert.

Ayliazarah swept her slender arm in a flowing arc. "This is where you were born. This is where your mother gave you the spark of life. Here is where all life began, and where it must someday end."

"So you know who my mother is?" His heart pounded.

She laughed and twirled around in an elegant dance. "Of course I do. She is the mother of all. And through her will, all life is given the spark of the divine."

"You can't mean…" He couldn't finish his thought.

"You, Darshan, are the last of our kind." She continued to dance, leaping impossibly high and landing without leaving a single footprint in the sand. "The mother gave you a part of her grace." She stopped abruptly. "And then left us forever." Her words now boomed and echoed like thunder. "She took Gerath into her infinite majesty, and through that union, you were born. The moment you came to be, our connection to the Creator was lost for all time. She sacrificed herself to atone for our sins."

Gewey couldn't accept it. It was impossible. "This cannot be. It would mean… It would mean…"

"It means that your birth heralded the end of the Creator." She turned and looked at Gewey. "Though her power remains, we can no longer hear her voice. It means that should you fail to defeat the betrayer and free the gods, all life will end. He will destroy the world and consign all that lives to eternal oblivion."

Gewey shook his head wildly. "No! This cannot be! Why would the Creator have done such a thing?"

She approached him and held his face in her hands. "We cannot know her mind or her motives."

"But so many have died," snapped Gewey. "Just because I was born. She could have prevented it. Why didn't she?"

"I dearly wish I had the answer," said Ayliazarah. "But even were I not merely a shadow of my true self, I would still be ignorant. But do not despair, for there is hope. Should you fulfill your destiny, our sins will be forgiven and our connection restored—and with it, the grace of her word to be spoken throughout all the lands."

Gewey looked into her eyes. "What must I do?"

She pulled him close and tenderly kissed his cheek. "You must return and protect those you love."

"But what if I fail?"

"I have faith in the Creator," she replied. "And I have faith in you."

Without thinking, he embraced her. "I am afraid."

She stroked his hair. "I know. But you will find the courage in your heart."

Slowly, the light around them dimmed until there was nothing but darkness. Then, the scent of honey and lavender returned, and he realized that he was back inside the small house. The Oracle was sitting on the rug, grinning up at him.

"It's over," he whispered.

"Did you find what you were looking for?" the Oracle asked.

"How long was I gone?" he said, ignoring her question.

"Minutes," she replied. "At least, from my perspective."

Gewey's head was spinning as he tried to understand what had happened. He stumbled toward the door but stopped just as he was reaching for the knob. How could he face Kaylia? How could he tell her what he had seen? How could she love him after she discovered what he had done? He could feel her concern through their bond. She was waiting for his return and was already experiencing his sorrow and remorse. He knew he could not hide it from her.

"Whatever you saw," said the Oracle. "It was what you needed to see."

Gewey looked over his shoulder. "I should have stayed," he said, turning the knob and opening the door.

Kaylia immediately rushed forward and wrapped her arms around his neck, but Gewey pushed her away.

"What is wrong?" she asked. "What happened?"

Gewey knew that he had to tell her. There was no way he could not.

"Your heart is heavy," said Felsafell. "Your mind burdened. But your love is a vessel that will help you bear it."

Gewey lowered his head and closed his eyes. For a full minute, he stood in silence. Finally, he looked up and told them what he had experienced. "I beg you to forgive me," he said after his tale was told.

Kaylia cupped his chin in her hands and kissed him lovingly. "You have saved us, my love. Now you know what is possible. You faced your weakness and still chose to fight. None of what you saw will come to pass—I swear it." She touched her belly. "Our child will be born in a world free of the perils that threaten to destroy us."

Gewey nodded and smiled. "Yes. Together we will prevail." He kissed her long and deeply. "But I beg you not to go in there."

"She must," said Felsafell. "As you faced your demons, she must also face hers. But not to fret. Fierce and strong is this one. Oh yes. One more kiss goodbye and in you go."

As Kaylia approached the door, she paused to look at Felsafell. "Have you ever been inside?"

Felsafell shrugged. "My demons have long ago been vanquished. Nothing for these old eyes to see. Oh no. But tell that dear girl in there that the hermit sends his greetings."

Kaylia smiled and entered the house.

"Are you sure she'll be all right?" asked Gewey.

Felsafell sat cross-legged on the ground. "An elf carries secrets, but the gods carry the world. She will face what she must face. But her mind is strong and her love without end. She will endure."

Gewey gathered some twigs and used the flow to start a small fire. He needed to take his mind off Kaylia or he'd drive himself mad. "Are you really as old as the Book of Souls says?" he asked.

Felsafell grinned. "Old I am. The first were my people to walk the earth and see the stars. And now I'm the last."

"The Book also said that your people warred with each other and nearly destroy the world," said Gewey.

"All too true," he replied. "Madness took immortal minds. Despair reigned. But I cared not for blood and fire. Found this place I did, oh yes. Long I dwelled inside its bosom. From time to time I ventured forth, but again and again my people failed to see reason. But when I emerged at last and forever, the gods had given my brothers and sisters the gift of death. Only our children remained, but madness soon took them as well. But these things you know. The Book of Souls speaks truth, it does."

Gewey tried to imagine what it must be like to live for so long, but the thought was too much for him to comprehend. He changed the subject. "Do you think I can defeat the Dark Knight?"

Felsafell held up his hands. "I know not the extent of your power. But you have weapons your enemy has not." He cocked his head and smiled. "You do not fight alone."

Gewey asked the old hermit what the world was like before elves and humans came, but his answers were confusing and disjointed, leaving Gewey even more confused. After less than half an hour, Kaylia emerged. Her face was grave and Gewey could feel that she was upset.

"Are you all right?" he asked.

Kaylia nodded. "I am fine."

He took her hands. "What did you see?"

"Only what I needed to see," she replied.

"Do not ask an elf to reveal her secrets," warned Felsafell lightheartedly.

Kaylia shook her head, smiling. "What I saw was private and had nothing to do with the task at hand." She kissed Gewey's cheek. "I will tell you once I have had some time to think. Until then, please allow me to keep my secrets to myself."

Gewey took her in his arms and hugged her tightly. "Of course. I was just afraid for you. The visions I saw nearly broke my spirit. I hated the idea of you enduring the same."

Kaylia looked at Felsafell. "The Oracle sends her greetings and reminds you of your promise."

Felsafell suddenly looked sad and careworn. "I need no reminder." He turned and looked up at the stars. "Come. My house is not far away. We shall rest in warmth and comfort, at least for a time."

He led them down the trail and back to the snow covered paths of the Spirit Hills. About an hour before dawn, they caught sight of Felsafell's home. It was just as Gewey remembered, though the thatched roof was in need of repair and the wicker chairs on the front porch were overturned and scattered. Felsafell bounded up to the door and disappeared inside. Before Gewey and Kaylia could catch up, he reappeared in the doorway.

"Go inside," he said. "Take your ease. Food we need, and none is left." With that, the old hermit skipped away and vanished into the forest.

Inside, Gewey found a cord of wood wrapped neatly beside the hearth and started a fire. The house had the empty feel of being long abandoned—he could see from the scattered clothes and hides on the floor that Felsafell must have left in a hurry. He and Kaylia unwrapped their blankets in front of the fire to enjoy the warmth, though even in the winter and with a damaged roof, the house still managed to keep out the cold rather well. By the time Felsafell returned, it was more than cozy, and Gewey could feel an overwhelming desire to sleep.

"Eyes open," called Felsafell. In his right hand, he held three rabbits, and in his left, a handful of wild onions. "Food first, then sleep you can."

Gewey struggled to his feet and helped to prepare the rabbits. Soon the house was filled with the scent of roasting meat and the sharp smell of wild onions. Kaylia crinkled her nose and walked out onto the porch, saying that the smell was too much for her. Gewey joined her just before it was time to eat. She was gazing into the depths of the forest, still wrapped in her blanket.

"Are you all right?" he asked.

Kaylia smiled. "I am fine. Onions never bothered me before, but I suppose being pregnant will have some disadvantages."

He stood behind her, holding her in his arms. "I imagine we will both need to learn quite a bit." He kissed the top of her head. "Are you afraid?"

"I would be a fool not to be," she replied. "But together we will face it."

Felsafell came outside and handed Kaylia a cup of thick purple liquid. "This should serve you well, my dear."

Kaylia put the cup to her nose. It smelled like wine-turned vinegar. She looked at Felsafell doubtfully, but the old hermit nodded. In a single gulp, she drained the cup. Her mouth immediately twisted in disgust.

"It tastes like..." she began. A moment later, a smile crept over her face. "I think I am ready for our food now."

They sat on the floor to eat while Felsafell rummaged through his pantries and found a bottle of honeyed wine. The rabbit was bland and simple, but Gewey and Kaylia devoured it as if they hadn't eaten in days.

"Now that you have learned so much," said Felsafell as he gathered up the dishes, "What will you do?"

Gewey thought for a moment. "In one of my visions, I was able to use the flow of the spirit to separate the soul of a Vrykol from its body." He couldn't bring himself to say it was Kaylia's body he spoke of. "If this is possible, then I have a weapon against Angrääl that they cannot account for." He looked up at Felsafell. "But to use this power otherwise is too dangerous. I have seen what happens when I try to change people with it."

"Then restraint you will use," said Felsafell. "As did your kin. Servants and madness were all they could create. Your choice is wise, yet I fear it may not help you. When pressed to defeat, your heart will grow desperate, and you cannot forget that his armies are vast. Should those you love face death, the temptation will be great to save them."

"I saved Aaliyah when she was poisoned in the desert," said Gewey. "But in my vision, I was unable to save Lee."

"Every spirit is different," explained Felsafell. "If an elf she is, then her spirit is free. Easy to save compared to a half-man. A gift left by the gods for them. A gift from your father and from my kin."

Gewey could feel fatigue in his mind and knew that Kaylia was feeling the same. He lay back on his blanket, his arm beneath his head. "Tomorrow I will return to Valshara. After what I witnessed, one thing is certain. The Reborn King intends to bring the hammer down hardest in Althetas, and I should be there to help."

Kaylia rested beside him, her heart troubled. Gewey pulled her close and listened as Felsafell sang a sweet melody.

It wasn't long before sleep took them both.

Kaylia awoke at midday and carefully slipped from Gewey's arms. She looked down at her unorem. His face was tense, constantly twitching from the nightmare she could feel he was wrapped within. She longed to comfort him, but knew she must leave him to rest. Felsafell was sitting at the table, humming softly to himself.

"Back to speak to the Oracle?" he asked, without even looking at her.

"Yes," she replied. "I was afraid to do so before. But I know now that I must, or be driven mad by what I saw."

"Afraid to speak?" Felsafell laughed softly. "Dread indeed, it must have been. Your fire blazes like the sun, and your courage steadfast as a mountain. What sights and sounds could make you falter, I wonder?"

"I am afraid that what I saw could come true." Her voice was a whisper. "And the fear is too much."

"Then the Oracle is the one who can help," he said. "If help can be found. Her eyes see much. More than an old man's can."

She walked to the door and looked back at Gewey's sleeping form.

"Worry not," said Felsafell. "He shall sleep far into the day. And you travel swiftly, with knowledge of the way."

Kaylia left the house and headed back to the path leading to the Oracle. This time, the distance seemed much less, as did the depth of the snow. Still, the cold bit hard, and she was grateful for the warmth that surrounded the path. As the house appeared, she could see that the door was again ajar, almost as if she was expected. For a moment, she considered turning back but quickly dismissed the thought, angered by her own fear. She silently cursed her weakness before entering.

The Oracle was still sitting on the rug, sipping on a cup of wine. She smiled at Kaylia and offered her a seat.

"I will speak to you now," said Kaylia.

"I thought you might return," she replied. "Your vision disturbed you, did it not?" She didn't wait for an answer. "As with anyone, even the young god, what you have seen reveals your heart. You cannot think of it as a window to the future."

"But it seemed as real as me sitting here now," Kaylia retorted.

"In a sense, it was," said the Oracle. "The choices you made were real. The possibilities were real. But you must try to understand that time is not what you imagine it to be, and our lives are not as simple as the result of a single decision."

Kaylia looked at her, confused. "Then what is this place? If what I witnessed cannot, or should not be, what is the point?"

The Oracle laughed. "The point? I've never been sure there is one. This place is as old as the world itself, and served a time and people long since turned to dust. Gewey needed it to see himself and the impact of his choices. You, on the other hand—if I were to guess—I think you saw the sadness he may be faced with, and that is breaking your heart."

Kaylia lowered her eyes. "I stood at the Temple of the Far Sky and watched him being dragged from this world by the gods. The war was won. Our child was born, but he could not stay. The pain I felt through our bond was without measure. He fought to remain with us, but the danger to the world was too great. I have never felt such despair. But that was not what disturbed me most."

"You knew it was for the best," said the Oracle, completing Kaylia's thought.

Kaylia nodded. "And more! I was glad. He had killed so many and would kill thousands more if he remained. The only thing I could think about was protecting our child ... from him."

The Oracle reached forward and took her hand. "The path you saw was what your heart fears most. You know better than anyone how powerful he is and will become. Other than the betrayer, he is the most dangerous being that has ever walked the earth. Even more so than the gods themselves. To bring about the end of the world with love and good intent is no better than ending it with fire. You were not given your vision as a punishment nor to blacken your heart. You were given it so that you may know yourself and to prepare for what may come."

"But I never thought I would take joy from our separation," said Kaylia. "Yet I did—I felt joy and relief. I was terrified of him. As I sit here now, I can feel his mind within me. It gives me strength. To think that this could be turned to fear is unbearable." She met the Oracle's eyes. "It is said that you have the gift of prophecy. What do you see for us?"

The Oracle sighed sadly. "The door to heaven is sealed, and with it, the substance of my power. But I can tell you this. You have the power within you to keep your love bound to this earth. You can keep his heart human. What you saw need not be. Many times I have been asked to foresee the destiny of the love between two people, and many times I have given to them words of tragedy. Yet I am faced with the unknown when I look at you and Gewey Stedding. Not because he is a god, and not that he is bound to an elf. When I see the two of you in my mind, I see a strength that only the Creator can fathom. So take courage. For never before have I encountered two people who could reshape the very meaning of the world through love and will alone."

Kaylia thought on this for a minute, then stood. Her anxiety was turning to relief and determination, and she was now grateful to have seen her vision. For now, she knew it was not a fate set in stone, nor was her heart unable to endure. "I thank you, Oracle."

She bowed. "Perhaps we shall meet again."

Kaylia bowed in return and left.

It was early afternoon when she arrived back at Felsafell's house, and she could feel that Gewey was still sleeping. Felsafell was sitting on the porch in a wicker chair with eyes closed and a sly grin on his lips.

"You look more at ease," he said.

"You see with eyes closed?" remarked Kaylia.

"I see more than you can guess," he replied. "I see that we will not leave these hills without incident." His eyes popped open. "The Vrykol are near."

Kaylia spun around, her hand flying to her blade.

Felsafell rose and moved beside her. "They will not attack us here, oh no. They wait. They watch. Tomorrow we face them. Oh yes. To arms, we go." He placed his withered hand on Kaylia's shoulder. "Worry not. Old Felsafell will keep the watch. Rest and be calm. Join your mate and ease his dreams. Torment is no way to spend your short moment of peace."

"Can you tell where they are?" asked Kaylia.

Felsafell nodded. "Even the powers that have corrupted my kin cannot hide them from my sight." He motioned for her to go inside. "Now go. Leave me to worry."

She took another full minute to scan the forest before finally doing as instructed. Gewey's face was still twitching from his nightmares, so she lay beside him and called out, bringing him from his terror into her loving embrace. Soon, they were both enraptured with the desire they shared.

All else was forgotten—at least for a time.

CHAPTER 17

King Lousis stared out over the expanse of the Western Abyss, half expecting to see enemy ships on the horizon. It had taken him most of the morning to ride from the city gates to the harbor, but he needed to see the blue water and taste the salty air. Two elf ships had been diligently patrolling the waters between Skalhalis and Althetas, but the Abyss was unfathomably massive, and in spite of elf reassurances, he still feared a surprise attack.

Althetas's own ships were now ready to sail for Baltria. With soldiers already starting to board their vessels, one hundred warships, led by elf power and skill, would soon be bearing down on the enemy. Lousis longed to join them, but his principal duty was to the city—the council had at least convinced him of that. Nehrutu was a capable leader and had been made admiral of the fleet. He had immediately assigned elf seekers to every ship, and through these, they were able to communicate without flags or smoke. Lousis smiled at the thought of Angrääl soldiers trying to match their maneuvers.

Ground preparations had also gone well. Lord Ganflin and other nobles had practically emptied their treasuries in order to strengthen the city's defenses, and the muster of both elf and human armies was complete. Nearly one hundred thousand troops were camped near Valshara. It had taken immense resources to keep them supplied, but Ertik had shown himself to be masterful at logistics and organization, so things had run smoothly thus far.

It had been suggested that they send the army south. Winter was sweeping through the lands north and west, and no invasion was generally expected until spring. Lousis, however, was not convinced of this. Knowing that the forces of Angrääl were from a harsh and frozen land, he felt that the comparatively meager snows that fell south of their home were unlikely to be much of an obstacle to them.

Seeing as how no word had yet come from Theopolou or Mohanisi, there was still concern regarding the elves of the Steppes. But there was little that could be done. If they had failed in their mission, Lousis would know soon enough. In the meantime, the northernmost kingdoms were keeping a watchful eye for any signs of attack.

Lousis's guard stood at his back. The elf elders, Lord Chiron in particular, had insisted that he double his protection by including elf fighters. The morale of the city hung in the balance. Should the Reborn King send assassins and the Althetan monarch be killed, fear and panic would grip the people like a vise, and that, they could ill afford. This rankled Lousis. He was a warrior and hated being coddled, but in his heart, he knew they were right.

"Your Highness," called the voice of Eftichis.

The elf lord had become a welcome companion during the past few weeks. He seldom spoke of the coming war, or of anything else that would likely cast a shadow over the spirit. Lousis had heard about his fight with Gewey at the Chamber of the Maker, and marveled at his deep sense of honor.

The king turned to see the elf's face darkened by worry. "What is it?"

"We have just received word that Angrääl has landed on the Tarvansia Peninsula and is already marching north," he replied.

A cold chill shot into his stomach. "How many? And how far have they gotten?"

"We think at least sixty-thousand. But there may be more. It is unclear how far they have penetrated. I imagine it will depend on how stiff resistance is."

"King Victis will not be easily defeated," said Lousis. He began walking swiftly toward his horse. His guard instantly surrounded him and kept pace. "What of the elf lands to the east?"

"Should they march east, they will find it well protected," said Eftichis. "Even with the bulk of our forces here, we are not undefended. But as of this moment, we have not heard anything that suggests their attention is focused on the elves."

"No," mused Lousis. "They'll take the port of Althetas first. Then your people will be unable to stop them."

"We cannot sail for Baltria until this attack is dealt with," said Eftichis. "If we do, we leave the city and harbor undefended."

King Lousis stopped short. A sly smile crept upon his face. "Yes. Indeed, it would." He continued with renewed vigor and speed.

The moment Lousis and Eftichis reached the manor, the king ordered his generals and admirals to gather in the council chambers. By the time they arrived, he was already poring over maps and charts laid out on the table.

Lord Chiron and Lady Bellisia were attended by several elf seekers. Lord Maynard Windcomber, Lord Brasley Amnadon and Lord Jeffos Windermere arrived with a few other human commanders, while Nehrutu was accompanied, as always, by Aaliyah.

"By now you all know that Angrääl has landed on the Tarvansia Peninsula," announced the king. Everyone nodded.

"Conventional wisdom will tell us to keep our ships here and surround the harbor while we march south from Valshara to meet them."

"That would be my recommendation," said Maynard. "If we sail south and they meet us on the open sea, or worse, somehow get by us, Althetas will be defenseless other than the city guard."

Nehrutu stepped forward. "They would have to sail very far from shore to avoid detection. If we spotted them, the navigators would be able to keep them from landing ahead of us."

"But neither of you is taking into account the speed in which this attack has come," countered the king. "It has taken us nearly a month to make ready. They have landed after sailing from Baltria in the same time." He looked around the room. "They must have departed while we were still fighting the first battle. Given that, we cannot possibly know how many ships may be coming."

"What do you propose, Your Highness?" asked Maynard.

"I think the Reborn King intends to crush us here and now," he explained. "To do so, he must take Althetas. I say we sail our ships out of harm's way and march fifty thousand soldiers north. Then we allow the enemy to enter the harbor and approach our gates. Once they arrive, we close in behind them. The rest of the army will go to Skalhalis in case I'm wrong, and they land there instead."

"But if they see the harbor is empty, they'll suspect..." Maynard began.

"They won't," said Lousis, cutting him off. "We will set a blockade of merchant vessels flying the Althetan banner. Once the Angrääl ships are spotted, the fleet will retreat into the harbor and dock. They'll think we are fleeing into the imagined safety of the city, frightened by their power. It will take them a full day to march an invasion force to the city gates. By the time they realize they have been duped, they'll be trapped."

Nehrutu nodded approvingly. "A sound plan. You keep our fleet out of danger and force them to engage on our terms."

"But, Your Highness," objected Maynard. "You will leave the southern kingdoms without support. Can you not at least send the other half of our army to their aid?"

Lousis grimaced. "No. Not until I know the strength of our enemy and the condition of our southern forces. If they are already defeated, and I'm wrong, I could be sending them to their death for nothing. We will need to be able to meet them with full strength. But if I'm right, this attack on the peninsula is a ruse designed to draw us away from Althetas. If they land in Skalhalis and it is undefended, they will have a foothold in the northern kingdoms."

"Should we send word to King Victis?" asked Maynard, clearly displeased.

"No," said Lousis. His voice was stern and commanding. "We cannot risk the plan being discovered." He turned to Chiron and Bellisia. "I need your seekers to head south at once and discover the strength and position of Angrääl."

They nodded in unison. Bellisia gave one of her seeker escorts a quick glance. He bowed and immediately sped away.

"I hope you're right, Your Highness," muttered Maynard.

"As do I," said Lousis.

They spent the next hour charting where the fleet would lay in wait, after which the meeting adjourned for the commanders to make their preparations.

"Where will you be?" asked Lord Maynard as they were leaving the chamber.

The king grinned. "Not hiding. I will take command of the guard."

Maynard scowled but said nothing.

King Lousis decided to go to the dining hall, but by the time he got there, six more soldiers were surrounding him. All were wearing the colors of Lord Maynard's personal guard. Lousis protested, but the guards merely apologized and remained, anyway. Whatever their commander had told them, it was clearly sufficient to outweigh the king's displeasure.

It took most of the day to organize the merchant vessels for the decoy. At first, some demanded extra gold or tariff exemptions in exchange for the use of their ships, but a short talk with Nehrutu quickly ended the debate. Chiron and Bellisia sent word to the main army and had seekers patrol around the city looking for spies that might give away the plan. By the next morning, the fleet was ready to sail and the merchant vessels were ready to take up their positions.

King Lousis ventured down to the docks to watch them depart. He was accompanied by his escort, which by now had grown to twenty men and elves. A cold chill ran down his spine as he watched the fleet slowly sail away. Part of him hoped he was wrong. Even if Angrääl fell into his trap, there would still be war inside his beloved city. He would need to allow them to land for the plan to work. That meant death and destruction for his people, not on some distant battleground, but right on their doorsteps.

He thought of King Victis and squeezed his eyes tightly shut. An army of sixty-thousand men was far more than the southern kingdoms could match without aid. He knew that many would die. Villages and towns would be burned, and cities sacked. But if he was right, this was their only hope. If Althetas were to fall, the war would be over. The path west would be clear, and Angrääl would have possession of the two largest ports in the world. If that happened, they wouldn't need to march. They could literally starve out any kingdom that opposed them.

Once the army arrived, Althetas became a beehive of activity. The city walls were reinforced and defenses were put in place around the harbor to slow the advance of invading soldiers. The moment everything was ready, Lousis ordered the gates closed and travel south forbidden.

Skalhalis was prepared as well. Although he knew an attack there was indeed possible, Lousis didn't think it likely. Still, he'd had the elves send seekers to keep watch on the city for signs of enemy scouts, or perhaps even an advance force.

But a week had now passed without any sign of attack. Lousis was becoming increasingly anxious and spending most of his evenings at the harbor staring out across the Abyss. With no news coming in via messenger bird, and the elf seekers yet to return, he was even beginning to make tentative plans to send forces south.

On the morning of the eighth day, there was a knock on his chamber door. Lousis donned his robe and rubbed his weary eyes. Lord Maynard entered wearing full armor, his face tight with concern.

"What is it?" croaked Lousis. He grabbed a cup of water from his bedside table to soothe his dry throat.

"You were right," said Maynard. "Angrääl ships approach from the southwest."

Lousis felt a wave of adrenaline rush through his aging body. "Are we ready?"

Maynard lowered his eyes. "Your Highness..."

"Spit it out!" he commanded.

"Three hundred ships," he said unsteadily. "At least three hundred ships will land within four hours."

Lousis swallowed hard. "So many." He shook his head. "It doesn't matter. While I live, they will not take this city. Check the defenses and man the walls—and have my armor brought to me at once."

Maynard bowed and hurried out.

Lousis's anxiety was now turning to dread. How could they have so many warships? How could Angrääl have mounted such a massive attack from just one port? He could hear orders being shouted from outside his door, together with the pounding of countless heavy boots running through the halls. He pictured the Althetan harbor in his mind, trying to see if he should change their plan of defense. He glanced up at the painting of his father. It stared at him tauntingly.

"Do you think you could have done better?" he shouted.

A young boy came in with Lousis's armor piled high in his arms, the sheer weight of it making the thin lad stumble. Lousis held back a laugh as he took it from him. Two Althetan soldiers entered a second later.

He looked at the boy and smiled. The blond youth wore a thick leather tunic stuffed with cotton. It looked far too big on him and gave him an even more awkward appearance. "What's your name, boy?" he asked.

"Fre ... Fredman, Your Highness," he replied nervously.

Lousis looked at the guard, his eyes unyielding. "You two wait outside. Young Fredman will help me into my armor."

The guards slammed their fists to their chest in a salute and left.

"So, lad," said the king. "Are you afraid?"

Fredman couldn't bring himself to look the king in the eye. "Yes, Your Highness. I'm ashamed to say that I am."

He gave the boy a fatherly grin. "No need to feel ashamed. I'm afraid as well."

This time, the boy met the king's eyes, a confused look on his face.

"What? You think a king can't be scared?" Lousis continued. "I just heard that three hundred ships are bearing down on my home. Only a great fool wouldn't fear that. Fear tells us when to fight, boy. It tells us when something is worth fighting for. I fear for the lives of my people, and the well-being of my city."

"Do you fear for your own life, Your Highness?" he asked.

Lousis paused for a moment. His eyes grew dark. "I do. But not because I am afraid of death. I fear only that my passing will herald the death of Althetas." He shook off his sudden melancholy. "But it is the same with any king.

We all imagine ourselves to be far more important than we really are."

"I think you're very important, Your Highness," replied Fredman. "I think the city would fall without you."

Lousis smiled and walked over to the painting of his father. "Do you know who this is?"

"I'm not sure, Your Highness," he replied.

Lousis chuckled. "No. I didn't imagine you would. This is my father. His reign lasted longer than any king in our history. When he died, the entire city despaired." He touched the image with his fingertips. "I was terrified. So much so that I couldn't properly mourn his death." He turned to Fredman. "The first week after my coronation, there was a massive fire in the merchant quarter. Fifty people died. I didn't know what to do. My father was gone, and I felt as if he had taken the heart of the city with him."

"What did you do?" asked the boy.

"I hid," said Lousis, with a laugh. "I hid in this very room, staring at my father's image. I begged the gods to bring him back to save me."

"What happened?" asked Fredman. It was clear he was having a hard time imagining the aging king hiding in his bedchamber.

"Eventually I was called out to speak to the people," he answered. "So I put on my bravest face and went down to the merchant quarter. I can still remember how scared I was. I just knew they were going to blame me for this disaster. I knew they would say it happened because my father was gone. But they didn't. I climbed atop one of the few buildings that had escaped the flames and looked out on the devastation, then down at the faces of the people. They were looking to me for solace and hope. Not my father—me. In that moment, I came to understand that the soul of the kingdom was inside of me, just as it had been in my father before, and his father before him. I fear that the city cannot survive without me because Althetas lives in my heart. With every single beat, it is forever here."

He placed a hand over his chest to emphasize his point before allowing Fredman to place the shining breastplate over his head. "And I'll do anything to keep that heart alive," he concluded.

With his armor donned, he dismissed the boy and called for his guard. An elf warrior entered wearing shining black leather armor with a white lily painted on its breast.

"We will see to the docks and then go to the command center," Lousis announced. Grabbing his sword from where it hung on the wall, he attached it to his belt.

When they arrived at the docks, he could see the sails of the massive Angrääl fleet stretching across the horizon. Their own merchant fleet was already docking and disembarking. Lousis chuckled to himself. The plan had been to let the enemy think they were afraid of their might. Well, at least that part of the trap was no longer a ruse. Troops scurried about, taking up their positions; the barking orders of their commanders sounding like an obscene melody.

"We must leave, Your Highness," said one of the guards.

Lousis took one last look before turning away and riding back to the city. The command center was near the city's main gate. It was well-defended, and even if Angrääl troops circled around, they would be hard-pressed to breach the walls or batter the gate down.

A large pavilion had been erected, in the middle of which was a round table with a map spread out on it. Standing alongside the table, Lord Chiron and Lady Bellisia were talking quietly with Lord Maynard. Aside from these three, plus a few soldiers and runners, the pavilion was empty. Most of the commanders were with their men. Everyone bowed as the king approached.

"All is ready, Your Highness," announced Maynard.

Lousis couldn't help but admire the old general. He knew he had family in the southern lands and desperately wanted to go to their aid, but never once had he mentioned them to the king.

"Then there is nothing for us to do but wait," said Lousis.

CHAPTER 18

Nehrutu ran silently through the forest with Aaliyah at his side and an army of elves at his back. The flow raged through him like a torrent, illuminating the night and making clear every detail of the trees and brush. Even though they were still five miles away from the city walls, he could already see the sky glowing red from flames. He hoped that Angrääl had not breached the gates, but as they drew closer, his hopes diminished.

The humans were still several miles behind. Even without their heavier armor, they would never have been able to keep up. Not that it mattered. The road from the harbor, though wide and well constructed, could not have accommodated their entire force at once. As it was, the fifteen thousand elves he had with him would be forced into a bottleneck. Speed was their only ally, and if the enemy were already inside the walls, it would certainly complicate matters.

He listened to the hushed footfalls of his kin, impressed by their dexterity, especially as this was achieved without the aid of the flow. He knew how fierce they were in combat and allowed himself a smile. Whatever they were about to face, they would certainly triumph.

The light from the flames grew brighter as they neared the city, and sounds of clashing steel could clearly be heard over the roar of a thousand battle cries. Nehrutu reached out for signs of Vrykol, but to his great relief, could find none. Pulling his blade free, he let out a primal yell. His brethren answered, their voices piercing the air like a thousand silver trumpets.

When they finally emerged from the woods and ran onto the harbor road, they were only half a mile away from the city. From here, Nehrutu could see that the massive gates had indeed been shattered, also that flames were rising from the market quarter just inside the walls. Angrääl soldiers were still pouring in through the broken gates, while Althetan archers positioned on the high walls above continued to rain down arrows. But this line of defense could not last for much longer. The archers would soon be forced back once the enemy reached the guard tower steps that would allow them access to the ramparts.

The elves struck before the Angrääl soldiers even knew they were there, ripping into their flank and causing sheer terror as they hacked their enemy to pieces with cruel steel. Nehrutu and Aaliyah let flames erupt into the soldiers nearest to the gates, scattering them like ants. From atop the wall, cheers rang out and the archers instantly redoubled their assault.

The elf attack penetrated deep, forcing the soldiers back. Even so, Nehrutu knew that once the enemy had recovered from the surprise, his fighters would be outnumbered by at least three to one. From the corner of his eye, he saw Aaliyah slicing through two men in rapid succession, then sending a ball of flame into the center line. Again and again, he pushed forward, killing at least a dozen soldiers with fire and steel. But the Angrääl commanders were now organizing their men much better. Soon the advance was halted, and Nehrutu was faced with an impassable wall of shields and spears. One by one, the elves began to fall.

In a massive counterattack, the Angräal soldiers suddenly surged forward. These troops were unlike any of those they had encountered near Skalhalis. With eyes bulging unnaturally large and crazed, they bellowed out their frenzied battle cries like men possessed. Several times, Nehrutu was only just able to avoid being impaled. His heart then gave an almighty jump as he glanced over to see blood pouring down Aaliyah's right shoulder. He cut down three men while maneuvering himself toward her.

"Pull back," he shouted, both aloud and through their bond.

She ignored him, instead casting another fireball directly ahead, igniting wood and flesh. Nehrutu looked to the walls. The Althetan archers were gone. "Pull back now," he repeated, this time even more forcefully. She glared at him, still unwilling to respond. There was nothing else for it. He moved in front of Aaliyah and forcibly pushed her away from the lines. "The archers have fled," he told her. "We must protect our kin."

Just as the words came from his mouth, he spotted Angräal bowmen taking up positions on the ramparts. Aaliyah saw them, too. She nodded and retreated to the rear, where elf bows were already bent and ready. The thwack of a hundred bowstrings sounded, sending white-fletched elf arrows streaking through the air. Bodies dropped from the walls, screaming on the way down. The return volleys were deflected by a tempest sent skyward by Aaliyah and Nehrutu. An instant later, it was calm again as the elf archers let loose another round of certain death.

In spite of this success, they were still being forced back as the Angräal soldiers gained more momentum. After half an hour, Nehrutu feared they might be forced into full retreat, but then he heard the clamor of steel and heavy boots coming from behind. He looked around. The humans had run far more swiftly than he would ever have thought possible.

The human reinforcements charged in, engaging the enemy with unparalleled fury and skill. Nehrutu knew that most of the men were from Althetas. The sight of invaders at their shattered gates and their beloved city in flames was clearly giving them unnatural strength and determination. Within minutes, they had regained lost ground and turned the tide of the battle. Nehrutu suddenly felt a deep kinship with all those who lived within the city walls. He imagined what he might feel should it be his land that was being invaded.

Angrääl had apparently run out of archers, and the ramparts were now clear. He ran to the left flank and ordered it to pull back. One of the human captains scowled when he heard this.

"We have them," the captain protested. "Why leave them an avenue for escape?"

"To save lives," Nehrutu replied forcefully. "Never corner a wild beast. They fight twice as hard. And I will not sacrifice lives unless I must. Let them retreat to their ships."

The captain grumbled briefly, then saluted. "As you say." He raced off to spread the word.

Nehrutu understood the captain's feelings. The light from the fires on the other side of the wall was becoming ever brighter. To watch one's home burn must be agonizingly hard to bear.

He joined Aaliyah and ushered her farther to the rear, well behind the archers who were still showering the enemy with arrows. From here, he ordered an area set up for the wounded.

"Our skills in battle are no longer needed. We should attend the wounded," he said. Much of his strength was now drained. Aaliyah's eyes, however, still blazed with the heat of battle. Never before had he seen her so fierce. It reminded him of Kaylia when they had first arrived on these shores. He wondered if Aaliyah's connection to Gewey had anything to do with this change.

Soon, the wounded were being carried to an area a few hundred feet back from the rear lines. Ignoring the still-fevered battle, they set about their work.

"We have done this far too often," remarked Nehrutu.

Aaliyah was tending to an elf who had been run through by an Angrääl spear. She looked up with a fragile smile, her warrior's face now replaced by that of a concerned parent. "This is only the beginning."

Another hour had passed when a young Althetan soldier ran up, jubilant. "My lord. They are retreating."

Nehrutu nodded, unable to smile. "As soon as you are able, send word of our situation to King Lousis."

The soldier bowed and sped off.

Nehrutu glanced up at the walls of Althetas. Indeed, the enemy was in retreat. The fires behind the walls made it easy to see. Dozens of elf and human healers had come to help, but more were still needed.

He closed his eyes and thought of home, wondering if he would ever see it again.

CHAPTER 19

King Lousis paced back and forth under the pavilion. He desperately wanted to be somewhere—anywhere but where he actually was. He glanced across at Lord Chiron, who just grinned with amusement. Striding over to a small table, he grabbed a bottle of wine and lifted it to his mouth. Something then caused him to hesitate. Letting out a curse, he replaced the bottle without having taken a drink.

"I do not think a small measure of wine will addle your senses," remarked Chiron. "In fact, it might do you some good."

Lousis didn't bother to look up. "I can't abide this waiting."

Chiron laughed. "Frankly, I could wait forever. If it takes our enemy a hundred years to arrive, it is still too soon for my taste. I have seen more than a full measure of war during my life and am in no hurry to see more."

Bellisia placed her hand on Chiron's shoulder. "Perhaps you could be a little less ... jovial."

Chiron chuckled. "My lady, since the moment Gewey told us what is written in the Book of Souls, I have had to look at life from a different perspective. And for my part, I will keep my spirits as high as my heart allows."

Bellisia looked at him crossly. "You should still be considerate."

"No," Lousis interjected. "He's right. Our hearts cannot be filled with darkness. That alone can defeat us." He reopened the bottle and this time took a long drink. "We have had one triumph, and now we will have another."

Chiron stepped forward and took the bottle. Bellisia did the same, albeit without the mirthful grin of Chiron. Maynard, who was standing in the far corner, grumbled at first, then shouted for more wine. For the next few hours until dusk, runners continued to bring news that all was prepared. Lousis stared blankly at the map of the city, wishing there was more he could do. But there was not. All that could be done had already been done.

Lousis tensed as he saw a messenger approaching with a fearful look. He handed the king a small piece of parchment.

"It has begun," muttered Lousis. He felt almost relieved.

For the next two hours, King Lousis and Lord Maynard received report after report of the enemy's assault. Mostly, they were doing nothing more than firing arrows over the wall from behind large wooden shields.

"Something tells me that they will unleash their real intentions soon, Your Highness," said Maynard. "For certain, they did not send so many just to shoot arrows at us from afar."

His words were proved correct. A few seconds later, a messenger arrived, pale and out of breath. "They've battered down the city gate," he gasped.

Lousis and Maynard exchanged shocked glances.

"That should have taken them hours, if not days!" Lousis exclaimed. "How did this happen?"

"They rolled up a battering ram," the messenger explained, fear in his voice. "One like I've never seen. The end was wrapped in white sackcloth..." He paused. "One strike. That's all it took. Just one strike before the gates burst into splinters and flames. The force instantly killed twenty men standing close by inside. It ripped them apart as if they were made of silk."

Lousis tried to picture the scene in his mind. "Are we holding the market?"

The messenger shook his head. "We have pulled back just beyond and are holding them away from the merchant and tavern districts."

Chiron touched Lousis's shoulder and pointed in the direction of the west gate. They could see the red glow of flames and thick black smoke rising. At that moment, his guard surrounded the pavilion.

"If they are within the walls," said Chiron, "we may be forced to flee."

"No!" shouted Lousis. "Nehrutu will still come. We will not lose Althetas!"

Reports of the enemy advance continued to pour in throughout the next hour. After the death of two guard captains, Lord Maynard left them to take direct control of the defense, while Chiron and Bellisia began treating the wounded that were being laid down around the pavilion.

It was nearing midnight when Maynard returned to the pavilion, his face covered in soot and his armor spattered with blood. He cursed and spat. "The devils are burning everything. Half the city is in flames."

"Any sign of Nehrutu?" asked Lousis.

"We are cut off from the west gate," explained Maynard. "There is a company of bowmen barricaded within the guard tower, but we can't get to them. If reinforcements have arrived, there is no way to know. We'll have to wait for them to break through."

A sweat-soaked soldier ran up and saluted. "The enemy is pushing toward your manor, Your Highness."

Lousis's hand instantly shot to the hilt of his sword. Maynard tried to step in front of him, but the king was having none of it. Pushing the commander aside, he set off at a run toward his home. His guards immediately chased after him.

"Bloody hell," grumbled Maynard, following on with Chiron and Bellisia beside him.

Smoke filled the streets, stinging Lousis's eyes and burning his throat. He knew he should have stayed at the command center, but the thought of invaders in his home—his father's home—was more than he could bear. As the manor came into sight, he let out a loud sigh of relief. Beyond the gates, several hundred Althetan soldiers had formed a protective ring around the building. On seeing their king, their cheers erupted and swords rattled against shields.

"This is foolish, Your Highness," said Maynard, finally catching up. "You would risk your life for bricks and mortar?"

Lousis fixed his eyes on Maynard's. "It is far more than just bricks and mortar. It is my home and the home of every king that will rule after me. Our history lives inside those walls, and I'll be damned if I'm going to let anyone destroy it."

The sounds of battle continued to echo throughout the streets as if the city itself was crying out in agony for each moment the invaders trespassed within its walls. The king's guard pushed their way through the lines, escorting Lousis to the rear.

An Althetan captain made his way to Lousis and bowed low. "We are honored to have you with us, Your Highness, but if the enemy attacks in force, we may not be able to protect you. Perhaps it would be best if..."

"Who ordered the king's manor protected?" asked Lousis.

The captain looked confused. "Ordered? No one."

"Then why are you here?" asked the king, at the same time looking to Maynard.

The captain's face showed pride and resolve. "This scum may burn the rest of the city to rubble. But they'll not touch the king's manor. As long as it stands, the city will live on."

"You see, Lord Maynard?" jeered Lousis. "It's not just bricks and mortar."

Maynard grunted. "You do realize, Your Highness, that the manor gate and fence were not designed to hold off an attack."

"If it slows them even a bit, it will help," countered Lousis.

Half an hour passed. The glow from the burning buildings drew ever closer and brighter until the flagstone street directly beyond the manor fence was reflecting vivid orange. Shadowy figures could be seen running back and forth between the large houses that surrounded them.

"Can you tell if they are ours?" Lousis asked Bellisia and Chiron.

Both shook their heads.

They could hear the thunder of boots drawing ominously closer. The glint of blades and armor then appeared from behind the houses. Moments later, hundreds of Angrääl soldiers charged toward them, their battle cries heralding their madness and fury. Dozens of shields crashed into the wrought iron fence, and just as Maynard had predicted, it gave way almost immediately before being trampled completely flat by enemy boots.

Lousis shouted a challenge. In response, his soldiers raced to meet the enemy, their fevered cries ringing with blood lust. Shields collided with ear-splitting cracks, and for a moment, both sides came to a thudding halt. Gradually, though, the overwhelming numbers of Angrääl began to inch the king's men back toward the manor walls. Swords sought flesh from behind shields, and men on both sides screamed in agony as the blades found their mark.

Lousis tried to move forward, but Bellisia placed herself between him and the fray, pushing him back.

"If we fail, go inside," she ordered. Without waiting for a response, she leaped to her left to help hold the flank.

Angrääl soldiers were now beginning to break through a few at a time. Half of the Althetan defenders had fallen as more and more enemy reinforcements came in from the streets. Lousis looked over his shoulder. The door to his beloved home was only a few yards away. A few feet in front of him, Bellisia, Chiron, and Maynard were fighting fiercely to hold off more than a dozen men. Even though his guard was now all but destroyed, those few remaining were still trying desperately to surround him. Just then, he heard an anguished cry and saw Maynard clutching at a sword that had pierced his gullet.

"No!" shouted Lousis. Without hesitation, he went running over. With a single swing of his sword, he hacked off the arm of his friend's killer.

Blind rage was engulfing him. Again and again, his sword lashed out as he pushed his way to the front. The voices of protest from his men became nothing more than a distant echo. Pain shot through his arm as his armor was laid open. Yet another blow knocked the helmet from his head. Still, he was undaunted, and three more men fell to his fury. Another enemy sword found the flesh of his left thigh, but the blood running down his leg only fueled his anger. Chiron and Bellisia appeared by his side, their eyes glowing red from the nearby flames. Lousis allowed himself a slight smile, then struck off the head of an Angrääl axeman.

All but about twenty of the Althetans were now slain, including Lousis's entire guard. This harsh reality gradually stifled his anger and quieted his madness. His sudden rage had surprised the enemy, forcing them to give ground. But he knew this could not last. Within moments, he and the others would all be dead. He braced himself to die like a true king in the final onslaught.

A trumpet sounded three times, its call instantly turning the heads of the Angrääl soldiers. For a moment, there was silence. The trumpet sounded again, reinforcing its message. The king watched in utter amazement as the soldiers first of all drew slowly back, then, as they passed over the fallen fence, turned and fled.

Without pausing any longer to wonder at this development, Lousis rushed straight over to Maynard's fallen body and kneeled beside him. His eyes were barely open, and blood trickled from the corners of his mouth, staining his beard. The Angrääl blade still protruded from his belly. Seizing hold of the hilt, Lousis pulled it free. Maynard cried out in pain.

"My friend," said Lousis softly.

Maynard looked up at the old king and smiled weakly. "My king. You were magnificent. I am honored to have seen you fight so bravely before I die."

Bellisia and Chiron stood over them, their faces grave.

"Save him," begged Lousis.

Removing the staff Gewey had given to her from her back, Bellisia kneeled and placed it over Maynard's wound. For several minutes she was motionless, her eyes shut. "I can do nothing," she finally said. "He has lost too much blood. I am sorry."

Lousis leaped up and grabbed one of his remaining soldiers. "Send for my physician. She is near the pavilion. Run as fast as your legs can carry you. Tell her she must hurry."

With a short nod, the soldier bolted off.

Bellisia reached out and touched Lousis's shoulder. "She will not arrive in time," she whispered. "And there is no human medicine that can help him now."

Tears welled in the king's eyes as he lowered his head. "I must try." He sat beside Maynard and rested the man's head on his lap.

"I am ready," said Maynard. His voice was distant and strained. "I have served enough." He grasped hold of the king's hand, his breaths now coming in labored gasps. "Please ... let an old soldier rest."

Choking back his sobs, Lousis nodded, squeezing Maynard's hand until it finally went limp. Reaching down, he gently closed the general's dead eyes. "Goodbye, my old friend."

Lousis wiped his eyes, stood up, and gathered his remaining soldiers. "See that Lord Maynard's body is taken inside the manor and cleaned," he ordered two of them.

He then turned to Bellisia and Chiron, who were already tending to the wounded. "When my physician arrives, have her assist you. I'm going to find out why we are still alive."

Lousis led the remainder of his men beyond the grounds and into the street. Cautiously, they followed the route along which the enemy had retreated. Some of the houses close to the manor were aflame. Clearly, Angrääl intended to leave nothing untouched.

They made their way to the edge of the garden district and halted in the shadows. The streets leading to the market were jammed full with Angrääl soldiers, their massive numbers impeding their hasty progress.

"They're fleeing, Your Highness," shouted one of his men with a combination of relief and confusion.

"Perhaps," said Lousis. "Or perhaps our reinforcements have arrived and they go to the greater fight."

They watched for a few more minutes before heading off in the direction of the pavilion. Everywhere they passed, the city seemed to be full of burning buildings and weeping people. The dead and dying littered every avenue, many of them calling out for help with their final breaths.

On arriving at the command center, Lousis could see several captains and commanders already gathered. Among them was Lord Brasley Amnadon. The king had hoped to see Eftichis there as well and immediately became concerned by his absence. Everyone saluted and bowed as he entered.

"The enemy is in retreat," announced Amnadon. His eyes were weary and his face smeared with blood. "I believe that Nehrutu has arrived. It is the only thing that can explain their pulling back. A few more hours and the city would have been all but lost."

"How many have died?" asked Lousis, not really wanting to hear the answer.

"I don't know, Your Highness," he replied. "At least half the guard, I would guess. But we made them pay. They lost far more than we. Had they not been able to smash the city gates so quickly…" His eyes burned. "I thought that only the elves and Darshan could achieve such a thing."

"If the description I heard was accurate," said Lousis, "I don't think it was caused by the same power as they possess. More likely it was some new weapon."

Lousis spotted the runner he had sent out to the west gate returning. He slid to a halt, out of breath. "Nehrutu has arrived, Your Highness."

Lousis squeezed the boy's arm in acknowledgment, then walked to the map. "Where are the rest of the men?"

"When the enemy began to retreat, I pulled them back to the southeast, near to the grain storehouses," replied Amnadon. "We were in no condition to give pursuit."

"And what is their condition now?" he asked sternly.

"They can resume the fight if you so command," he replied, though with a hint of uncertainty.

"Then have them attack at once," Lousis ordered. "We will not lick our wounds while Nehrutu still fights." He looked over all his commanders. "Gather your courage. Lord Maynard is slain. Let his name be our battle cry as we chase Angrääl back to the pits of hell."

The news of Maynard's death caused everyone to stir. Tears filled nearly every eye. Faces twisted in anger and sorrow.

Drawing his sword, Amnadon called out at the top of his voice.

"Maynard!"

His cry was taken up by all. Still chanting their dead general's name, they stalked into the city to take their revenge. Lousis smiled inwardly at the honor and bravery of his people. But he could feel the pains seeping into his muscles, and his legs were growing heavier with every passing minute. Dragging himself over to a chair, he sat down hard and let out a long, weary sigh. His head was swimming, and for a moment his vision blurred.

"Are you all right, Your Highness?" asked a nearby soldier.

Lousis forced a smile. There was no guard smothering him now, he noticed. With a heavy grunt, he pushed himself up to his feet. "Find some wine and drink with me," he told the soldier. His legs wobbled, causing him to drop back down into the chair. "I am old and haven't fought so hard in many years." As the soldier ran off, Lousis caught a fresh scent of the flames engulfing his beloved city. He let out a mighty roar of anger.

The soldier returned with the wine and they sat together briefly, drinking to the memory of those who had died. The cool liquid soothed Lousis's throat and warmed his belly. He wondered if peace was now within reach, or whether his life would be forever plagued by war. After dismissing the soldier, he shouted for another bottle. He no longer cared to keep his wits. The taste of the wine helped to ease his mind a little, though it did nothing for the heaviness in his heart.

"They are retreating to their ships," came a voice.

At first, Lousis didn't respond. He drained the bottle he was holding and tossed it to the ground alongside the three others already discarded.

"Your Highness."

This time, he looked up. It was Eftichis. Lousis smiled, his spirits lifted. "I feared you dead."

"Many times this night I nearly was," he replied.

Lousis looked around and wondered how long he had been sitting there. He held out his hand and Eftichis helped him to his feet. "My city burns."

"We will put out the flames," said the elf. "And we will rebuild your city. Do not despair. We have cast out the enemy and wounded them deeply. Though many have died, we are victorious." He noticed the king's unsteady legs and the wounds he'd sustained in battle. "Why have you not been treated?" Before Lousis could respond, he raced off. A few minutes later, he returned with Lady Bellisia.

Lousis had all but forgotten his injuries. Bellisia cleaned his wounds, using the flow to make certain the bleeding had stopped.

"You are very fortunate Nehrutu taught me this skill," she said, noticing the empty wine bottles. "Wine thins the blood. You could have bled to death."

Lousis chuckled. "My time has not come just yet. I still have work ahead. I will see my city rebuilt and the war won. Only then will I allow myself the long sleep and join my forefathers."

"You need rest, Your Highness," said Eftichis. "At least for a short while. You cannot continue as you are."

Lousis wanted to protest, but his voice abandoned him. Slowly, he lowered his head and allowed Eftichis to lead him to a bedroll that had been prepared a few yards from the pavilion. All of a sudden he felt old and weak, power-less to keep his eyes from closing before his head had even touched the pillow.

Even so, sleep was briefly denied. For a short time, his mind would not release him from thoughts of the battle in front of his manor, nor of his holding the dying Lord Maynard in his arms.

"And there I have left my strength," he whispered. Seconds later, his breathing was steady as he entered a dreamless slumber.

The light of the dawn awoke him. His muscles still ached, and the wine had left his head pounding. In spite of all this, his mind was clear. He sat up and stretched.

"Good morning, Your Highness," It was Aaliyah. She and Nehrutu were standing a few feet away, together with Eftichis and Lord Amnadon.

Lousis struggled to his feet and looked up at the smoke still billowing from the smoldering buildings. "It is good to see you all. But you should have awakened me sooner."

"There was no need, Your Highness," said Amnadon. "Angrääl has been defeated and we have already begun putting out the flames. Nehrutu has set up a hospital just beyond the east gate and the wounded are being brought there."

"Where are Lord Chiron and Lady Bellisia?" he asked, half yawning.

"Resting," said Aaliyah. "I had to insist. They are not nearly as powerful as Nehrutu and I, and even we are very nearly drained to the point of collapse. There are many injuries. Far more than the few kin I have with me can treat in a single day."

Her words struck at Lousis's heart. "How many?"

Aaliyah sighed despondently. "Tens of thousands. Angrääl did not spare your people their wrath. They made no distinction between a soldier and a citizen."

"Also, we just received word from the south," said Amnadon. "The peninsula is theirs, as well as half of Tarvansia. It seems that King Victis has managed to stop their advance for the moment, but how much longer he can hold them is uncertain.

Lousis's anger began to rise. "How soon can we be ready to march?"

"We can be ready in two days if pressed," Nehrutu replied. "But I suggest you wait a few days to repair your defenses. The city is still vulnerable."

"You have three days," said Lousis. "Then we go to expel Angrääl from our lands once and for all." Suddenly, his limbs were revitalized and his fatigue was gone. "I want the commanders gathered in the council chambers an hour before sunset. And send word of our intent to Skalhalis."

All bowed in unison and watched as Lousis strode away. His tall frame looked regal and strong—his steps sure. Amnadon motioned for a few soldiers to follow, but they were very nearly forced to break into a run to keep up with their monarch.

The thought of King Victis fighting desperately to defend his people was steeling Lousis's resolve. He swore on everything he believed in that he would drive this scum into the sea and save the people of the Western Abyss.

Even if he were to die achieving it.

CHAPTER 20

With Shen standing silently at his side, Mohanisi looked at the distraught faces of the elders gathered inside the former home of Oliana. It had taken several weeks for all of them to arrive, and most looked distant and confused. The light of the lanterns made evident their pale, unhealthy complexions as if a foul disease had stolen their spirit.

"I know many of you are still uncertain as to why you are here," said Mohanisi in a clear, deep voice.

A thin elf woman stepped forward. "What is uncertain to me is how we are here. I have no memory of my journey—or of much else. It is as if my life has been ripped apart and cast into the wind. I can barely see the faces of my own children."

"The destruction of the Reborn King's evil has touched each of you differently," explained Mohanisi.

A short male wrapped in a thick fur blanket shook his head wildly. "I cannot accept what has happened. I saw my brother engulfed in darkness and my village tear itself apart."

"The object your brother carried was tainted by evil," explained Mohanisi. "And it would seem that all these objects were connected. When I destroyed the dagger possessed by

Oliana, this somehow destroyed every one of them. I am sorry. I did not know that would happen."

"And had you known?" asked another.

"It would have changed nothing," he admitted. "I did what needed to be done. And though you are in pain now, you are free. And in time, you will heal."

Shen touched his shoulder. "They are too wounded. They need more time."

"We have no time," he replied sharply. He turned to the gathering. "I know you are confused, but the enemy who trapped your spirits will not wait for you to regain your strength. He marches on your brethren in the south and seeks the destruction of our entire race."

A dark-haired elf man in gray robes spoke next. "I am Frenil, elder of the Lor Nabi tribe. I watched as my father died and my people went mad. In my grief, I swore revenge on whoever had brought this evil down upon us. But it is not the death of my father, or the pain of my people that drives me. It is that our will and spirits have been stolen and corrupted. We killed our brothers and sisters. We made war on our kin. For these sins, I cannot seek redemption."

He turned to meet Mohanisi's eyes. "When I received word that the same thing had happened throughout the Steppes, and that the elders were gathering here, I hoped to find a way to unburden the rage in my heart. I prayed to the Creator that I would learn what had happened to my people. You have given me what I sought."

Spinning around, he addressed the others. "I will fight, wounded or not. If I must, I will go alone, but this Reborn King will pay for what he has done."

Murmurs of agreement mixed with those of fear and doubt.

"You have told us that our kin have arrived from across the Western Abyss," Frenil continued, "and that they fight with our people in the south. Also, that it was their power..."

He turned again to Mohanisi. "Your power, which freed us. It can be no coincidence that our legends tell of our bygone kin returning to show us what we have lost." He paused and lowered his head. "For that reason alone, I would go to war."

"And what of the humans?" cried an angry voice.

Frenil's eyes scanned furiously for the source of the objection. "Our hatred of humans is what weakened us. Do you not see that? Our fear. Our clinging to old ways. It was what allowed the Reborn King to blind us in the first place." He pointed to Mohanisi. "If this noble elf who has saved the souls of everyone in this room, fights with humans—so shall I." With this final statement, it was as though he had expended his final bit of energy. With sagging shoulders, he returned to his seat.

Shen leaned over to whisper in Mohanisi's ear. "We should allow them time to discuss this alone."

Mohanisi nodded, then rose. "I leave in two days. You have until then to decide." He strode from the room, Shen at his heels.

The morning was frigid, though the wind was calm. The dim light of dawn revealed the depth of sorrow set upon the village by the curse. Elves wandered aimlessly with vacant expressions, occasionally stopping as their eyes grew full of tears. Some dropped to their knees and wept, while others cursed and spat angrily. But even this was an improvement over the insanity of the first few days. Some had torn out their eyes and slashed their own throats. Others had run into the sea and drowned. A few seekers such as Shen had managed to hold their minds together sufficiently to gather the children before any harm could come to them. Gradually though, the madness had subsided, to be replaced by utter despair.

"I will speak with the prisoner again while we await their answer," said Mohanisi.

Shen frowned. "He has not uttered a word since his capture, nor eaten a morsel. How he still lives…"

"His spirit remains possessed," said Mohanisi. "For whatever reason, the destruction of the dagger did nothing to help him."

"Why are you obsessed by this?" asked Shen.

"He was important to Theopolou," he replied earnestly. "He intended to save him. So if I can, I will."

Shen sighed. "I wish I had known Theopolou better. My mind was so clouded when last we met, I can scarcely recall the encounter."

Mohanisi smiled. "You should be proud. Even when possessed, you behaved with honor. You stood as his second and ensured your people's redemption."

"It is strange." Shen's voice was now a whisper. "I can recall days—weeks at a time. But then there are gaps. Time I have lost to oblivion. I remember you. I remember Theopolou's fight with Oliana. I can even remember wanting her to be defeated. But it is like remembering moments from my early childhood. The memories appear distant in my mind."

Mohanisi touched his shoulder fondly. "The poison lingers, and it will take time for it to completely drain away. But you are strong and of good heart. You will see it through."

They walked to the small building where he and Theopolou had been held when they first arrived. One of Shen's fellow seekers guarded the door.

"Has he eaten?" asked Shen.

The seeker shook his head. "Nor has he made a sound. If I could not see his breathing, I would think him dead."

"In a way, he is," remarked Mohanisi. "But I hope to restore him to the land of the living." Reaching to his belt, he removed a small flask. While he took a long drink, the scent of jawas tea filled the air. He could feel the fire running through his veins as the tea strengthened his power.

"How?" asked the seeker.

"By attempting the impossible," he replied.

He opened the door and light flooded the room. The glow orb had ceased to work, and the lanterns left inside to replace this lay shattered in the corner. In the center, a ragged figure was curled up on the floor. Mohanisi filled himself with the flow and shut the door behind him.

"Are you willing to talk?" he asked. There was no movement or response. "Malstisos. Speak to me."

Mohanisi reached out to touch his mind but was met by fierce resistance. He'd tried this several times before during the past week but had been unwilling to attempt to force his way through. But now he knew he must. He pressed in, breaking down the barriers and overwhelming his spirit.

"Enough," cried Malstisos, desperately clutching at his head. He rolled over and faced Mohanisi. His features were gaunt. His skin was pale and blotched. "What do you want of me?"

Mohanisi sighed. "I only want to save you."

Malstisos let out a disdainful laugh. "Save me? Perhaps you should save yourself."

Mohanisi shrugged. "Perhaps. But Theopolou held you in high regard, and I will do what I can."

"Theopolou was a fool," he replied.

"Theopolou was many things," said Mohanisi, steel in his tone. "But a fool was not among them."

Malstisos sneered. "And you are an even greater fool. You follow a false hope and a false god. You will bring doom to all who are willing to listen to your words." He sat up and brushed the dust from his shirt. "Your efforts to enter my mind will continue to fail, too."

"Perhaps," he replied thoughtfully. "But I have come to believe that you cannot be free of your curse unless I use more..." He paused. "More intense means."

Malstisos huffed. "You are powerless. Unless you intend to torture me. And even that will do you no good. I will not betray my master."

Mohanisi leaned forward. "I have no intention of torturing you. What I am about to attempt may very well kill us both. Only Darshan is powerful enough to draw from the spirit of the world, yet I must try."

The name Darshan caused Malstisos to wince, but he remained defiant. "Do what you will, fool."

Mohanisi drank what jawas tea remained in his flask, then sat down on the floor. Taking a deep breath, he closed his eyes. For several minutes, he was completely still as he searched for the flow of the spirit.

Eventually, he heard a soft hum. Distant at first, it grew closer and closer until it completely surrounded him. Then the hum changed to bells and laughter. The sounds were so small and delicate that at first, he thought he was imagining them. He reached out to touch them with his spirit, but they were elusive—just beyond his grasp. Summoning up all of his skill, he reached out again until the limit of his power stopped him short. The sounds were still soothing, but as unreachable as before.

Finally, he sighed in defeat and relaxed his mind. But to his amazement, this seemed to encourage the spirit to come closer. He reached for it, but it pulled away. Again and again, it danced around, just out of reach, as if taunting him. He recalled Aaliyah telling him of the time she had touched the spirit of the world. She told him it was tender and pure—that it wrapped around her like a mother's arms.

He opened his eyes and surrendered his will. At that moment, he felt it. The pure spirit of the world. It was as warm and joyous as an elf child's heart. Tiny lights twinkled and danced all around him like the reflection of the moon's glow on a calm sea.

He looked over to Malstisos. He was surrounded by a shadow of bile and corruption.

"I see your pain," whispered Mohanisi.

"Stay away!" screeched Malstisos. His eyes turned dark and menacing.

Mohanisi ignored his words and reached out with his spirit. The shadow of filth darkened and swirled as he came near. Then, just as he touched it, the world around him abruptly vanished. His vision blurred and his head began to swim.

When his eyes slowly regained focus, he could see that he was standing in the ruins of a ravaged city. But this was like no city he had ever seen before. The three-story buildings were made from pitted and worn black stone. Gruesome thorny vines snaked around the buildings in sinister patterns to form ancient elf letterings, each spelling out foul curses. The narrow streets were covered with dirt and ash and smelled of rotten flesh and putrid earth. Smoke rose from the rooftops, yet no flames could be seen.

"Is anyone here?" called Mohanisi.

His question was answered by a series of ghastly screams that echoed off the forbidding stone walls and then quickly faded.

He took a tentative step. The grit of the street crunched beneath his boot. Another scream pierced the air, and this time he could almost make out words within the agonized cry. He reached for his sword, but it was not there. He tried to draw power from inside himself and found nothing but a foul emptiness. It was then he realized that he was virtually defenseless. Fear began to grip his heart.

Steeling his nerves, he continued walking down the street, his eyes shooting back and forth from building to building. Shadowy figures appeared in windows but vanished before he could tell what they were.

"I am being hunted," he whispered. He stooped to pick up a jagged piece of rubble. "But I will not be easy prey."

Again he heard a scream, and this time the word "pain" could clearly be heard within the wretched cry. He tried to make out where the voice was coming from, but the echoes dulled his hearing. On and on he walked, the feeling of being stalked growing ever stronger. Each building looked more decrepit and broken than the last until after he had walked for about a mile, they were nothing more than massive mounds of shattered rock and dust.

A great wind rose up, stirring the ashen street and stinging his eyes. He gripped the rock tight. He knew it was only a matter of time before...

He stopped. "Where am I?" he muttered. "How did I get here?"

He felt a gentle tug on the left leg of his trousers. Jerking away, he raised the rock to strike. But there, shielding his eyes from the ash-filled wind was an elf child. Barely as tall as Mohanisi's waist, the boy was dressed in a gold silk robe. His long, silvery blond hair was blowing wildly. He looked up with frightened eyes that were on the verge of weeping. Slowly, Mohanisi lowered his rock and kneeled down.

"How did you get here?" he asked.

The child whimpered, then threw himself into Mohanisi's arms. "They are after me." His tiny voice trembled as he clutched at Mohanisi's shirt. "They want me dead."

He held the boy, trying to comfort him. "Who wants you dead?"

"I cannot say it," he cried. "Do not make me. If I say it, they will find me."

Mohanisi eased the boy back and held his gaze. "Where are we?"

He sniffed and sobbed. "Please help me. Do not leave me."

He brushed the ash from the child's face and smiled. "I will not leave you. But..." Just then, the bells and laughter returned, and he remembered. He eyed the boy suspiciously. "Who are you?" His voice was now harsh and commanding.

"I do not know," he admitted through his tears. "I do not know who I am. Please do not leave me."

Mohanisi thought for a moment. He looked around at the rubble of the ruined city. "This is not real. It cannot be." He focused on the child. "I will save you. But you must help me. You must guide us from this place."

"If I do," said the child timidly, "they will kill you too."

Mohanisi dropped the rock and reached confidently to his belt. He grunted with satisfaction as he felt the cold hilt of his sword back where it should be. "They will try."

"Arrogant elf!" came a shrill voice from behind a pile of stones to his right.

Mohanisi sprang up and freed his blade. The howl of the wind increased, swirling up ever more fiercely the ashes and dust that seemed intent on blinding him. A dark figure crawled out from the rubble on all fours. It moved like a great spider, nimble and deadly, with pale skin hanging loosely from a skeletal frame. Its only clothing was a black cloth tied at the waist and reaching down to bony knees. It held a long triangular dagger; the blade notched and rusted. With black eyes fixed on Mohanisi, the creature advanced. The moment it touched the road, it stood up straight, grinning maliciously with sharp, jagged teeth.

"Be gone, beast!" shouted Mohanisi.

It hissed and laughed, pointing to the child. "You think to save this creature? Malstisos belongs to us, and we will never release him."

"I do not need you to release him," he shot back. "I will take him, anyway."

It cocked its head and twirled the dagger in its hand. "Do you think you can? You have not the power. That you are even here at all has pushed you to your limits. Can you not feel that your strength is gone?"

Mohanisi felt his arms growing heavy for a moment, but he clenched his jaw and focused his mind. His strength quickly returned. "Your tricks will do you no good. I am taking him from this place."

The air suddenly went still and cold. The creature sprang forward, its knife slashing at Mohanisi's throat. He ducked and spun, bringing his blade across the creature's back, causing it to cry out in pain. It turned, its face ablaze with fury. Again, it charged, but Mohanisi easily moved aside and took off its arm with a quick strike. The limb flopped and twitched in the dust, still gripping the dagger.

"You think you have victory?" it scoffed. An instant later, it vanished from sight.

Mohanisi looked over at Malstisos. To his surprise, his child form had grown several inches taller and appeared older. Mohanisi took his hand and continued down the street.

"That was not all of them," said Malstisos. "They will not let me go."

"Do you know who you are?" he asked.

Malstisos looked up with a pitiful expression, tears welling in his eyes. "I..." He lowered his head and wept.

Mohanisi gave his shoulder a comforting squeeze. "All will be well. But I need you to be strong."

Malstisos sniffed and wiped his eyes on his sleeve. "I will try. I promise."

They had only continued for a few more yards when the buildings began to fade, to be replaced by a dead forest. The gnarled, withered trees were twisted and bent, and the black ground was covered by jagged rocks. Just ahead of them, a line of thin flames spewed up from the earth; some were only a few inches high, others shooting up several feet.

Mohanisi pulled Malstisos behind him and scanned the area for foes. Once again, he could feel eyes upon him. "Reveal yourself," he commanded.

All at once, the flames shot skyward and disappeared. A few yards ahead, there stood a snarling wolf. But this was no ordinary beast. At least twice as large as a normal wolf, its black fur bristled to reveal a row of vicious-looking spikes running all the way down its spine. Its eyes glowed green as it flashed razor-sharp teeth within its gaping maw.

"Leave the whelp," came a disembodied voice that seemed to echo from all directions. "Leave him and we will allow you to live."

Mohanisi glared at the wolf contemptuously. "You will release Malstisos from your foul grip. I do not fear you."

A malicious laugh carried on a sudden wind. Almost as if this was a signal to attack, the wolf raced forward, its jaws snapping and foaming. Mohanisi crouched and brought up his sword defensively. The wolf was fast—much faster than the first creature he had fought. He could hear Malstisos's panicked breaths behind him, and the deep growl of the wolf's anger. He expected it the leap for his throat, but instead it bit at his left leg and then rolled its back. Pain shot through him as the spikes tore into his flesh. He thrust his blade straight down, but the wolf twisted away and jumped clear.

"Now do you understand?" the voice taunted. "Do you see your death approaching?"

Blood seeped from the wounds left by the cruel spikes. Pushing the pain of these from his mind, Mohanisi braced himself for another attack. He didn't have to wait long. The wolf ran in, teeth bared, again going for his legs. This time, Mohanisi stepped in and slashed crossways. His blade cut through the wolf's right front leg, but the momentum of its massive body kept it hurtling forward. Savage teeth sank into Mohanisi's right thigh. The beast's jaws clamped down, and it shook its head violently, sending blood flying in all directions. Drawing in all of his remaining strength, Mohanisi thrust his sword clean through the wolf's neck. With the blade still protruding from the top of its spine, the beast reared up violently, tossing the elf high into the air. He landed on his side with a thud. After a breathless moment, he tried to scramble to his feet, but the injury to his leg was too severe and he was only able to kneel.

The wolf thrashed and rolled in horrifying death throes. Finally it went still, and like the creature before it, suddenly vanished from sight. Mohanisi heaved a sigh and then examined his wounds. Blood was gushing out, spilling onto the barren earth. He knew he couldn't continue for very long with such a bad injury. In a short time, his loss of blood would make him unable to fight.

He looked over to Malstisos. Again, he looked older; now like an elf in his mid-teens, at least. He tore a strip of cloth from his shirt and bound his wounds. "Help me up," he ordered.

Malstisos walked over to him with awkward, frightened steps. He grabbed Mohanisi's arm and helped him up. "How bad is it?"

Mohanisi shrugged. "If we were in the real world, I would not be worried. But here..." A thought struck him. "Perhaps you can heal me."

Malstisos shook his head. "I cannot. I do not know how."

The cloth around Mohanisi's wound was already soaked through and blood again trickling down his leg. He began to feel lightheaded and was struggling to keep his feet. "You must."

Flames exploded around them, threatening to burn them alive. Malstisos screamed and curled into a tight ball at Mohanisi's feet.

Mohanisi kneeled down, though the pain was taking him to the limits of his endurance. Seizing Malstisos's face in his hands, he forced the youngster to meet his eyes. "You must be strong. You must not allow fear to rule you."

The flames raged, and the heat intensified. Malstisos trembled and wept, but nonetheless got slowly to his knees.

He looked down at Mohanisi's wounds and placed his hand over the unbandaged leg where the spikes had struck. At first, nothing happened, then a soft glow began to shine from beneath his palms.

Mohanisi grunted and hissed. His leg felt as if it were being bathed in fire. He reached out and clutched at Malstisos's arm. Then, just when he was on the verge of crying out, the pain ceased. He gave a loud sigh of relief, but it was a brief respite. A moment later, Malstisos touched the other leg, and the agony returned. As it did, the flames around them grew even more intense. The ground began to shake, and a roar like the battle cry of a savage beast rumbled through the air.

Mohanisi pushed Malstisos away and leaped to his feet. When he glanced at his legs, he could see that his wounds were completely healed. Reaching down, he helped Malstisos up. But he was no longer a boy. He stood as an adult elf, powerful and proud.

"Healing you has healed me," said Malstisos. "You have banished my fear."

Mohanisi smiled while discarding the blood-soaked bandage. "I am pleased to see it, and grateful that you are as strong as Theopolou believed you to be. Come. I'm certain that there is more for us to face before this is over."

Malstisos gave a smile in return. "There is. But I must face it alone. The devilry that ensnared my spirit will not be so easily dispatched. I can feel it closing in even now, trying to recapture me." His face was stone. "But this time I will not be taken." A sword appeared at his side and the blade sang as he pulled it free. "Should I survive, I will thank you properly for your kindness. But should I awaken still possessed, I would ask you to end my life. For if I fail, there will be nothing of me left to salvage."

Mohanisi nodded. "I swear it."

"I can see your thoughts," said Malstisos. "I know who you are and from where you have come. I look forward to getting to know you and your kin." He gripped his sword tightly. "Until then, farewell."

As these words faded, the laughter and bells returned. The world around Mohanisi dimmed, then grew dark. He found himself once again on the floor of the small prison room in front of Malstisos's unconscious body. He shouted for the guard to bring lanterns and food.

Shen joined him. He looked down at Malstisos and could see his face twisted, as if in great pain. "What happened?" he asked.

Mohanisi recounted what he'd experienced. "Now all we can do is wait and hope."

"And if he is unchanged?"

Mohanisi lowered his eyes. "Then I will fulfill my promise."

It was nearly an hour later when Malstisos stirred and his eyes fluttered open. Propping himself up on his elbows, he looked at Mohanisi and Shen with a blank expression for what seemed like a very long time. Then, slowly, a smile crept up from the corners of his mouth. Though his skin was still pale, his eyes were bright and aware.

"I am hungry," he said.

Mohanisi handed him a piece of bread and a bottle of honeyed wine. "How do you feel?" he asked.

Malstisos forced a small laugh. "That depends. I am free from the curse, but my mind and spirit are worn and tired."

"Then it matches your appearance," remarked Shen jokingly.

Mohanisi could feel great relief, but was still cautious. "Are you certain you are free?"

Malstisos shrugged and tore off a piece of bread. "As certain as I can be. Only time will tell for sure."

"Then perhaps you can tell me how this happened," said Mohanisi.

Malstisos nodded, then took a sip of wine. He moaned with satisfaction. "To taste wine again..." He took another sip and closed his eyes, savoring the sweet liquid. "Food and drink were like ash. You cannot imagine." He sat the bottle down and told them of his journey with Maybell. His voice cracked when he spoke of the two brothers and their tragic duel. "My heart despaired and my thoughts became darker each day. Soon I began hearing whispers in my mind. They told me that my soul was doomed for what I had done. At first, I thought I was imagining it, but they grew louder and louder as more time passed.

"Then one night I heard something stirring near to where we had camped. Maybell was sleeping, so I went to see what it was. It did not sound like an animal, but neither did it sound like a man or an elf. I stalked it for an hour, but it was always just beyond my sight. Finally, I gave up and started back. That was when they attacked me. Three Vrykol came out of the shadows and knocked me to the ground. I was sure they would kill me, but they only held me down.

"I remember how furious I was with myself. I could not understand how they had managed to sneak up on me. I had encountered their kind before, and knew their scent. But these were different. Better, is the only way I can describe them. They wore the same black robes, but they smelled ... well ... it's hard to say. Not like a human, and certainly not like an elf. In fact, there was almost a complete absence of scent about them."

He shook his head and shuddered. "I thought to cry out to warn Maybell, but one of them put his hand over my mouth. Then I heard a low hum. It took me a moment to realize that it was coming from the Vrykol. The one holding my mouth leaned in close and let out a foul hiss. I struggled to free myself, but they were too strong. A few moments later, there was a bright flash and all three of them burst into blue flames. I scrambled to my feet and tried to run, but something was holding me. Some unseen force had gripped my mind."

He looked from Mohanisi to Shen. "That is the last thing I remember until you freed my spirit." A stricken look washed over his face. "Please tell me I did not harm Maybell."

"She is well," replied Mohanisi. "You delivered her safely to Althetas."

Malstisos sighed with relief. "Thank the Creator. I would have never forgiven myself had I done her harm." He rubbed the bridge of his nose. "Please excuse me, but I would like to rest for a while. If you will allow me just a few hours."

Mohanisi bowed. "Of course. I shall return tomorrow. If you feel the need to leave this room, a seeker will guide you."

"I thank you," he replied with a fragile smile.

Once outside, Mohanisi left the guard instructions to escort Malstisos everywhere he went should he desire to leave the building.

"Is he not cured?" asked Shen.

"Perhaps," replied Mohanisi. "But I cannot risk the possibility that he is deceiving us. And even if he is no longer possessed, he is badly wounded. I will not have him wander alone in his weakened condition."

They walked through the village to a small garden at the west end and sat on a wooden bench. The flowers were not in bloom, but the wilted petals that littered the ground still gave the air a hint of spring.

"What will you do with him?" asked Shen.

"I must take him with me," he replied. "I cannot leave him among your people, especially after the ordeal they have already been through."

"Is taking him with you not a risk?"

Mohanisi nodded slowly and smiled. "But I feel it is the right decision. I am responsible for him now. I feel a connection between us; that is how I know the extent of his wounds." He leaned back and breathed deeply. "I do not think he is false. At least, I do not think he believes himself to be. But our enemy is cunning. Once I reach Althetas, I will enlist the aid of my kin, and with their help, we can heal him further."

They sat in silence for several hours, just listening to the chirp of the crickets and looking up at the stars painted across a clear sky. Mohanisi filled himself with the flow, enabling him to experience every nuance of the village and the surrounding landscape.

"The elders have adjourned," he said. "I can hear them leaving the house."

"Can you tell what they have decided?" asked Shen.

Mohanisi chuckled. "I am afraid I cannot see into their minds, and they are not talking amongst themselves."

They left the garden and walked back to Oliana's former home, stopping on the way to see that Malstisos was still resting. Shen had already taken upon himself the duty of being Mohanisi's personal guard, so remained in the house with him overnight. After lying down, it took only a few minutes for Mohanisi to find himself in a deep slumber.

He awoke with the dawn and took a light breakfast before sending for the elders. Only Frenil showed up. His countenance was determined.

"The others have returned to their villages," he announced. "Some to gather their forces, others to defend their homes. I could not convince all to join you."

Mohanisi smiled and bowed. "That you tried is enough. And those who choose to fight are welcome. How long until they are prepared?"

"It will take at least three weeks to muster," he replied.

"How many will come?"

"Nearly thirty-thousand, I should guess."

Mohanisi nodded and stood. "Then I will leave at once and let the others know you are coming. They will be anxious for news by now."

"I will go with you," said Shen. "Frenil, make sure that those who choose to go south are as well prepared as possible. It may be some time before they see their homes again."

"I will see it done," said Frenil. He left without another word.

"I will gather our supplies and inform the other seekers of our departure," said Shen.

Once Shen had left, Mohanisi went to where Malstisos was still resting.

"Can you travel?" he asked.

Malstisos was sitting up and staring at the dim light of the lantern. He looked at Mohanisi and nodded. "I can. Though I have yet to recover my full strength, I will be able to keep pace."

"Good," said Mohanisi, opening the door. "Then prepare yourself. Very soon we will make our foes pay for what they have done to you."

CHAPTER 21

Maybell had finally come to terms with what had happened to Malstisos, though his plight did still enter her dreams from time to time. She kneeled beside her bed in silent prayer, just as she did every night before sleeping. More and more, though, she was finding it to be an empty ritual.

She prayed earnestly for an end to the war, and for the people who suffered its ravages. But she knew there could be no answer. The gods were trapped, and she was alone. Even the many duties High Lady Selena had given her to do could not make her forget that fact. A lifetime of faith—faith in beings that were themselves flawed and weak—had been turned upside down.

Even though life in Valshara was fulfilling in its own way, each day her desire to leave became a little stronger. But there was nowhere for her to go. Her years had been spent within the confines of the temples. She had nothing else. If she left Valshara, she would be homeless. But worse than that, she would be completely alone. At least here she had others to tend to and duties to perform.

But each night her heart was heavy. She had once thought that to acquire knowledge was a gift. She never imagined that too much knowledge could be a curse. Once, the origin of humankind had been a mystery, whereas now it was a known history. The place the gods held in the world was thought to be certain and definable, but now a different picture lay before her. Even the mystery of the elves had been solved. She wondered if they knew that it pained her as much as it did them when they tried to ask her for advice and understanding. That she had traveled with Gewey, who many now called Darshan, made them believe she could help. They were wrong.

She finished her prayers half-heartedly and climbed into bed. Just as her eyes closed, there was a light rap at the door. Maybell sighed irritably, got out of bed, donned her robe, and turned up the lantern.

"Come in," she called, trying to keep her voice pleasant.

The door opened and High Lady Selena entered. Maybell curtsied in her usual formal manner and offered her a seat. Her room was far more luxurious than what she was accustomed to, boasting a small mahogany dining table, a hearth, and four soft chairs. There was even a large bookcase stocked with dozens of historical tomes. It was a palace when compared with typical temple quarters.

"How are you faring?" asked Selena. A slight twitch on her smiling face betrayed her deep concern.

"I am well," she lied.

Selena took notice of her attire. "I'm sorry to disturb you at such an hour, but this cannot wait." She reached inside her robes and pulled out a small piece of parchment. "This was delivered to me this morning. I thought it was meant for my eyes, but it was not. It is for you."

Maybell took the parchment and read it carefully. Her stomach knotted as the meaning became clear. "I understand. I will leave at once."

"I truly am sorry," said Selena.

Maybell's apprehension slowly turned to relief, and a tender smile grew from the corners of her mouth. "There is no need. I have been distraught. Now my life may have meaning."

"I will send knights..." Selena began, but Maybell's eyes halted her words.

"I go to meet my destiny alone," Maybell said. "And I will meet it gladly."

Selena nodded and sat in silence for a few minutes. She then rose and bowed low. "I will pray for your safe return."

"Thank you, High Lady Selena," said Maybell. "For everything."

After Selena left, Maybell began gathering her few belongings, the last of which was her priestess robe. As she held it up in front of her, a single tear fell. Brushing the moisture from her cheek, she folded the garment neatly and laid it on the bed.

After opening the door to leave, she took one final sad look back to where it lay. Then, clutching the parchment, she steeled her wits and moved on.

CHAPTER 22

Gewey and Kaylia sat on Felsafell's porch listening to the song of the few birds that populated the hills in winter. The snow surrounding them was unblemished. Icicles hung like crystal prisms, catching the light of the morning sun and bathing the ground in color.

Neither of them was anxious to depart. The road ahead held many perils, and the here and now was like a sanctuary of peace. The Vrykol that lurked in the woods would not dare approach, and Gewey guessed that any soldiers would only be able to find the house if Felsafell allowed it.

Even after having read the Book of Souls, the old hermit was still a mystery to Gewey. Every time he thought about the vastness of Felsafell's life, his mind boggled. The knowledge he possessed must be beyond measure. And yet, at times, he seemed as innocent as a child.

The door flew open and Felsafell came bounding out. "Are you ready?" He carried their packs in his arms and tossed them over as Gewey and Kaylia got to their feet. The scent of bread and honey reached their noses, promising at least one decent meal during the long journey back to Althetas.

"You aren't bringing anything?" asked Gewey.

"My path differs from yours," he replied. "Again, I must seek my own answers."

Gewey's heart sank. "Where will you go?"

"To clear the way, oh yes." His eyes sparkled and his voice was a song. "But again we will meet. I think it will be so. Destiny has a role yet for us both."

A musical laugh echoed off the trees. They turned to see the Oracle of Manisalia walking gracefully through the snow, her bare feet barely leaving an imprint. "Your destiny?" Her tone was teasing, yet kind. "Old hermit. Your destiny is the most clouded of all. When even the mountains call you father, your past always overshadows your future."

"What are you doing here?" snapped Felsafell.

Gewey and Kaylia were startled by his harsh tone and sudden anger.

But the Oracle took no notice. She stepped onto the porch. "I did what I must."

Felsafell's expression softened. "But they will see you. They will know where you are."

She touched Felsafell's cheek. "That they will, my love. But it could not be helped." She turned to Gewey and Kaylia. "Fresh word has come to me. You must not go to Althetas. If you do, all will be lost."

"Then where should we go?" asked Gewey.

"Your enemy has begun his assault on the west," she explained. "And soon the west will fall unless help arrives quickly. Your friends have joined with the elves of the desert and hurry to their aid, but they will not make it in time. Not unless you are there with them."

"Where are they now?" asked Gewey.

"I only know they march west," she replied. "But I suspect an army of elves will not be difficult to find."

"How is it that you know this?" asked Kaylia. The idea of meeting the desert elves excited her. "I thought your abilities were limited now that the gods are trapped."

"The shadow of Ayliazarah still retains certain powers," said the Oracle. "And clearly she wanted me out of my sanctuary. Otherwise, I would have had this knowledge to pass on to you when first we met." She let out a cheerful laugh. "So now my destiny is a mystery as well. Perhaps my end has come at last. The Vrykol will brave anything to capture me. Even the house of Felsafell."

Felsafell took hold of her hands. "I will protect you."

Gewey and Kaylia stared at him in wonder. The hermit was transformed. No longer was Felsafell a bent old man with a scraggly beard and crooked teeth. He was tall, at least a foot taller than Gewey, with a slim yet muscular frame. His flawless ebony skin accentuated his piercing gray eyes. His ears were twice as long as an elf's, swooping up to a slender point, and his hair was like polished silver shining in the morning sun as it fell to his waist. The familiar animal skin clothing was now a purple and gold robe made from the finest satin. Embroidered on this with gleaming silver threads were a series of undulating and intricate circular patterns.

"They will not touch you, my darling," said Felsafell, looking into her eyes with intense affection. His voice had become a deep and powerful baritone.

"Then I will never again leave your side," she replied. "We will meet our fate as immortal fools, then return to the Creator's loving embrace together."

He leaned down and kissed her lips, lingering for several long moments before releasing her hands.

And then it was over. Once again, the old Felsafell they knew stood before them. Gewey could only stand there, mouth agape. The Oracle giggled like a young girl. "My love is handsome, is he not?"

"How did you do that?" asked Kaylia, her eyes fixed on Felsafell.

"I showed you his true self," she replied. "Did you truly think the eldest so bent and frail as he appears to you now?"

"I thought your kind were unable to use the flow," said Gewey. "How is it you changed your appearance?"

Felsafell shrugged awkwardly. "I need not the flow to affect my body. I appear as I choose without glamour and illusion."

"But why ... this?" asked Gewey.

Felsafell grinned. "Easier to pass through the world unseen and misunderstood. The world could not fathom me. Nor have they ever seen my kind in true form. Trouble enough between elf and man without me stirring the pot."

"But even your manner of speech was different," said Gewey. "In this form, you speak in riddles."

"In this form, I speak your language," he said. "You heard my true tongue uttering from my lips. Not this harsh tangle of misunderstandings."

"You understood because it is your native language as well," explained the Oracle. "And Kaylia because of your bond."

Gewey shook his head, laughing at the thought of what people saw when looking at Felsafell. If they only knew what lay behind his comical form.

A loud screech tore through the air, snapping him to attention.

"They come for me," said the Oracle. "They will not wait for you to leave."

"Then go inside," said Felsafell. "And let them come to their doom."

The Oracle kissed him on the cheek and obeyed.

Felsafell turned to Kaylia. "Follow her and guard my treasure. Should they pass, only you can save her."

Kaylia hesitated, then nodded in compliance. "And you guard mine."

Gewey drew his sword and allowed the flow to enter. "You have no weapon."

Felsafell's eyes were dark and menacing. "A weapon I do not need. The enemy has good reason to fear this place."

They took a few steps in front of the house and waited. Gewey could feel the Vrykol approaching.

"There are more than twenty," he said. "Maybe you should..." But Felsafell had vanished without a sound, leaving no footprint behind.

A few seconds later, Gewey spotted dark figures with blades in hand darting back and forth between the trees. There were enough to hinder his abilities, but he had no intention of using fire to destroy his enemy, nor earth to slow them. The playful sound of the spirit surrounded him and the wisps of light danced and swirled. Reaching out, he touched the corrupted spirit of the nearest Vrykol. It recoiled, and he could feel sudden resistance. Gewey smiled inwardly as he reached in and ripped the tainted soul from its body. Its piercing shriek cut through the woods, tearing at Gewey's ears as the body crumbled to black dust. The other Vrykol paused, and Gewey could feel their fear. He laughed out loud.

"I thought the Vrykol did not feel fear," he challenged. "Come. Today is your last."

Infuriated by his mocking, they charged as one. But when they were about fifty yards away, Gewey saw a gray form fall from the treetops and land on the shoulders of the leading Vrykol. It was Felsafell. In a single swift motion, he tore the head from the beast and then sprang atop another, gliding as if weightless. In just a few seconds, six Vrykol had fallen.

Gewey destroyed three more, but the rest were on him in moments. His sword came to life in his hands. With two strokes, he sent heads rolling on the ground. Cruel blades sliced at his neck as he stepped back and spun around. But by now the Vrykol had closed in. The tip of a jagged sword sliced through his left arm. Ignoring the pain, he ran another through and jerked up, splitting the beast in half. Another Vrykol strike found the back of his right shoulder, this time deep enough to scrape bone. Gewey cried out. Knowing that another blow would quickly follow, he leaned forward to lessen its cut.

But no blow came.

When he turned around, he saw Felsafell standing in the midst of the remaining Vrykol, their headless bodies scattered all around him.

"Not fast enough to save you pain, I'm afraid," said Felsafell, seemingly calm. "But healing is near, as well as a moment more of peace."

The pain from his wounds was burning fiercely as Gewey stepped over the bodies and entered the house. The two women were sitting by the fire, Kaylia with her long knife resting across her lap. She sprang up and was across the room to him before he had barely crossed the threshold. Taking off his ruined shirt, he cleaned his sword while she examined his injuries.

Felsafell joined the Oracle and sat beside her. They spoke in hushed whispers as Kaylia used the flow in the way Nehrutu and Aaliyah had taught her to heal Gewey's wounds.

"Another night you should spend," said Felsafell. "Recover your strength and eat hearty tonight."

Gewey put on another shirt. "I suppose that would depend on what the Oracle has to say."

She smiled and took Felsafell's hand. "One night will force you to press your pace. But the reward is worth the risk. And I am no longer the Oracle. Once, long ago, I was called Basanti. I think it is time I was called that again."

Gewey smiled and bowed. "As you wish, Basanti."

Felsafell left for a time, returning with a wild turkey and herbs. By nightfall, the wine was flowing, and the meal was prepared. Soon, they were all sitting around the table with spirits lifted. For one evening at least, their troubles were forgotten.

"If it is not too personal," said Kaylia to Basanti. "Were you ever human?"

"I was indeed," she replied. "When humans left the sands in the east, I was among the first of the children born unto them. And until the gods asked me to serve, I lived on a small farm with my parents and brothers."

"Why did the gods change you?" asked Gewey.

"The goddess Pósix came to me one spring afternoon." Basanti's eyes were far away, and a tiny smile crept upon her rosy lips. "She was so beautiful, I thought I had wandered into a dream. I was picking herbs in the forest near to our house when the figure of a young woman appeared. But of course, this was no ordinary woman. I can't describe how it felt." She looked to Gewey and Kaylia. "Can you recall how you felt when you met the essence of Ayliazarah?"

"It was like love and passion were things I could hold in my hands," answered Kaylia. "It was almost too much to bear."

"Then imagine the goddess of the dawn and light," she said. "The real goddess. Standing before you. She looked at me and smiled." Basanti laughed softly. "I actually fell to my knees and wept, overcome with joy. I knew at once who she was, but couldn't imagine why she was there.

"She took my hand, dried my tears, and asked me if I loved my family. Her voice was enough to make me weep again, but I told her that, of course, I did. Then she asked if I would be willing to sacrifice everything to serve them— to keep them safe from harm. I didn't understand what she meant, but naturally, I said yes, anyway.

"It was then I felt my spirit leaving my body. The earth was the same, but above me was a light so bright and pure that it made my heart swell. It took me a minute to under- stand what had happened, and when I did, I was terrified. I thought this meant I was dead. But Pósix rose from the earth and took my face in her hands. She explained that I would only die if I chose to, but first, she had something to show me.

"Needless to say, I was unable to refuse, so I let her lift me up until we had passed through the light. And that is when I saw them ... the gates of heaven."

Kaylia gasped. "You saw them with your own eyes? How is such a thing possible?"

"How is Darshan walking among us?" she replied simply. "To me, that is just as wondrous. I did, in fact, see them, but they are not as you might think. The gates of heaven are not actual gates. At least, not in the way a mortal might imagine them. It was more like a great tempest of light and color, infinitely large and impossibly deep. I had thought the beauty of Pósix was beyond anything I could ever fathom, but she was plain and ordinary by comparison. It was as if I were seeing the heart of creation in all its majesty. I could neither move nor speak. I longed to touch it and pass inside, but she held me fast. She told me that, if I chose to, I could be one of its guardians. Beyond lived the souls of all human-kind, but to reach this place, they needed help and guidance. I was to be given the gift of prophecy to shepherd them along the right path.

"The gate grew distant, and I wailed and cried to see it one last time. But in an instant, I was back inside my own body. I screamed and sobbed at the loss of such untempered grace. Pósix sat beside me, stroking my hair and singing softly in my ear until I regained my wits."

A single tear fell down Basanti's cheek. "She asked me again if I would serve her. Instantly, I said yes. That was when I died. At least ... when my mortal self died."

"That is when she made you a Vrykol?" asked Gewey.

Basanti shot him an angry glance. "Please do not call me that. The stories of the Vrykol were an invention of the elves. They feared us and sought to destroy us. And for the most part, they succeeded."

"I am sorry," said Kaylia. "I regret that my people have wronged you."

She gave Kaylia a forgiving smile. "Thank you, my dear. But that was long ago, and I do not hold you or your kin accountable."

"Did it hurt?" asked Gewey. "You know—when she killed you."

She cocked her head. "It was strange, to say the least. But I would not say it hurt. Pósix changed my spirit and wove it back into my body. From that moment to this, I have been unchanging, immortal ... and alone."

"Alone no longer," Felsafell objected. "The old hermit do you have as your servant."

She leaned over and rested her head on his shoulder. "And for that, I am grateful." She took a sip of wine.

Felsafell tenderly stroked her hair. "But the time for tales has come and gone," he said. "The time for sleep is now. The morning comes quick, and I would walk with my lady under the stars." He pushed back his chair and led Basanti to the door.

Gewey and Kaylia prepared a bedroll in front of the fire. They sat there quietly, watching the flames dance and pop.

"The wonders of this world seem never-ending," remarked Kaylia after a spell of comfortable silence.

Gewey nodded, then gently placed his hand on Kaylia's belly. "And there are more to come. Of that I am certain."

CHAPTER 23

The next morning Gewey awoke to find Felsafell and Basanti gone. A folded note had been placed beside his bedroll.

Kaylia was still sleeping, a wry grin on her face. He was tempted to touch her mind to see what she was dreaming of, but the light shining in through the window told him that they needed to depart. Unfolding the note, he held it near to the dying fire.

Darshan,

Your path is clear and we wish you speed on your journey. We would have stayed to see you and Kaylia off, but Felsafell did not want to draw more Vrykol down on you, and my presence would certainly have done that. Felsafell and I must flee in order to avoid the agents of the betrayer, so we may not see you again until this horrible conflict is done. I wish I had more wisdom to give you other than this—stay close to those who love you. I intend to do the same. I do

hope we will meet again before our time is at an end,
but if we do not, know that all our hopes are with you.
Your heart is indeed true, and that is a weapon your
enemy will never possess.

With sincere wishes,
Basanti
PS. Felsafell reminds you of the key he once gave
you and hopes that you have not lost it.

Gewey refolded the paper and reached into his pouch. There he found the tiny silver key Felsafell had given to him when they were standing outside the Chamber of the Maker. After nearly leaving it behind on several occasions, he was now very glad that he had not.

As Kaylia began to stir, he noticed their packs beside the front door, as well as two plates of bacon and bread on the table.

"Good morning," she said, stretching her arms wide.

Gewey showed her the letter. "I still have the key, though I have no idea what it's for."

Kaylia shrugged. "I am sure you will figure it out when the time comes."

They ate their breakfast and left the house. A light snow was now falling, but the wind was still. Gewey reached out with the flow to see if foes were about. Unable to detect any, he sighed with relief.

"What route shall we take?" asked Kaylia.

"There is a town two days' walk away once we reach the Old Santismal Road. I have enough coin with me to purchase horses. From there, we should head due east and cross the Goodbranch just south of Helenia."

"We could run faster than horses can carry us," objected Kaylia.

Gewey scowled. "As you also carry our child, I would prefer you ride."

Kaylia glared daggers at him, sending waves of anger through their bond. "You apparently know nothing of elf women. When we are with child, our strength and endurance double. I would be able to run until the day I give birth if I desired."

Gewey searched for a suitable response, but none came quickly to mind. Sighing, he shook his head. "Then I have no choice, do I?"

"Finally, a sign of intelligence," said Kaylia. Her anger lessened as she took his hand. "I swear to you that I will do nothing to harm myself or our child. But you must remember that your experience, if you have any at all, is with human women. An elf is very different."

"I believe you," said Gewey. "And I trust you. However, I still think it would be better to ride until we reach the other side of the Goodbranch, if for no other reason than we will attract less attention. From there on, if you wish to run, I will not object."

Kaylia pursed her lips, but finally nodded her agreement.

They began by heading east through the thinnest part of the forest, then, after finding a lightly worn trail, switched south. At first, they walked, but after an hour, Kaylia glanced across at Gewey, a mischievous grin on her face. Before he knew it, she was speeding away from him at a dead run. He could feel the flow racing through her. And even though he was using it too, it still took him more than two minutes to close the gap between them. But her game was not over yet. The moment he drew within touching distance, she let out a loud laugh and ran even faster. He could feel the adrenaline coursing through her and couldn't help but join in with her laughter. The forest whizzed by for more than three hours until they eventually reached the road.

"Feel better?" asked Gewey playfully.

"I do," she replied. "But you look out of breath."

They both laughed some more and held each other for a short while before moving on. The road was quite busy, considering the season. They passed several traders and craftsmen along the way but were thankful to see no soldiers about.

The first night, they made camp in a small forest clearing just away from the road. Gewey quickly set about drying the ground and building a small fire. Felsafell had packed them enough dried fruit and jerky to last at least a week, and as they huddled together, the wine warmed their bellies.

Knowing that each step took them closer to their enemy, Gewey was unable to sleep. Though he had no doubt that they could deal with a few troops, he didn't relish the idea of traveling through the heart of enemy territory with an entire army on the lookout for them. By now, Kaylia had donned her headscarf and was also wearing her hood.

They reckoned to reach the village of Charo by the next afternoon, and from there onward, Gewey felt he could be a bit more at ease. Two people on horseback would attract far less attention than two fools tramping through the snow.

"You know there are ruins to the south," said Kaylia. "And hidden roads that lead far enough east to conceal us for many miles."

"Are you suggesting we bypass Charo?" he asked.

"Perhaps," she replied sleepily. "The roads are too rough and weathered for horseback. They were used long ago by Felsafell's people, I would imagine. Humans fear the spirits that are said to dwell there, and the elves only use it as a respite when traveling. Angrääl soldiers certainly would not be there."

"The Vrykol might," countered Gewey.

"Yes," agreed Kaylia. "But they could be anywhere. Even along this road. At least there we would not attract notice if we had to fight."

"Your mind is set on this, isn't it?" he said, sighing.

Kaylia didn't respond, and soon her breathing was slow and even. Gewey kept watch until dawn, all the while listening to the sounds of the forest.

Kaylia woke, looking invigorated. "So the ruins it is?"

Gewey chuckled. "As you wish, my love."

The forest south of the Old Santismal Road was considerably less dense than the woods of the Spirit Hills. Kaylia had said that they could easily reach the ruins by mid-afternoon and that the road east would leave them six days from Helenia.

They wound through the woods at a quick jog. After a few hours, Gewey began to notice pieces of broken granite from long-forgotten buildings protruding from the earth. It was just past noon when they came upon a large clearing. In the center stood a ring of white marble columns, each one twenty feet tall. Within the ring was a smooth black tile floor that gleamed and shone as if time and weather had never touched it.

"I wonder what this was?" mused Gewey. The hairs on his neck stood up as he felt the presence of eight elves approaching from the south. He reached for his blade, but Kaylia grabbed his arm.

"They are from the Steppes," she said. "I do not think they mean us harm."

As she spoke, he remembered the healer who had told Kaylia of her pregnancy. She had mentioned then that they were in search of the ruins. He looked at Kaylia with irritation. "You knew they would be here, didn't you?"

"I thought they might be," she admitted. "Wait here. I will speak with them alone." She walked toward the columns.

When she reached them, a single elf appeared from the tree line and joined her. Gewey could feel that she was relaxed and sure of herself as she spoke, though he chose not to listen in on the conversation, focusing instead on the other elves, who were waiting just out of sight.

After a short talk, Kaylia returned. "They have warned us to stay clear of the ruins. They have seen Vrykol in the area and fear attack. Only a few elves still remain. The rest have continued east."

"What about those?" said Gewey, nodding his head south. "Why are they still here?"

"They have decided to return to the west and seek refuge among my kin." Her voice was compassionate and sad. "They are a lost people with nowhere to call home. If we had come a day later, they too would have been gone."

"Then I think we should heed their advice and avoid the ruins," said Gewey. He stretched his senses to their limits. No Vrykol.

"We can still use the road," said Kaylia.

"Then you will get your wish," said Gewey. "We will run."

"Follow me," she responded, flashing a smile. "I know the way."

For two more hours, they raced through the forest until reaching the ancient road. Grass and weeds sprang forth through the cobbled stones, and small chunks of rock were scattered all along their path. In spite of there being snow covering the landscape on either side, only a few small patches of white had settled on the relatively flat and even surface of the road itself. Without hesitation, they turned east, their power and skill enabling them to navigate the minor obstacles caused by eons of neglect. As they ran, Gewey actually began regretting that they would not get to see the ruins.

They stopped to eat just past midday. Kaylia's speed and endurance had left him amazed.

"You were certainly right about elf women," he remarked while munching on a strip of jerky. "I've never seen you run so fast for so long."

Kaylia grinned and tossed him a flask of water. "There is still much for you to learn if you are to be a good unorem. And I know you wanted to see the ruins, so you will be happy when I tell you there are others farther along this road, though they are not quite as grand. We should reach them by nightfall."

Gewey couldn't help but feel excited. "I wonder if it really was Felsafell's folk who built them."

"If we see him again, we will ask."

They continued on for a few more hours, Kaylia growing stronger with each step. Then, just as the sun was dipping below the tree line, almost in unison, their faces twisted in disgust. The foul presence of Vrykol was close. Skidding to a halt, they ducked into the nearby brush and drew their weapons.

"There are hundreds," whispered Gewey. He could virtually see them—a mass of Vrykol, twisting and writhing like a pit of vipers. He concentrated even harder. There were also humans among their number, but not soldiers. He could feel their fear and despair. After a time, he decided to risk touching one of their minds.

"Slaves," he said after a moment. "The Vrykol have human slaves." His fury began to rise and boil, but one look at Kaylia calmed him. "We should go around."

"I think we should see why they gather in such great number," countered Kaylia. "And why the Vrykol need slaves."

"We can't risk it," argued Gewey. "There are too many."

"Risk what?" she argued. "If we are seen, there is no way they could catch us. Besides, we will not be seen."

Gewey clenched his jaw but could feel her determination. "Then we wait for nightfall and run at the first sign of trouble."

"Agreed," she replied.

They waited in the brush until just past midnight. The Vrykol were about a mile ahead, and despite their vast number, appeared to be contained in a very small area. Gewey touched the minds of the slaves several times but could gather little more than their sheer terror. Some were so broken that their inner voices were nothing more than a constant scream.

They checked their weapons before creeping forward through the shadows. Gewey was reminded of when they first met, and how she had trained him to become one with the darkness. Now she followed him, his powers far beyond any seeker alive.

It took about twenty minutes to move close enough to see where the Vrykol were located. The sight startled them. The ancient ruins had been swept aside, and in their place stood a great citadel of gray and black granite.

The curtain walls were twenty feet tall, spanned two hundred feet in each direction, and were topped with razor-sharp iron spikes. The guard towers located at each corner rose a further ten feet and bore dozens of small rectangular windows. Rising up from within the fortress, a single spire towered above all else, with only a catwalk and a single window showing at its very top. The gates were flung wide open, and the vicious points of the raised portcullis peaked down from inside the archway. Not a single light shone anywhere.

The foul stench of death and decay filled Gewey's nostrils. Dozens of black figures stood motionless about the outer yard, mostly near the gate, but he could feel many more were inside.

The search for the human captives didn't take him long. Thirty yards from the north wall stood a massive steel cage where at least fifty men and women were being held. They appeared to be unguarded. For a full hour, he and Kaylia watched, seeing only the occasional Vrykol moving about. Otherwise, the citadel was still and quiet. Slowly, they backed away and retreated far enough not to be heard.

Gewey could feel what Kaylia was thinking before she spoke and quickly cut her off.

"We are going around," he said, using his most commanding voice.

"And you will leave those people here to suffer and die?" she asked, appalled.

"There are too many," he said. "There is no way to free them without being discovered, and I cannot fight so many Vrykol."

"The humans are unguarded," she countered. "We can release them and get away without making a sound."

"Then they will hear the prisoners escaping," he shot back. "We can move silently. They cannot."

"If that happens, we can hold off the Vrykol long enough to let them get away." Her voice was hard and unwavering. But Gewey would not be swayed. She moved in close and held his gaze.

"Why do you want to risk everything for this?" he asked, his frustration growing.

Her face softened. "Because once, not so long ago, a young farm boy did the same for me when I was held captive by bandits. At the time, I thought he was a fool. But now I understand why he did it. We are fighting to free the world from this kind of evil. How can we claim to be on the side of good when we are afraid to take action in the name of that good?" She touched his cheek. "I will not leave the innocent to die. The person I was who could do that was changed by you."

Gewey sighed, exasperated to the point of surrender. "Very well, we will try. But only on two conditions. If the alarm is raised, you must swear to run—regardless of the slaves' fate. Also, you must let me free them alone. I want you far enough away to escape." He reached down to touch her belly as a reminder of what they were protecting.

Kaylia started to object but could see that it was the only way he would agree. She smiled lovingly. "I swear it."

"Now I know what Lee must have felt like back then," he told her, grinning.

They crept silently around the citadel until they were directly behind the cage. Gewey was grateful that there was still no sign of movement from the Vrykol. The top of the wall and the windows of the towers were all empty. Clearly, they didn't deem it necessary to keep a vigilant watch. But then, who would approach this place? There was no city nearby that could challenge them, even if their presence was known. Their overconfidence would be Gewey's greatest ally.

The cage was about thirty yards from the tree line. Motioning for Kaylia to wait where she was, Gewey inched his way forward. The nearest Vrykol was just beneath the west tower, the rest scattered beyond. After each step, he scanned for signs that he had been seen, but the cloaked figures remained still.

He was only a few feet away from the cage when he felt Kaylia's sudden alarm and fear. Spinning around, he saw a Vrykol holding her from behind. It was pressing a dagger to her throat.

He was back to the tree line in seconds, sword drawn and with the flow raging through him. To his rear, he could hear many others moving in his direction.

"Be still, whelp," ordered the Vrykol. "Or I will slit her throat."

Kaylia's eyes were defiant, but he could feel her terror growing.

"Release her or I will destroy you," roared Gewey.

The Vrykol laughed harshly. "You arrogant fool. You thought your power could hide you from us? Now you have delivered both yourself and your elf mate into our hands. The master will be very pleased. He has sought you for some time."

Twenty Vrykol were just behind him and more were on their way.

"Drop your blade," the creature ordered. "Give yourself to us and she will live. Do it not..." He pressed the blade against Kaylia's flesh, drawing a thin trickle of blood.

Gewey's rage was uncontrollable. "Free her now," he thundered.

Barely were these words out of his mouth when the power within him exploded with a force far beyond anything he had ever known before. The world around him slowed right down. He could feel his body actually rising up from the earth. Now he could see deep into the heart of the Vrykol's corrupt spirit, and it served to fuel his rage to even greater heights. But it was not only the Vrykol holding Kaylia that he saw. He could see them all. And his hatred for these foul creatures erupted.

He no longer feared for the safety of his wife and child. Fear was something he could no longer understand. His name—his true name—echoed over and over in his mind. He was Darshan, and he would make them pay for their existence. All of them.

He could see the look of horror on Kaylia's face and feel her desperation through their bond. The laughter of the flow of the spirit was now a cacophony of woeful cries. The blade on Kaylia's throat began to move just a fraction. But in the slowed-down world below him, he had all the time in the world to act. Long before the blade could sink deep, he ripped the Vrykol's spirit from its body. It writhed and squirmed in the air above him, and Gewey laughed with delight as he crushed it to nothingness.

The other creatures behind him were charging in, but his power made them seem like fumbling children. Without even looking back, he reached into all of them; the flow spreading like fingers on a gruesome hand, each one piercing a Vrykol and annihilating its spirit.

He turned, and with righteous fury, shouted, "I am Darshan!"

Those he had not destroyed immediately turned and fled. He could sense everything within the citadel. Hundreds of Vrykol were streaming out, hearing the dying cries of their brothers and realizing the doom that was upon them.

But Darshan would not allow them to escape. The flow shot forth like a bolt of lightning, striking at the Vrykol and sending them into oblivion. The power was no longer within him. It was him. He could see the caged humans cowering and felt disgusted by their weakness. He was tempted to reach into them to make them see, but some small part of his mind resisted.

Many of the Vrykol had fled to the forest, but Darshan had no intention of allowing them to escape. His wrath was absolute and unbending. His gaze fell upon their wretched fortress, and he knew it was built from the labor of human slaves.

"This must fall!" His voice boomed, shaking the very foundations of the earth.

The west wall exploded, sending huge chunks of stone flying in every direction.

Come back to me. A tiny voice in the corner of his mind was calling to him. Please, my love. Come back to me.

He realized it was Kaylia. She was standing behind him, calling out through their bond. She wanted him to surrender the power. She wanted him to be human. But he was not human. Not any longer.

Come back to me. Her love for him stabbed at his heart and flowed freely into his spirit. Come back to our child.

He felt the ground touch his feet and the power inside him waning. Visions of Kaylia weeping as he was forced to abandon them flashed through his mind. He was dangerous—far too dangerous and powerful to remain in such a fragile world. If he stayed, he would be no better than the Dark Knight. The human side of him would be gone forever and a vengeful god all that remained.

"This need not be," cried out Kaylia. "Come back to me."

He looked into her eyes. Her fear had now been replaced with terrible sorrow. This is what she had seen in her vision when visiting the Oracle. He would be dragged from this world ... and she would be glad. His heart ached at the thought. Yet, no matter how deep and painful the ache was now, he knew this would be nothing compared to the pain he would suffer for eternity should he ever allow this vision to become a reality.

Slowly, the flow of the spirit dissipated completely. "I'm sorry," he whispered. "I'll never let that come true."

He could feel the relief flooding through Kaylia as she touched his cheek and kissed him lightly. "I know. I will never allow it either."

He took her in his arms and held her tight. The Vrykol were all but forgotten. Only the persistent sobbing of the slaves snapped him back to reality. He released Kaylia and walked to the cage. They pressed themselves into the far corner as he drew near, terror-stricken.

"Please," said Gewey, holding up his hand. "There is nothing to fear. I am here to help you."

The slaves simply stared at him, too traumatized to respond. Gewey sighed. With a mighty pull, he ripped the cage door from its hinges, but this only terrified those inside even more.

"You are free," he announced. "Run home and tell your people that help is coming. Those that enslaved you will not go unpunished."

Stepping away, he returned to Kaylia. Together they watched as the slaves gradually summoned up sufficient courage to creep toward the enticingly open door. But even when on the very brink of freedom, they hesitated, as if fearful of a trap. Then one found the will to make a break for it. Another quickly followed. In an instant, the stampede began. More than fifty men and women surged forward in the desperate rush for freedom.

Gewey could not sense any Vrykol lurking nearby. Apparently, those that had survived his wrath were still fleeing.

Once all the slaves were away into the night, he and Kaylia walked to the citadel gate. The ground was covered in the gray ash of destroyed Vrykol and chunks of the shattered wall.

"I know we should go inside," said Gewey. "But after what I did just now..."

"What you did saved my life, and that of our child," she replied.

"I can never let something like that happen again." He lowered his eyes and took a deep breath. "I nearly lost myself."

Kaylia nodded. "I know. I could feel it. But what matters is that you held on to who you are and came back to me ... to us."

He turned and took her hands. "But next time I may not be able to do so. You are the only reason I am not completely Darshan already. You brought me back from... I don't know what. And I don't want to know. The price of victory cannot be the unleashing of such terrible power on the world."

She leaned in and kissed him with deep love and passion. "Together, we will see to it that the world is truly free. Free from the Dark Knight ... and free from Darshan." She looked at the citadel and frowned. "Let us leave this place. The stench of death is too much for me."

Though Gewey's heart was still troubled, he managed a tight smile. As one, they broke into a rapid run, heading due east toward the ancient road. Kaylia sent him feelings of love and comfort, and soon dark thoughts gave way to the quest at hand.

They had to reach the desert elves in time.

CHAPTER 24

Lousis sat tall in his saddle and looked out over his army with pride and optimism. The gleam of steel caught his eye, while the scent of oil and leather filled his nostrils. Thousands of multi-colored banners fluttered on a chill east wind, and the call of war could be heard in the ringing of smiths' hammers reverberating off the cliff walls that encased the passage to Valshara.

More elves had come up from the south, ready to fight. Although aware of Angrääl's army landing in Tarvansia, they had brought no news of the battles or details about the extent of the destruction. Lousis had heard that the enemy was still being held in check but feared the remnants of the force that attacked Althetas would tip the balance once they arrived. He could understand Nehrutu's decision to allow their retreat, but he wasn't sure it was the right one. The lives saved in Althetas may well be lost in Tarvansia.

The repair of Althetas's city gates was already near completion, as were the new outer defenses suggested by Nehrutu. The fleet was also gathered and ready to sail. Led by Nehrutu and Aaliyah, they hoped to land on the south-east tip of the peninsula and attack the Angrääl rear just as Lousis was engaging them from the north. It would take his army at least three weeks to reach King Victis unless he was being forced north—an eternity to resist when faced with such a superior force. Lousis prayed that his fellow monarch could hold out until he arrived.

Since the siege, his personal guard had grown to a ridiculous number. Twenty-five men and elves on horseback were lined up behind him. Though they were certainly worthy warriors, he couldn't help but be irritated by their constant attention and caution. He was accustomed to moving about freely, but that was currently out of the question.

A runner approached and bowed low. "Your majesty, High Lady Selena wishes to speak with you before the army departs."

Lousis scowled. "I am no emperor. Your Highness is how I am to be addressed."

Under the king's sharp eye, the runner instantly became flushed and nervous, unable to speak. After a moment's silence, he lowered his head and ran off.

This added level of deference to Lousis had become increasingly common during the past few days. At first, he thought it was simple fatigue and stress from the invasion making him imagine things, but then he began hearing the stories circulating. People were saying that he slew a hundred men while defending the manor and that he single-handedly repelled the final Angrääl charge before driving them from the city. It didn't matter how many times he told the true account, his legend continued to grow. Some people even wanted to turn the Stone of the Tower into a statue of him. Of course, he ordered it not to be touched. But talk of a monument in his honor still continued.

He spurred his horse on toward Valshara. His guard quickly surrounded him, and cheers rose as he made his way through the ranks. He did his best not to look displeased.

As he approached the passage, he could see that a large white tent had been erected a few yards off to the side of the entrance. Resplendent in her robes, Selena was standing just in front of it, smiling broadly.

Lousis dismounted and bowed, a grin on his face. "You are a welcome sight indeed, High Lady."

"I'm flattered to hear such kind words from a living legend," she teased.

Lousis sighed and frowned. "It does me no honor to have such nonsense spread. Many good men died that night, and I was fortunate to have fought by their side."

"It gives the people hope," she countered. "Now more than ever, they need heroes, and who better than their king?" She motioned toward the tent. "But rest assured, in here you can just be Lousis."

Lousis looked at his guard, who had already begun to surround the tent. "You lot stay out here," he instructed.

Two chairs and a small table had been set up, and two glasses of brandy had already been poured. Lousis took a seat, then held one of the glasses under his nose, savoring the aroma.

"I suppose you won't be enjoying very much of that for a while," said Selena.

"I'm afraid not," he replied, taking a sip. "The comforts of home will be in short supply. But I imagine you didn't call me here to discuss brandy."

"Actually, I did," she replied. "You have defended both of our homes, and I would not have you march to war without a proper farewell."

Lousis visibly relaxed. "You have no idea how glad I am to hear you say that. I was afraid you were going to ask me to take Ertik along with me, or some other such nonsense."

"I think your mind is burdened quite enough," said Selena. "And while Ertik may not complain about going to

Althetas, to have him go as far away from Valshara as you intend would surely send him into a panic."

"Have you enough men and supplies?" asked the king.

Selena frowned. "Valshara is well defended and supplied. But in truth, it now feels more like a fortress than a temple."

"It will be as it was once again," Lousis assured her. "You have my word."

She forced a weak smile. "Perhaps. But I think when that day comes, my usefulness will be at an end. When this war is over, I intend to return to my childhood home and retire. Hopefully, I'll be able to visit my grandson from time to time."

Lousis sat his glass on the table and stroked his beard while thinking. "Perhaps you would consider living in Althetas?"

Selena laughed merrily. "And what would I do there?"

"Be my queen," he replied, almost without hesitation. His eyes fixed on hers and his lips formed a sly grin.

This brought forth even more laughter from Selena, but her amusement faded when Lousis's expression did not change.

"Stop teasing me," she chided.

"I am not teasing you, High Lady," he said. "Nothing would honor me more, and I can think of no better way to spend the rest of my days than with you."

"We are far too old for such things," she replied with an uncharacteristic blush. "Besides, I think you would be in need of a queen capable of bearing you an heir. I am well beyond that."

Lousis reached over to touch Selena's hand. "And I am well beyond caring about such petty matters. I will leave Althetas with a capable leader when the time comes. There are many who could take up the mantle. But I have no desire to spend the rest of my time in this world alone."

Selena lowered her eyes and smiled sweetly. "Neither do I. But if I agree—and I'm not saying that I do—you must promise me one thing."

"I am at your command," said Lousis.

She looked into his eyes and squeezed his hand tightly. "You must survive."

Leaning down, he kissed the tips of her delicate fingers. "You have my word." He gave a playful smirk. "At least my guards will be happy."

"And more numerous," she added. "I'll be sending three knights of Amon Dähl to accompany you."

One look at her face told Lousis that it was useless to argue. "As you wish," he said.

They spent the next hour in pleasant conversation, leaving behind troubled thoughts and dark dreams. But it was not to last. A messenger arrived to inform Lousis that the army was ready to depart.

"You never gave me your reply," he said, rising from his chair.

"Keep your word by returning alive and you will have it then," she replied. "Until that time, know that you will remain in my thoughts and prayers."

"And you in mine, High Lady." Bowing low, he left the tent.

The army had formed lines, awaiting only Lousis's command. As promised, three knights showed up to join his guard. Lousis smiled inwardly, picturing the sweet face of High Lady Selena.

"Lads," he shouted, turning to the guards. "I have a great need to return home alive. Don't let me down."

He nodded to the herald, who sounded a mighty blast from a silver trumpet. This was met with a thunderous cry as the army slowly moved forward.

With a new hope for love and companionship beating in his heart, Lousis prayed for peace to come soon.

CHAPTER 25

Yanti sat admiring the décor in the living room of Lee Starfinder's former home. It saddened him to think that he was soon to return to the barren halls of Angrääl, though he would certainly be taking a few select books along with him.

A young girl was dusting the mantel, making a point of avoiding eye contact with him. The people of Sharpstone were far more accommodating than he'd expected. Likely, they had been told not to resist; an intelligent move if they were to have any hope of survival. The master would not tolerate resistance from this lot. Not from Darshan's hometown. They were lucky the village was still standing after what had happened to the faithful. Fifty men from Baltria had come to burn it to the ground in retaliation. Yanti took another look around and crossed his legs. He was glad he'd stopped them. Certainly, this house would have suffered the same fate as the rest of the village, and the treasures here were far too beautiful to be destroyed at the hands of that rabble.

"Did you know Gewey Stedding?" he asked the maid.

She stopped and turned, but did not look up. "I did, my lord. Everyone here knew him. It's a small village."

Yanti nodded. "Of course. Tell me, what was he like?"

She shrugged awkwardly. "He was nice—like his father—and he worked hard. Most people thought well of him. He used to help my grandmother when something needed fixing. Oh yes, and most of the girls thought he was handsome."

Yanti chuckled. "I'm sure they did." He pulled a copper from his pocket and tossed it to her. "That will be all for today."

The maid curtsied and hurried away.

The moment the door closed, Yanti felt the foul presence of a Vrykol approaching the house from the east. Grumbling at this intrusion, he poured himself a glass of wine and sat down to wait. Within minutes, a black-cloaked figure entered and took a seat opposite him.

"Deliver your message and leave," ordered Yanti. "Your company offends me."

The Vrykol pushed back his hood, revealing his elf features. "I had heard you were a pretentious snob."

Yanti sneered. "Just because you look less disgusting doesn't mean you are any different from the rest of your kind."

The Vrykol laughed mockingly. "And because you were created by the gods and not our master, that doesn't make you any better than me ... or the rest of our kind."

Yanti waved his hand dismissively. "Just tell me why you're here."

The Vrykol sighed and leaned back in his chair. "Your sister has been found."

"I know," he replied. "I can sense her. Please say you didn't come here to tell me that."

"You are to find her and bring her to the master," he continued. "At once."

"Me?" said Yanti. "She's harmless. Why send me? Certainly, you or one of the others could do it just as easily."

"She is protected by the hermit," he explained.

"Felsafell," Yanti growled. "Yes. Then I am certainly the only one who could do this. I hope you will not be joining me."

"I have my own duties to perform," he replied, his tone boastful. "I am to kill Darshan."

Yanti doubled over in laughter. "The master is sending you? Other than he, I am the only one who can stand against the son of Gerath. Is this some kind of joke?"

The Vrykol reached inside his cloak and pulled out a small gold box with the symbol of Angräal engraved on the lid. He sat it on the low table positioned between them and pushed it forward. "I will not fail to kill him as you did."

Yanti glared angrily. "I beat him. Only the elves prevented my total victory. Besides, the master merely wanted him incapacitated, not killed."

"That has changed," said the Vrykol with an air of smugness. "And you could no longer defeat him. The master is certain that Darshan has discovered our weakness. He would rip your spirit from your body before you could lift your sword."

Yanti thought on this for a moment. "I still fail to see why he has sent you. If we are no longer a threat, then only the master himself can defeat him now."

The Vrykol motioned to the box. "The answer to that is inside."

Yanti eyed him skeptically before lifting the lid. One glance was sufficient. With a gasp, he pushed the box away and leaped to his feet. "Where did you get that?"

"It was unearthed when we were building an outpost near Hazrah," he replied, amused by Yanti's reaction. "I am surprised you are so upset."

"Do you know what that is?" Yanti stepped forward and looked inside once again. "Have you any idea what that could do to you?"

The Vrykol reached into the box and took out a tiny crystal dart, no longer than his little finger. Only their keen eyes could see the symbols of the nine gods etched along the shaft. At the tip was a shard of gleaming steel, and though the metal itself was barely visible, it shone bright and steady as the noonday sun.

"Be careful with that, you fool!" shouted Yanti.

The Vrykol smiled, tilting his head and feigning innocence. "It would seem the mighty Yanti is not without fear after all. And to think that such a little thing could cause you to tremble." He lifted the dart in front of his face for a few seconds before returning it to the box.

Yanti sat back down, visibly shaken. "I have good reason to fear. And that you do not, only shows me your ignorance."

"Then perhaps you will enlighten me," it mocked. "Being that you are so wise and powerful."

Yanti's hatred boiled. It was taking a supreme effort just to stop himself from killing the creature. "That is one of the Fangs of Yajna. If you so much as touch the tip..."

"Unlike you," interrupted the Vrykol. "I do not fear death."

"Death?" Yanti huffed and shook his head. "It will not be death that you will face, you fool. Your spirit will be sent to a place where even the gods fear to tread. It is a realm of eternal torment and horror made at the beginning of time by the Creator herself." His eyes remained fixed on the box. "No ... it is not death that I fear."

The Vrykol laughed. "You believe those tales? If such a place really exists, it is unknown to anyone but you. More likely it's a story told to scare young children."

Leaning forward, Yanti leveled his gaze at the Vrykol. "There are only two beings on this earth older than I, both of whom I am now commanded to seek. And only Felsafell is my true elder. I have seen things beyond your limited imagination—powers so great that they shook the foundations of the world. I was there when the Sword of Truth was forged in the fires of creation and Amon Dähl set to be its protector." His eyes blazed. "To me you are but a speck, and that you doubt what I say, matters not in the least." He rose from his chair. "I no longer wish to speak with such a fool. If there is nothing more, you can leave."

The Vrykol stood, scooped up the box, and walked to the door. "One last thing," it said, smiling. "If I were you, I wouldn't fail again. I would hate to see anything happen to..." It paused ominously. "You know ... one of my own kind."

The instant the door closed, Yanti's temper exploded. Picking up his chair, he hurled it across the room, smashing it to splinters against the far wall. Only a moment later, he sighed with regret for having destroyed such a beautiful thing. He sat down in the other chair and closed his eyes. A second sigh quickly followed.

He called out to her with his mind. "Sister, you should have stayed hidden." He felt her spirit. It was full of sadness and pity.

"I am sorry, brother," came back her reply. "And I love you. No matter what has been done to you, or what you have done to others, I will always love you."

A single tear fell down Yanti's cheek. He wiped it away and then stared at his wet finger as if he had never seen a tear before. Slowly, his sorrow turned into rage. Springing up from his seat, he retrieved his sword.

"I am coming," he muttered. "Perhaps to both our ends."

Storming out of the house, he walked with long, even strides into the village. Fearful stares followed him as he passed the villagers on the street. With each step, his blood-lust was growing and his desire to destroy Sharpstone was nearing obsession. This was the fault of the godling. All of it. And rather than have the joy of killing him, he must now hunt down and destroy the one person he had long ago sworn to protect—an oath he was now being forced to break.

As he reached the market and the entrance to the docks, he paused to look back. He knew he could track down the Vrykol and steal the dart. It could be he who defeated

Darshan, not that mongrel. He could return with his ravaged body and hang it right here in the market square for all to see.

Yanti took a step back the way he had come. "Yes," he whispered. "I will be the one."

A searing pain shot through his head, forcing him to his knees.

Do not defy me!

The voice felt as if it would shatter his skull. He let out a primal scream. His fists pounded into the slate, sending shards of rock flying.

"Are you all right?"

Yanti felt a withered hand touching his shoulder. He looked up to see an old man looking at him with kind eyes.

"Do you need help?" he asked.

Rising quickly, Yanti drew his sword and ran it straight through the old man's gullet. There was barely time for a gasp and a gurgle before the man slumped into Yanti's arms. Throwing the body to the ground, he hurried to the docks where a cargo vessel from Baltria had just finished unloading.

"Cast off," he commanded as he stepped aboard.

A skinny deckhand stepped forward nervously, noting the bloody sword still in Yanti's hand. "The captain isn't back yet from..." His voice cracked and faded as each word came out.

Yanti took a step, his eyes ablaze.

"Yes, my Lord," the deckhand said, hurrying away.

In less than a minute, the boat was off the docks and heading downriver, Yanti standing on the bow.

"I'm coming." He sent his thoughts once more before closing his mind from his sister's view.

CHAPTER 26

Lee sat atop a hill, gazing down at the elf army. Music and laughter filled his ears as the wedding celebration reached its third hour. He had tried to join in, but thoughts of his wife tormented him.

He saw Jacob approaching, a bottle of wine in each hand and a broad grin on his face. Forcing his melancholy aside, he waved to his son.

"Why did you leave the party?" asked Jacob, plopping down beside him.

"I suppose I'm just getting old," he lied.

Jacob nodded and sighed. "It's mother, isn't it?"

Lee put his arm around his son, his eyes far away. "It just reminds me of our wedding day. The entire city turned out to celebrate. It was the grandest wedding Hazrah had ever seen."

"People still talk about it," said Jacob. "They say you spent half of your fortune on that one day."

Lee chuckled. "That may be a bit of an exaggeration. But your mother was worth it. I wanted to impress her so much. She had left everything behind to be with me, and I was afraid she would be disappointed with life in such a remote city. I wanted to show her that I could give her anything she desired."

Jacob laughed. "I can only imagine what she must have thought. She was never one to hold wealth as important. By the time I came of age, she had given away most everything we owned helping the poor." His laughter went away. "I called her a fool for that."

There was a brief silence as they both contemplated their personal memories. Lee then grabbed one of the bottles from Jacob and took a long drink. "She always did have a kind heart. When I first met her, Millet told me that she was far above my station. Did you know that her family had land-holdings in all five of the Eastland kingdoms? As rich as I was, they made me look like a pauper. But that's not what he meant by above my station."

"She never spoke of her father," said Jacob. "Or anyone else in her family."

Lee took another drink. "I'm not surprised. They dis-owned her when she decided to marry me. Her father even tried to have me killed. I can't say I blame him for that. I was actually a lot like you." He grinned. "Only even more arrogant and foolhardy."

"Millet has told me," said Jacob, smiling. "He said that it is a miracle you survived."

"He's not wrong," said Lee. "But don't let his overblown sense of responsibility fool you. He has had his own moments of reckless abandon. He even fell in love once."

Jacob raised an eyebrow. "Millet? In love? What happened?"

"She married another," replied Lee. "It broke his heart."

Jacob shook his head in bewilderment. "I can't imagine Millet in love. He seems so cold and unemotional."

This time it was Lee who raised an eyebrow. "Millet is anything but that. His passions run deep and his friendship is unwavering. The woman he loved, loved him in return. But her family had chosen another."

"If she had loved him as mother loved you," said Jacob, "surely she would have ignored them and married him, anyway."

"It wasn't that simple," said Lee. "The woman's family was in debt and nearly ruined. Her marriage to this other man was the only thing that could save them. Millet sacrificed his own happiness for the good of others."

"Just as you did," Jacob remarked solemnly. He paused for a moment before adding: "You told me that the Reborn King may have brought mother back. Is it possible she can be saved?"

Lee shook his head. "No. If it is true, then she is little more than a slave with her soul subject to the whim of the Dark Knight. Her only salvation will be his death."

"What about Gewey?" asked Jacob, hope rising in his voice. "Could he save her?"

"I don't know," Lee replied. "Perhaps. Perhaps not. I have thought long on this. If I could bring her to him, he might be able to do something, but I have no idea how to accomplish this. A return to Angrääl would only result in my capture, and that wouldn't help her at all. And I can't ask Gewey to risk everything by going there himself." He closed his eyes. "I can only hope that in the end I find a way to save her."

Jacob chuckled softly.

"What's funny?" asked Lee.

"I hated you for so long," he replied. "I never imagined I'd be able to forgive you for abandoning us. Now all I think about is how I don't want you to die, too."

Lee pulled his son close and embraced him. "That means more to me than you can understand. And I wish I could tell you I'll survive this war, but fate may have other plans."

They sat drinking their wine until they saw Millet coming up the hill, looking unusually cheerful. He snatched the bottle from Lee and took a long swallow.

"You may have heard, Jacob, that lords of the house Nal'Thain are notorious drinkers," joked Lee. "It is good to see that our reputation is secure."

Millet tossed Lee the bottle. "I doubt I could ever match your escapades." He groaned as he sat down. "Did you know that your father was one of the most loved and yet hated men in all of Hazrah? Before he met your mother, every woman in the city swooned whenever he passed by, and not all of them unmarried maidens. He must have given out a king's ransom in gifts by way of apologizing for his misdeeds. It was a good thing he was rich."

"Millet," said Lee. "I can't remember the last time you were this drunk."

"We all cope in our own way," he replied, his face turning serious. "I know why you came up here alone. I mourn her too." He smiled at Jacob. "Another thing you may not know about your father is that when he met your mother, not a single woman in the city dared hope to catch his eye again. This would have made him very popular with the men if not for the fact that your mother was by far the most beautiful, kind, and graceful woman they had ever seen. The luckiest lord in Hazrah they called him—and they were right." A tear fell down his cheek. "I loved her as well, you know."

"I know," said Lee, a sad smile forming. "And she loved you in return."

Millet wiped his eyes and cleared his throat. "But that is not the reason why I climbed this bloody big hill. Linis and Dina are to be bonded, and Dina's mother expects us to be there."

"Bonded?" said Jacob. "Didn't we just see them married a few hours ago?"

"This is different," explained Millet. "The elves of the west are able to bond their spirits together as one. The desert elves don't—or can't—do this; I'm not sure which. But whatever the case, they're gathering not far from here, and you, Lee Starfinder, have the honor of standing by Linis's side."

"I may have missed Gewey's bonding," said Lee. "But I will certainly not miss this as well."

Millet stood up, albeit on slightly unsteady legs, to lead Lee and Jacob down the slope and around the edge of the encampment. To the west, atop another hill, Lee could see Linis and Dina standing beside Dina's mother. They were dressed in tan cotton robes with stitching that formed blue angular patterns. Linis wore a matching blue sash around his waist, while Dina had delicate yellow flowers adorning her hair. Nahali was wearing a long, flowing black dress with a blood-red belt. In her hands, she held a small, gold-handled dagger.

Lee bowed respectfully as they crested the slope.

"No need for such formality," said Linis. He gave Lee a rough, friendly embrace. "I am happy you are here, my friend." He looked at Millet and Jacob. "And you as well."

Lee reached out and took hold of Dina's hand. "You are a vision of beauty."

She leaned in to kiss him on the cheek. "Thank you. Though I do wish I had brought along something more appropriate to wear."

"Nonsense," Millet interjected. "You have never looked lovelier."

She smiled before kissing him on the cheek as well. "I see you have been enjoying the celebration."

Millet blushed and lowered his eyes. "Forgive me. I may have taken just a bit too much wine."

Dina's laugh was light and sweet. "Not at all, my dear friend. This is the happiest day of my life; I want you to drink and be merry. There should be no sad faces tonight."

She looked at Jacob. "And I am honored that you are here too, Jacob."

Jacob bowed low. "The honor is mine."

Lee took his place beside Linis, and Millet beside Dina, while Jacob stood a few feet away. Lee couldn't help but envy Linis as the couple dropped to their knees and Nahali performed the ceremony. Once the final ancient word was spoken, he could see a visible change in them both. It was as if their love had instantly multiplied many times over and their understanding of each other had become infinite. Slowly, they rose up. With a tender smile, Nahali took their hands and led them away into the night.

"A marriage tent was erected just before the celebration began," remarked Millet. "I suggest we return to the others. I hear Bevaris has challenged Weila to a wrestling match."

"I would like to see that," said Lee, smiling.

Ignoring the fact that Linis and Dina were no longer present, the celebrations continued well into the night. In the desert elves' eyes, the wedding ceremony that had taken place earlier had been a mere formality. They were far less constricted by dogma and tradition than the elves of the west, or even humans for that matter. To them, all that really mattered was mutual consent. Weila had told Lee that many marriages were performed while traveling in the desert, and that it was the celebration of the union that was most important. This was normally held within a month of the marriage, as it is not always practical to do so right away. Lee liked the way they did things. It seemed somehow innocent and wholesome.

Bevaris did indeed wrestle Weila—losing three out of four bouts. This spawned a dozen more good-natured challenges. Lee refused several times before finally agreeing to wrestle a young dark-haired youth. The elves were impressed when he won quite easily, and cheers of admiration and friendship were called to him long after the sport was over.

A few hours before dawn, the music finally ceased and everyone bedded down for what remained of the night. Millet had continued enjoying the wine right until the end, so Lee and Jacob helped him to a small area close to the edge of the camp. After Lee had settled into his own bedroll, he looked over to Millet and Jacob, both of who were already fast asleep. He regretted the burden he had thrust upon Millet. Being lord of the house Nal'Thain was not a responsibility he would have wished on anyone in such dark times. Yet Millet was truly the only one who could bear it.

"Lord Starfinder," came a voice from a few yards away.

Lee rolled over and saw an elf sentry, his face grave. He sighed before sitting up. "Is something wrong?"

He nodded sharply. "A spy has been captured just outside of the camp."

Lee quickly got up and fastened his sword to his belt. "Where is he?"

"A few hundred yards to the west," the sentry replied. "He is being held there until it's decided what to do with him."

"Then I will go there immediately," Lee said. "Meanwhile, have some of your people surround Linis and Dina's tent. Do not get too close. I don't want them disturbed on their wedding night unless there's no other choice."

The elf sped off to do his bidding while Lee headed to the western edge of the camp. Atop a low hill, he could see three elf sentries with swords drawn. They were standing guard over a dark-haired man wearing a jet-black shirt and pants. The prisoner's pale face was smeared with charcoal and soot. His eyes were wide with fear. As Lee approached, one of the elves stepped forward and bowed.

"We caught him spying," he said.

Lee nodded, then squatted down in front of the terrified man. "What are you doing here?" His voice was hard and menacing. "Speak now!"

"I ... I was sent by King Luccia," he stammered, his fearful eyes never leaving the elves. "We had heard of an invasion coming from the east."

Lee rubbed his chin. "And who told your king this?"

"I don't know," he replied. "I just came to see if it was true. That's all."

Lee looked up at the elves. "He speaks the truth. Leave us."

At once, the elves set off down the hill.

"Now," continued Lee, "you only have me to fear. And as I mean you no harm, you can surely relax." He put on a friendly smile. "First, I would know your name."

"Normak," he replied, still trembling. "My name is Normak."

"Normak," said Lee. "I am Lee Starfinder, and what you see is not an invasion. In fact, we come to assist your king if he wishes it. And if he does not, we ask only to be granted leave to pass through his lands."

"You're here to fight the Reborn King then," he said.

"And what do you know of him?" Lee asked.

"Nothing, I swear." With the elf sentries now out of sight, Normak was visibly calming. "Just that Angrääl is at war in the west. Rumor says that it's with the bloody elves."

"Only a fool listens to rumors," said Lee. "The Reborn King is at war with the whole world. Has King Luccia joined with him?"

"No, sir," he replied. "Our king isn't about to get us caught up in a war. Sure, we sometimes traded with Angrääl, but we're not about to go marching off to fight."

Lee thought for a minute, then stood up. "I need you to take me to King Luccia."

Normak looked at Lee incredulously. "You think I'll just take you straight to the king? Are you mad?"

"I've been told so, yes," Lee grinned, pulling Normak to his feet. He began to descend the hill, not bothering with his captive.

"So you're just letting me go?" Normak called after him.

"You'll wait for me here," said Lee over his shoulder. "Or if you prefer, you can run and see if the elves can catch you again."

Normak opened his mouth, but no words came out. With a defeated expression on his face, he sat back down on the ground.

Lee woke Bevaris and Tristan and told them what had happened.

"Then we should depart at once," said Bevaris. "Tristan. Stay with the men."

Lee then woke Millet and Jacob.

Millet struggled to his feet, rubbing his bloodshot eyes. "I shall go with you."

Lee laughed. "As you wish, my lord. If you think you are able. But Jacob, you must stay here. If this is a trap, it would be best if one of us is still free."

An hour later, they gathered on the hill where Normak stood quietly, waiting with Bevaris. A few feet away from them, Lolin and Weila were talking to Linis and Dina. That the newlyweds had risen from their wedding bed brought a frown to Lee's face.

Linis waved as Lee approached. "You did not think to leave without us, did you?"

"There is no need for you to come," said Lee. "Enjoy a few days of peace."

"I would, my friend," he replied. "But my unorem insists on representing Amon Dähl, and I will not allow her to leave my side."

"Normak here tells me that the king is definitely at his estate in Xenthia," said Bevaris. "I told the men to lead the army a day's ride west of the city and wait there for our return."

Tristan and two of his men approached, leading horses for everyone but the desert elves. However, Linis had made a habit of running alongside the others, so refused the steed brought for him.

"We should arrive in four days," said Normak, eyeing the elves suspiciously. "But I think you waste your time bringing elves. King Luccia will not see them."

Bevaris stood nose to nose with the man. "King Luccia will honor the request of Bevaris, knight in the order of Amon Dähl, just as his father did before him. And you will speak with a bit less contempt in your voice unless you wish to test my patience."

Normak averted his eyes and mounted his horse.

"Thank you," said Lolin. "But there is no need for anger. Understanding and trust are earned and will come in time. We do not hold those who fear us out of ignorance responsible. Ignorance can be remedied."

Bevaris chuckled and motioned to Normak. "Yes. But what of stupidity?"

All but Normak burst into laughter.

"For that, we have yet to find a cure," replied Lolin, smiling.

"Let us hope that the king does not suffer such an ailment," remarked Weila.

They set off down the hill before turning northwest. A cold wind chilled Lee's face and the Weeping Mountains were barely visible. Suddenly, he felt a powerful sense of foreboding. He gripped the reins tightly.

"Is something wrong?" asked Bevaris, riding beside him.

"I'm not sure," said Lee. "I hope not. But I suppose we shall find out soon enough."

CHAPTER 27

The four-day ride to Xenthia was uneventful. Taking into account the speed of the elves, Lee reckoned that their army would be no more than a day and a half behind them.

Earlier, the landscape had become increasingly hilly as they neared the shadow of the Weeping Mountains. Soon it became obvious to everyone how they had earned their name. A great mist poured down from the many peaks, shrouding their bases. Lee explained that an immense hot spring was to the north of the range. Clouds formed above this, rising higher and higher until eventually falling down on the other side. It gave the mountains a ghostly quality that over the centuries had spawned many a grizzly tale.

On arriving at the city, Lee noticed at once that it had only limited defenses; just a short wall and flimsy gates, though at least fifteen guards were standing in front of these and eyeing them suspiciously as they approached. As soon as the presence of elves was detected, the sound of steel sliding free from scabbards grew loud.

Normak spurred his horse forward and scrambled from the saddle the moment he was able to. Within seconds, he had disappeared inside the gate.

Bevaris took the lead. "We are here to seek an audience with King Luccia." His voice boomed with bold assertiveness.

"And who are you?" demanded the guard captain. "And why do you bring elves to my gate?"

"I am Bevaris, son of Vrinda," he announced proudly. "And who I bring to your gates is my own affair. I suggest you tell King Luccia I am here. That is ... if you wish to keep your head attached to your shoulders."

The captain glared furiously and stood unmoving in silence for what seemed like an eternity. But Brevaris's sheer presence finally overwhelmed him. With a loud growl, he spun on his heels and marched off, roughly pushing aside his guards as he went.

"Was that wise?" whispered Lee. "Perhaps it would be best not to antagonize the locals."

"I will not have my comings and goings in my own home-town questioned," he shot back. "I know that man, and he knows me. He was a stuffed shirt when he was young, and a captain's chevron has only made his condition worse."

His words cause sniggers from the other guards.

Just over an hour passed before the captain returned with a self-satisfied look on his face. "You are to be disarmed and arrested ... Bevaris. If you resist, you and your friends will be killed."

Bevaris leaped from his saddle, causing the guards to shift nervously. "If the king wishes my arrest, so be it. As for my friends..."

"They will comply as well," completed Millet.

The company dismounted and began to remove their weapons.

"If any harm comes to them," warned Bevaris. "I will settle accounts with you first."

"Mind your tongue," replied the captain. "Or it may be your head that is in jeopardy."

Bevaris sneered while taking off his massive sword. "I should ask you how your sister fares, Captain Konnor. I have missed her company. As I'm sure she has missed mine."

The other guards could not hold back their chuckles and stifled laughs.

The captain fumed. "Be quiet! All of you!" He pressed his face close to Brevaris's, but the knight was unmoved. "Take them away," Konnor finally ordered.

They were immediately surrounded, and their mounts seized.

"This is not exactly how I hoped it would go," remarked Lee.

"It is to be expected," offered Weila. "With an elf army of unknown intent at your door, they may feel a show of strength to be prudent."

Bevaris shrugged. "Prudent or not, the hospitality of Xenthia has suffered."

The guards led them into the city. Lee could see that the once well-tended white stucco buildings were now showing distinct signs of decay, and also that the many small flower gardens that used to line the avenues had been filled in with pebbles and dirt. Trash and debris were piled up between the houses and shops, amongst which rats scurried about feasting on the refuse. The people of the city looked haggard and emaciated, staring suspiciously at the new arrivals as they passed by. Whispered words of war floated to Lee's well-tuned ears.

"Hardship has befallen these lands," he remarked. "Even in winter, this used to be a beautiful place. Now…" He shook his head sadly.

"It grieves me to see it so," said Bevaris. "Trade with Angrääl has clearly not gone well."

The word Angrääl caused the guards to pause momentarily and look at one another.

"I see that name is well known here," observed Millet.

They were taken to a guard post at the southern end of the city and placed inside a small windowless room. As the door slammed shut, Lee could hear a guard mentioning the words "ambassador" and "execution."

"We may be in more trouble than we first thought," he said.

Several hours passed before the door reopened and Captain Konnor stepped inside.

"The king will see three of you," he stated. "Bevaris and two others."

Lee looked to Millet.

"I think it best you go," said Millet. "Your reputation may help our cause."

"I wouldn't count on that," mocked Konnor. "We know of you, Lee Starfinder. Don't think your skill with a blade will allow you to impose your will here."

Lee ignored him.

Weila also stepped forward. "I will speak for my people."

The captain gave a mocking laugh. "An elf, a has-been warrior, and a scoundrel. This will indeed be amusing to watch."

Konnor led them out into the street. With the sun waning, the smell of torches and unwashed bodies filled Lee's nostrils. They weaved their way north through the city until the road began to gently slope upward. Soon, the king's manor came into view.

Though only a single-story building, it was at least two hundred feet wide, built from polished blue stone, and topped with a black tile roof. An imposing marble archway stood at the head of a path leading up to double doors made of oak. Panels of white latticework surrounded the yard, while marble fountains close to each corner of the house spouted crystal clear water. The yard itself was well-manicured, with dozens of circular flowerbeds and a multitude of peach and apple trees.

"It would seem at least this house has escaped hardship," muttered Bevaris disapprovingly.

"I'll be sure to mention your compliment to the king," sneered Konnor. "I'm certain he'll be pleased to hear of it."

The hall inside was wide and spacious. A polished wood floor shone like glass. Stained panels decorating the walls were of superb craftsmanship, covered in art from both the western and southern kingdoms. Life-size marble statues of the nine gods stretched across the far end, every one magnificent in its artistry. To the right were a dozen chairs set in a semi-circle, each separated from its neighbor by a small round table. Fine blue lace curtains covered an archway directly in front of the visitors, while above their heads, huge glass panels allowed the night sky to be clearly seen. By day these would flood the hall with light, though at present it was illuminated by three crystal chandeliers.

Konnor led them through the curtains into an antechamber with several plush chairs set against the wall. "Wait here," he ordered before exiting through another door to their left.

Two guards remained, standing stiff and silent. Another hour passed before Konnor returned. This time, his face was red with anger. "King Luccia will see you now," he said sharply.

He led them through a series of hallways to a round chamber with a large oval dais at the far end. Four rows of chairs were facing this stage, on which two men and three women dressed as Baltrian pirates were performing a comedy for a lone audience member.

"That's enough," commanded the solitary spectator, clapping his hands.

The actors stopped at once and bowed respectfully. As they hurried away, they glanced fearfully at Weila, while completely ignoring Lee and Bevaris.

"They've never seen an elf before," said the man, rising from his seat. "But of course, neither have I."

He was short, though not frail or slight, with thick wavy brown hair, oiled and pushed back in Baltrian fashion. His ruddy complexion and green eyes gave him a friendly bearing. Though not opulent, his blue and green shirt and blue pants were clearly of fine quality. Several gold rings on the fingers of both hands spoke of his wealth.

"Your Highness," said Bevaris, bowing. "It is good to see you again."

King Luccia scrutinized the group. "So this is what dear Captain Konnor was so worried about. I recognize the name Lee Starfinder. My father spoke of you with great admiration."

Lee bowed. "Your father was a kind and wise leader. I held him in the highest regard."

Luccia smiled. His eyes then settled on Weila. "And an elf. Amazing! I would be overjoyed if there was not an army of your folk heading in this direction."

Weila stepped forward and bowed low. "I am Weila, Your Highness. And let me assure you that my people mean you no harm. Our fight is elsewhere."

"Yes," said Luccia. "You go to challenge the powers of the north." He allowed a hint of disdain to seep into his voice.

"That we do," she replied.

Luccia chuckled. "If only we had your courage."

"Then Angrääl is the cause of your woes?" asked Bevaris.

"Angrääl is a storm," said Luccia. "One I fear we cannot weather. But before I speak of these matters, I will hear your tale in full, Bevaris. Captain Konnor is convinced of your ill intent. Tell me why he is not to be believed."

Bevaris stood proudly. "Aside from the fact that the captain is a fool, and always has been, I will say only this. I have ever been a man of honor, and no one in this city has just cause to dispute that. I was a friend to your father, and to you. I only wish to bring hope and life to these lands—things which I have noticed you do not have in abundance at present.”

“Konnor may be a fool,” said Luccia in a reprimanding tone. “But he is a good captain and a loyal subject. He only serves to protect our life and lands.” The king’s face then cracked into a smile. “However, I can only hope he is able to do a better job at that than he did protecting his sister’s honor.”

Bevaris grinned. “Actually, Your Highness, those rumors were...” He hesitated. “Well—a little bit exaggerated, perhaps. At least, some of them were.”

“Your Highness,” cut in Lee. “What of our companions? Will they be released?”

All traces of the king’s humor vanished. “Once I have heard your story and am satisfied you speak the truth, then I will let them go. Not a moment sooner. I am sorry if you take insult to my actions, but these are dark times.”

“Then let us not dally,” suggested Lee. “The tale is long and our friends, uncomfortable.”

“Quite right,” agreed Luccia. “Please be seated.”

For the next two hours, Bevaris, Lee, and Weila took their turn telling the king their stories. His interest increased noticeably when hearing about the elves of the desert. Once everyone was finished, Luccia got up and walked to the door. After a quick word with the guard, he returned to his seat.

“I am having your friends released at once,” he said. “Though I am afraid they must not move about the city unescorted. They will be brought here and given a proper room.”

“I thank you, Your Highness,” said Bevaris. “And now that you have heard our tales, I would hear what has happened to my beloved home.”

“It is as you see it,” said Luccia sadly. “We are all but cut off from the world.”

“But your scout told us you traded with Angrääl,” said Lee.

"And we did," affirmed Luccia. "But no longer. When representatives of the Reborn King first arrived, we thought it a boon. They had goods, skilled craftsmen, and no lack of gold. Then I learned that they were recruiting my people to serve in their army. When I ordered them to stop, they complied—at first. But very quickly it became apparent that they did not respect my rule. When I threatened to expel them from my kingdom, I was told that unless I relented, all trade would be cut off and we would surely starve."

He sighed deeply before continuing. "They had already taken control of Survia's ports, and that is the only coastal kingdom in the Eastland. Later, to my dismay, I heard they had taken Baltria as well." His tone became even more melancholy. "Baltria was the first city I ever visited outside of my own lands. Half of the goods we receive come through there. Even the cities along the Goodbranch are under their control."

"But I see that didn't stop you from throwing them out," remarked Lee.

"What choice did I have?" His sadness became anger. "I am the rightful king, and will not shame my father by cowering before this villain."

"Then you will fight?" asked Bevaris.

Luccia laughed. "Fight? Are you mad? I have no more than a volunteer force of five thousand swords. Angrääl would sweep us aside like so many dead leaves."

"You could raise an army," suggested Lee. "Certainly the other four Eastland kingdoms would come to your aid."

"You speak without knowledge, Starfinder," snapped Luccia. "I would defend my lands if I could, but the people here are afraid and on the brink of starvation. They will not answer the call to arms. And, as far as enlisting aid from the other four kingdoms—their rulers have already allowed themselves to become vassals of the Reborn King, so I would be fighting them as well. No. Soon my rule will end and my people forced to serve Angrääl; that much is clear."

"Is there nothing you can do?" asked Bevaris, deep sadness in his voice.

"I am afraid my only hope is to either submit or pray for the gods to intervene," said Luccia. "And as neither of these things will happen, I expect that one day soon I will find a dagger in my back, or perhaps poison in my cup."

"Help may come in ways you never expected," said Lee. "And your prayers may not go unanswered. There is one who walks the earth with the power to challenge the forces of darkness. One who even the Reborn King fears."

"You speak of Darshan," said the king in a whisper.

Lee smiled. "Word travels fast."

"I have heard rumors," he replied. "Men fleeing the war in the west speak the name. They say he killed fifty thousand soldiers with a wave of his hand, though I find that a bit hard to believe. It's more than likely he's a half-man." He looked at Lee's calm expression and leaned forward. "You know him, don't you? I can see it in your eyes."

"I know him," Lee admitted. "I know him well. And I can tell you that he is not a half-man, as indeed I am. He is far more powerful than I."

Luccia chuckled. "I always suspected that of you. The stories that surround your name are too fantastic for you to be anything else. My father told me that he saw you kill ten men without unsheathing your sword. And he was not one prone to exaggeration."

"I remember that," said Lee. "Your father tried to come to my aid, and would have done so had his guards not held him back. But the truth is that I was only unarmed because Millet wouldn't allow me to carry my sword when I took drink at the taverns. Otherwise..."

"Otherwise you would still have bested ten men," interrupted Luccia lightheartedly. "They were marauders from out of the Weeping Mountains, I was told. I also heard that you sailed with Baltrian pirates."

"I did," he admitted. "But I assure you that I took no part in any crimes."

"I'm sure," said Luccia with a wry grin. "But if Darshan is not like you, then what is he?"

"He is the herald of a new world," said Weila. "The child of heaven who has come to set the world to rights."

Luccia took a deep breath. "If you are saying what I think you are, then I have lived to see impossible times. He is then, as the rumors claim? Darshan is truly a god?"

Lee nodded slowly. "That is why Angrääl moves so quickly, and why you should not give up hope."

"I cannot imagine meeting such a creature," said Luccia, rubbing his temple. "Tell me about him. What is he like?"

Lee chuckled. "If you meet him and expect anything other than a man, you will be disappointed. He is no different from you or I. He eats, sleeps, and breathes just like everyone else. But his heart has a purity that I have yet to see in anyone I have ever encountered. And, in spite of all his power, that is his greatest weapon."

Lee went on to tell him of Gewey's life in Sharpstone, and how he had discovered who he really was.

"A simple farm boy," said Luccia with a smile as Lee finished. "You have given me reason to hope. But I still can do little to help you. Until this Darshan is victorious, my plight remains the same. But I will gladly grant you passage through my kingdom, and tonight we shall feast."

He turned to Bevaris. "And just so you know, it is the people who have chosen to maintain my gardens with what little they still have. It is their only reminder that we are still a free people."

Bevaris turned red with embarrassment. "Forgive me, Your Highness. I spoke from ignorance."

King Luccia smiled and clapped his hands. Two guards approached from the door. "Show them to their rooms and tell the kitchen that we are to host honored guests tonight."

"Thank you, Your Highness," said Bevaris.

"And once we have eaten, we shall watch a play about Baltrian pirates." Luccia looked at Lee, smirking. "I'm sure you will find it amusing."

Lee laughed. "I'm sure I will."

They all bowed and allowed the guards to lead them through the halls to their rooms. Lee pulled off his boots and lay down on the bed, staring at the ceiling. Speaking about Gewey so openly had made him realize just how much had happened in such a short time—and how much was yet to unfold.

A light rap at the door brought his mind back to where he was. Weila and Millet entered.

"I am grateful you were able to secure our release," said Millet.

"King Luccia is a good man," said Lee. "As was his father. I pray this war is over before it reaches him."

"As do I," agreed Millet.

"He asked to speak to one of the elves," said Weila. "So I sent Lolin. It would seem the king does not fear us, though I cannot say the same for the rest of the people here."

"It will take time," said Lee. "Fear is banished through understanding, and King Luccia has obviously not allowed his ignorance of your people and their ways to cloud his mind or foster paranoia. His qualities as a ruler would show him the wisdom of knowing you better."

"If only all people were so open-minded, war would never trouble the world again," said Weila.

"Hopefully, we will see the last of it," said Millet.

"Until then, we must plan our next move," said Lee. "Being that King Luccia cannot give us aid, we must move quickly to cross the Eastland and make our way to Althetas."

"The army should be where we told them to be by morning," said Weila. "Unless your mind is changed, I assume we will go southwest to the river crossing."

"I see no better way," said Lee.

"Nor do I," added Millet. "We can only hope that we make it there unnoticed, or at least unchallenged."

Lee shook his head and gave a cynical half-grin. "How often have we had such luck?"

Millet sighed. "Not often."

The feast was not lavish by any standards, though the food was well prepared and the wine plentiful. Only a few officers, including a most unhappy-looking Captain Konnor, attended. Bevaris made a point of staying clear of the man, though they did exchange several angry glances. To keep the peace, the king eventually ordered Konnor to organize a patrol of the city.

After dinner, they returned to the theatre. The audience for the play was made up mostly of local citizens, seemingly of all classes. Merchants sat beside laborers as the actors regaled them with a tale of a blind Baltrian pirate who sought the love of his life—a woman whom he knew only by the smell of her perfume. After the entertainment was over and the actors had taken their bows, King Luccia invited Lee and the others to join him for a drink in his parlor. They found a warm fire and comfortable chairs there to greet them.

"Did you enjoy the play?" asked Luccia, savoring the sweet scent that rose from his glass.

"It was very well done," remarked Millet. "But I must ask about your audience. They seemed a rather diverse group."

"Our plays are one of the few distractions left to us," Luccia explained. "Every citizen is invited to attend regardless of social standing. Names are picked at random each morning, then posted in the market square. It has become extremely popular. So much so that I plan to move it outdoors to accommodate more people."

"Your Highness," said Weila. "I have given consideration to your concerns over your personal safety, and have decided that Lolin shall remain here with you. You will not find a more capable elf, and he will not allow you to come to harm."

Luccia smiled and bowed. "I do appreciate the gesture, but I think having an elf guard may upset some of my people a bit more than is needed at this time."

"No one will ever know I am here," Lolin insisted. "I can remain hidden from all eyes but those of Your Highness. Only if your life is in danger would I make myself known."

"You could consider it a bond between our people," suggested Weila. "And as this world is in dire need of courage and heart, I would see to it that you remain alive to care for your kingdom."

"What do you think, Bevaris?" asked Luccia.

"You could ask for no better protector," he replied earnestly. "And if the Reborn King seeks your demise, it could make the difference between life and death."

Luccia thought for a minute. "I would have to inform Captain Konnor, of course, and I assure you that he will not be pleased. But that aside, I think you are right. No one would expect me to have an elf protector." He bent his knees and gave Lolin a sweeping formal bow. "I am honored to have you with me, and I am in your debt."

"A debt to be paid only with friendship," said Lolin. "I would speak to your captain as soon as my companions are away."

"I must say that I am eager to see his reaction," said Luccia with a devilish grin.

There was a knock on the parlor door and a messenger entered. He handed King Luccia a folded piece of parchment. As the king read, his face darkened. "A force of sixty thousand soldiers is approaching from the west," he told the others. Fear was in his eyes. "They are only two days away."

The room went silent for a moment.

"Then we should leave now," said Lee. "We will do our best to draw them away from the city."

Without another word, everyone hurried off to retrieve their belongings. Six guards escorted them to the front gate, where King Luccia was waiting beside their horses.

"Will you be able to defeat such an army?" the king asked, desperation in his voice.

Lee mounted his steed. "We must. And we will. Even so, you should prepare your defenses as best you can."

Linis climbed in the saddle behind Dina, while Lee pulled Weila up behind him. His stone stare denied her any objection. The night was an empty chasm of fear as they galloped off to join their army.

"Do not despair," said Weila. "It is not we who should fear them."

Lee grunted and urged his horse on even faster.

CHAPTER 28

Lee was stunned by the speed at which the elves now traveled. Their mobility had impressed him even before this latest situation, but once they were told of the Angrääl army approaching, the renewed pace they set made their earlier efforts seem like a mere leisurely stroll. Moreover, their mood was nothing short of jubilant, with not the slightest hint of fear. For two days, they had scarcely rested for more than an hour. Lee began to suspect that even when they did choose to rest, it was far more for the benefit of the humans and horses than due to their own fatigue.

They turned northwest in the hope of gaining high ground, but scouts reported that the enemy had marched south, parallel to Xenthia where the land was flat. Here they had halted. It was clear they knew that the elves were coming and had chosen their place to fight. This concerned both Lee and Bevaris. Though not vastly outnumbered, they had no heavy horses, and the enemy could set lines that would be difficult for the lightly armored elves to break.

The evening before they were due to engage the enemy, Bevaris and Lee sat together at the edge of the camp, pondering on their best plan of action. A few yards away, three elves were shooting arrows at a thin pole they had stuck in the ground, regularly hitting the nearly impossible target from more than thirty yards away.

"Amazing archers," said Bevaris with sincere appreciation.

"There are none better," agreed Lee. "If only we could win a battle with bows alone."

"Indeed," he replied. Bevaris watched for a time, then a wave of inspiration washed over his face. Springing up, he ran over and spoke to the elves for several moments.

Lee watched curiously as Bevaris nodded and smiled excitedly. He then called Lee over.

"I take it you have a plan," said Lee.

"Don't move from where you are," Bevaris told him. He then winked at one of the elves, who took off running until he was swallowed up by the night. A minute or so later, a high-pitched whistle sounded from some distance away. Bevaris whistled in return. A brief silence followed, quickly broken by an ever-increasing hissing sound that seemed to rip through the air. Lee barely had time to blink before a white, fletched arrow buried itself into the ground less than three feet away from where he was standing.

"That was from six hundred yards," said Bevaris.

Lee pulled up the arrow and smiled with keen under-standing. "That is incredible news. We should inform the others."

As morning broke over the field of battle, the elves sang merrily of their impending victory. By contrast, the army of Angrääl stood silent and firm, their banners flying high in the brisk morning air. The elves lined up in long rows, with archers in front and the rest in staggered columns behind them. Lee and Bevaris glanced at each other with knowing smiles.

Jacob had taken it upon himself to be Millet's personal guard, and, along with Tristan, insisted on keeping him far behind and clear of the fray. To Linis's dismay, Dina insisted that he stay with her at the rear as well.

"There will be other battles," she had said, feigning sympathy. "I will not tempt fate and have you risk your life before we've even been married a week."

Reluctantly, he had agreed.

When they reached six hundred yards from the enemy lines, a trumpet blast called for a halt. In seconds, the archers had notched their arrows and were ready to fire. Lee raised his arm and silence fell. Then, with one fluid motion, he gave the signal. Thousands of arrows raced skyward. Even before these missiles struck their target, the elves were already sending another volley. Again and again, with remarkable speed, they shot death at the enemy. Within moments, the Angrääl lines were scattering. The cries of their dying carried clearly all over the field.

For a short time, it looked as if the battle would be over quickly. But the enemy commanders soon recovered their composure. Soon they were reforming their ranks and sending out a wave of heavy horses. Long, steel-tipped lances glinted in the morning sun, their advance on the elf army bringing forth a vengeful roar from the Angrääl soldiers. The elf archers adjusted their fire, but the thick armor on both the horses and men deflected most of the deadly shafts.

Lee looked over the field and saw the enemy footmen running headlong at them. "They're closing the gap." He unsheathed his sword and glanced at Bevaris. "Their commanders are cleverer than I had hoped."

Bevaris shrugged. "I have always desired to die in battle. Perhaps today I will get my wish." His massive sword rang out as he freed it from its scabbard.

The archers dropped their bows and drew their swords just as the horsemen drove deep into the lines. Lee, Bevaris, and the few other human soldiers they had with them charged in. Lee felled three men in an instant and unhorsed four more.

Bevaris swung his blade repeatedly, hewing through armor and flesh as if it were wet parchment.

Despite many elves falling during this initial onslaught, they still managed to halt the advance, and before long, were even beginning to force the cavalry back. But then the Angrääl foot soldiers arrived, smashing their way into the gaps. Though the elves fought fiercely, it was becoming obvious that the sheer force of numbers was going to win the day.

Lee's horse reared as a spear pierced its neck, throwing him from the saddle. Only his half-man dexterity kept him from landing on his back. Two more soldiers were quickly cut down by his fury as he carved a path to the center of the battle. But he could see that their line was collapsing. Any moment now, the elves would be split in two. Blood trickled from cuts to his forearm and neck, but years of training made him able to dismiss the pain.

Then, from seemingly out of nowhere, an almighty explosion sent shock waves thudding into his ears. A huge column of fire erupted at the rear of the Angrääl army. For a second, the battle paused as all eyes turned to witness the terrible sight. Another blast followed, then another and another, each one more devastating than the last.

Roaring and spitting destruction in every direction, a massive wall of flames nearly fifty feet high ripped through the enemy, cutting them in twain. Black smoke billowed up, and the nauseating smell of burning flesh hung heavy in the air. The elves, unsure of what was happening, simply pulled back and watched while their foes were roasted alive. In less than five minutes, the Angrääl forces were in full retreat, screaming in terror as the blazing inferno continued to chase after them.

Lee scanned the horizon. He knew of only one power that could do this. On a tall hill, just beyond the battlefield, he spotted two figures. One an elf woman, the other a human male. His spirits lifted at once. As the last of the retreating enemy disappeared into the distance, the two figures began moving toward them.

"Gewey!" yelled Lee. "Kaylia!"

Cries of jubilation arose from the elf ranks as the two came near. The name of Darshan began echoing off the hill-tops. Gewey and Kaylia raised their arms in greeting.

Without a word, Lee threw his arms around Gewey, all but taking his breath away.

"I'm happy to see you too," Gewey gasped once Lee had finally released him. He looked over the field at the fallen elves. "I only wish I could have arrived sooner."

Lee smiled and took Kaylia's hand. "I see you are still as beautiful as ever."

"And I see you still think you are charming," she replied, laughing.

Linis, Dina, Millet, and Jacob soon joined them as the rest of the army closed in to shout out their salutations and thanks. After responding to countless warm greetings, they began to make their way through the crowd to the rear. Lyrial and Weila greeted them with a friendly smile.

"I told you we would come, Darshan," said Lyrial. "Though it seems as if it is you who has come to our aid."

"Believe me," he replied, bowing. "Your help is desperately needed in the west. The enemy is on the move, and time has run out."

"So it seems," said Lee. He threw an arm around Jacob's shoulders. "Gewey, this is my son, Jacob."

Gewey nodded. "It is an honor to meet you."

Jacob lowered his eyes. "My father speaks of you as a son. So I will look upon you as my brother."

"Nothing would give me greater pleasure," said Gewey. "But I'm afraid there are wounded who need healing. Stories and reunions must wait."

Lee looked at Gewey in wonder. "You have changed so much. Even your words seem different."

Gewey seized Lee's shoulder fondly. "Much has happened since we first started out from Sharpstone. And still, there is much to do."

Gewey and Kaylia set about healing those they were able to, not stopping until dusk. Exhausted, they were led by Linis and Dina to a small fire where the others waited. The army was camped about a mile away, and Lyrial had commanded that no one should disturb Gewey until the following morning.

"If you are too weary, talk can wait," offered Linis.

Gewey shook his head. "No. It can't. I can manage for a time. My strength isn't completely gone."

They took their place beside the fire, where a bowl of hot stew and a bottle of wine were waiting. Once they'd finished their meal, Gewey leaned in and stared into the fire.

"I never thought I would see so much bloodshed," he muttered. "And there will be more to come."

"How is it you are here?" asked Dina. "We thought you were in the west."

"The Oracle of Manisalia told me to come," he replied. "She said you would be destroyed if I did not."

"The Oracle?" said Lee. "I had heard she vanished."

"She was in hiding," said Gewey. "She is with Felsafell now, though she sacrificed her safety to send me to you."

"The Oracle... Felsafell..." Dina shook her head. "So many things have happened since we saw you last."

Gewey nodded and recounted his adventures, omitting only Kaylia's pregnancy. The tale continued on well into the night, and soon it became clear that his fatigue was growing. When he finished, Lee stared at him for a moment before bursting into boisterous laughter.

"It is little wonder that we have heard your name spoken of so often," he said. "An entire fortress of Vrykol destroyed, the Oracle revealing her true nature, and as for Felsafell—I always suspected that there was something odd about him. But to think he has walked the earth for so long…"

"Your power is amazing," said Linis. "And it is no surprise that the enemy fears you. Still, you cannot be everywhere at once. What do you plan to do next?"

"Once I have seen you safely to Althetas," Gewey replied. "I will seek out the Dark Knight and destroy him."

"How will you reach him?" asked Lee. "You can't simply walk into Angräal and knock on his door."

Gewey shrugged. "I might do just that, though I hope he will come to me."

Jacob cleared his throat. "I'm sorry, but I must ask you this." He paused, unsure what to say next.

Lee squeezed his son's shoulder and told Gewey what had happened to his wife. "If what I was told is true…"

"If I can help, naturally I will," said Gewey. "But I must tell you that I am only just discovering the extent of my power. And so far, the flow of the spirit has been difficult for me to control. I cannot promise that I would not do her more harm than good."

"All I ask is that you try," said Jacob.

"I swear it." Gewey forced a weary smile. "Now, before all of my strength is gone, I would hear your tales."

Each took their turn in telling Gewey and Kaylia what had happened to them. Gewey scowled when hearing about the invasion of Sharpstone, but his heart lightened when he was told of the marriage between Dina and Linis, and of Dina's reunion with her mother.

"And where is your mother now?" he asked her.

"With Lyrial," Dina replied. "You will meet her soon."

When all the tales had been told, Gewey leaned back and smiled.

"It would seem we have all had adventures worthy of songs," said Linis. "And now we are all back together again."

"All but Maybell," corrected Gewey. "Though I am glad she is not here to share in our hardship."

"Based on the short time I knew her," said Jacob. "I would wager she could keep pace."

"There is little doubt of that," agreed Millet, smiling. "But I do wish her peace and safety. She has earned it."

"Agreed," said Gewey. "And once we arrive in Althetas, it will be our duty to see that she gets it."

"I must admit," said Lee. "Until I saw you on top of the hill today, I thought my end was at hand. Now hope is renewed, and I feel in my heart that our victory will come soon."

"Hear, hear," said Dina as Linis pulled her close. "Now that we are together again, nothing can stand before us. Especially not with the mighty Darshan leading the way. Though to me you will always be Gewey."

"I never wanted to be anyone else," he said. "At least, not in the eyes of my friends. And regardless of how strong I may become, my true power flows from all of you."

There was a long silence.

"I think it is time we slept," said Kaylia, dragging Gewey to his feet. "We have a long road ahead and plenty of time for talk."

After bidding everyone else goodnight, they walked a few yards to where two bedrolls had been placed around a small bundle of wood. Gewey lit a fire, and they laid down, allowing the warmth to soothe their bodies. The others were still gathered together, talking quietly, the excitement of the day still running hot through their veins.

"Your mind is troubled," whispered Kaylia, stroking Gewey's hair.

"They seem so different now," he replied. "In a way, almost fragile. Even Lee. It's strange."

"You see them through different eyes now, that is why," said Kaylia. "Compared to you, they are fragile. At least in body. But their power is in their spirit and love for each other. And for you."

Gewey peered into her eyes. "And I love them all in return. Though not as I love you." He kissed her lips with tender passion.

"Of course not," she said, the hint of a laugh in her voice. "But still, it is enough. It is the one thing our enemy lacks, and it is his greatest weakness. He exists without love."

"I know." Gewey closed his eyes, allowing himself to drift. "I just fear that when the time comes, love won't be able to protect them. Nor will I. Or possibly to do so will mean that Gewey must die, and Darshan must live."

The memory of Kaylia's vision shot through their bond and a pang of anxiety entered them both.

"I will not allow that to happen. I will keep you with me." Kaylia's voice tensed with resolve.

"But at what cost?" Gewey's voice trailed off, his mind wandering into the realm of dreams.

Kaylia stared at his sleeping form. "I will keep you right here." She closed her eyes, knowing that the morning would herald the beginning of their final march. Once they reached Althetas, Gewey would seek his destiny.

Then, one way or another, the war would finally end.

End Book Four

BOOK CLUB QUESTIONS

1. Who is your favorite character? Why? And what about them make them enjoyable to read about? Has your favorite character changed since the last book?

2. How well does the author follow the formula of the hero's journey while making the story unique in its own right? Has the journey held true from book to book?

3. How well developed do you feel the character arcs are? And how do you think they develop throughout the book and series?

4. Do you feel Gewey will be the savior he is prophesied to be or will he succumb to the temptations of power? Have your feelings on this changed since the last book?

ACKNOWLEDGMENTS

Jonathan and Eleni Anderson, George Panagos, Vincentine Williams, Gerald and Donna Anderson, Hunter and Sarah Anderson, Bobby and Bobbie Anderson, George Stratford, The Ramos family, the DiBatista family, the Gnyp family, Helen Paton and "K", Cassidy Webb, Tom Riddell, Jen Frith-Couch, Alex Harris, Jacob and Elizabeth Bunton, Jenny Bunton, and everyone who has supported me.

I love you all!

ABOUT THE AUTHORS

Brian D. Anderson was born in 1971 and grew up in the small town of Spanish Fort, AL. He attended Fairhope High, then later Springhill College, where his love for fantasy grew into a lifelong obsession. His hobbies include chess, history, and spending time with his son.

Jonathan Anderson was born in March 2003. His creative spirit became evident by the age of three when he told his first original story. In 2010, he came up with the concept for The Godling Chronicles. It grew into an exciting collaboration between father and son. Jonathan enjoys sports, chess, music, games, and, of course, telling stories.

Discover more at
4HorsemenPublications.com

10% off using HORSEMEN10